Praise for the novels of Susan Johnson

"Susan Johnson is a queen of erotic, exciting romance who soars to new heights with each novel."
—*Romantic Times*

"Johnson delivers another fast, titillating read that overflows with sex scenes and rapid-fire dialogue."
—*Publishers Weekly*

"A spellbinding read and a lot of fun . . . Johnson takes sensuality to the edge, writing smoldering stories with characters the reader won't want to leave."
—*The Oakland (MI) Press*

"Sensually charged writing . . . Johnson knows exactly what her devoted readers desire, and she delivers it with her usual flair."
—*Booklist*

"Fascinating . . . The author's style is a pleasure to read."
—*Los Angeles Herald-Examiner*

"Flat-out fabulous, sexy [novels] so textured they sometimes compare . . . to the phenomenal Judith Ivory."
—*All About Romance*

Berkley Sensation Books by Susan Johnson

HOT PINK
HOT LEGS
HOT SPOT
FRENCH KISS
WINE, TARTS, & SEX
HOT PROPERTY
GORGEOUS AS SIN
SEXY AS HELL

TWIN PEAKS
(with Jasmine Haynes)

SEXY AS *Hell*

SUSAN JOHNSON

BERKLEY SENSATION, NEW YORK

THE BERKLEY PUBLISHING GROUP
Published by the Penguin Group
Penguin Group (USA) Inc.
375 Hudson Street, New York, New York 10014, USA

Penguin Group (Canada), 90 Eglinton Avenue East, Suite 700, Toronto, Ontario M4P 2Y3, Canada
(a division of Pearson Penguin Canada Inc.)
Penguin Books Ltd., 80 Strand, London WC2R 0RL, England
Penguin Group Ireland, 25 St. Stephen's Green, Dublin 2, Ireland (a division of Penguin Books Ltd.)
Penguin Group (Australia), 250 Camberwell Road, Camberwell, Victoria 3124, Australia
(a division of Pearson Australia Group Pty. Ltd.)
Penguin Books India Pvt. Ltd., 11 Community Centre, Panchsheel Park, New Delhi—110 017, India
Penguin Group (NZ), 67 Apollo Drive, Rosedale, North Shore 0632, New Zealand
(a division of Pearson New Zealand Ltd.)
Penguin Books (South Africa) (Pty.) Ltd., 24 Sturdee Avenue, Rosebank, Johannesburg 2196,
South Africa

Penguin Books Ltd., Registered Offices: 80 Strand, London WC2R 0RL, England

This is a work of fiction. Names, characters, places, and incidents either are the product of the author's imagination or are used fictitiously, and any resemblance to actual persons, living or dead, business establishments, events, or locales is entirely coincidental. The publisher does not have any control over and does not assume any responsibility for author or third-party websites or their content.

SEXY AS HELL

A Berkley Sensation Book / published by arrangement with the author

PRINTING HISTORY
Berkley Sensation mass-market edition / January 2010

Copyright © 2010 by Susan Johnson.
Excerpt from *Sweet as the Devil* by Susan Johnson copyright © by Susan Johnson.
Cover art by Aleta Rafton.
Cover design by Diana Kolsky.
Interior text design by Tiffany Estreicher.

All rights reserved.
No part of this book may be reproduced, scanned, or distributed in any printed or electronic form without permission. Please do not participate in or encourage piracy of copyrighted materials in violation of the author's rights. Purchase only authorized editions.
For information, address: The Berkley Publishing Group,
a division of Penguin Group (USA) Inc.,
375 Hudson Street, New York, New York 10014.

ISBN: 978-0-425-23020-6

BERKLEY® SENSATION
Berkley Sensation Books are published by The Berkley Publishing Group,
a division of Penguin Group (USA) Inc.,
375 Hudson Street, New York, New York 10014.
BERKLEY® SENSATION and the "B" design are trademarks of Penguin Group (USA) Inc.

PRINTED IN THE UNITED STATES OF AMERICA

10 9 8 7 6 5 4 3 2 1

If you purchased this book without a cover, you should be aware that this book is stolen property. It was reported as "unsold and destroyed" to the publisher, and neither the author nor the publisher has received any payment for this "stripped book."

CHAPTER 1

London, January 1892

OSMOND, BARON LENNOX, was known for his luck at cards. Oz would call it skill, but regardless of the reason, there was no doubt he was on a winning streak tonight. A crowd had slowly gathered round the table as the stakes rose, and Brooks's members, gamesters to the core, were hazarding wagers on how long Elphinstone would last. Viscount Elphinstone had been losing heavily. While his père could afford it, Elphinstone was clearly rankled. He was slumped in his chair, coatless, disheveled, red faced, and looking pugnacious—although that may have been due to the family's propensity to breed true on their bulldog features.

Elphinstone's major opponent at the table was lounging back in his chair, his dark eyes amused, a half smile on his handsome face, nonchalance in every lithe contour of his tall, lean frame. Or rather, indifference some might say; Lennox never seemed to care whether he won or lost.

"It ain't fair, Oz. You always get the good cards," the young Marquis of Telford groused, staring at his cards with obvious disgust.

Lennox glanced up. "Lady Luck's been good to me tonight," he murmured, taking a card from his hand and drop-ping it on the green baize.

"As usual," Elphinstone growled.

A servant approached and bent to whisper in Lennox's ear. The baron nodded without looking up from his cards. "Your turn, Harry. This is my last hand."

"Nell getting tired of waiting?" Harry Ogilvie waggishly queried.

Oz's heavy-lidded gaze met his friend's droll glance for a telling moment. "Are you talking to me, Harry?"

The Earl of Airlie's youngest son grinned. "Hell no. Slip of the tongue."

"Someday an irate husband is going to have you horse-whipped, Lennox," Elphinstone muttered.

"Only if he's not man enough to call me out," Oz drawled. The viscount's wife was a pretty little hussy; could he help it if she was in hot pursuit?

A sudden hush greeted Oz's soft-spoken challenge.

The eyes of the crowd locked on Elphinstone, wondering if he'd respond, or more to the point, *how* he'd respond. Lennox was young and wild, his temper as easily provoked as his lust, and while he'd been screwing his way through the ranks of London's fair beauties the last two years, he'd also had more than his share of duels.

With not so much as a bruise for his exertions.

Elphinstone finally growled something under his breath, his nostrils flaring, his narrowed gaze two pinpricks of anger. Then not inclined to end his life or be maimed, he scanned the breathless crowd. "You won't see blood tonight on my account," he spat. Turning back to Oz, he snarled, "I'll raise you a thousand," recklessly wagering his father's money rather than stake his life.

Held breaths were released, a collective sigh of relief wafted round the table; Elphinstone wouldn't have stood a chance at ten paces. Or even a hundred. Ask Buckley, who'd barely survived his recent ill-advised challenge.

Oz almost felt sorry for Elphinstone, who'd no more meet him on the dueling field than he'd satisfy his wife in bed or even know enough to be decent to her. *Almost* felt sorry. "I'll raise you another thousand," he gently said, the cards he was holding as near perfect as the law of averages allowed. *What the hell; the ass doesn't deserve my pity.* "Make that two."

Five minutes later, much richer and in a hurry, Oz was in the entrance hall and a flunkey was holding out his coat for him. "It's still raining hard out there, sir."

"That's England," Oz said with a smile, sliding his arms into the sleeves and shrugging into his grey overcoat. "More rain than sun." Handing the man a sovereign, he turned and strode toward the door. Standing outside under the portico a moment later, he watched the rain pouring down as though the heavens had opened up, felt the wind tugging at his coat skirts, surveyed the distant treetops tossing in the gusts, and was suddenly reminded of Hyderabad during the monsoon season. Christ, he must have drunk more than usual tonight—too many of those old memories were surfacing. Shaking off the unwanted images, he dashed down the stairs and entered his waiting carriage. "Drive like hell, Sam," he said, dropping into a seat with a smile for his driver who had been taking refuge from the storm inside the conveyance. "I'm late as usual."

"I'll get you there right quick." Sam slipped out the opposite door.

As the well-sprung carriage careened through the streets of London at a flying pace, Oz half dozed, his life of late slightly deficient in sleep. With Nell's husband in Paris, she'd been consuming a good deal of his time. In addition, he had a shipping business to run, he'd been working at translating a recently purchased rare Urdu manuscript, and of course, Brooks's was a constant lure to a man who loved to gamble.

Once Lord Howe returned from Paris next week, Nell would be less persistent in her demands. He smiled faintly. Not that he was complaining. She had a real talent for acrobatics.

As the carriage drew to a halt before a small hotel, newly opened by a gentleman's gentleman who had recently retired with a tidy sum, Lennox came fully awake, shoved open the carriage door, and stepped out into the downpour. "Don't wait, Sam," he shouted and ran for the entrance.

A doorman threw open the door at his approach. Swiftly crossing the threshold, Oz came to a stop in a small foyer. He smiled at the proprietor behind the counter. "Evening, Fremont. Damn wet out there." He shook the raindrops from his ruffled hair.

"Seasonal weather I'm afraid, sir. Would you like a servant to run you a hot bath or bring up a hot toddy?"

"Perhaps later. Which room?"

"Thirteen, sir."

Nell had chosen Blackwood's Hotel in Soho Square for its seclusion, and they'd been coming here with great frequency the past fortnight. Taking the stairs at a run, he considered his apology. He couldn't say the game was too exciting to leave; he'd have to think of another excuse.

He strode down the hallway, glancing at the passing brass number plates until he arrived at the requisite room. He opened the door and walked in.

"You're late."

A soft, breathy tone, with a touch of impatience. Knowing well what stoked Nell's impatience—the randy tart liked it morning, noon, and night—he answered in a suitably apologetic tone. "Forgive me, darling, but one of my ship captains arrived just as I was leaving the house." Christ, it was dark. Why was just a single wall sconce in the far corner lit? Was Nell in a romantic frame of mind? But then he saw her toss back the covers and pat the bed beside her, and rather than question the degree of darkness, he quickly shed his wet coat, his two rings, and stripped off his clothes.

"I like your new perfume," he murmured as he climbed into bed. Dropping back against the pillows, he pulled her close. "Are you cold, darling?" She was wearing a nightgown.

"No."

"In that case, we can dispense with this." Pushing the silk fabric up over her hips with a sweep of his hand, he rolled over her, settled smoothly between her legs, and set out to apologize to Nell in the way she liked best.

A door to the left of the bed suddenly burst open, a gaggle of people trooped in, the bedchamber was suddenly flooded with light, and a portly man in the lead pointed at the bed. "There!" he cried. "You are all witnesses to the countess's base and lewd moral turpitude!"

Lennox stared at the woman beneath him. *Not red-haired Nell. A blonde.* "What the hell is going on?" he growled.

As if in answer, the spokesman declared with an oratorical flourish to the cluster of people crowded round the bed, "If required, you will testify in court as to exactly what you have seen here tonight—to whit . . . a clear-cut case of moral turpitude and venery! Thank you, that will be all," he crisply added, dismissing the motley crew with a wave of his hand.

His eyes like ice, Lennox surveyed the female under him. "I don't believe we've been introduced," he said with soft malevolence. Obviously he'd been gulled for someone's monetary gain.

"Nor need we be," the lady cooly replied. "You may go now. Thank you for your cooperation."

Lennox didn't move other than to turn his head toward the only other man remaining in the room. "Get out or I'll shoot you where you stand." He always carried a pistol—a habit from India.

Isolde Perceval, Countess of Wraxell in her own right, lying prone beneath the very large man, nodded at her barrister. Not that he was likely to put his life at risk for her, but should he be considering anything foolish, she rather thought she would prefer to deal with this hired actor herself.

As Mr. Malmsey shut the door behind him and quiet prevailed, Isolde gazed up at the man who'd come to rest be-

tween her legs with a casualness that bespoke a certain acquaintance with dalliance. "I thought Malmsey explained
what was required of you," she said. "But if you'd like an
additional payment, kindly get off me and I'll be happy to
fetch my purse and pay you whatever you wish."

Oz's brows rose. "Is this some farce?"

"Far from it. With your cooperation, of course. As Mr.
Malmsey no doubt pointed out, your silence is required."

Silence about what? Through a minor alcoholic haze, Oz
speculated on how he'd landed in this bizarre scenario.
"What room number is this?"

"Thirteen."

Then where was Nell? Still waiting somewhere. *Merde.*
"Don't move," he said. "I'll be right back." His expression
was grim. "If you wish my silence, I suggest you comply."

"There's no need for belligerence. I'm not going anywhere."

You had to give her credit. The lady wasn't easily rattled,
although having organized this performance—with witnesses
to boot—bespoke a certain audacity on her part. He slid off
her and rose from the bed. Lifting his overcoat from the chair
on which he'd dropped it, he slipped it on, buttoned it, then
exited the room and made his way downstairs to speak to the
proprietor.

Isolde debated dressing, but should he return quickly, she
ran the risk of being caught in some degree of nudity, and
with a forward fellow like this actor, she was safer where she
was. Her purse was within reach. Furthermore, there was no
doubt in her mind that they could reach a monetary agreement. Malmsey had already paid him for his night's work,
but the life of an actor was one of financial insecurity. So
she'd simply ask him what he required to forget that he'd
been here and she'd pay it.

Downstairs, Oz was offering the proprietor of Blackwood's Hotel a rueful smile. "A slight problem has arisen,
Fremont. Room thirteen is occupied by an unknown person."

"My apologies, sir." The trim, dapper man quickly flipped through the guest ledger and a moment later glanced up with a genuinely pained expression. "My most *profuse* apologies, my lord. I should have said room *twenty-three*." His face was beet red. "I most *humbly* beg your pardon."

"Rest easy, Fremont," Oz replied good-naturedly. "No great damage has been done. Although, if you'd be so kind as to inform the lady in room *twenty-three* that I'm unable to meet her tonight, I'd appreciate it. Tell her that a business matter of some importance has delayed me."

"Naturally, sir, as you wish, sir." Relieved he wouldn't meet with the baron's wrath, the proprietor deferentially added, "Would you like me to express your regrets to the lady?"

"I would, thank you. And see that she has a carriage waiting for her."

"Yes, sir. Consider it done." Fremont gave no indication that he knew Lennox was nude beneath his coat. The baron was a very generous man, his gratuities commensurate with his fortune. Not to mention his forgiving nature tonight was a profound relief.

Oz turned to leave, then swung back. "You don't happen to know the name of the lady in room thirteen?"

"A Mrs. Smith, sir," Fremont answered, one brow lifting at the obvious fraud.

"Ah—I see. Thank you."

Not prone to self-reflection after an evening of drink, he gave no more thought to the lady's pretense. Taking the stairs at a run, he returned to room thirteen, slipped inside, and shut and locked the door behind him. There she was—right where he'd left her. That she'd not taken the opportunity to run suggested this situation was critical in some way. Interesting . . . as was the lovely lady. Shedding his coat, he walked to the light switch by the connecting door, flicked off the intolerably bright overhead fixture, and moving toward the bed, turned on another wall sconce.

A touch of apprehension appeared in Isolde's eyes. Even in worldly London, even with an actor from the free and easy world of the theater she'd not expected such shamelessness. "What are you doing?" Seated against the headboard, she jerked the covers up to her chin.

"Coming to make a bargain with you." While he was not entirely sure what had motivated his reply, the persuasive influence of a beautiful woman, opportunity, and considerable liquor couldn't be discounted. Not to mention that on closer inspection, her charms were even more impressive.

"Kindly do so once you're dressed."

"You're not in a position to give orders," Oz gently noted, thinking he really must have drunk too much tonight that the alarm in the lady's eyes was so perversely satisfying. Prompted by his thoughts, he looked around the room. "Is there any liquor here?"

"No."

But he spied a tray with decanters on a table in the corner. He walked without haste to the table and poured himself a brandy. Returning to the bed, he raised his glass to her. "See—you were mistaken. Would you like some?"

"No, I would not," Isolde replied in quelling accents. "Kindly inform me of this bargain of yours so we may both be on our way."

Since his intentions weren't entirely clear or rather of a chrysalis nature, he climbed back into bed, took a seat beside her, and said, "First tell me why I'm here—because clearly the man Malmsey hired is not." Lifting the glass to his mouth, he drank half the brandy.

Good God, he isn't the actor! "I have no idea on either score," she tersely said, rattled by this unexpected turn of events. "If I did, you wouldn't be here annoying me and some anonymous actor would have long since left."

"An actor?" Oz grinned. "Did the poor man know what he was getting into?"

"I'm sure he did. He was well paid for his role."

"Apparently he was," Oz drolly noted, "considering he didn't show up for his performance."

"Obviously, there was some mistake. But," Isolde mockingly added, "since you performed well, all turned out in the end."

"*If* I agree to accommodate you." The word *perform* was triggering rather explicit images.

"You already have."

"Not completely." This lady along with her story piqued his interest. Or maybe he'd become bored with Nell.

"If it's money you want," she said with a touch of impatience, "just say so and we can stop playing games."

Oz lifted his glass to her. "I haven't even begun playing, Countess," he silkily murmured.

"I find your innuendo shameless *and* irritating," Isolde snapped, bristling with indignation, her ready temper on the rise. The man was equally shameless in his nudity; he didn't even *attempt* to cover himself.

"Now, now," Oz murmured, fascinated by her willful personality, "there's no reason we can't be friends. Where are you from?" He hadn't seen her before, and if she was indeed a countess, he would have met her—and more to the point, wouldn't have forgotten so splendid a woman. She had the face of an enchantress—sensual blue eyes dark with storm clouds, a fine straight nose, soft, cherry red lips that fairly begged to be kissed, and a stubborn little chin that was infinitely fascinating to a man who knew far too many willing females. A glorious halo of pale hair framed her features, and even with their brief bodily contact, her voluptuousness was conspicuous.

"I have no intention of being your friend, nor need you know where I'm from." She must extricate herself from this unexpected and potentially disastrous predicament—and quickly. Her plans didn't include someone who might talk out of turn. Everything depended on a nameless lover who couldn't be found and cross-examined.

"Then perhaps," Oz drawled, "I should tell Mr. Malmsey that I don't choose to cooperate with this scheme and if he persists I'll sue him for every penny he has."

"You're the one who barged in," she argued, more calmly now. This man would eventually name his price; everyone did.

"And you were the one who said I was late." His lazy smile was full of grace. "Surely I'd have been remiss to keep a lady waiting."

"How very smooth you are. But impertinent, sir."

"While you're quite beautiful," he softly countered. "Although I expect you already know that. Tell me, is this little drama perpetrated to give your husband cause for divorce? If so, I don't understand why your lover is willing to expose you to all the prurient interest and scandal on your own. Where's the scoundrel's backbone?"

"So you would assume responsibility if your lover were exposed in court?"

"Certainly. Any honorable man would."

"Why then would an *honorable* man toy with another man's wife?"

Oz's dark brows shot up. "You can't be serious. Or perhaps you live in a cave. Although, if you do," he cheekily murmured, surveying the portion of her nightgown visible above the covers, "you have a fashionable modiste in there with you. That's quality silk you're wearing." Anyone in the India trade knew silk.

"Who *are* you?" she asked, suddenly curious about a man acquainted with grades of silk.

Perhaps she did live in a cave; he was well-known for a variety of reasons, some of them actually acceptable. "You tell me first."

She watched him drain the rest of his drink, wondered in passing why her alarm had seemingly disappeared, and wondered as well where he came from with his deeply bronzed skin. "Are you drunk?" Would he remember any of this? How much should she divulge? And how honorable would he be if she related her tale?

He hesitated a fraction of a second. "I'm probably not completely sober."

"Are you dangerous?" Even as she spoke, she realized how useless the question if indeed he was.

He shot her a look. "To you? Hardly."

"I'm relieved."

He smiled. "I'm relieved you're relieved. Now tell me your name."

"Isolde Perceval."

"From where—the ends of the earth? I haven't seen you in society."

"I avoid society."

"Apparently." He dipped his head. "Osmond Lennox. Pleased to make your acquaintance, ma'am."

"Now that the courtesies have been observed," she said, "kindly tell me what you want, so we may end this charade and go our separate ways."

"You."

Her eyes flared wide. "You can't be serious."

"I am." There, certainty—his plans no longer moot— although wealthy noblemen were as a rule unrestrained in their whims. "Think of it as recompense," he said with a small smile, "for the shock to my system. When your witnesses barged in I thought someone was seeking vengeance for my many sins. Or about to horsewhip me."

"Well, no one was seeking revenge. You're quite unharmed. And what you ask is naturally out of the question."

"Surely you can't claim to be a virgin."

"I hardly think that's any of your business."

"You're right of course," he drawled. Although, if she'd been a virgin, she would have been quick to say so. Also, a divorce case with witnesses was about adultery. She couldn't possibly be a virgin. "Since you prefer not discussing virginity, at least explain how you plan to use your obviously hired witnesses?"

She chewed on her bottom lip.

"While you're deciding on your reply, excuse me while I get myself another drink. It's been a very odd night"—he grinned—"at least so far."

She should have averted her eyes, but she couldn't help watching him as he walked away from the bed in all his nude splendor. Not that she'd ever been overly concerned with the shibboleths of society. Truth be told, he was quite beautiful in face and form—with an unmistakable brute virility beneath his charming manner. He'd threatened to shoot poor Malmsey and seemed quite capable of doing so. She'd have to pay her barrister an extra premium for that fearsome threat.

As he returned to the bed with his refilled glass, Oz was pleased to see that the lady was no longer clutching the bedclothes to her bosom. "Now," he began pleasantly, taking his place beside her once again, "I think I deserve some minimum explanation." He held her gaze for a moment. "Particularly if this goes to court and I happen to be involved."

"It shouldn't go to court."

"Shouldn't or won't?"

She made a small moue. Frederick had threatened a breach of promise suit among other extortion demands.

"That's what I thought. So is this about your marriage?"

"No."

He shot her a sharp look. "No?"

"I'm not married."

"But you were." She'd been designated a countess by the barrister.

"No."

He softly sighed. "I'm not leaving until I know what's going on, so you might as well tell me. I can stay here as long as Fremont keeps bringing up liquor."

"You know the proprietor?"

"Yes, Mrs. Smith," he replied cheekily.

"He shouldn't have disclosed that."

"I pay him well."

"For his silence about your assignations."

He nodded.

"So you're a lothario," she said with distaste.

"No, I'm a man. Now—an explanation."

His voice had taken on an edge.

"Very well, if you must know—"

"I must," he brusquely interposed.

"Then I'll tell you. I'm a countess in my own right, but as you know in situations such as mine, I simply hold the title as steward for the next male in line to inherit should I die childless. In my case, a cousin has decided he doesn't wish to wait—I might outlive him, you see, or marry and have children. So *he* intends to marry me to gain access to my funds."

"What of a marriage settlement?" They were written to protect family fortunes.

"First, I loathe my cousin and wouldn't marry him if he was the last man on the face of the earth. Secondly, Frederick's pursuit has been persistent and very determined since his gambling losses have mounted. I expect coercion would be involved with a marriage settlement. He's completely unscrupulous."

"Have you no one to protect you?"

"Naturally, I could hire guards, but I'm hoping it won't come to that. My plan, in which you recently participated, is to so completely ruin my reputation that even Frederick will be forestalled at least in his marriage plans. What other tactics he might employ to make claim on my property Malmsey can handle in court." Her voice took on a derisive tone. "I doubt he'd be personally moved by this scandal, but fortunately for me he has a domineering mother who prides herself on virtue and decorum."

"In the scramble for a fortune, people have been known to

overlook even the most egregious scandals," Oz drily said. "How can you be sure your scheme will serve?" He really meant, *How can you be so naive?*

"I can't be, of course. Not completely." She smiled for the first time. "Yet you've not met Lady Compton."

"Actually, I've had the misfortune," he replied with a grimace. "My condolences on your prospective mother-in-law."

"Bite your tongue," she retorted. "If all goes well, I shan't be saddled with her or her despicable son. My little drama, as you call it, will be published in all the scandal sheets tomorrow—without naming my partner, of course, only myself. You are quite safe, you see. Now, if you wish payment, I'd be more than happy to pay you. Money," she quickly added.

"I don't need money." As heir to the largest banking fortune in India he could buy a good share of the world if he wished. And he retracted his naive assessment. The scandal sheets could ruin a lady. Although someone with large gambling debts might overlook even that degree of infamy.

She shifted slightly under his gaze. "Surely you wouldn't take advantage of a woman."

"I doubt I'd have to."

Her brows arched. "Is that unimpeachable certainty usually effective?"

He smiled. "Always."

"Such arrogance." She glanced at his crotch. "And yet—I see no visible signs of your interest."

"I was raised in India. I'm capable of controlling my, er, impulses." He grinned. "Although, if you'd like to see interest"—he swept his hand downward—"observe."

The transformation was not only instant but also profound. Wide-eyed, she took in the provocative sight.

"Is that better?" he said, his voice velvet soft.

She slowly wrenched her gaze from the flaunting display, his enormous erection stretching from crotch to navel, his blood pulsing wildly through the tracery of tumescent veins standing out in high relief on his resplendent length. "You're definitely a flashy fellow," she said, meeting his amused gaze, fully aware as well of the soft tremors beginning to flutter through her vagina. "Still, I think I'll restrain myself."

"At least keep me company for a short while." His voice was well mannered, his gaze amicable. "Thanks to you, I seem to have missed my assignation. Surely, that's not too much to ask." He recognized the look of longing in a woman's eyes. He knew as well that her taut nipples pressing through the silk of her gown had something to do with his erection and her desires—restrained as they might be. Only temporarily restrained if he had his way. "Would you like a drink? Fremont set out a nice assortment of liquor."

The smallest of hesitations.

"Why not," she said, thinking to humor him and better gain her ends.

"Then I'll be right back, ma'am." He glanced at her over his shoulder as he slipped off the bed. "Correction . . . miss." He casually strolled away as if he wasn't nude and blatantly aroused, she wasn't a stranger, and they'd be sharing nothing more than a game of whist when he returned. "You have a choice," he offered, standing at the liquor tray a moment later. "Sherry, cognac, brandy, or hock."

"Cognac. Just a little."

"How are you getting home?" he asked as he poured her drink. "Could I drive you somewhere?"

"No, thank you," she replied, trying not to stare at his enormous erection. "I believe Malmsey is waiting for me."

He nodded toward the door through which the surprise party had entered. "Waiting in there?" He preferred not being monitored.

She shook her head. "Downstairs."

Good. "So does Malmsey know Fremont as well?" he queried, moving back to the bed.

"I'm not sure. He might."

At least he does now. Fortunately, Fremont was the soul of discretion; Miss Perceval's intrigue was safe. Not that it should matter to him one way or the other, yet she shouldn't have to suffer the unwanted machinations of her cousin. Nor should she be required to resort to such drastic measures to retain control of her title and wealth. "Would you like me to call out Compton?" he abruptly asked, handing her a glass. "I could see that he never bothers you again." While dueling was illegal, it was privately practiced.

The casual certainty in his voice gave her pause and quite inappropriately, pleasure as well. "While I appreciate the offer," she more prudently replied, "I don't think it would serve."

"It would serve perfectly. He'd be dead—not a great loss if you ask me; the man cheats at cards. Your reputation would remain unscathed and"—he grinned as he settled back on the bed and rested against the pillows—"you might be inclined to thank me in some agreeable way."

She laughed. "I admit there's a certain appeal to your plan, but, no, I couldn't be party to something so crass." If he could urbanely disregard his erection, she should be able to as well.

"As if his wanting to marry you for your money isn't crass."

She smiled. "So bloodthirsty, Lennox. Is it your Indian upbringing?"

"Hell no. Dueling is a European foolishness wrapped up in a mantle of honor. In India if you want someone murdered, you hire assassins or a poisoner and have the job quietly done." He shrugged dismissively. "It's different here."

"My goodness. You quite alarm me."

"No I don't. Not unless by alarm you mean something else entirely."

"Such as?"

"Your nipples," he said, nodding at her breasts; he didn't mention her veiled glances at his erection. "They've been signaling your aspirations for some time now."

"Aspirations don't necessarily equate with actions."

His lashes lowered faintly. "In our case, why not? We're alone. I'm thoroughly aroused, as you can see," he politely said as if she hadn't noticed several times already. "I can tell that you're not exactly indifferent to me. What's the point in denying ourselves?"

"So blunt, Lennox," she sardonically observed. "No sonnets or odes to charm a lady?"

"Ah Love! Could you and I with Fate conspire. To grasp this sorry scheme of things entire. Would not we shatter it to bits. And then remold it to our heart's desire. I could also recite it in the original Persian if you like." He smiled. "Is that better now? Or would you like more verses to entice you?"

"I'm not sure I wish to be enticed."

"Why not? Making love is one of life's great pleasures."

"Or sorrows."

He could have asked, but he didn't want to know. Even while he understood the merits of asking in terms of facilitating a seduction, he didn't. There was something about her, a kind of intrepid heroine willing to stand up for her rights no matter the consequences that reminded him of things he'd rather forget. Right and wrong had nothing to do with the reality of the world, he'd discovered. You could be moral to the core and right as rain and no one cared.

He had his own sorrows when it came to love.

All he wanted tonight was sex.

And if not with Nell, Miss Perceval would do.

CHAPTER 2

SLIDING DOWN ON his spine, he rested his glass on his chest and shut his eyes for a moment, suddenly struck by a wave of fatigue and melancholy. Maybe he'd been running from the past too long; maybe the heavy rain tonight had brought old memories to the fore. Perhaps he was feeling nothing more than ennui, finding himself as he did in bed with another woman he barely knew.

Or possibly, using sex as a diversion from reality had finally exhausted him.

Was he sleeping? Isolde wondered. Would this be a good time to leave? Or was she obliged to stay so he wouldn't sue Malmsey or be difficult in some other unknown way? How much did she have to fear from him? And why was he sleeping if indeed he was? Not entirely without vanity, she found herself mildly vexed at his indifference. While she lived away from society, she was not without influence in her country sphere, nor was she without suitors. Heavens! Why was she even considering such nonsense! It didn't matter one whit whether Lennox liked her or not. She had much more serious issues facing her.

But sensible rationale aside or perhaps because of it—he

could prove to be troublesome—she chose not to leave. Although her decision may not have been completely rational—a thought that didn't bear close scrutiny in terms of good judgment.

As for scrutiny of another kind, however, her companion's stunning looks were difficult to ignore. Not that she didn't try. She'd seen naked men before, she reminded herself. There was no need to examine this particular one.

Seated against the headboard, she sipped on her cognac and looked everywhere but at the nude man lying beside her. She counted the squares on the Greek fretwork molding above the fireplace twice, uselessly estimated the number of roses on the chair upholstery, followed the Byzantine maze design on the carpet with her gaze, and was about to tally the medallions on the mirror frame when temptation became too great.

She turned and looked.

My lord, he is gorgeous! Silky black hair, fashionably cut, lay on the pillow in ruffled waves. His features were finely formed, stark rather than harsh, austerely male, high cheekbones, firm jaw, the line of his nose arrow straight, his mouth . . . She paused in her inspection, as if drawn to forbidden fruit. No austerity there—a sensual ripeness to his lips that was explicitly erotic. Quickly looking away, she focused her gaze on the dark slashing line of his brows; no erotica there—a hint of menace instead.

Even in slumber, he exuded a barely suppressed brute energy, as if one was in the presence of a young Mars, God of War—or more likely a heathen god with his deeply bronzed skin and exotic eyes. He was powerfully muscled by any measure, his long-limbed athletic body taut and honed, the capacity for violence only thinly veiled even in the dissolving glow of the wall sconces.

No fashionable, effete beau lay at her side.

Nor was there any suggestion of the more conventional English lord in his manner. No man she knew would be sleeping at this point. They'd be hell-bent on wooing her.

Perhaps Lennox's indifference intrigued her most, although his great beauty and bold audacity couldn't be discounted. But whatever the particular or sum total of his allure, she found herself sorely tempted to take him up on his brazen proposition.

Although he might not be *entirely* indifferent, she decided, surveying the length of his rampant erection—unless he was dreaming, of course.

As if in answer, his grip loosened on his brandy glass and the tumbler began to slide off his chest.

Isolde snatched it up just as it was about to overturn.

Coming awake with a start, Oz's scowl turned into a smile as he glanced up and recognized her. "Forgive me for nodding off." He held out his hand for his brandy. "I haven't slept much lately. Was I snoring?"

"No. Although," Isolde lightly said, "I thought you might be ignoring me."

"On the contrary"—he offered her a wicked wink—"I was dreaming about you." He glanced down before meeting her gaze once again. "As you may have surmised."

"What facile charm, Lennox. I almost believe you."

"*Believe me*, my dear Miss Perceval." He was pleased that she was flirting with him, the shift in her behavior gratifying. "It was a warm summer day in my dream, you were swinging on a rustic swing high above me, and I was lying on the grass enjoying the view. Considering the weather outside," he added with a quirked grin, "you can't fault me for improvising."

"Your fantasy does sound rather nice with the rain pounding on the windows and the wind wailing."

"I'd be more than happy to let you into my dream," he murmured.

"I've been thinking about—"

"Enjoying yourself?"

Her lashes lowered, and she gave him a considering look. "Why would you think that?" She was still undecided, wasn't she?

"As I mentioned before"—he tipped his glass toward her breasts—"your peaked nipples are conspicuous." He didn't say he could smell her arousal, too, for fear of scaring her off, but the familiar fragrance was pungent in his nostrils. "Come, darling, what's the point of playing the innocent maid? You obviously would rather not. As for myself, my interest is clear and it's a cozy warm bed we're in on this stormy night. We might as well be equally cozy."

"You make sex sound warmly genial."

"Why shouldn't it be?" She hadn't tried to argue her indifference, nor could she honestly do so when her body was obviously willing. Suddenly weary of artifice and games when he knew they both wanted the same thing, he drank down his brandy, dropped the glass on the floor, took hers from her hand, and did the same. Turning his head on the pillow to more fully meet her gaze, he smiled. "Now then, Miss Perceval, I'm about to touch you, so don't scream."

She laughed. "Do most women usually scream?"

"Not at this point," he drolly replied, brushing his hand down her arm to her wrist, circling it with his long, slender fingers, lifting her hand to his mouth, and gently kissing each fingertip with the same lazy indifference that so marked his demeanor.

She should resist. Now was the time to say no. Make clear she was not available to him.

But she didn't. Perhaps because she wasn't flameproof.

Nor would he have let her. Because he wanted what he wanted.

"Come a little closer, darling," he softly cajoled, unclasping her wrist and reaching up to lightly cup the back of her head in his warm palm. Rising slightly from the pillow in a ripple of taut abdominal muscles, he pulled her head lower, lifted his mouth to hers, and brushed her lips with his. It was a sweet, undemanding kiss—one designed to soothe a lady's conscience.

"There now," he murmured, "that wasn't so frightening, was it?" Letting his hand drop away from her head, he lay back. And waited.

He tasted of brandy and lust, a combination that might have been frightening if not for the undisguisedly flamboyant burst of desire that not only burned through her senses but also served to seriously whet her appetite for more. Not that she was completely defenseless against his allure. She still had wits enough to tamp down her skittish passions and cooly survey temptation lounging before her.

He looked back calmly, shameless and assured.

"I shouldn't," she said, but she half turned and rested her hand on his shoulder as she spoke, and a treacherous little voice reminded her that just because Will had married didn't require she forgo sexual pleasure.

"Yes, darling, one always should," Oz softly returned, covering her hand with his as it lay on his shoulder. "Life doesn't give one second chances."

And well she knew, having lost the man she loved. The warmth of Lennox's hand was strangely comforting, and leaning closer, she no longer weighed impulse or motive, seeking respite instead from the cold and rain outside, from the sense of loss that had been plaguing her, from the evil designs of her relatives—or perhaps it was nothing more complicated than she wished to enjoy this glory of a man smiling up at her. Dipping her head, she kissed him in a much less gentle way than he had her. Too long celibate, or maybe having finally jettisoned equivocation, she was in her own way as audacious as he. Her kiss was restive and high-strung, provocative in its what-do-you-have-for-me silent query.

Oz was more than willing to give her what she wanted.

He'd been waiting to do so since shortly after entering the room.

Lightly gripping her shoulders, he eased her away from him enough so their eyes met, so he could be sure she understood. "You have to tell me when to stop," he said, recognizing the nature of her kisses but not entirely sure she did. "Because I'm in a strange mood tonight"—he smiled— "or you're the cause of my strange mood."

"Should I apologize?"

He smiled at the impudence in her tone. "No, darling, you're perfect in every way."

Her brows rose faintly. "Available, you mean."

He didn't say that was a given in his life, nor that she was a saucy little bitch. He shook his head instead. "I could be anywhere. But I'm here with you," he added with smile. "And that's a good thing."

"Along with the cozy warm bed on a cold wet night," she pleasantly reminded him.

"And the lady of my dreams to keep me warm." He grinned. "Now in terms of getting warmer, are you amenable because I have a night of excess on my mind?"

"I am," she said with candor because her body had shamelessly opened in welcome at the word *excess*, a night of sexual prodigality suddenly alluring. As recompense for her loss. Or more aptly because Lennox was carnal temptation in the flesh.

"Good," he replied with equal frankness, and coming up off the pillows with muscular grace, he rolled over her, slid her under him with an effortless strength, came to rest between her thighs, and put an end to what had been a record period of politesse for him. Not that he begrudged her uncertainty considering the perilous state of her affairs.

Braced on his forearms, lying lightly above her, he said with a cheeky smile, "A last check now, Miss Perceval; if it's all right with you, I'll be coming in."

"It's very much—all right, my dear Lennox," she breathlessly replied, the riveting display of brawn and muscle she'd witnessed in his swift shifting of their positions, male supremacy—pure and simple. "My lord, you're strong," she whispered.

Her words were throaty and hushed, and whether it was fear or not he wasn't sure. "I won't hurt you," he said, sure of that at least.

"I didn't mean that. It's just that you're"—she caught her breath as a flurry of longing streaked through her senses—"very powerful."

"I lead an active life." He planned on becoming more active very soon.

"Doing this, you mean," she said, touching him because she couldn't help herself, lightly tracing the line of his collarbone with her fingers, her skin startlingly pale against his.

"Partly." He was no hypocrite about his amusements. "Now if you're warm enough," he unnecessarily said with her cheeks flushed rosy pink, no longer in the mood for conversation, "your gown is in my way." He reached for the small pearl buttons at the neckline without waiting for an answer and deftly unfastened them while her breathing accelerated. As impatient as she, he quickly rose to his knees, slid his hands under her arms, and pulled her into a seated position. "Lift your arms, puss."

His soft command was the most banal of orders. There was no reason his words should have registered with such force. Yet they did, her overwrought response out of all proportion to his simple statement. With shocking violence, a lustful jolt of desire spiked through her body, slammed into every vulnerable, frenzied nerve ending, streaked up her spine, and left her trembling. When she never trembled. When sex was about euphoria and gratification. Not mindless hysteria. "This never happens to me," she whispered, unnerved and shaken by her rash, predacious need.

Tossing her gown aside, Oz eased her back down. "Life's absurd, darling," he gently said, settling between her legs once again. "Everything's not always rational."

"But it always has been." Her eyes were wide with bewilderment.

"Not tonight, sweetheart," he gently said. "Blame the storm. Because I'm planning on burying myself inside you and staying there til morning. I found my safe haven from the tempest outside," he added with a teasing smile.

Still struggling to bring her senses to heel, disquieted by his presumption and her lack of choice in his plan, confused by her body's instant response to his mention of safe haven, she took issue with his bold assurance. "You didn't ask if I agree."

"I already know the answer. But if we're still playing games, let me put it this way. You don't have a choice." He was beyond teasing foreplay—or whatever she called it.

She stared at him, astonished. "You'd coerce me?"

"I doubt it'll come to that."

"Get off me," she ordered with the imperiousness granted those of ancient title and vast fortune. "We're done."

"No we're not." A soft, patient reply.

"Damn you, Lennox!" she spat out hotly.

"Too late," he said through his teeth. "I'm already damned."

Struck by the sudden bleakness in his eyes, conscious as well that he was more right about her willingness than she chose to admit, she grimaced and sighed and after a lip-nibbling pause, finally said, "This is insanity, you know."

"No, darling," he answered in frank demur. "It's simple passion."

"Morals aside." Although she wasn't disturbed by morals so much as by her outrageous desires.

He shrugged. "If you believe in such things."

"You don't."

He didn't answer, although his dubious look was answer enough.

Coming to the conclusion that a splendid man like Lennox was rare, understanding as well that the blissful heat of his body lightly touching hers was an extravagantly lush sensation she'd never come near to feeling before, knowing he wasn't the only one in search of safe haven tonight, she reached up and framed his beautiful, ascetic face in her hands. "Give me pleasure and oblivion, dear Lennox, and I'll stay."

Pleasure he could guarantee; he also owned the map to oblivion after years of searching for mindlessness in count-less women's arms. And he'd known all along she was stay-ing. "Thank you," he politely said as if he'd only been waiting for her sanction. "I'll happily give you both."

"Lucky me, you *splendid* creature." She smiled, comforted by his understanding, charmed by the random hand of fate that had brought him into her bed tonight. Strangely enticed by the rarified enchantment he offered.

No tyro at love with her casual reply. How very convenient. Resting easily between her outstretched thighs, instead of anticipating another night of casual amour, he experienced an unaccountable desire to see that she found full measure of the pleasure and oblivion she sought.

He gently brushed his finger over her nipples. "I think it's time I tasted these—if that's all right with you?"

She smiled. "Am I allowed to say no?"

He grinned. "You're not big enough or strong enough."

"Do women always yield to you?"

He shook his head and lied. "Of course not, but humor me. You won't regret it," he added, capturing one nipple between his thumb and forefinger and squeezing it ever so softly.

"Arrogant man," she whispered, but his arrogance was tantalizing and the pressure of his fingers was beginning to command the attention of her genital nerves, a seemingly direct path from nipple to vagina, encouraging added moisture to flood her tissue. Or was it the compelling presence of his rigid penis crammed against her vulva that incited her body's response?

"Not without reason, puss." He'd not wasted his time in the boudoirs of the world. Slipping his hand down between her legs, he slowly measured the length of her slippery cleft with his fingertip. Her small gasp was affirmation and permission he decided, and shifting slightly, he lowered his head, drew one nipple into his mouth, and tenderly sucked.

With a soft moan, she slid her fingers through his dark hair and held him firmly at her breast while her breathing changed to soft little pants, a heated glow melted through her body, and she wondered with frenzied rapture and poetic license where he'd been all her life.

Recognizing her soft whimpers meant he'd been given carte blanche, he slid two fingers into her slick sex and gen-

tly explored the sleek interior. *No virgin.* Not that he'd
thought she was, but he was gratified not to have miscalcu-
lated. Although in his current, highly unusual state of
arousal, he would have mounted her, virgin or not. An aber-
ration he deliberately ignored.

It must have been too long since she'd had sex. Surely
that was why she wanted him so madly. Why she was so lost
to reason. And whether having rationalized away her monstrous desires or simply given into sensation, she surrendered
to the piquant incitement of Oz's mouth and stroking fingers,
raising her hips in invitation, signaling her urgency by pressing her throbbing cleft against his palm. "I want *you*," she
whispered, frantic to feel him inside her, reaching for his
erection. "I want *this*," she said, brushing her fingers over the
swollen head of his cock. *"Now."*

"Soon," he answered, his voice in contrast, serene. They
had all night; he was in a rare quixotic mood, poised between
genuine emotion and wildness. Also, he'd learned long ago in
a culture that equated sexual expertise with spiritual enlightenment that speed was a deterrent to carnal pleasure.

And he was a genuinely enlightened man.

She protested, but he ignored her, and Isolde soon relented,
Oz's versatile skills not only sumptuously satisfying but also
incredibly arousing. Not that Will, the love of her life, hadn't
been a tender lover, nor that they hadn't together explored
passion and desire, but Lennox touched her differently. With a
sybaritic, refined exactitude, he fondled, stroked, massaged,
and sucked with such exquisite versatility that he kept her hov-
ering, suspended in a state of bliss just short of orgasm.

By the time he slipped a third finger inside her, she was
literally shaking. "Try this," he whispered, and applied himself to making her heated cunt even more hospitable. Gently
exploring the honeyed passage, he examined every overwrought crevice and fold, plumbing her depth with his long,
slender fingers, titillating and tantalizing until flushed and
breathless, she reached the volatile point of no return.

"Are you ready?" he unnecessarily inquired, his fingers running wet, her body taut with need, her eyes shut tightly against the flame-hot lust scorching her brain.

It took a moment for his words to register, overwhelmed as she was with rapacious desire. And another moment for her to try to find the breath to speak. She nodded instead, incapable of more with the steady, pounding ache between her legs obscuring all else.

"Do you know my name?" For some inexplicable reason, he took umbrage at her fevered frenzy, but even as she tried to speak, he mentally stepped back from the iniquitous brink and smiled. "Don't bother, darling," he soothed, telling himself to count his blessings. Whether she knew who she was fucking or not, a night of pure excess was not to be disparaged.

Dispensing with further unwanted emotion, he guided his cock into her silken cleft, slowly invaded her, and set about bringing this particular stage of their amorous encounter to an end.

Long past any notion of leisurely sex, Isolde swiftly slid her hands down his back, cupped his firm buttocks, and with surprising strength propelled him forward. "More," she ordered, as a countess in her own right was wont to do, the single word faint but audible.

Perhaps more familiar with accommodating females or less familiar with demanding ones, or maybe taking issue with her blind carnal need, Oz gruffly said, "You want *more*?"

Her eyes opened briefly at the low, guttural sound.

Not quite sure why he bridled at the lady's explosive sexuality, nor currently reasonable enough to resolve his peremptory impulses, he instead relinquished further thought, plunged forward, drove into her with barely restrained violence, and gave her what she wanted.

Her scream rocked him back on his heels.

"No, no, no!" she precipitously cried, desperately clutching his hips to drag him back.

Quickly scanning her face—although there was no mistaking her fierce grip—he decided she wasn't in pain. "Hush—here, I'm back," he whispered, gliding in again, bottoming out in her intoxicating heat, resting engulfed and motionless in her snug cunt while a raw, spine-tingling ecstasy bombarded his senses.

Her small, blissful sigh brought a smile to his lips, her soft exhalation strangely touching. Although why it struck him so was a mystery. But not enough of a mystery to alter his irrepressible carnal focus. Grasping her hips firmly, he drove in that slight intoxicating distance more—where the world disappeared and only pure feeling held sway.

Her manifestation of pleasure was no high-pitched scream that time but a series of whisper-soft gasps punctuated with little breathy moans that echoed lewd and sibilant in the quiet of the room.

And the reason that explicitly needy, salacious little sound was drifting into his ears, he pleasantly thought, giving himself up to the soul-stirring rapture, was because his cock was buried in her delectable cunt. Because he'd found safe haven in this soft-as-silk enchantress. Because he'd discovered a measure of paradise in room thirteen of Blackwood's Hotel and suddenly, inexplicably all was right with the world.

He felt curiously *alive* for the first time in ages. There was no explanation, nor was he actually interested in one. A practical man, he was rather more interested in reconstituting the indescribable, all-encompassing, cosmic bliss. Slowly withdrawing in order not to upset the lady, he drove back in again. And then again. And once again—with deftness and ingenuity, with competence and expertise garnered in temples throughout India. The path to ecstasy had been refined over thirty-five centuries, and with conscientious study he'd come to appreciate the concept of the divine body as the source of infinite delight.

The countess feverishly clung to him as he masterfully

transported them toward orgasm, meeting his downstrokes with wild eagerness, whimpering softly each time he withdrew, distrait, wanting more.

Then she'd sigh as he filled her again, her little sumptuous exhalation inevitably making him smile. Miss Perceval, he cheerfully decided after her second riotous climax, was a damnable gift from the gods, a unique blend of joyous innocence and shamelessness, sweetly and sometimes not so sweetly asking him for more, always taking what he gave with a voracious appetite.

Gentleman that he was, he saw that she came several more times before he allowed himself fulfillment. Well trained in his youth by the mystics as well as the courtesans in Hyderabad, he was capable of withholding his orgasms. But not forever.

Even in extremis, though, he was practical.

He came on the countess's stomach.

Having seen too many illegitimate children in India struggle for identity in the ambiguous no-man's-land they occupied, he didn't want to add to that population. There or here.

Once his breathing returned to a semblance of normal and reality reaffirmed itself, he wiped the countess's stomach with the sheet while she lay, eyes shut and unresisting—other than a soft groan when he rubbed her dry between her legs. To which sound his cock instantly reacted, as if her voice alone was magnet to his lust. Drawing in a breath of restraint, he reminded himself that the night was still young and proceeded to wipe himself off rather than plunge back into her enticing little cunt.

Tossing the soiled sheet on the floor, he dropped into a comfortable sprawl, put his arms behind his head, and gazing up at the tester, basked in an agreeable surfeit of excess. And rare contentment.

So rare he found himself subscribing the feeling to some mystical force that had come into play in this hotel room in London.

"I'm so pleased that actor didn't arrive," Isolde whispered, lifting up on one elbow to smile at him as though in answer to his musings. "You're quite lovely in every imaginable way."

He wasn't about to say, *You make me feel strangely content,* so he said, "I consider myself fortunate to have blundered into your room."

"It must be fate."

"Indeed." *And a certain degree of motivation on my part.* "Although, I'm not finished yet," he said, putting his odd feelings into a more familiar context. "We've plenty of time til morning."

"How nice," she said, running a light fingertip across his muscled chest. "I didn't dare ask for fear of appearing too forward."

His gaze was amused. "Really—after your repeated demands for more?"

"Mock if you wish, but I hardly know you. I didn't feel I could ask for more now . . . I mean, now that—you've finished."

Her lovers apparently hadn't had stamina. "I'm just pausing for a moment. So demand away," he pleasantly declared.

"You're not annoyed?"

"No. Gratified certainly, annoyed—not likely. You're a captivating little puss, Miss Perceval. Tell me," he said, curious when he never was, "do you do this often?"

"I don't see that it's any of your concern."

"Forgive me," he suavely returned. "Naturally, it's not."

"Do you do this often?"

"Too often. You're a damned refreshing change."

"Another jaded gentleman. Why am I not surprised?"

"If it's any consolation, jaded is not a feeling I recommend."

"Then why do you do it?"

"Boredom, ennui, who knows," he finished with a shrug. "You must live in the country," he added, preferring less-encumbered subjects.

"Yes."

"And you don't wish to disclose where."

She sighed. "I don't know why. After the papers come out tomorrow morning, you'll know anyway."

"So?"

"I live near Cambridge."

"That's not very definitive."

"Two miles north of town."

"Better. What do you do there?"

"Take care of my estates."

His brows lifted faintly. "For your despicable cousin to inherit."

"Don't remind me," she grumbled.

"Why not marry? That would solve your problem."

"Are you asking?" she playfully inquired.

"Lord no." For a frightening moment he wondered if his earlier fear of being gulled had been mere prologue to this authentic gulling. "Don't say you planned this for I tell you straight out, no one can make me marry."

"Rest easy, Lennox. I don't wish to shackle you or myself for that matter."

Reassured, Oz drew her into his arms and set out to please her and himself in the bargain.

They made love that night slowly and gently, fiercely and wildly, like young lovers learning the other's likes and dislikes for the first time. Neither were innocents, and yet they experienced simple long-forgotten pleasures in each other's arms. They talked as well with a degree of candor neither had previously offered their lovers. She discovered he was alone in the world, his family gone. He discovered she was living an equally solitary life without close family. Maybe their common singleness put them in sympathy, or maybe it was their declared ambition to remain unmarried that prompted their unusual accord.

They both meant it, too, for possibly similar and unspoken reasons.

Near sunrise, they finally fell asleep in each other's embrace after what could only be characterized as a night of extraordinary pleasure.

CHAPTER 3

Exhausted, they slept late. And so they would have continued if they'd not been wakened by Malmsey shouting and pounding on the adjoining door.

"He's your barrister," Oz grumbled, levering his eyes open. "But I'd be more than happy to tell him to go to hell."

Dragged from a glorious dream starring Lennox, Isolde struggled to come awake, to make sense of Malmsey's clamorous outcries. Then she heard the name Frederick and instantly came alert. "It's about my cousin," she muttered, pulling away from Oz's embrace, sitting up and throwing her legs over the side of the bed in one swift motion.

"The loathsome one," he muttered, fully awake now, tossing aside the covers.

"The same." Dashing to the armoire, she snatched up her dressing gown and called out, "I'll be right there, Malmsey!"

Oz had already left the bed and was stepping into his trousers, proficient at dressing rapidly after being surprised in numerous boudoirs by irate husbands over the years. Slipping on his shirt, he quickly rummaged through his overcoat pocket, pulled out his pistol, and checked that it was loaded.

"Good God, don't use that," Isolde declared, casting a nervous glance his way as she knotted the belt of her dressing gown and ran for the door.

"Only if I have to." He didn't believe in turning the other cheek when it came to survival.

Isolde was unlocking the door as he spoke and didn't have time to take issue with Oz's reply. Jerking the door open, she took one look at Malmsey's terror-stricken face and crisply said, "Is he on his way here?"

"Worse, my lady. He's downstairs with a brace of bullies at his back. Only Fremont's burly footmen are holding them at bay."

"How did he find me?" A brisk query, collected rather than fearful.

"He must have a spy—in your household I suspect."

"Has he seen the papers?"

"Indeed, my lady. He's brandishing a copy of the *Belgravia Gazette* and fit to be tied, he is."

"Let him up," Oz directed, coming up beside Isolde. "Don't look at me like that," he said, meeting Isolde's startled gaze. "I'll send the blackguard on his way and you'll be rid of him."

She swung back to Malmsey. "How many men are with him?"

"Five or six."

"It doesn't matter," Oz asserted. "Cowards never stand their ground, retinue or not."

"I don't know," Isolde equivocated. "What if they're armed? Perhaps we should flee."

"He'll follow you wherever you go," Oz gently observed. "Let me take care of this." He glanced at the barrister. "Tell her I'm right, Malmsey."

The barrister was ashen. "I'm not sure, sir—that is . . . Lord Compton has so many ruffians with him."

"Then I'll shoot Compton first," Oz said in a level voice. "Once he's dead, paid hooligans won't stand their ground."

"Dead? Good God, Lennox, don't say such things!" Isolde exclaimed.

"Darling, he's trying to take everything you have. He doesn't deserve a great deal of charity."

"Still . . . dead?" Her eyes were huge. "I find the prospect too awful to even contemplate!"

But a moment later, any further argument became moot as the heavy tramp of feet echoed up the stairs and a confrontation became inevitable.

"In or out, Malmsey?" Oz crisply queried. "I'm shutting this door."

"Really, Robert, you needn't become involved," Isolde declared.

"No, miss, I couldn't leave you unprotected." The rotund little barrister pulled himself up to his middling height and tried to look fierce.

"Excellent," Oz politely remarked, waving the little man into the bedroom, hoping he wouldn't faint and cause a distraction. Quickly shutting the door behind him and locking it, he turned to his companions. "I want you both to stay out of sight. I've dealt with men like Compton before. Don't argue, darling," he firmly added, holding Isolde's gaze. "You'll only get in the way."

"My dear Lennox," Isolde said as firmly, "this confrontation is exactly what I need to confirm the story in the papers. I think he *should* see me. *You* stay out of sight, although it would be useful if some of your clothing was visible."

Oz smiled. "You can't be serious. Do you actually think I'd remain out of sight while he threatens you?"

"I'll simply inform him that the gossip reports are true and he can go on his way."

"Suit yourself." He chose not to uselessly argue. The heavy tread of footsteps was almost upon them.

The knock on the hallway door a moment later was a rough tattoo, followed by Frederick's petulant cry. "Open the door, Isolde! I know you're in there!"

Isolde shivered, the thought of facing Frederick suddenly less auspicious. "What if I don't?" She studied the oak-paneled door. "Do you think it will hold?"

"Of course it'll hold. But then you'll be prisoner in here until—" Oz blew out a breath. "Darling, he's not going away."

"I agree, my lady," Malmsey murmured. "Lord Compton was in high dudgeon when I caught a glimpse of him downstairs."

"I'm going to send him on his way," Oz calmly said, moving toward the door. *Or shoot him where he stands.* "I'd like you both to stay back, but suit yourself."

Turning the latch a moment later, holding his pistol in a deceptively slack hold, he opened the door. "What can I do for you, Compton?" he lazily drawled, his pistol barrel aimed at Frederick's paunch, his gaze swiftly surveying Frederick's burly entourage. "Make your comments brief because my pistol has a hair trigger and I'm testy after being wakened from a dead sleep."

Frederick seemed to shrink into his skin at the sight of Lennox, his rage at Isolde's public scandal subsumed by terror. The feeling increased along with his pallor as his gaze flicked to the pistol Oz held aimed at his stomach.

"You'd best be on your way, Compton," Oz gently said.

But the prospect of Isolde's vast fortune firmed Frederick's spine, as did recall of his hired thugs backing him up. One man against six; the odds were in his favor. "I'm not here to see you," he said with a hint of his normal haughtiness. "I came to speak to the Countess of Wraxell."

"The lady's indisposed at the moment, Compton. She's rare tired after last night," he added with an insolent smile.

Flushing red with anger, Frederick glanced over his shoulder to assure himself his hired roughs were in place. "Nevertheless, I must insist on speaking with her," he said, the extent of his gambling debts prompting him to stand his ground. "This is a civilized country, Lennox," he added, the obvious slur referring to Oz's Indian background. "I have simply come to call on the lady."

"With bully boys at your back." Oz nodded at the menacing crowd. "If you recall, Compton, I shot Buckley last month for irritating me. So don't fucking irritate me or I'll shoot you where you stand." *What the hell is he doing with a frock-coated minister?* The man suddenly hove into view behind a brawny ruffian.

"I have armed men to protect me," Frederick blustered. As if mention of his bodyguard gave him fresh courage, Frederick foolishly added, "Step aside, Lennox. I have business with Lady Wraxell."

"If you wish to see her, you'll have to go through me," Oz silkily said. "I have six shots. One for you and the rest for your thugs if they choose to die today."

The men hired by Frederick lived in a hazardous, dog-eat-dog world; they were survivors or they'd never have lived to adulthood. None of them questioned the cold-blooded malevolence in Oz's eyes or the steadiness of his pistol hand.

"There now, that's a sensible lot," Oz said. Not one man so much as shifted his stance. "I have some money in my coat pocket, Malmsey. Give it to these gentlemen so they might have a pint or two on me." He calmly waited, his finger on the trigger, while the barrister found the coat and the money and hurried over to the door.

"All of it, sir?" the barrister quavered, holding up a thick bundle of large notes.

"Yes, I'm in a charitable mood." He was patently undisturbed, his voice unemotional. "Buy the wife and kiddies a present from me, too, gentlemen." Taking the bills from Malmsey's outstretched hand, he tossed them well down the passageway.

As Frederick's guard melted away in raucous pursuit of the windfall, Oz nodded at the minister who'd not been touched by the greed of lesser men. "Come in, sir. I have need of you. It's not a request," he gruffly added as the man hesitated. "Although, if you do your duty by me," Oz said with a pleasant smile, "your parish will be richer for it."

Ah, there are calibrations of acceptable greed, he thought as the minister walked toward him. "Good day, Compton." He waved him away with his pistol. "Although, I'm more than willing to put a bullet in you if you want to argue the point."

Left to face the formidable Lennox alone, Frederick could do little but glower. "You won't get away with this disgraceful behavior, Lennox! I shall have my revenge on you *and* my cousin!"

The man must be obsessed by the prospect of Isolde's fortune that he dared threaten him. Most men would have been more prudent. "Not, I think, before I have mine, Compton," Oz returned, a plan having leaped full-blown into his mind at the sight of the minister. And so saying, he shut the door in Compton's fat face and locked it securely.

Turning, he set his pistol on a small table and offered Isolde a graceful bow. "Fear and money, darling—an incomparable combination."

"Very effective. My compliments and thanks."

"You're welcome, but you heard him. He's not about to give up without a fight."

She shrugged. "I've dealt with Frederick for years. I'll manage his next threat when it comes."

"He owes money everywhere. I'm not sure he's going to be manageable this time. I have a proposal. A business arrangement as it were—temporary and capable of permanently discouraging your contemptible cousin."

Isolde's gaze flicked to the minister, then back to Oz in warning.

"Malmsey, would you be so kind and take the minister—" He stopped and nodded toward the frock-coated man. "Lennox, sir."

"Pelham, sir."

"You have a marriage license, I presume."

The man flushed. "I was told the marriage was by mutual consent, Mr. Lennox."

Oz didn't correct him; he wore his title lightly. "If you'd leave us for a few minutes," Oz submitted. "This won't take long."

Once the door closed on Malmsey and the minister, Isolde snorted in disgust. "The vile pig. He thought to marry me by force! I'd rather die!"

"Which would only serve his ends," Oz drily said. "As for his scheme to marry you, once the words were spoken, you might not have had recourse."

"Of course I would! It would have been an unspeakable outrage, not to mention a crime!"

"Come, sit with me." Taking her hand, he drew her to a small sofa. "You need to make some plans." Oz was more aware than most men of the finer details of marriage law after listening to his many lovers' conjugal complaints.

"My plan is to avoid the despicable blackguard. I'll hire an army if I have to in order to keep him off my land."

"That might work," he diplomatically replied, sitting and pulling her down on his lap. "But I have a better scheme. A foolproof one."

She smiled. "If this has to do with sex, we have rather too many guests at the moment."

"I'll get rid of them soon." He grinned. "And then we can have sex as man and wife—don't look so shocked. It's an excellent idea. Now, listen."

Afterward, she said, "Hmm," and he was encouraged.

"It's strictly a business arrangement." His voice was soft and even. "We'll have whatever legal documents you want drawn up to protect your property. I have no need of your wealth, nor do I want it. I've plenty of my own. I'll live with you temporarily so all looks right and tight, and once Compton is off the scent, we can divorce easily enough. It only takes money, a good barrister, and patience."

She grinned. "Is that all?"

"Darling, consider, Malmsey will be thrilled to take on such a lucrative commission. And admit," he added, amusement in his gaze, "no one else will have you now that the papers have come out."

"A blessing as you well know. But you needn't be so chivalrous. It's quite too generous, particularly for a man of your—"

"Selfishness?"

Her brows rose. "I was about to say a man of your sybaritic tendencies—all of which I adore by the way. But still, it would be a horrendous imposition for you even temporarily. I don't think the lovers I assume you have will care to drive up to Cambridge to sleep with you."

He didn't say he'd be more than content with her for the immediate future—his driving motivation after a night of uncommonly fine sex. "It's not permanent, darling, so it's not an imposition. As for my lady loves, they'll be in London when I return."

"Are you sure?"

"About them?"

"About this marriage proposition of yours."

"Right now I am. I suggest you seize the opportunity while you may." He grinned. "I may sober up and change my mind."

"Seriously, Lennox. Do you know what you're doing?"

"I always know what I'm doing," he softly said, his gaze crystal clear. *I'll be fucking you for at least a month.* "Compton will be checkmated—which I admit will satisfy me. I dislike cheats. Your fortune will be secure. Not to mention society will buzz with excitement trying to account for our hasty marriage. Need I add," he said, dropping his glance for a moment, "the heart of gossip will center on your stomach and whether or not you're increasing. Particularly now after the scandal sheets have conveyed news of your denouement."

"Will that bother you? The stares and speculation?"

He laughed. "Naive child. That's for me to ask you."

"Nothing bothers you?"

"Nothing in *this* world. Now, come," he briskly said, thrusting aside the affliction he drank to forget, "think of the lovely tumult we will cause. Denouement or not, no one would expect me to marry for fear of scandal. My entire life is lived under a disreputable cloud. The speculation will be intense."

"So my scandal will be a mere bagatelle next to your indiscretions."

"Everyone will consider you a saint for marrying me. So now, Miss Perceval, will you do me the honor of accepting my ardent, heartfelt proposal or reject me and cast me into eternal gloom?"

His roguish smile offered delight. Unrivaled as she well knew. But while his audacious proposal would solve her immediate problems, she was more sober than he since he'd had a bottle close at hand all night. And, she suspected, she was incomparably more responsible drunk or sober. "You're very sweet, but—"

"I'm not in the least sweet. Even knowing that, unlike you, none of the women I know would consider equivocating over my proposal."

She smiled. "They would squeal with delight, shriek 'Yes!' and drag you to the jewelers."

His gaze from under half-lowered lashes was sardonic. "Rich men are much coveted by unmarried females."

"Rich, *handsome* men even more."

"Then you understand the great honor I do you," he said, softly teasing.

Shifting on his lap, she faced him more fully—indecisive, uncertain, yet not unaware of the benefits of his proposal. Including the extravagant sexual pleasures he offered. "What if I were to agree to your reckless offer?"

"Then I'd suggest we finally end this discussion, call in the minister, and embark on the blissful state of matrimony."

His lip curled lightly in mockery. "Naturally, I'd expect due compensation for my charitable impulses."

"To that I would willingly comply," she laughingly replied.

"And to the marriage? Come, darling, enough dithering. Think of it as sport."

She gazed at the prodigal young man pinning her with his dark, high-strung gaze. "As everything is with you."

"You can't say you didn't enjoy last night."

"No," she honestly answered. "But I don't know you."

In the only respect that mattered to him, she did. "Consider, darling, would you rather get to know Compton in my stead?" He glanced at the door to the adjoining room; the man of the cloth's voice was raised in hectoring accents. "Darling, we're keeping the minister waiting."

"I'm trying to decide," she muttered.

"Would it help if I reminded you of Compton's paunch, foul breath, and of course, his grievous luck at cards? He owes a fortune to the moneylenders."

"Oh God, don't remind me."

"Sorry, but he won't give up. Not with the moneylenders snapping at his heels."

Drawing in a small breath, she hesitated still. Then exhaling, she said, not without sufficient trepidation to cause a slight catch in her voice, "Very well. I accept your kind offer."

"I'm deeply honored," Oz said with polished grace.

"And drunk."

"Perhaps a little," he lied, and, turning his head, shouted for the minister.

CHAPTER 4

MR. PELHAM'S RESERVATIONS were overcome with a generous gift to his parish, Malmsey's with a quickly scrawled note by Oz in which he relinquished any interest in Isolde's property, and shortly after, in room thirteen of Blackwood's Hotel, with Malmsey and Fremont as witnesses, Miss Perceval and Baron Lennox prepared to outmaneuver Frederick Compton.

"Make it short," Oz instructed the minister. At Pelham's frown, he thought him an ungrateful bastard considering the sizable sum he'd donated to his church, but rather than argue about the man's lack of appreciation, Oz turned to Isolde and gently said, "Unless *you* prefer the entire ritual, darling. Although you really shouldn't be standing that long."

He was brazen and shameless out of bed as well, Isolde thought, as a blush pinked her cheeks at his insinuation. But she answered with cool equanimity. "A short ceremony would please me."

How like her, Oz reflected, recalling that same mild tone from their first meeting. "As you see, Mr. Pelham. The lady wishes brevity."

But as the minister grudgingly flipped through the pages of his prayer book to the essential passages, Isolde reflected on the stark difference between this humble ceremony and what she'd once envisioned for her wedding day. Like every young lady of wealth, her dreams had been romantic and starry-eyed. The family chapel would have been filled with fragrant summer flowers, she would have been radiant in a magnificent couturier design instead of her travel gown, scores of guests would have been in attendance, and of course, a different bridegroom would have stood at her side.

But then Will had been obliged to marry Anne Verney.

Frederick's coercion had taken a dangerous turn.

And here she was—harsh reality dispatching romantic dreams.

Oz chose not to consider the bizarre occasion other than as a temporary solution to a lady's dilemma that offered him at least a month of deeply satisfying sex. As for romantic dreams, his had been buried in India two years ago. When the minister paused at the point in the ceremony where a ring was required for the bride's finger, Oz pulled off his gem-cut signet ring and slid it on Isolde's finger. It was less suitable perhaps than the emerald on the fourth finger of his left hand, but that ring was too precious to relinquish.

Once the ceremony was over, Oz saw that Isolde took possession of the marriage certificate, then he thanked the various participants and politely ushered them from the room. Shutting the door, he leaned back against it and looked at his new wife, his lashes at half-mast, his gaze unreadable. "So," Oz spoke softly. "How are you feeling?"

She was silent for a moment. "Filled with doubt," she quietly said. Plucking up her spirit because she wouldn't become some vaporish female now that the deed was done, she added in a more normal tone of voice, "What about you?"

He shrugged, more sober suddenly than he wished. "It's over. Let's get out of here. We'll wait at my house for the more definitive documents from Malmsey. We'll have some champagne to celebrate the happy occasion," he offered, hoping to lift her spirits—although he could use a bottle or two himself right now. "I have an excellent library if you like to read, a china collection of my mother's I'm told is good"—*women like china collections, don't they?*—"I also have a damned fine chef who'll cook you anything you want. From cakes and tea to bloody beef and anything in between. Are you hungry?"

She wrinkled her nose. "Do I look so forlorn you must cajole me?"

"Like a lost puppy, darling." His voice was idle as if his thoughts were elsewhere. "Come, we'll discuss Compton's blighted hopes over breakfast," he said, the familiar amusement back in his tone. "That should please you."

She smiled ever so faintly as he moved toward her. "How blighted are his hopes? Lie if necessary."

"Blighted beyond redemption. No lie. And as your savior," he said with a wicked wink, taking her hand in his, "I shall expect my reward in short order." *Better sex than morbid reflection*—his mantra of recent years.

"Shameless libertine," she accused, although her voice held a hint of levity. "Don't you ever think of anything else?"

"Not with you around." Taking the marriage parchment from her hand, he dropped it on a chair and pulled her close. "See?" His remedy of choice to moments of chagrin.

Lacing her arms around his waist, she moved her hips against his rising erection and, gazing up at him from under her lashes, saw the familiar smoldering flame in his dark eyes. "You're always ready to oblige a lady, aren't you?" she murmured, a familiar glow beginning to warm her senses.

Sliding his hands down her back, he pressed her into his rigid length. He couldn't say sex had been his substitute for feeling the last two years. "Why don't we pull down the carriage shades," he said instead, "and entertain ourselves on the drive home."

"You *do* know how to cheer me up."

"What's a husband for if not that?" he offered with a grin. "My God," he exclaimed, "I'm going to engage in carnal relations with my *wife*."

"Your *temporary* wife."

His grin widened. "I wouldn't have it any other way."

But their plans were curtailed once they reached the lobby for Malmsey was waiting for them. "Forgive me," he said with a rueful smile, "but I still have questions to put to you both before I can draw up the settlement papers."

Oz glanced at Isolde, who stood at his side, her gloved hand resting on his arm. "Do we have time?" She was less inclined to forgo her pleasures than he.

She hesitated.

He was about to make some excuse to Malmsey when she leaned into him and looked up from under the hood of her blue velvet cloak. "It's up to you."

It made no difference to him one way or the other; he'd be fucking her soon enough. But Malmsey's hopeful expression couldn't be overlooked. "Ride with us and ask your questions," he kindly offered. "You need paper and pencil, don't you? Fremont!" He gestured as if writing. "Fetch a pencil and paper!"

The distance to his home wasn't sufficient for Malmsey to interrogate them fully, so Oz invited him in.

As the trio ascended the shallow bank of stairs, the front door of Oz's mansion opened before them with smooth efficiency, and Oz ushered Isolde over the threshold into an entrance hall of palatial proportions, considerable colored marble, and an impressive display of gold gilt.

A majordomo of indeterminate age and considerable consequence stood at attention before them in a simple black livery.

"Good morning, my lord." Neither his expression nor manner indicated the singular occasion. Oz did not bring his lady loves home. "Would you be needing refreshments?"

"Yes, please." Relieving Isolde of her cape, Oz handed it

to a footman. "I have a small announcement," he remarked with the tranquility of a man long accustomed to indisputable power. "Allow me to introduce my lady wife and your new mistress, Lady Wraxell." His gaze moved from his retainer to Isolde. "Josef will cater to your every whim, darling, as he has to mine for as long as I can remember. You may wish us happy, Josef," he finished with a smile.

"May we offer you our most hearty congratulations, sir," the tall majordomo said without so much as a glimmer of surprise in his cool, grey gaze, nor a glance at the disheveled state of the newlyweds' clothing. "What a great pleasure it is to meet you, my lady," he added, turning to Isolde with a look as bland as that he'd offered Oz. "I know I speak for the entire household when I wish you both much joy."

Oz dipped his head. "Thank you, Josef, and thank the staff as well. I'm afraid we're both tired and hungry. It's been a busy, energetic many hours. If someone could show Mr. Malmsey to my study," he added with a glance at the barrister, "we'll join him there."

As Malmsey was led away, Oz looked at Isolde. "Now, is there anything you'd like, darling?"

She blushed.

He smiled, mouthed the word *soon*, then shifting his gaze, addressed his majordomo with imperturbability. "See that my lady's valise is brought in and put in the ivory chamber. We both need a bath drawn. Have coffee and some small nourishment brought to the study. Brandy for me." He took Isolde's hand. "This shouldn't take long, darling. We'll send Malmsey on his way in short order."

As they walked away, Josef turned to the several footmen on duty who displayed varying levels of shock. "I suggest you stop gaping and see to your duties. Have the lady's valise brought in, see that she has a servant waiting in her chamber, and inform Achille that our master is home, hungry, and newly married."

"A prodigious surprise," the elderly hall porter said, his

long-standing employment in the household allowing him such frankness.

"But a pleasant surprise," Josef murmured. "The boy has long needed a companion."

"As if he ain't had enough of those," a footman said under his breath.

"That's quite enough, Ted. Mind your tongue." Josef clapped his hands. "I believe you all have duties to perform. We wouldn't want our new mistress to find the household deficient in any way."

But once everyone had dispersed, Josef allowed himself a pensive moment. He'd been with the young master since birth, having served his father before him. He hoped the boy hadn't made too hasty a decision. He hoped above all that the new Lady Lennox would bring their headstrong master joy. Two years ago, young Oz had lost the woman he loved as well as his parents in the space of six months. He deserved some happiness.

COMING TO A stop outside the door of his study, Oz pulled Isolde close and stole a kiss. "Mmm—you feel good. Don't go far."

She smiled up at him. "Since I seem to be addicted, you needn't worry."

He drew in a quick breath, let his hands drop away, and reached for the door latch. "Let's get this over with. I don't want anything of yours. Correction, anything material. *You* I want. Ready?" At her nod, he shoved open the door, waved Malmsey back into his chair, and escorted Isolde into his book-lined study. The room smelled of leather bindings and hashish, of masculine cologne heavy with musk. Of brandy most of all. He spent his evenings here reading and smoking before his nightly excursions into London's clubs, society, or stews.

"We're at your disposal," he courteously said, conducting

Isolde to a leather wing-back chair and dropping into a chair beside her. "Ask away, Malmsey, although you only need protect your client's property. I'm not concerned with mine. I have more money than I need. I own the largest merchant bank in India." He smiled at Isolde. "Unlike your cousin, I only want you."

Since he'd already signed away any interest in her property, she hadn't been concerned, but *my goodness, the largest merchant bank in India?*

Apparently, Malmsey was equally impressed. He had to clear his throat several times before speaking. "I see. Would that be the National Bank of Delhi?"

"That's one of mine, yes, although our headquarters are in Hyderabad."

"And you're active in the operation?" Isolde inquired, startled.

"Yes." He grinned. "Are you surprised?"

"Frankly, yes."

"Then I'll have to educate you in that enterprise as well."

She blushed. He'd meant her to. "I'm familiar, indeed overfamiliar with legal documents," he said to Malmsey, allowing his wife a moment to regain her composure. "You need only show me where to sign."

"I understand, sir. Nevertheless, certain procedures must be followed."

Oz said no more; barristers were of a suspicious nature. He settled back to politely endure the inquisition.

Once his brandy was carried in, he suffered the occasion with considerably more forbearance.

"I'll have the papers drawn up and delivered to you this afternoon," Malmsey said at last, clutching a fistful of papers covered in spidery script and rising from his chair.

Coming to his feet, Oz put out his hand. "Thank you for your able assistance in the recent turmoil."

Isolde smiled at her barrister from the depths of the burgundy leather wing-back chair, her hair like spun gold against the dark leather. "Thank you, Robert, for being so helpful. I'm in your debt."

"It's a pleasure to serve you, my lady." Malmsey's bow was quite elegant for a portly little man.

The door shut with a small click a moment later, and Oz turned to his new bride.

"At the risk of offending you, darling, that took so long I do have to eat now. I'm starved." He dipped his head in a deferential gesture. "We can eat breakfast in bed if you like, but eat I must. You drove me damned hard last night."

She smiled at the heated memory. "I'm feeling a little peckish myself."

He blew out a breath. "Thank you."

Her brows rose. "Am I that difficult?"

"No, not at all—the thing is . . . honestly—I don't usually have a lady in my house. More to the point—a wife." He raked his fingers through his hair. "I'm improvising. Look," he abruptly said, "let me call Achille, you tell him what you want for breakfast, then we'll go upstairs and bathe and change while he's doing whatever he does in the kitchen."

"Did my valise come in?" She'd brought a single change of clothes with her to the hotel since she'd planned to return home the morning after her staged denouement.

He nodded. "I'm sure it's upstairs." Josef had risen to the occasion with his usual aplomb on being introduced to Isolde; not so much as a raised eyebrow had testified to his shock. But then Josef had been with Oz a long time; nothing shocked him anymore.

As they ascended the broad marble staircase, Oz softly swore. "We forgot to have Malmsey see to the marriage announcement for the papers. My secretary will arrange it," he promptly resolved. "It's simple enough."

"Must we?"

He shot her a look. "Cold feet?"

She took a small breath. "There's a certain finality to an announcement in the *Times*."

"But not as final as Compton stripping you of your fortune," he said drily.

"I know—you're right."

"I would have been more right if you'd given me leave to kill him."

"Please, don't even think it!"

"Sorry, I'll say no more." But he and Compton were going to have a little talk. "Much as I'd like to join you in your bath," he murmured, deliberately changing the subject as they moved down the corridor, "I'm going to beg off. If we were to bathe together, we wouldn't be eating anytime soon."

She smiled. "And you're starving."

"An understanding wife is a blessing," he drolly said, stopping before a door and opening it.

"As is a husband who does his conjugal duty by his wife." Isolde offered him a playful wink as she walked past him.

"Once we eat, consider me at your disposal for my husbandly duties. I'll clear my schedule."

She turned around to reply only to see the door close. After having his warm body next to hers all night, she felt strangely bereft. Not a sensible feeling considering the pragmatic nature of their arrangement, nor one she should dwell on. Instead, she scanned the large chamber she'd entered. The decor was exotic—the walls composed of carved ivory panels, the furniture, inlaid mother of pearl, the upholstery and draperies vividly colored silk. She was surrounded by the splendor of India. She must ask him more about his family.

"Your bath is ready, my lady."

A young maid appeared from behind a latticework screen.

She lived more simply in the country. Not that Oak Knoll wasn't a sprawling Tudor mansion filled with relics from the past, but Oz's home was resplendent of wealth, from the huge staff to the glorious furnishings suggestive of eastern potentates.

"My lady, the water's cooling."

Prodded from her reverie, Isolde quickly said, "Thank

you. I'll be right there." But she would do well to remember that a marriage of convenience had no room for emotion. Especially with a man like Oz.

Driven by hunger, Oz sped through his toilette, and fifteen minutes later, bathed and dressed, his wet hair slicked back, he entered the breakfast room and inhaled the welcome fragrance of hot coffee and bacon.

"Congratulations. I hear she's very lovely." Achille was standing beside the sideboard.

"She is, thank you. I need coffee." Oz made for the table, where his chair was occupied as it was most mornings by a two-year-old, fair-haired boy who at the moment was smiling at him through a mouthful of jam-filled pastry, the remnants of the cruller held out to Oz in one sticky hand.

"At your place. I ground it myself. What can I get you this morning?"

"Two of everything—make that three. Morning, Jess. Is that good? It looks good." As the little boy vigorously nodded and chewed, his uplifted face shining, Oz picked him up, sat down with the toddler on his lap, and reached for his coffee cup. "Thank you, Achille," he said, his gratitude plain as he lifted the cup to his mouth. "I *need* this."

"Try dis!"

Narrowly averting an ungentle meeting between pastry and coffee cup, Oz swept his cup aside just as the much-handled cruller struck his chin. He laughed. "You missed—here," he said, bending his head, "try again."

"Me wike." A wide, jammy smile. "You wike, too."

This time the pastry was on target to the satisfaction of one chubby-cheeked toddler who liked Oz as much as Oz liked him. The son of a new member of his staff, Jess often enlivened Oz's mornings.

"Not much sleep last night?" Achille set two plates before Oz.

"Very little."

"I thought so. I made the coffee strong."

The men were of an age and friends of long-standing. Oz had found Achille in the Maldives years ago where the cook had been stranded when his employer along with his employer's yacht had been sunk by the pirates who plagued the eastern waters. A long way from his home in Marseilles, Achille had been cooking in a waterfront dive; Oz had hired him on the spot.

Quickly draining his cup of coffee while Jess busied himself running his sticky fingers down the gold buttons of Oz's waistcoat, Oz set down the empty cup. "*That* was a lifesaver. Now some food and I might survive another day."

"She must have been delightful, but you don't usually marry them."

"It's a long story. One I can't divulge at the moment. But in time, all will be revealed."

"Sounds mysterious." Achille reached down, picked up a damp cloth, conveniently set on the table for just such a purpose, and quickly wiped Jess's fingers as the toddler struggled against his grip.

Oz shook his head, chewing a mouthful of very wet scrambled eggs done just as he liked them. "Not mysterious," he said a moment later. "Just a minor crisis. Soon to be resolved."

His attention diverted from the buttons, Jess recalled more important issues. "Me toy, me toy, me toy!"

It was a daily ritual. "Look in this jacket pocket." Oz pointed. "And tell me if you know what's in there." While the boy was plunging both hands into Oz's pocket, Oz asked, "Is that the bacon from Normandy? It is? Give yourself a raise. I thought you couldn't get any more once Monsieur Battie died." He speared a thinly sliced round.

"His grandson came home from Paris and took over the farm."

He smiled without looking up. "Obliging boy. Give him a raise, too."

"You're in a damned good mood for a man who vowed never to marry."

Oz said, "It's your food, Achille," before turning his attention to the boy in his lap.

Having pulled out two small, brightly painted animals, Jess was frowning at them.

"Do you know what they are?" Oz gently asked.

"Cows?"

"Dinosaurs. There's more in the other pocket. Set them on the table and I'll tell you their names."

As Jess was digging in Oz's other pocket, he returned to his breakfast.

"I think your good spirits might be because of something more than my food," Achille remarked, Oz's marriage as shocking as his casual disregard of the event.

"Don't get all intuitive and sensitive on me," Oz scornfully said, scooping up another forkful of eggs. "You're wasting your time."

"As you say," Achille acceded, Oz's reply exceedingly blunt. He changed the subject. "I hope my lady likes Madagascar chocolate."

"God knows. We'll find out. Here, Jess, line them up here; there should be five. Can you count to five?" He looked up. "What did she ask for? I didn't listen."

"Steak and kidney pie if I had any in the larder."

"For breakfast?" Oz shrugged. "Did you have any?"

"Of course. And cake."

"She wanted cake? I suppose you had that, too."

"Need you ask?"

Oz grinned. "No, you smug bastard."

"You keep an excellent kitchen, mi'lor," Achille said with a smile.

"Do I indeed? Glad to hear it. On a serious note, though, we're going into the country soon, and I need you along. Her cook won't know how to prepare Indian food. There's one more, Jess. You have to find one more."

"I'll start packing supplies after breakfast."

"We leave either tomorrow or the next day." Oz glanced

up as the door opened, bent to whisper in Jess's ear, quickly came to his feet, and left the little boy in his chair, busy with his dinosaurs.

With a bow for his new mistress, Achille returned to the sideboard to fetch Isolde's breakfast.

Oz moved to greet his wife and, meeting her in the center of the large room, casually said to the question in her eyes, "He's the son of my sous-chef's sister. He likes to breakfast with me. By the way, you look good enough to eat." He took her hand and brought it to his lips. "I like your girlish gown."

She wore a simple morning dress of raspberry silk with a matching ribbon in her pale, frothy hair. It was the only gown she'd packed, and the traveling dress she'd worn to London needed pressing.

Since nonchalance seemed to be the order of the day, not to mention perhaps the usual mode of living for her new husband, Isolde lightly said, "You clean up rather nicely yourself." His tweed jacket and buff trousers were casual morning attire, his gleaming half boots testament to his valet's competence. His crisp linen was immaculate, his foulard waistcoat smeared with jam the only flaw in the elegance of his dress.

"Two-year-olds," he said, noting her glance. "The bane of my valet. Although I'm assuming we'll be undressing again soon anyway. Malmsey won't be back until afternoon."

"How tempting," she said. "You do know how to—" Isolde paused at a knock on the door.

A young man entered at Oz's bidding, and after escorting Isolde to her seat at the table and resuming his, toddler on his lap, Oz introduced her. Jess was devoted to lining up dinosaurs on the linen cloth.

"Darling, this is my secretary, Charles Davey. Charles, my lady wife. You have the announcement I see." Oz nodded at the sheet of paper in Davey's hand.

"For your perusal, sir, and"—he dipped his head toward Isolde—"my lady."

It was a brief two lines giving their names and the marriage date. Oz glanced at it, handed it across the small table to Isolde, who surveyed it and gave it back.

"Have it published in all the papers tomorrow," Oz instructed, holding it out to his secretary. "We should be gone from the city before the news is broadcast."

"Very good, sir. Are you home today?"

Oz looked at Isolde. "Are we home?"

She shook her head.

"We are not it seems," he said with a smile for his wife. As his secretary walked out, Oz gestured at a small gold coffer of medieval character, set with large cabochon gems. "Pick out a more appropriate wedding ring. My mother kept some of her jewelry in London. There should be something suitable in there."

"I don't need a ring, but thank you. I expect you want your signet back." Quickly sliding the ruby cut with the Lennox cipher off her thumb, she handed it to him across the small table.

"Don't argue. Think how tongues will wag in the ton if I don't bestow a suitably lavish symbol of my affection on my new bride. Be a good girl," he quietly said, "and take one."

She'd not yet come to know how much he disliked resistance, but understood beneath the softness of his voice was a well-mannered command.

"Very well, but you may have it back later," she said with equal imperiousness, at which he smiled and said, "Of course. As you wish."

Then he committed himself to entertaining Jess, speaking low, explaining the names of the dinosaurs, helping the toddler rearrange the figures to his satisfaction, not so much as glancing Isolde's way as she selected her wedding ring from a sumptuous collection of jewels.

"There, are you happy now?" She held out her hand, a heart-shaped ruby sparkling on her ring finger.

There was a small pause while Oz obliged Jess by moving a figure slightly to the left before he turned to his new bride and smiled. "Very well behaved. Thank you." Then his smile changed to one of lethal charm and he said, "Forgive me for being childish. I'm afraid I'm not used to a wife. That was one of my mother's favorite rings by the way. It suits you."

"I apologize as well. We are both singularly determined."

"I remember that," he softly said, delight in his gaze. "A quality I much admire in you."

She flushed deeply and nervously glanced at Achille.

"Achille hears nothing, darling. Do you, Achille?" Oz murmured with a raised brow to his friend standing by the sideboard.

"Excuse me, sir?"

Oz turned back to Isolde. "There, you see? We are quite alone, especially while Jess is transfixed with his toys. Now, come, darling," he placidly said, "enjoy your breakfast."

But even as the newlyweds breakfasted with a noisy, busy toddler, rumors of Lennox's marriage were racing like wildfire through the ton. A servant at Blackwood's Hotel had spoken of the surprising marriage to his cousin who valeted for the Duke of Buccleuch—disclosing the news in the strictest confidence, of course. The duke's valet whispered the juicy bit of gossip into the butler's ear who in turn conveyed the astonishing tidbit to his counterpart in the Earl of Derby's household. And so it went, the shocking event made known to the whole of society in less than two hours.

As reports of their marriage were touching off shock and wonderment in boudoirs and breakfast rooms around town, Oz and Isolde shared a companionable meal, finding that they could converse easily like friends of long-standing rather than recent acquaintances. Jess had been diverted with his toy chest, which was conveniently at hand under the sideboard, and was oblivious to the adults as only a toddler fully engaged in play could be.

Oz, having eaten well, was at ease, his wife's presence across the table surprisingly soothing—a revelation for a man who'd always carefully avoided morning-after occasions. It occurred to him that she was very restful. She didn't disrupt his normal routine or look askance at Jess, who hadn't yet warmed to a new acquaintance at breakfast; nor did she introduce a jarring note into what had always been for him a tranquil time. She quietly read the paper, commenting from time to time on some topic that actually interested him, intelligently answering his infrequent remarks with a degree of acuteness that made him conclude that he might have been amusing himself with very shallow females prior to Miss Perceval.

Isolde was equally surprised she was so comfortable with a man she barely knew. Furthermore, a man of such notable seductive skills hardly seemed the type who would entertain a child at breakfast and manage to exude tranquility across the breakfast table as well. And yet he did. Like an old shoe, she incredulously thought.

CHAPTER 5

WHILE THE NEWLYWEDS were breakfasting *à trois*, two people in London were particularly hard hit by the news of Oz and Isolde's nuptials.

Compton was somewhat the worse for drink despite the hour, but then he'd been roughly handled earlier that morning and had just cause for imbibing. On being given the inauspicious tidings by his valet, he swore roundly, poured himself another drink, drank it down, then sent for a shady fellow and a shadier solicitor he knew.

At her maid's mention of Oz's new wife, Nell's shriek echoed all the way down to the kitchen, the servants throughout the sprawling house flinching at the sound. Lady Howe's temper was fearsome. Her next scream—freezing the blood in all within range of her voice—was for her carriage to be brought round. Then, hurling her breakfast tray on the floor, she leaped out of bed, bellowing for her abigail.

In the course of her toilette, she took out her fury on the poor woman, unmercifully threatening and upbraiding her at every turn, finding fault with all her words and actions, using the young maid servant as a convenient target for every item of clothing, bit of jewelry, comb, brush, or hairpin that offended her. By the time Nell finally stalked from her boudoir, the floor was littered, but London's reigning beauty was modishly, even dashingly attired. Her fox cape and black velvet gown served as stunning foil to her pale skin and red hair; pearls the size of pigeon eggs glistened at her throat and ears, and a small beaded bonnet was picturesquely perched on her upswept curls. With her pert chin high, her cherry red lips pursed, she sallied forth to ferret out the truth.

The instant the bedroom door closed on her mistress, the abigail, ashen and shaking, collapsed in tears. As she loudly sniffled and sobbed, she vowed to seek out another position even if it meant taking a post at some lesser establishment. Even if she was reduced to working for some arriviste mushrooms.

For her part, Nell was vowing to get to the bottom of the ridiculous, outrageous rumor making the rounds of London. She had no intention of giving up a virile, captivating, obscenely handsome lover like Oz! None at all!

IT WAS NO surprise to at least one of the occupants enjoying coffee in the baron's morning room sometime later, when a distrait servant burst in stammering an apology, followed closely by a beautiful, glowering woman in red fox and black velvet who swept into the room like a whirlwind.

"Sorry, sir," the servant quavered, sweating. "She weren't—"

"Never mind, Jack. You did your best." A master at awkward situations, Oz rose from the sofa to face his irrate lover. "To what do we owe this early-morning visit, Nell?" he blandly inquired.

"Tell me you didn't actually *do* it!" Nell retorted, ill-humored and sulky, swiftly advancing on Oz, her porcelain brow marred by a scowl.

"News travels fast below stairs it seems."

"As you well know! Is it true? It can't be!" Halting before him, she raked him with a glance. "You *did*, didn't you! How *could* you?" she cried, stamping her foot and swatting him with her beaded purse.

"Allow me to make my wife known to you, Nell," Oz remarked, not about to respond to her outburst. Taking a step back, he glanced at Isolde seated on the sofa. "Countess Wraxell in her own right, meet Lady Howe. Nell and I are old friends."

If looks could kill, Isolde thought with amusement as the stylish redhead raked her with a murderous glance, her husband would have been widowed on the spot. As for old friends, it was obvious they were rather more than that. "Good morning, Lady Howe. Would you like coffee or do you prefer tea?"

Oz smiled at his wife, charmed by her poise.

"Don't be ridiculous," Nell snapped. "I didn't come here for tea." Flushed with anger, she turned to Oz. "I came to speak with *you*."

"Say what you like," he answered.

"I doubt your wife would care to hear what I have to say." Snobbish and snide, she dismissed the young woman in the unfashionable gown.

"I'm sure Isolde won't care; we deal well together."

Shock and chagrin registered for a flashing moment on Nell's face, his fondness plain when he mentioned his wife. *Impossible; not Oz. It must have been a lapse of some kind.* "Very well, suit yourself," Nell said sweetly, shifting her tactics, although the quick look she cast Isolde's way was anything but sweet. "The truth now, darling," she murmured, brushing Oz's arm with her gloved finger in a proprietary gesture. "Surely, this must be some jest."

"Not in the least."

She tried to interpret his tempered tone. "Is it some absurd wager?"

"No."

His placid reply and faint shrug left little doubt he spoke the truth. "I can't believe you *actually* married this, this— little nobody from nowhere," she petulantly accused, volatile and sullen once again. "You were supposed to meet *me* at Blackwood's last night!"

"Believe it, Nell," he gruffly said, suddenly impatient. Oz was never in the mood to deal with Nell's sulks, and this morning was no exception.

Nell met his chill gaze, recognized the restive look in his eyes, and understood there were men at her beck and call and others like Oz who never would be. Sensibly dismissing his marriage as irrelevant, she shrugged her fur-draped shoulders, ceased pouting, and smiled. "Whether you're married or not doesn't really signify, does it, dear? Everyone knows a leopard doesn't change his spots," she added with a little laugh. "I wish you good fortune in your marriage, Countess." She threw Isolde a pitying glance, for who better than she knew of Oz's plans the previous night. Gently touching Oz's hand, she softly said, "Do call on me, darling, whenever you have time. We always have such fun together. You amuse me in so many—"

Oz caught her arm in a vicious grip. "I'll see you to your carriage," he growled, forcing her toward the door before she said more.

Isolde heard him swear as he exited the room, and while she had no business feeling smug, she couldn't help but experience the veriest bit of satisfaction at her husband's gallantry. True, he might only be acting the part to convince Lady Howe the marriage was real. But he seemed genuinely irritated by his tantrumish lover.

The beautiful redhead was *quite* splendid, though, her fiery temper notwithstanding.

Then again, Oz might prefer tempestuousness in bed.

Which was neither here nor there, Isolde sensibly decided.

Her husband would do as he pleased, married or not.

Lady Howe was right. Oz wasn't likely to change his spots.

NOT THAT HE wasn't trying at the moment. "Goddamn, Nell, what the hell were you thinking?" he muttered as he hustled her down the stairs. "Don't show up here again."

"Don't order me about! I'll do as I please!" She gasped. "You're hurting me!"

"I'll strangle you with my bare hands if you come back," he curtly said, unmoved by her gasp, shoving her across the entrance hall toward the door. "It's not an idle threat, Nell." The strength in his fingers was leaving deep bruises. "You're bloody irritating me."

While he seemed immune to his retainers' stares, Nell tried not to swoon before the several flunkeys in the hall.

Signaling for the door to be opened, Oz propelled her toward the open threshold and reaching it, let her go. "Don't come back," he said loud enough so his servants understood she wasn't to be admitted again.

Then he turned, crossed the entrance hall in swift strides, and took the stairs at a run.

Returning to the morning room, Oz apologized for Nell's intrusion.

"She's a vain, self-indulgent baggage. But we won't be bothered again. I promise." Dropping beside Isolde on the sofa, he stretched out his legs, slid into a comfortable sprawl, rested his head against the cushions, and softly exhaled. Nell was a handful. She always had been.

"You're quite free to pursue your personal amusements," Isolde quietly remarked. "You know that."

He turned his head enough to smile at her. "I know. However, we should appear the newlyweds for the moment at least—to put Compton off the scent. As for Nell, it won't happen again."

He spoke with a rough brusqueness at the end, and Isolde

recalled him offering to shoot Frederick for her. Her husband had a callous streak she'd do well to remember. "Once we're in the country, we'll be under less scrutiny—from Frederick or your friends."

He nodded, only half listening. Nell would spread the news of his marriage far and wide, including his savaging of her—which would only increase the tittle-tattle. "If you're up to it, I think it might be wise if we're at home today. Our marriage is the current overnight wonder; the most avid of the curiosity seekers are bound to call. It would serve your purposes to let the multitudes come and see"—he smiled— "the woman who so swept me off my feet, I was induced to renounce bachelorhood and allow myself to be caught."

"Please, a stalking female is such a cliché. Would you be averse to the proposition that *I* was pursued and caught."

"Cliché it may be, but it's true," he grumbled, having evaded every form of female pursuit since arriving in London, including being surprised in his bed. "I understand, though. Our marriage will be the result of love at first sight on my part. How's that?"

"Very gracious of you." Isolde softly sighed. "I have a confession."

"Good God. Don't say you're my sister."

She laughed. "Rest easy. But your love-at-first-sight fiction *is* useful to me for another reason." She took a small breath, glanced away, clearly discomfited.

"Go on, darling," Oz prompted. "I'm unshockable."

"It's not actually shocking." Her voice was subdued. "In fact, it's quite common I suspect—a betrothal gone awry."

His brows lifted. "Yours, I presume."

She nodded. "It turns out"—she grimaced—"the man I planned to marry had been promised by his family to another. He felt honor bound to marry her."

"In this day and age?"

"Country ways are more traditional."

"Ah."

"It's true," she insisted.

He put up a hand. "I didn't mean to disagree." He smiled. "As I understand it then, you'd like *your* husband—me—to be head over heels for you as compensation for all the local gossip you had to endure with this, er, foiled betrothal."

She looked down briefly before she met his gaze. "Do I seem silly and foolish?"

"Not at all." He knew about wanting things that could never be, about the cruelty of gossip. *Do you love him still?* he thought, knowing how much he missed Khair. Not that any of it mattered. "In truth, posing as your lovesick husband will actually serve as explanation for my extraordinary behavior. I was a confirmed bachelor; everyone knew it."

She smiled, relieved for inchoate, possibly stupid reasons. "Thank you. It shouldn't be for long in any event."

"No." *Especially after I scare the hell out of Compton.*

"Now then," she said, cheered by Oz's casual chivalry, "do you think we'll have many visitors?"

Shoving himself upward, Oz reached for a bottle Achille had conveniently left for him. "I know we will," he said, uncorking the bottle.

And he set about fortifying himself for the ordeal.

CHAPTER 6

BEFORE LONG, THE busybodies, scandalmongers, and a great many of Oz's inamoratas came to call, all morbidly curious to see the clever, artful woman who had managed to lure Lennox into the marriage trap. They smiled and bowed and offered their felicitations; they took tea and made idle conversation—all the while frantic to know the reason for Lennox's marriage.

"She's but a child," the matrons whispered, Isolde's girlish gown offering up an image of innocence. "And clearly unworldly, wearing a simple gown like that without a speck of jewelry. Where did she come from? Where's her family?" And then their eyes would narrow, as if the answer to this odd marriage would be revealed with closer scrutiny.

The men discounted innocence, their focus instead, male-like, on sex. "Lennox lusted after that buxom, young maid," the men murmured, surveying Isolde's curvaceous body with heated gazes, envying Oz his voluptuous, new bride.

"The bitch. The clever bitch," Oz's resentful lovers hissed under their breaths, their veiled glances sullen. How had she brought him to the altar when so many had failed? Although, she'd have competition soon enough they didn't doubt. Which thought consoled and heartened them.

"Have you known each other long?" the visitors invariably asked, each arrival—thanks to Nell's *on dits*—sensible of the startling suddenness of the marriage. *It must have been a necessitous marriage*, they all thought. *Why else would a cheeky young profligate like Lennox marry?*

The first time the question of their acquaintance was posed, Isolde turned to her husband. "Oz likes to tell the story," she said with a smile. "It's quite romantic."

"We've known each other since we were children," he blandly lied—repeating the fiction often in the course of the day. "A family connection—distant, of course. Isolde always wrote to me over the years, didn't you, darling," he fondly murmured, lifting her hand to his lips at that point for a gentle kiss. "And then suddenly, I found my little Isolde all grown up and I fell head over heels in love."

She blushed prettily.

The room always went quiet for a second at such blatant affection from a man who'd seduced women far and wide but never loved them.

"She's shy," he'd say, smiling fondly at his bride. "An admirable quality in a wife."

Another moment of shocked silence would ensue.

Oz had always preferred audacious women.

And so the at-home visit went, Isolde smiling through it all, accepting society's spurious good wishes and pointed glances at her belly with grace, Oz discharging his role of doting husband with careless panache. All the while the servants keeping the cake plates and teacups replenished.

It was a long, albeit productive day.

Until finally, an old roue made the mistake of saying, "If I was twenty years younger, Lennox, I'd vie for the lady's favors myself."

"If you were twenty years younger, Wilkins, I'd call you out," Oz said, his expression uniquely unpleasant. "Consider yourself lucky." As if suddenly reaching some indefinable breaking point, Oz rose to his feet, surveyed the social herd he despised, and said with cool precision, "My wife is fatigued. I trust you know your way out."

No one debated staying with the grim set of Lennox's mouth. The room emptied in minutes.

"No one else gets in, Josef," Oz ordered, nodding at his majordomo, who'd held the drawing room door open for the departing guests. "Not God himself."

"Very good, sir. Would you like a brandy?"

"Another bottle if you please." He'd moderated his drinking while they had guests, fearful of losing his temper before all the breathless voyeurs. But he'd finally run them off, and dropping onto the settee beside Isolde, he unbuttoned his coat and waistcoat and loosened his cravat.

"Champagne for the mistress?"

Oz glanced at Isolde.

"Cognac, please."

Oz grinned. "We deserve it."

"Indeed. You were everything a loving wife could wish for. Thank you."

"You may thank me later in a more personal way."

She laughed. "My pleasure."

He grinned. "I know."

But when the fresh bottle arrived, she watched him drink with a kind of reckless speed that was disconcerting. Noticing the apprehension in her eyes, he lifted his glass to her and offered her a glittering smile. "After hours of posturing and guile, darling, I need to wash the bad taste from my mouth. Don't be alarmed. I'm never difficult until my third bottle."

"Perhaps you should eat something."

"Very wifely," he murmured, pouring himself another brandy. "But I'm not hungry."

A timid knock on the door was shouted away.

Josef was brave enough to open the door and announce, "A Mr. Malmsey, sir."

"I'll see him," Isolde said, jumping to her feet.

Oz lunged and caught her wrist. "Stay. Send him up, Josef. Sorry, did I hurt you?"

Rubbing her wrist, Isolde shook her head.

He gave her credit for courage; he'd have to be more careful. "Why don't you order us some food," he suggested in atonement. "I probably should eat. Anything," he added to the query in her gaze. "You decide."

He consciously set out to be civil, greeting Malmsey with good cheer, thanking him for his quick service, signing each document without looking at it, his bold scrawl dwarfing Isolde's fine copperplate script. "Would you like a drink?" he asked when the last paper was back in Malmsey's leather portfolio.

He caught Isolde shaking her head behind his back and grinned. "My wife is alarmed at my drinking, so I won't insist you join me. Is there anything else?"

It was dismissal no matter the softness of his voice.

But Malmsey glanced at Isolde, wondering if she required his help.

"I'm perfectly fine, Malmsey," Isolde said. "My Lord Lennox assures me he's not difficult until his third bottle."

Oz lifted the brandy bottle from the table. "Two, Malmsey. Your client is quite safe."

But he didn't eat when the food arrived, and when he broached his third bottle, Isolde said, "I think I'll see about finding a book to read in your library."

As she made to rise, he put out his arm, forcing her back. "Talk to me instead. Tell me the world is good"—he smiled tightly—"discounting the fashionable world, of course. Parasites all," he muttered.

"You've been too long in the ton. Country society is not so brittle."

"But is it good? Convince me of that with your betrothed—what was his name?—leaving you at the altar."

"He didn't precisely leave me at the altar."

Oz looked at her and snorted.

"Well, I suppose he did in a way."

"His name is?"

"I'm not grossly wounded, Oz. His name is Will, Baron Fowler, and you needn't snarl."

"I wasn't snarling. I was grumbling. Achille brought you cake I see. Was it to your liking?"

"Everything he makes is to my liking."

"Good, because he's coming with us."

"When?" The papers were signed.

"Tomorrow morning. The roads at night can be treacherous. Traveling by day is safer for you."

"You're not coming?"

He smiled at the hint of wistfulness in her voice. "Of course I'm coming. Would I miss meeting Will?"

"Don't be difficult now. I'm quite reconciled to the situation."

"I'm never difficult."

"You're always difficult."

"How soon a wife turns shrewish," he drawled. "I might have to teach you some manners."

"You'd have to first know what manners are."

He laughed. "Then I'll have to teach you something else."

"There at least you have competence."

He dipped his head. "So I've been told."

"By all your lovers who glared at me over tea. How did you manage to service them all?" She'd counted at least a score in the course of the day.

"A robust constitution and a fondness for women."

"For sex, you mean."

"Yes, for that."

"Will they come calling again?"

"Josef won't let them in."

"But they'll try."

He shrugged. "It won't do them any good." He flashed a wicked grin. "I'm a happily married man."

She couldn't help but smile back. "You were wonderful

this afternoon. I mean it." She kissed her fingertips. "It was a beautiful sight."

"I'll surpass what you saw today when Will comes to call."

"I shouldn't be so shallow, but—"

"You are," he sardonically finished. "As would anyone be, darling, in the same situation. I know what country society is like—incestuous, exclusive, everyone knowing everything. Did you go to the wedding?"

She shook her head. "I couldn't."

"There's your mistake. Never show your feelings. That's when the claws come out. You must have been bloodied."

"I have good friends. In some ways, incestuous as country society may be, it's not so vicious as the ton."

"Yes, it is. You must be well liked."

"I like to think I am."

"I'm curious. Did this Will marry an heiress richer than you?"

"Yes, but that's not why he married her."

"If you say so."

"Don't look at me like that. He didn't marry her for her money."

"Does Will have money?"

"Some."

"Ah."

"Don't look so smug. He has sufficient wealth."

She was becoming distrait. "I need a nap," Oz said, coming to his feet and holding out his hand to Isolde. "Come keep me company. We didn't sleep much last night."

"You shouldn't have said that about Will," she murmured.

"I'm sorry. Truly." Reaching down, he grasped her hand and pulled her to her feet. "I'll make it up to you. Tell me what you want."

"Because you're so rich you can give me whatever I want."

He grinned. "As long as we understand each other."

She punched him.

He dragged her close, wrapped his arms around her, and held her tightly. "We're two lost souls, darling. Let me entertain you. At least for now."

Resting her chin on his chest, she gazed up at him, debating whether to take issue with his characterization. Not in the mood for argument, however, she softly sighed. "You *are* entertaining . . ."

"Damn right I am." He'd honed his skills to a fine art in recent years, dissipation his remedy for painful memory. "And I have what—a fortnight at least to play congenial husband. Maybe more if Compton proves obtuse. You must tell me what you like best in the way of amusement."

"Surely you know better than I if all the lustful ladies who came to call today are any indication of your competence."

In his experience, discussing other women with a lover was never beneficial. While disclosing other females' sexual preferences was not only ill-bred but suicidal. "As I recall, you like to come a few times before you settle into a rhythm," he offered.

She grinned. "Are you avoiding my question?"

"I certainly am."

"What if I want specifics? Say about Lady Livingston who never stopped staring at you. Or the Honorable Miss Childers who looked near tears."

"Why don't I show you what they like," he said in order to put an end to her catechism.

"With names attached?"

"I don't know why, but if it appeals to you, certainly."

"You're lying."

He had a discerning little wife. "And you're much too persistent. Should I ask you to tell me how you and Will made love? Ah, it's not quite so amusing now."

She had the grace to look nonplussed.

"I apologize," she said. "Although you must admit," she said with the tenacity he'd found common to women on this subject, "*that* many distressed lovers begs the question."

"Look, darling, every one of the ladies who came to tea today is bored. I alleviate the boredom, that's all." He allowed himself more honesty with her. But then, having done her the notable service of marrying her, he expected *her* to be more accommodating to him.

She understood all the ladies wanted Oz for more than that, but she also knew when to call it quits. "So you'd be willing to exert your imagination and finesse for me as well," she lightly said.

"With pleasure." Although, there had been a time in his life when making love had been about love and not about lust. "Now, would you like me to bring your cake upstairs?" He appreciated his wife's good sense. Some women lacked such self-restraint. "I'm taking that," he said, nodding at the brandy bottle.

"Then, yes. I'll indulge my gluttonous desires in addition to relieving my boredom."

"We both will," he said with a roguish wink.

After showing her into his bedroom, he set down their provisions and waved her toward a chair. "Would you like the services of a maid?"

"Not unless you're leaving," she drolly replied.

He turned, the brandy bottle in his hand. "Not likely."

As he went back to pouring his drink, she surveyed Oz's bedroom. It was more austere than the room she'd bathed in that morning, the draperies and carpet cool tones of blue, the walls adorned with muted, bucolic murals reminiscent of Claude Lorrain. The furniture was large in scale, the chairs sized to a man, the four-poster bed a Chippendale piece from the previous century.

"Crème anglaise on your cake?" Oz asked without turning around.

"Yes please." He might have been her husband of many years so casual his query and tone—like his easy manner at breakfast, or more to the point, like his suave affability with all his fawning lovers who'd come to call today. He was comfortable with women.

He swung around, his drink and her cake in hand. "I suggest we dine in bed. If your sensibilities aren't averse to such casualness."

"As you may recall, my sensibilities are rather unencumbered."

He smiled. "Maybe that's why I proposed. I found your, shall we say, eagerness charming."

"While I found your, *shall we say*, stamina charming," she returned in teasing mimicry.

"Allow me to put that to good purpose once again." He nodded toward the bed. "After you eat your cake—or before. Or *during*," he said over his shoulder.

She watched him walk away with a degree more infatuation than was advisable considering the practical nature of their marriage. But he was sinfully handsome and devilishly good in bed—the answer to any woman's dream, which was reason enough if indeed reason even entered the equation in their bizarre arrangement.

And if the sheer beauty of his person wasn't enough of a lure, she mused, his tailor further enhanced his many charms, the width of his shoulders displayed to advantage beneath his handwoven tweed jacket, his long, muscular legs impeccably showcased in slim-fitting trousers, his linen dazzling white in contrast to his bronzed skin. In deference to Isolde's limited wardrobe, he'd not changed from morning dress to meet their guests. He was a considerate husband—*particularly* while making love.

She found herself suddenly comparing Oz to Will—to the former's detriment—and immediately chastised herself for fickleness. How could a single night of lovemaking nullify what she'd previously perceived as an enduring attachment. How *could* she be so shallow?

"If you're going to daydream, darling, come do so in bed." Oz had set down the brandy and cake plate and was shrugging out of his jacket. "We can interpret your dreams according to that fellow Freud—society's newest conceit."

"Or we could interpret yours," she lightly returned, reminding herself this was nothing more than amorous sport for her husband.

"Uh-uh. My dreams aren't for the faint of heart."

"Pshaw—you don't frighten me."

"Nor do I intend to," he suavely remarked. "I promised to entertain you, I believe."

"As if I've forgotten. I'm afraid I'm no different than all the ladies lusting after you over tea," she said, untying the ribbon in her hair as she approached him. "Just add me to your list."

"You forget, I'm a happily married man *without* a list," he sportively noted, holding out his hand.

"Your many lovers wouldn't agree. I believe they're ever hopeful." She dropped the twirl of pink ribbon into his open palm and shook out her pale tresses.

"Let them be. I don't care. I like your hair loose," he said, deliberately changing the subject. "You remind me of a fresh-faced country lass. *My* country lass," he murmured, dropping the ribbon on a table. Reaching out, he slid his fingers through the soft silk of her hair and held her gently captive.

She smiled up at him. "And you're *my* irrepressible temptation."

"A mutual dependency in that regard," he said a trifle gruffly, surprised at the urgency of his desire. He let his hands drop.

"You don't like the feeling."

"No. On the other hand," he more sensibly acknowledged, turning her and beginning to unhook her gown, "my libido has a narrow focus when it comes to feelings."

She glanced over her shoulder. "And those feelings are—"

"Likely to keep you up all night."

"How nice. I never have to wait with you."

"I can pretty much guarantee that."

But he undressed her without haste, unhooking, unbuttoning, untying with a smooth, deft competence, taking his time. He wasn't a novice, nor in the mood for slam-bang sex; as for his languid pace—it was a matter of self-discipline.

Less seasoned in the lists of love, Isolde was acutely aware of his touch—the casual drift of his fingers over her skin, the warmth of his palm sliding her dress sleeve down her arm, the occasional brushing contact with his erection as he moved behind her. Each time his hard, solid length grazed her bottom or hip, little anticipatory tremors quivered deep inside her, warming her blood, stirring her skittish senses, making her fully conscious of the heady phrase *insatiable longing*.

Prior to their meeting at Blackwood's, she'd always considered sex a pleasure and delight, but never a craving. And now Oz had but to mildly bestir himself and she was instantly in rut. If it didn't feel so gloriously divine, she might consider being mortified by her shameless response. Maybe later, she decided, wallowing in a voluptuary warmth.

"I should make you wait," Oz said, well versed in female arousal. Dropping her chemise on the carpet, he turned her around and calmly surveyed her lush nudity. "You'll thank me for it when you climax."

She flushed. "So cool and collected. Am I boring you?"

He flicked a glance downward. "Does it look like I'm bored?" he said, laughter stirring in his eyes.

His cool equanimity was infuriating but provocative as well, and whether prompted by lust or vexation, determined to ruffle Oz's unruffled calm, she threw herself at him.

He grunted softly at the sudden impact but otherwise appeared unmoved, save for his libido, which reacted predictably to a nude female in close proximity.

"Umm, he noticed me . . ." Wrapping her arms around Oz's neck, Isolde melted into his hard, lean body and rising on tiptoe, kissed him with wild, wanton spontaneity.

"There," she whispered long moments later, dropping back on her heels and leaning back against his light embrace. "Even *you're* not completely impervious."

"Hardly. For your information, I'm not in the habit of asking women to marry me."

She smiled faintly. "So you're a little enamored of me."

"Of course," he said as if he meant it, knowing what was expected in amorous play. "Now, do I gather we're in race mode again?" Her eagerness was charming. "No foreplay, no waiting, no cake or brandy?"

"If you don't think me too rude." Isolde fluttered her lashes in sham demure.

Oz chuckled. "You're going to wear me out."

"*He* seems in fine form." She slipped her hand downward and ran her fingers up the length of his erection, patently obvious under the soft wool of his trousers.

"It's the last thing to go," he said with a grin.

"If you're tired, I could just use him. You needn't do anything."

He spread his arms wide. "Who could refuse?"

"So I'm in charge?" she airily remarked, taking a step back.

"You're in charge." The truth was always flexible in situations like this.

"Didn't you say that to Lady Mortimer at the Dorchester hunt?"

"I don't recall." Damn Lizabeth. He hadn't thought Isolde had heard her whispered comments at tea.

"You were probably too occupied at the time to notice— what with Lady Mortimer's very devoted attentions and the possibility of discovery imminent. What was that stable boy's name?"

Silently cursing Lizabeth's brazen impertinence, he said, "She was trying to embarrass me. Ignore her."

"I must say, the image she provoked was intriguing. Do you do things like that often?"

"Christ, can we not talk about Lizabeth?"

"Lizabeth? Is that her name?"

His gaze narrowed. "Where are we going with this?"

Dropping to her knees, Isolde glanced up at Oz. "I thought we might go to an imaginary stable where no stable boy's likely to walk in and interrupt us."

"Need I brace myself?" A guarded note echoed in his voice.

"Heavens no. Why would I harm the instrument of all my pleasure?" Isolde brightly said, beginning to untie one of Oz's shoes. "Our relationship is completely laissez-faire anyway, so what you did with Lady Mortimer is strictly your business. Lift your foot."

For an inexplicable moment he wasn't sure he liked the sound of the phrase *completely laissez-faire* when it came to his wife. But as quickly as the thought surfaced, he dispelled so outré a notion. Isolde was perfectly right about their personal freedoms, and what was even more perfect—she was about to perform fellatio on him. How very wifely.

What was also perfect—as in beautiful to behold—was his wife's provocative pose. She was kneeling at his feet, all lush, pink flesh and shapely charms, her pale, frothy hair loose and tumbled, the nape of her neck exposed—in a primal vision of submission.

An utterly captivating image.

Deferential and compliant.

He was hard-pressed not to rip open his trousers, tumble her back onto the carpet, and mount her like some randy animal.

Sucking in a breath, he restrained himself. He could wait.

Or *maybe* he could wait. Having disposed of his shoes and socks, Isolde had suddenly risen to her knees and her upturned face was inches from his crotch.

"You don't *mind* being used, do you?" She smiled. "Not that it matters whether you do or not since I'm in charge." She gently squeezed the bulge in his trousers. "Umm . . . do you think he's getting bigger?"

A rhetorical question, he supposed as his erection surged higher and he wondered where she'd acquired her coquettish flair—the combination of breathy innocence and voluptuous splendor highly erotic.

"You're not asleep, are you?" she playfully asked when he didn't reply.

He smiled and shook his head.

"Then let me know," she said, intent on disturbing her husband's damnable composure, "if I'm too rough." Having witnessed the full extent of Oz's impressive harem over tea, she was feeling a stab of jealousy—useless but real. "Although if I interpreted Lady Mortimer's comment correctly you don't mind a little roughness." She began opening the buttons on his trouser fly. "Or did she say *roughhouse*," she sardonically queried, "which is something else altogether?"

"You don't seriously think I'm going to fight with you?"

"I was just wondering how common this is for you."

"With a wife? You tell me."

"And you tell me if I'm doing this right," she said with equal impudence, sliding the last button free. "Oh hell."

"I'll do it," he offered, interpreting her expletive, swiftly releasing the small pearl closures on his underwear, experiencing the fierce untrammeled lust specific to the provocative Miss Perceval so recently become his wife. *And oh hell to that, too—in spades.*

He clenched his hands at his sides as she struggled to draw his engorged penis from the confines of his clothing, her untutored efforts stirring previously unstirred emotions, her naivete captivating to a worldly man. She elicited a tender regard quite different from what passed for feeling in the beau monde.

Then his erection sprang free, Isolde gasped, wide-eyed, and Oz took solace in the fact that he wasn't alone in his singular fixation.

Her grip tightened, and he tensed against the prodigious shock to his senses. There was no reasonable explanation for his fierce response, even less to the near-orgasmic jolt that streaked up his spine when she forced his engorged cock away from his belly, slid her fingers up the long, rigid length, whispered, "He's *huge*!" and opening her mouth, availed herself of Lady Mortimer's favorite plaything.

Sheer will along with years of practice kept Oz from instantly ejaculating when her mouth slid over the hypersensitive head of his penis. Stepping back from the orgasmic brink, he slipped his fingers through her pale curls, held her prisoner between his large hands, and said, taut and low, "Let's see how much you can take."

His terse, brute authority registered with dazzling impact in the liquid core of Isolde's body, that coercion along with the forceful advancing pressure of his cock, perversely intoxicating. Conscious only of the hot, pulsing ache deep inside her, wet with longing, openmouthed and submissive, she struggled to swallow more of his enormous penis.

"Slowly, darling . . . slowly—there you go . . . that's a good girl."

His deep voice was perfectly modulated, soft as silk, yet he was imposing his will, demanding obedience, and where in other circumstances—more rational, cool-headed ones—she might have resisted, seething and overwrought, Isolde willingly capitulated.

His grip on her head was gently determined, the pressure inexorably driving his erection deeper into her mouth, his domination rousing her every sexual nerve, tantalizing and titillating, inciting a hot flood tide of ecstasy to spread outward from her pulsing vagina. And rather than offend, his authority only further fomented her overwrought passions, touched her to the quick, left her trembling.

Feverish and needy, her thighs clenched hard to contain the seething rapture, the head of Oz's cock suddenly struck the back of her throat.

She choked.

Under ordinary circumstances her muffled utterance would have gone unnoticed. But in the throes of a single-minded obsession, Isolde's small gurgle was consent to a man well beyond prudent deliberation, and with a monstrous lack of control Oz abruptly climaxed.

Held firmly by his large hands, Isolde swallowed and gulped and swallowed again, the hot gushing deluge of semen inciting some primal dynamic of male-female affinity that triggered her own wild orgasm. The convulsive spasm swept upward through her body, ravaged her quivering senses, left an indelible, thrilling imprint on every throbbing, impressionable nerve ending, raged and seethed red-hot and exquisite until overcome and overwhelmed, with a last breathless shudder, she collapsed.

Oz instinctively caught her, his consciousness more fully absorbed by feverish sensation, and for a considerable length of time only the soft rasp of heavy breathing echoed in the large, high-ceilinged room. Neither was capable of moving, each preoccupied by the glowing bliss of sated pleasure, the unexpected ferocity of their passions.

Less given to emotion, Oz yielded first to reason, and gently easing his penis from Isolde's mouth, he lifted her into his arms and deposited her limp form on the bed. Bending, he kissed her flushed cheek. "I apologize for climaxing so quickly." He never did.

"Anytime," Isolde whispered, her voice the merest breath of sound, her eyes half-shut. "Force majeure is intensely arousing."

"So it appears," Oz muttered, restive under his novel impatience. He gazed at his wife as she lay on his bed, naked and rosy pink, her legs languidly disposed, her pouty sex luring the eye, and any chafing scruples he might harbor gave way to his own fervent feelings about force majeure. Jerking open the buttons on his shirt front, he dragged his shirt over his head, shoved his trousers down his hips, and a second later, stepped out of his underwear.

High-strung, disturbed by a heretic intensity of feeling, he stood motionless for a moment beside the bed.

Looking up from under the pale drift of her lashes, Isolde whispered, "Do I get *you* now?"

"In a minute," he replied, turning to pour himself a drink in an effort to restore some sanity to what could turn out to be an afternoon of savage debauch if he didn't control himself. He wasn't sure his recent bride was up to such hard use. Draining his drink, he glanced at Isolde. "Would you like your cake now?" A technical pause, a moment of reason, a means of clearing the lewd anarchy from his brain. "And some brandy to rinse out your mouth?"

She smiled and nodded as though he'd asked perfectly normal questions. Then she dutifully took a sip of brandy as he held a glass to her lips. Lying back against the pillows, she ate as he sat on the edge of the bed and fed her, as if that too was ordinary. As if he was always so unselfishly obliging.

Up was down and down was up was more the case.

He fed her Achille's torte between kisses, playing the gentleman with ease, conversing in banalities, urbanely charming and amusing.

She answered if somewhat tardily at times—often replying only when Oz lifted his brows and said, "Don't go to sleep on me, darling. I have plans."

"Never fear—not when *that* awaits me." And she'd reached out and fondle his upthrust erection.

It always took a moment afterward to rein in his more prodigal inclinations, but he did because he still could. Then he'd offer his wife another forkful of cake as if his chivalry might translate into an equally bland sexual gallantry.

Undeterred by any need for restraint, Isolde considered herself exceedingly fortunate to be the recipient of Oz's splendid sexual expertise. In fact, she was quite willing to overlook any number of her husband's lovers in order to take advantage of his lovely virility and talents. Which delectable thought encouraged a heated tremor to shimmer up her vagina.

Heavenly days! Being fed chocolate torte with crème anglaise by her gorgeous husband while experiencing a rush of desire surely must be counted as one of life's beautiful moments. Oz was, without doubt, the most irresistible of aphrodisiacs. She glanced at his seemingly indefatigable erection pressed hard against his belly and shivered in pleasure.

Oz met her gaze and set down the cake plate. "Ready again?"

"Always with you," she answered simply. "I hope you don't mind."

"Not at all. I can't remember when last I contemplated fucking myself to death."

"I never have, yet the notion's vastly appealing. Do you think marriage does that to one?"

He laughed so long she had her answer, or at least his answer. "You're no romantic, I see."

Swallowing his last chuckle, he swept the back of his hand across his mouth to stifle his lingering smile. "No, nor is any man of my acquaintance. A fundamental difference between the sexes I'm afraid."

"Even while sex itself is *always* compatible," Isolde drolly countered.

"With some women at least. You in particular. Move over a little and I'll demonstrate our unique compatibility."

As she made room for him she was suddenly struck by the randomness of fate that had brought them together. "Do you realize we were thrown together completely by chance? What if I hadn't stayed at Blackwood's? What if I'd left with Malmsey?"

Dropping into a sprawl beside her, Oz said, "I wouldn't have let you go."

Her eyes widened a little. "You don't say."

"I do. I wasn't finished with you."

"I beg your pardon?" That was beyond callous. "Did *my* feelings come into account at all?"

"Are you trying to start a fight again?"

"No, we're *discussing* the fact that your wishes superseded mine."

"I rather had the impression our wishes were in accord," he said, soothingly. "Or do you have wild sex with any man who walks into your room?"

"Of course not."

"How do I know?"

She had the grace to blush. "Well, I don't."

"Excellent because I'm in a possessive mood. God knows why, but there it is."

"Unfortunately I don't care to be possessed."

He grinned. "Sometimes you like it a lot."

"I don't happen to at the moment. Maybe I should leave," she said pettishly, more coolheaded postorgasm.

"You could try." He knew the difference between willingness and unwillingness. Not that the latter figured largely or at all in his life.

"Don't say that." But even as she spoke, she felt a powerful surge of prurient craving and a flush of arousal crept up her neck in rosy denial.

"Then why don't I say I'm going to fuck you until I can't fuck anymore." Sliding upward into a seated position, he flexed his fingers in a gesture of taut restraint. "Or is that in bad taste?" he drawled, looking down at her.

She turned her head on the pillow and met his gaze. "Arrogant bastard."

"Fuck me anyway."

"I should refuse."

"You don't want to, and I won't let you in any case. Let me apologize in advance. I'm not in the mood for resistance. Perhaps it was the long afternoon of worthless, vain, and empty conversation. Now, come here," he said, crossing his legs easily in a yoga pose, knees wide, feet together. "Sit on my lap."

She should take offense at his volatile presumption and bluntness, and yet every impressionable nerve in her body was not only in full compliance but shamelessly eager. "On your lap?"

"A euphemism, darling. I expect you'll sit where it pleases you best."

"What if I said your brazen insolence is wearing?"

"I'd say come here anyway. I want to feel you around my cock."

"Maybe I won't."

He should have coaxed or cajoled; he knew perfectly well how to do both. But the long afternoon of tea and malice had left him thin-skinned and restive and he wasn't in the mood. "Sure you will." Leaning over, he smoothly lifted her onto his lap facing him. Ignoring her scowling protests, he wrapped her legs around his hips, quickly slid his hand under her bottom, raised her enough to adjust his cock precisely under her sleek cleft with his other hand, and shifting his grip to her hips, rammed her down his rigid length.

He knew, she knew, they both knew, protests aside, all was forgiven the moment he was completely submerged and her honeyed sweetness fully engulfed his rampant erection.

A strumming, mutual enchantment brought the world to a standstill.

"How do you do this to me?" she finally whispered. "Make me want you and need you—with or without cake," she finished with a smile. "I'm ravenous for you."

"Perfect. Hush, now, don't move—listen."

He spoke to her, softly, softly, explaining how to feel her heartbeat, her pulse, the tingling nerves in her fingers and toes, him inside her, the liquid heat that bathed their sex. His voice was hushed and low, his hands warm on the small of her back, his erection swelling inside her as he sat motionless and held her stationary.

Then he spoke in a language she didn't understand, the phrasing and syntax lyrical, melodic, the tenor of his voice seeming to touch her inside—slowly at first and diminuendo. Harder and stronger after a time, each syllable alive, a fingerprint on her senses, eclipsing reality, taking her deeper and deeper into a fathomless pleasure where lust devoured temperate emotions and only boundless, heart-stirring passion held sway.

When it finally happened, she climaxed with starry-eyed wonder and wanton artlessness and a very soft, breathy cry.

She lifted her lashes after a time and met Oz's placid gaze.

"How did you like it?" he said.

"Was that poetry?"

He nodded.

"As you already know, I'm sure, considering your many talents, I liked it very much indeed. I'm sorry I can't return the favor."

He raised her up his erection. "You can return the favor just fine," he whispered and slid her back down his rigid cock. "This won't take long."

It didn't, but then Isolde wanted more and then he did and so it went through a long and bewitching night.

It was almost morning when Isolde said, "For something that began as a temporary solution, I seem to have become rather dependent on your stud services."

He dropped a kiss on her forehead as she rested on his shoulder. "I'm not complaining. Don't worry about it."

"I'm not worried so much as trying to understand what's happening to me."

"We're enjoying each other's company, darling. That's all."

"You're right. There's no need to decipher every nuance."

"Speaking of nuance—once more before morning?"

"I'm going to die of pleasure."

"I won't let you. I'll be gentle. I'll barely move."

He didn't and he *was* gentle and she nearly died of pleasure.

She fell asleep shortly after, and content and gratified, Oz watched over his new bride.

She was the first woman in a very long time who'd engaged his interest.

Perhaps naive country girls were a welcome change from the hothouse flowers of the ton. Perhaps her charming artlessness appealed. Or the fact that when roused, she was really quite remarkable. Or maybe it was nothing more than the fact that he was dealing out justice to a cur like Compton.

He smiled. Or all of the above.

Whatever the reasons, he found himself contemplating the future with a new degree of pleasure.

That he even thought beyond the moment was a radical change for a man who'd lived by a carpe diem philosophy since arriving in England.

And even more surprising, toward dawn, he fell into a restful sleep, something that had long eluded him.

CHAPTER 7

ISOLDE WOKE THE next morning to find herself alone in bed.

But not alone.

A young servant girl was standing at the foot of the bed, staring at her.

"Good morning, ma'am. Did you sleep well?" The words were obviously rehearsed, the delivery so conscientious and exacting.

Isolde smiled. "Thank you, yes."

"I'm to tell the baron when you wake." A pondering frown flitted across the girl's brow, and then her expression brightened at sudden recall. "He'll be up directly, ma'am." She displayed a gap-toothed smile. "That be all he said, ma'am. Now, I'm to go get him right quick." Spinning around, she dashed from the room.

How long had the child been standing there watching her sleep? Isolde wondered. Her new husband was remarkably thoughtful of her comfort, and not only in this regard. He'd given her a night of unparalleled pleasure.

The heavy drapes had been drawn back from one of the

large windows—to aid in her surveillance, no doubt. Rain drummed on the glass, the grey sky heavy with scudding clouds. But a fire crackled on the hearth, warming the room, mitigating the dreariness outside. Not that the inauspicious weather impacted Isolde's unclouded mood. Her honeymoon night—however fanciful the marriage—had been pure rapture.

She even more fully understood why all Oz's lovers had glared at her yesterday.

They hated her for stealing away their favorite playmate. Although, she suspected they knew it was just a matter of time before Oz tired of marriage. Most aristocratic husbands did.

Before she could long lament the inevitable, the door opened and *her* favorite playmate strode into the room. He was splendidly attired, his dark frock coat beautifully tailored, his pale grey cravat tied with careless perfection, his ruffled curls restrained by his valet's attentions. The large sapphire on his watch fob sparkled in the subdued light; his smile was equally dazzling. "You're up."

"You've apparently been up for some time."

"Business before pleasure. Or so they tell me, and Davey gets up with the sun. How did you sleep?"

"Like the dead."

She had the look of a tomb effigy as well, he humorously thought, her hands crossed over her breast, her pose quiescent. "I hope marriage won't be too exhausting for you." Taking a seat on the edge of the bed, he covered her hands with his. "If I was too demanding last night, I'm sorry."

"I wouldn't dream of complaining," she said, smiling.

"Nor I. No man could have asked for a better bridal night." His smile was as graceful as his turn of phrase. "However," he said, drawing his hand away, "events of the day must be addressed."

A small trepidation flitted through her senses at his painstakingly deliberate tone.

"Achille is pacing in the breakfast room, awaiting your arrival. Something about strawberry crepes that are no longer at optimum temperature. I told him I'm sure you wouldn't care. I've already entertained Jess, who couldn't wait. By the way, you must try Achille's mango custard or he'll pout. So, the first question is—would you like your bath first or food?"

"You first would be nice."

"I agree. If only I didn't have people waiting to see me in my office."

She wrinkled her nose. "Already abandoned on my honeymoon."

"Not for long. We'll become reacquainted this afternoon." Leaning forward, he gently kissed her. "In the meantime," he said, sitting up, a note of restraint evident now in his voice, "I have another question to put to you. Would you mind being introduced to the ton in a more formal way than yesterday? Let me explain," he added at her instant frown. "It seems that Compton is spreading rumors that our marriage is a farce." Oz had a well-paid spy network here and abroad; a necessity in the world of banking where competitors often overlooked ethics. "I thought it might be best to have you make your bows at an official reception so the entire ton can see we are not only married but in love. You'll look adoringly at me, I'll return the favor, and we'll foil these mischievous rumors while Compton stews in the corner."

"You'd invite him?"

"Of course. Our most skeptical doubter must have a front-row seat."

"Along with Lady Howe, I presume."

"That I leave up to you. If you don't wish to see her, I understand. On the other hand—"

"She's your most skeptical doubter."

"Yes."

She pulled a face. "Must we?"

"Since you won't let me put a bullet through Compton,

yes we must. The man's a scoundrel to the bone," he said with a touch of impatience.

"I'd just prefer a less public way of dealing with him." She frowned. "I'd have to be polite to him in front of everyone. I was hoping never to see him again."

"You've led too sheltered a life, darling. Between marriage to me and your denouement in the broadsheets you've stepped into the glare of notoriety. There is no less public way," he said with composure. "Especially since Compton's spent considerable effort denouncing our marriage as a fabrication. Let me take care of this for you. Agree to this reception."

"You're sure there's no other way?" Reluctance in every syllable.

"Nothing so conclusive as the public spotlight. You were excellent in your role at tea yesterday. You can do it again. I'll be beside you to give you your cues."

"You make it all sound so reasonable."

He gave her one of his lavish smiles. "It is. A few hours and it's over."

She softly sighed. "I suppose if we must."

"Excellent." Oz smiled. The invitations had already been sent out.

"When exactly are you planning this reception? I want to return home soon."

"Tonight."

Her eyes flared wide. "Tonight! Surely no one will come on such short notice."

His lips twitched. "Of course they will. I have a reputation for being unmanageable. They'll want to see if you can manage me."

"I can't, of course."

"Tonight you can."

"In that case," she said with a sudden smile, "I must plan my strategy. The thought of you as a tractable husband quite boggles the mind."

"Be gentle." His gaze was angelic.

Pushing up into a sitting position, she playfully said, "Mock me if you dare. I'll be holding the whip hand over you in public."

The covers had fallen away as she sat up, exposing her sumptuous breasts, their soft ripeness and rosy warmth close enough to touch. Oz's libido reacted instantly. Fully capable of controlling his impulses, however, his voice was well ordered when he spoke. "Consider, my pet, once everyone is gone, I might be interested in whips as well."

"I'm not sure that's all bad," she said with wink.

He laughed. "I should have met you before and saved myself from a good deal of boredom."

"And I as well," she airily replied when short days ago she wouldn't have thought herself capable of sexual familiarity with a man she barely knew. "Do you really have people waiting in your office?"

He almost said no, the plaintiveness in her voice clear. If Sam wasn't waiting for instructions, if Davey wasn't impatient to have him reply to the morning's telegrams, if he wasn't routinely engaged in banking business at this time of day, he might have. "I do, I'm sorry," he gently said. "But you have an appointment as well after breakfast. A modiste is coming to fit you for a new gown."

She frowned. "What if I'd said no to your reception?"

"Then you simply would have had a new gown. If I've offended you, I apologize."

"You'd better. I suppose my entire day's scheduled?" she fretfully said, irritated with his apparently inexhaustible authority.

He put up a calming hand. "Feel free to do as you please."

"Except for the modiste."

He smiled. "If you don't mind. She'll be here at eleven. Now, if you'll excuse me." There was no point in useless argument when his plans were fully *en train*. He came to his feet. "Davey's waiting."

CHAPTER 8

MRS. AUBIGNY, THE most sought-after modiste in London, a woman fully aware of her consequence, was brought into what Josef referred to as the sewing room, precisely at eleven. Introductions were made, the door closed on Josef, and the fair, stylishly dressed Frenchwoman surveyed Isolde with a keen, assessing gaze.

Then she smiled warmly.

"Allow me to offer you my congratulations on bringing Lennox to heel," she pleasantly said, an undercurrent of French in her pronunciation.

"Do I say thank you to such frankness?"

"But of course, my dear. It's a compliment. When Lennox's man came to me I didn't quite know what to expect, but I see now"—the modiste's gaze narrowed in a considering way—"you're *quite* out of the ordinary. Your pale, blushing beauty bespeaks a *sans peur et sans reproche*—what do the English say—purity, virtue? A change for his lordship."

"You know his lordship personally?" Isolde inquired with her own candor. Was she dealing with another of Oz's paramours?

"*Non, non*, my lady. You misunderstand. His lordship merely patronizes my shop."

"Quite often I suspect," Isolde said. *Oh dear, how childish.* She instantly regretted her comment.

This little bride was clearly jealous of her husband's past—poor dear. "His lordship favors our establishment on occasion," Mrs. Aubigny equivocated rather than reveal that Lennox was her best customer.

"I appreciate your tact."

Ah, a woman of intuition. "One learns in this business, my lady."

"One learns that men and women approach marriage differently," Isolde returned with equal honesty.

"Not necessarily. In your case, you and his lordship were obviously in accord."

It was impossible to reply truthfully. "My husband is quite convincing when he wants to be."

"You must have been convincing as well, my lady. While his lordship's fondness for women is well-known, if you'll pardon my bluntness, he's never been inclined to marry them. Everyone will view you with legitimate wonder."

"A position I do not relish."

Lennox's bride spoke with distaste. Any society belle so clever as to have captured Lennox would have vaunted her conquest. "It's only natural you'd find the full glare of society disquieting after having lived in the country so long," Mrs. Aubigny kindly said, au courant on gossip. "But then that's why I've been commissioned by his lordship. I'm to see that you're not only dressed to perfection for your debut but also properly showcased. I assure you, you'll dazzle the ton."

"Did my husband so decree?" An instant, knife-sharp query, Isolde's antipathy plain.

Is there a struggle for supremacy in the marriage? Who would have thought the little miss had such courage with a man like Lennox? "His lordship simply wishes to acknowledge you as his wife before the world," the modiste smoothly replied. "Any and all decisions apropos your toilette are natu-rally yours to make," she diplomatically added. "His lordship was quite specific. I'm here merely to assist you."

Isolde softly sighed; there was no point in airing her grievances before a stranger. "Forgive me," she said, silently taking herself to task for her ill-advised outburst. "I do ap-preciate your help, of course."

And so you should, my dear, dressed as you are in that de-mode country gown. "You'll be magnificent tonight, my lady," Mrs. Aubigny bracingly pronounced, knowing she had her work cut out for her with the time allowed. "And you and his lordship will make an absolutely stunning couple." The modiste kissed her fingertips with a flourish, envisioning the handsome pair with an artist's eye. "The delicious contrasts—wildness and innocence, dark and fair, Lennox's powerful virility—*la,* my sweet, taming him will be exciting. There now, I've made you blush," she murmured. "Come now, enough of my flights of fancy. We must bestir ourselves," she briskly added, indicating several fashion books on a nearby table, "*You* decide which de-sign most appeals to you, my dear."

Grateful for an end to the modiste's embarrassing obser-vations, Isolde put to rest her lingering resentment over Oz's dictates and followed the dressmaker. Taking a seat beside her a moment later, Isolde set about perusing the beautiful illustrations, while the Frenchwoman kept up a running commentary, offering pithy judgments with her usual vigor.

Amused at the fiction that the decision was hers to make, Isolde waited to see which design Mrs. Aubigny would deem appropriate.

"Certes, pink is too youthful for a wife," the modiste firmly declared, wrinkling her nose at a pink confection of a gown. "As is this pastel shade of blue, *non, non,* completely unsuitable"—another page flipped over—"this daffodil yel-low as well—not with your fair skin. Umm—this rose and the sea green—I think not. They're both too precious by half. A woman of mettle such as yourself who's taken on a brute

like Lennox requires *je ne sais quoi*—a bit more drama."
Three more pages discarded. "What I'd really like to see you
in, my sweet, would be a diaphanous white, wholly feminine
creation, but it's hardly appropriate on such a cold night," she
went on, turning over several more pages. "Black, too, would
be wonderful with your coloring, but not quite right I think
for a lady of your, shall we say, grace. Nor do I think his
lordship would like you in something so seductive." To
Isolde's quick look, she added, "He'd find the sensual impli-
cations unsuitable."

"I doubt he's so pious."

"He isn't, but he'd prefer his wife not attract lustful
glances." Or so his note had asserted—although less directly.
He'd used the word *lurid*.

"You no doubt know him better than I, but still I'd disagree. His lordship is degage about women."

But not about a wife apparently. There was no point, however, in continuing the argument, so Mrs. Aubigny crisply
said, "I'm sure you're right. Tell me now, what do you think
of this cobalt blue velvet?" She tapped the illustration with
her manicured nail. "In the midst of winter, with the chill and
rain, the soft fabric and diamant ornament offers a cozy sense
of luxury and warmth."

More than willing to defer to Mrs. Aubigny's expertise,
Isolde yielded without argument. She'd never been a martinet
to fashion in any event. Country ways were considerably less
modish. "If you think it suitable, then I agree."

"It's perfection." Mrs. Aubigny made a circle with her
thumb and forefinger and briefly held it aloft to underscore
her point. "We have a bit of dashing spectacle, but not too
much. The sumptuous fabric draws the eyes, the shade of
blue is perfect against your pale skin, the décolletage, if I
might say so, is everything that's proper, yet revealing
enough to discretely display your lovely breasts."

Her attention called to the low neckline of the gown,
Isolde murmured, "You don't think it too shocking?"

"*Non, non*—it's the perfect compromise. Wifely, yet alluring."

"Very well." Isolde wasn't overly concerned with gowns in general. Had they been perusing photos of new breeds of cattle, her attention would have been more engaged.

The necessary approval granted, Mrs. Aubigny immediately rose from her chair, clapped her hands, and called out, "*Vite, vite,* my little helpers!" The door to an adjoining room opened and the room was soon awash with pretty young assistants. Isolde was quickly stripped to her chemise and petticoats and placed on a small dais that had been carried in with all the paraphernalia required for a fitting. Mrs. Aubigny commenced cutting then draping blue velvet on Isolde while a dozen chattering young women expertly pinned and basted the fabric in place.

The gown was taking on structure and form when the door quietly opened and closed.

Isolde looked up, Mrs. Aubigny turned, and a dozen seamstresses went motionless en masse.

"Don't let me disturb you," Oz affably said. "Very lovely, darling," he softly added, moving to a chair. Sitting, he leaned back, stretched out his legs, and gazed at Isolde from under his long lashes. "That cobalt blue velvet is perfect with your coloring."

"You're well versed in women's fripperies," Isolde observed.

He knew what she meant; he also knew Mrs. Aubigny was discreet. "I told you—fabrics are part of my shipping cargo. Even Venetian velvets like that, although my trade is mostly in Eastern silks." He almost said, *Is that better?*

"Consider yourself fortunate, my lady, to have a husband who notices such things," Mrs. Aubigny interposed, conscious of the small heated note in Isolde's voice, hoping to forestall a contretemps. She had very little time to create a gown of suitable magnificence for Lennox's wife. "Most men care nothing for the subtleties of dress."

"Or undress."

"Behave."

The single word was softly spoken, almost a whisper of sound, the authority beneath it giving rise to Isolde's sudden high color, Mrs. Aubigny's increased anxiety, and an explosion of gasps among all the wide-eyed seamstresses.

"Now, now, children," Mrs. Aubigny swiftly intervened. "Need I remind everyone of our time constraints? I think not. Charlotte, hand me my shears. This train is a bit too long."

Isolde bit back the remark on the tip of her tongue.

Oz's assent took the form of a faint smile.

And possible disaster was averted.

For his part, Oz was more than content; the view was enchanting, his plans were well in hand, and if his wife chose to show a bit of spirit in public, he had no complaint. In fact, her audaciousness was one of her many charms. Although, at the moment, he was rather more drawn to her shapely breasts exquisitely mounded above the blue velvet drapery.

"A little less fabric on the shoulders, Mrs. Aubigny. If you please."

Isolde flushed under his assessing gaze and the bluntness of his injunction. He could have been some prince of the blood directing his minions with the bland assurance in his voice. And while she took intellectual issue with his explicit command, unfortunately the deep timbre of his voice provoked and stirred her senses, his stark beauty tantalized—as usual, as always, and quite against her will, a small heat began to warm her blood and pulse in the core of her body. Damn him—how dare he simply look at her and make her want him without so much as lifting a finger? How dare he turn his smile on all the pretty little seamstresses and tantalize them with equal ease.

Familiar with adulation, more familiar of late with that rosy flush rising up his wife's throat, Oz pushed himself upright in his chair and out of concern for Mrs. Aubigny's schedule, interfered with Isolde's warming passions. "I actually came here on a bit of business, my dear, for which I beg your indulgence. It seems the jeweler will be here at three. I know, another appointment to ruin your day," he added at her frown. "It won't take long. What do you think? Sapphires with that gown or would a contrast be more appropriate?"

"If I might make a suggestion," the Frenchwoman smoothly interjected. "Pearls would be the perfect complement."

Oz held the modiste's gaze for a fleeting moment before turning to his wife, Mrs. Aubigny's perception acute. Pure white, matchless pearls resting on those soft mounded breasts, the contrast discreet, erotic, was a perfect symbol of marriage—romantic and carnal love in harmony. He wondered if Mrs. Aubigny had heard Compton's rumors. "It's up to you, of course, my dear."

"Is it really? I doubt it. Nothing has been so far," Isolde tartly said, bristling at her husband's artful pretense when nothing about this entire occasion was up to her. "I'm not your pawn to be moved hither and yon," she heatedly added. It was not a role with which she was acquainted. Although, what provoked her most—disobedient jealousy defying reason—were the looks of longing on the faces of all the pretty seamstresses gazing at her husband. To which he was profoundly indifferent.

A lesson there.

If her task wasn't so formidable, Mrs. Aubigny might have enjoyed the power struggle she was witnessing. She glanced at Lennox, wondering if she dared interfere. Perhaps not, she decided. She'd seen him like this before when he was out of patience with one of his inamoratas.

"I didn't realize you felt that way," Oz quietly said, his jaw set.

"Then you didn't listen to me this morning. Or did and chose to ignore me."

"I must have misunderstood." The faintest twitch slid along his jaw.

"No, you didn't. But I've had enough of this charade," Isolde waspishly said. She turned to Mrs. Aubigny. "Unpin me."

"Would you excuse us for a moment?" Oz spoke with exquisite courtesy, his glance at the dressmaker barely perceptible. "One of the footmen will show you to the conservatory Tell him to bring you tea."

He might have been God himself for the speed with which the room emptied.

He waited silently until the door closed. "What seems to be the problem?" he asked with a cool and deliberate civility, hoping to appease his wife before the situation turned into open warfare.

"The *problem*," she caustically said, "is you giving me orders and your obsequious dressmaker pretending you're not, *and* the fact that I'm opposed to *all* of this as you well know! I *want* to go *home*!" Partial truths. The rest having to do with all the wistful seamstresses didn't bear closer reflection. Since yesterday she'd come to understand that Oz didn't pursue women; it was the other way around. And stupidly, it irritated her.

"We went over this before," he said with restraint. "You can't go home just yet."

"I certainly can. Just as soon as I'm unpinned from these bloody yards of velvet," she pettishly muttered, plucking out pins.

Oz blew out a breath, his exasperation showing for the first time; Josef and everyone else were moving mountains to see to this night's work. "Don't be a child. You can go home tomorrow."

She glared at him in the midst of her unpinning. "Since when did God appoint you his authority on earth?"

His smile was impudent. "It's been a while. Any other questions?"

"Tell me honestly, how can any of this possibly matter?" she said, lowering her voice, trying to match his restraint.

"Compton's going to believe what he wants to believe regardless of this spectacle." *While I'm going to have to watch all your lovers stalk you tonight, like the breathless little seamstresses gazing at you with such hope.* She jerked out a handful of pins.

"We're going to change his mind tonight."

She paused in her unpinning. He was speaking to her softly as he would to a recalcitrant child, damn his bloody composure! "I don't happen to agree with you," she snapped, her effort at restraint melting away. "Do you *hear* me!"

His nostrils flared. "The entire household heard you. Let's not argue, though," he smoothly said, focused on achieving success tonight. "I apologize for anything I've done to offend you."

"I don't want your apology. I want to go *home*! Don't look at me like that. And don't speak to me like I'm a bloody child. I'm not obliged to agree with you on everything. For one thing I think I know my cousin slightly better than you. And more importantly, you can't tell me what I can or cannot do."

He didn't blink or move so much as a muscle. "You're tired," he said, his voice level. "I'll tell Mrs. Aubigny to finish without you."

"She can't. Handle *that* by imperial fiat," Isolde spat, sullen and pugnacious.

Rather than rise to the bait, Oz shrugged. "Mrs. Aubigny must have your measurements; she can do her best." He was paying her enough; she'd have to manage. "Here, let me unpin you," he calmly added, coming to his feet and moving toward her.

"Don't touch me!"

He stopped, drew in a breath, and slowly exhaled. "You're my wife." An act of excessive charity on his part, he rather thought. "I'll touch you if I wish."

"You'll do no such thing!" His air of command was exasperating to someone who laid claim to an equal authority in her own life.

He stopped before her and smiled, a faint, humorless twitch of his lips. "Is the honeymoon over?"

"It certainly is! But I'm sure you need only lift your finger and any of Mrs. Aubigny's seamstresses would be more than willing to accommodate you. Perhaps Mrs. Aubigny would herself."

Oz lowered his lids faintly. "Is *that* what this is about?"

"No, it's about me going home!" A half truth, a lie, her own tangled web of emotions beyond comprehension.

Now that Oz understood their argument wasn't exclusively about Isolde going home, in the interests of conjugal peace and the two hundred guests arriving in a few hours, he set out to cajole. "I promise you can go home at the crack of dawn," he said, soft-spoken and conciliatory. "The minute the last guest leaves tonight if you prefer. Be reasonable, sweetheart. Think of all Josef's work."

"I'm not your sweetheart."

"You were last night," he gently said.

"I'm *not* anymore!"

She sounded so much like a child throwing a tantrum that he couldn't contain his smile.

"I'm sure it's all very amusing to you," she huffily muttered.

Wiping the smile from his face, he said with punctilious gravity, "Not at all. I want only to serve your interests."

"What the hell does that mean?"

"Whatever you want it to mean," he answered in an ordinary voice.

"Because you're always amenable to women."

He generally was but this wasn't the time to admit it. "It means"—he hesitated and added *sweetheart* anyway—"that I want to give you whatever you want in order to have you at my side tonight. Name your price. I'll willingly pay it."

"I suppose women always say jewelry."

He supposed they did. "Just tell me what you want." He

wasn't stupid enough to mention other women. "I'm throwing myself at your mercy because the reception is that important." Because of Compton's whisper campaign and also because, at base, he didn't like to be gainsaid.

"You already promised to be tractable tonight."

"Ask for something else then." Compton was coming; below stairs was already buzzing with the news.

"Something expensive?"

"Christ, Isolde, I don't care."

This time she was the one who smiled. "When was the last time you faced dissent?"

"Never. Is that what you want to hear?"

"I thought so," she jibed, triumph in her voice.

"And I didn't think you could be so bloody stupid," he cooly returned, suddenly weary of this senseless polemic. "This reception is meant to establish the authenticity of our marriage. It's simple. You smile, I smile, we assure everyone we're madly in love, your cousin in particular, and after everyone eats and drinks all the food and liquor they go home. Then remind me not to play good Samaritan again," he said flatly. "Especially with an ungrateful bitch like you."

She slapped him so hard she thought she'd broken her wrist.

He flinched but otherwise didn't move, fighting to control his temper as any number of unacceptable options raced through his mind. Then he turned, walked to the door, locked it, and swiveling back, surveyed her with an icy gaze.

"What are you doing? Unlock the door."

He didn't move. He'd lived an untrammeled life too long.

"I'll scream."

"Scream."

"Because no one will come."

"You're not stupid after all," he flippantly noted. "Now let's get those pins unpinned because I'd like some recompense for all my bloody trouble. Or my Christian charity if you like or"—he smiled tightly—"more aptly, my misplaced altruism."

She crossed her arms over her breasts, as if so small a gesture would serve as shield. "I refuse to be compensation for some perceived misjudgment on your part." She lifted her chin and stared daggers at him. "I won't!"

"Of course you will," he said. "You like to fuck." He pushed away from the door and languidly moved forward, his smile sunshine bright and boyish now. "And I like to fuck you. Really, darling, we're a match made in heaven. You have to agree."

"I agree to no such thing!" She clutched her bosom tighter as he neared. "What do you think you're doing?"

"Taking advantage of my spousal privileges."

He came to a halt before her. Even standing on the dais as she was, he towered over her, intimidating and impressively male, and her voice when she spoke held less conviction than she wished. "You can't always do as you like, Oz," she said, a small breathlessness of something other than fear in her words.

He noticed. "But you like it, too, darling. I won't keep you long." Lifting his hand, he gripped a handful of soft velvet draped over her shoulder, his slender bronzed fingers slowly closing. As she tensed against his onslaught or his allure or her own base desires, he swept his arm downward and with an effortless strength ripped out pins and basting, dismantling half the gown. A second quick wrench of his arm and the remaining velvet lay at her feet. "Now," he said, with infinite serenity, "would you like to save your chemise and petticoat or should I destroy those as well?"

Chafing beneath the small avaricious flame kindling deep inside her, resentful of her susceptibility to a man who aroused desire without even trying, she freezingly said, "Uncouth barbarian."

He smiled faintly. "I've been called worse. Now, answer my question. My patience is limited." It had been a busy morning dealing with his shipping and bank business, weighing the significance of the rumors Compton was spreading, making plans for Isolde's defense—all the while trying to ignore the image of his sumptuous wife asleep in his bed. And here she was, aroused, defiant, and within reach—the first and third qualities of particular interest. "Answer me."

The two words were crisp and uncompromising. Oz was in some hotspur, intransigent mood. She could expect no help from her husband's household, where he ruled like an autocrat. Furthermore, she'd lavished hours of embroidery on her lingerie, she pragmatically reflected, and more craven yet, her senses were in the grip of a rash, reckless, and rising passion. "You have an exaggerated sense of your importance," she muttered, beginning to unbutton her chemise. "But I'd prefer you not shred my chemise. I have no intention of responding to your boorish behavior in any event. I'm not like all your strumpets," she said, angrily resigned but still glaring at Oz. "Do with me what you will. I shall remain unmoved."

He suppressed his smile with effort. "Really."

"You find that humorous?"

"I do. You're one hot little piece."

Glancing up from her unbuttoning, she shot him a furious glance.

"An observation only. But in any event, you're giving *me* an instant hard-on, so at least one of us will enjoy this."

She shouldn't have looked. She instantly flushed, and when she lifted her gaze, he was smiling at her.

"You *do* like it, don't you?" he murmured.

"Don't they all," she snapped, reminding herself she was one of an endless multitude.

"Some more than others. You more than most. Don't stop your undressing. I find myself damned impatient."

"Aren't you always."

"Only with you, darling," he silkily observed. A revelation had he taken the time to acknowledge it. But driven by lust, he was more intent on seeing her devoid of clothing. To that purpose, he said, "Relax now. I'm going to help you."

"I could fight you."

"You think so?" But his voice was benign, as was his dark

gaze; her breathing had changed, her nipples were taut, the rosy flush of arousal colored her skin.

"I *certainly* do."

"Then I'll have to be on guard," he mildly noted, untying the ribbon at the waistband of her petticoat with a brisk dexterity. He understood her willingness better than she. Letting the fine batiste petticoat slide down her hips, he reached for the buttons on her drawers. "Buttons." He glanced at her. "That's different."

"I'm sure you'd know."

"I've just never seen buttons before." Ignoring her sullen gaze, he smiled. "Is it a Cambridgeshire tradition?"

"Do you really care?"

He shook his head and watched her drawers drop to the floor. "Now this I care about," he murmured, gently brushing her mons with his fingertips. "I've been thinking about you—about this . . . all morning," he said, stroking her pale pubic hair, "about the feel of you as you take me in—your heat, warmth . . . the way you whimper when I'm deep inside you." He looked up and met her fevered gaze. "Does that interest you?"

She clenched her fists. "Not in the least."

"I'll wager you a thousand pounds it does," he said, sliding her chemise down her arms and disposing of her last item of clothing. "Think about it," he added, lifting her in his arms and scanning the room for a suitable piece of furniture. "If I'm mistaken, you'll be the richer for it, and if I'm not, I'll donate my winnings to your favorite charity. This little episode could be a profitable venture for—" He grunted as she sank her teeth into his earlobe. Curbing his temper and his urge to strike back, he drew in a restraining breath. "You're drawing blood," he grimly said of the warm trickle running down his neck.

Little episode indeed! Isolde enjoyed a moment more of satisfaction before releasing his ear. Leaning back in his arms, she cooly surveyed the damage she'd done. "I don't respond well to authority," she said.

He felt like saying he disliked aggressive women. But he had blood dripping down his neck, which indicated she wasn't in a reasonable mood, so politesse would better serve his purposes. "I apologize of course."

"You don't mean it."

"I might."

"And I might bite you again."

He sighed. "I wouldn't recommend it."

"Am I supposed to be frightened?"

"Christ, Isolde, can we stop this wrangling?"

"Someone's going to have to wash those blood stains from your collar," she said instead, reminding him of her little triumph.

"Maybe *you* could."

"If only I knew how."

"I could have someone show you," he said in a tone of voice any of his dueling opponents would have recognized.

"I doubt I could learn."

"What a defiant little wife," he unpleasantly said, considering forcing himself on a woman for the first time in his life. "Then again, you're always more manageable after a few orgasms."

"Not today."

His brows lifted slightly. "Why is today different? You were always ready for sex yesterday."

"Because I despise you today," she peevishly said. But her traitorous body was considerably less hostile, Oz's allusion to her sexual readiness triggering a flood of lubricant in her vagina, her unruly senses effectively priming her for intercourse without so much as a by-your-leave from her brain. "Damn you, Oz," she hissed, trying to quell her ruinous yearning even as her arousal spread and pulsed through her blood with every beat of her heart. "I hate you. I hate your arrogant assumption that every woman wants you. And that insolent smile. Stop it. Do you hear? You needn't look so bloody smug."

"I can smell you, that's all. You need me."

"So I should jettison my principles."

"We're talking about sex, darling—not principles. You feel good, I feel good, we feel good together. Don't make it complicated."

"What a romantic soul," she sneered.

"I didn't know it was romance you wanted. I thought it was hard cock."

"And you're here to serve me."

"You could have had two orgasms by now." He didn't say, *I don't have all day*, but that's what he meant.

Quite independent of logic and good judgment, the word *orgasms* was instant impetus to another flame-hot wave of prurient sensation, her body reminding her flamboyantly and graphically of the inexpressible bliss of sexual congress with the glorious Lord Lennox. "Very well," she briskly said. "I yield to your pragmatism and *irresistible charm*," she acidly added. "But Mrs. Aubigny will never forgive you."

He was tempted to ask her whether her crosspatch tone precluded screaming during orgasm but decided against it in the interests of speed and future harmony. "Don't worry about Mrs. Aubigny. I'll deal with her."

"After you deal with me."

He smiled. "I have my priorities."

"Sex first, last, and always."

"Same as yours."

"Just for the moment," she matter-of-factly said, having come to terms with her insatiable desire for her husband, the fierce pulsing between her legs a potent reminder of the immense pleasure he delivered.

"At last we agree. So tell me what you want," he murmured, moving toward a large red damask, down-cushioned sofa. "Slow, fast, nothing but orgasms, or playtime?" Bending, he deposited her on the scarlet cushions.

She looked up at him with a mocking smile. "You're giving me a choice?"

"Of course." He had what he wanted; the menu was hers to choose.

"First, a few orgasms," she neatly said. "After that—playtime."

As if he didn't know. "My pleasure, sweetheart," he blandly replied, sliding his frock coat down his arms, undressing with more than his usual speed.

But she was trembling when he lowered himself between her legs, her sex his current Nirvana, and it took no more than a second to bury himself to the hilt in her tight little cunt. They both stopped breathing for an instant while the earth steadied on its axis and more practiced, or perhaps more impatient after so much useless resistance, Oz moved first. But she wouldn't let him withdraw, her grip on his back sensationally strong. "Stay," she whispered, inundated by bliss.

Since he was infinitely stronger *and* single-mindedly intent on pleasure, he broke free and launched himself into a driving rhythm of thrust and withdrawal he was confident she'd like even better.

It was like an explosion of bodies the first time, forceful and wild, predatory, neither interested in anything but taking and taking. Isolde was wet with craving and lust, voracious; Oz's cock was so hard his eyes were slits against the agonizing ache. Both were frenzied, impatient, resentful, too, of their mutual compulsions, engaged in something more than fornication as they hammered their way to a violent climax that ended with Isolde in tears.

Dragging her into his arms, Oz kissed away her tears, whispered apologies that were more courteous than penitent, and wondered why sex with her was so different. Lurid instead of lucid, crude, rude, and barbarous—a desperate onslaught he was unable to contain. And the more he fucked her, the more he wanted her. Not his usual pattern where tedium quickly extinguished desire.

But Isolde suddenly twined her arms around his neck, pressed her soft, lush body against his, began kissing him back with sweet fervor, and his thoughts focused on more pertinent issues.

Soon their skin was slippery with sweat, Oz's hair was damp, Isolde's blonde tresses clung in coils on her face and neck as they explored sensory overload in a swift succession of orgasms. Not that anyone was counting orgasms or was even rational enough to count. Not that even a scintilla of thought was involved in their continuous, frantic coupling.

She shoved Oz away once, pushed him on his back, and straddled his hips with a kind of purposeful concentration that brought a furrow to her brow.

Lying spread-eagle on the sofa, Oz flicked his wet hair behind his ears with his forefingers and grinned at his rosy-cheeked wife, who was up on her knees, absorbed in conducting the head of his penis to her slick cleft. "Don't I get time to catch my breath?"

"No," she said without looking up, in the process of lowering herself over his undiminished erection. A moment later she came to rest on his thighs with a contented sigh and met his amused gaze. "You're my new toy. Mmm." She shifted slightly to experience the full measure of his massive size.

He groaned, his libido highly charged and infinitely resilient in close proximity to his wife. She was a damned fine jockey, too, he decided soon after, watching her ride him, feeling a deep sense of gratitude as she languidly slid up and down his erection. And when her desires reached that wild, impassioned stage he was beginning to recognize, she shut her eyes, threw back her head, and rode him full tilt. Grabbing her hips, he secured his hold on her slippery skin, saved her from tumbling off, and saved himself from unnecessary injury.

In their frenzied search for sensation that fine winter day, desire and lust melded in a tempestuous composite of slick skin and melting friction, sweet stickiness and sweeter rapture, redolent scents and lush tastes, heartrending touch, all faintly wild, fresh, and new. New even to a jaded man.

For Isolde, every sensation was new.

She'd led a different life than Oz.

"I'm broadening my horizons," she playfully murmured much later, trailing kisses over Oz's face as he rested briefly between bouts. "Does that feel good?"

"Do fish swim?"

"Perfect. Hmm . . . you have such beautiful eyes." She brushed her mouth over his dark brows. "And a perfect nose." A light kiss down the bridge of his nose. "And of course your delicious mouth." When she finally lifted her lips from his, her breathing was labored and her lips were pursed in a sulk. "Must you do everything so damned professionally?"

He laughed. "Is that a compliment?"

"I'm practically climaxing after a kiss for God's sake."

"If it makes you angry, I won't kiss you anymore."

"That's not the point."

He knew what the point was and he wasn't going anywhere near the subject

"How many women have there been?"

He silently groaned. "Need I remind you that you're not actually my wife?"

"Don't be so reasonable. I'm not in the mood."

"I could probably put you in a better mood. Come, dear," he softly said, "this is a foolish argument."

Drawing in a small, restorative breath, she reminded herself of their temporary arrangement, reminded herself as well that taking issue with the women in Oz's life was useless in countless way. "You're right; I stand corrected. I'm fine, really. Where was I?" Returning to her amorous play, she kissed the firm line of Oz's jaw, dipping her head lower after a time to lightly caress the smooth curve of his shoulder blades, his hard, muscled shoulders.

Relaxed now with Isolde's brief resentment resolved, Oz lay and watched her from under his lashes as she suddenly came up on her knees and pressed her mouth into the little dip at the base of his throat.

And began sucking with vigor.

He lightly touched her head. "You're going to leave a bruise."

"I know," she said against his throat, the vibration drifting down his nerve endings in lush temptation, mitigating a portion of his unease. "I want to," she whispered, moving upward slightly, adorning his throat with a second brazen imprint.

She was deliberately leaving bruises on his neck when he'd never allowed the London ladies such latitude. His policy was a hands-off one when it came to proprietary claims. The little puss was bold and cheeky. On the other hand, he knew where her trail of kisses would end.

By the time Isolde had satisfied her jealous pangs and paid homage to her husband's splendid body—kissing and caressing his bulging pectorals, his nipples, the hard ripple of his abdominal muscles, the dip of his navel, the crisp black hair at the juncture of his thighs, Oz was in a cold sweat, curtailing his climax by sheer will alone.

Circling his penis with her fingers, Isolde drew it away from his stomach and met his hot gaze. "You're not going to last much longer, are you?"

He shook his head.

"Then I suppose it's up to me to do my wifely duty."

"Sooner rather than later or you won't have to," he said on a suffocated breath.

"But of course I want to. Wait—wait!"

He was almost undone by her wistful zeal, and as she quickly obliged him and the crest of his penis slid into her mouth, he felt an unparalleled suffusion of spine-tingling pleasure. Whether it was her accommodating mouth, the continuous assault on his libido, or the rare level of delirium she incited, the fierceness of his ejaculation coursed through his body like a shock wave.

When Isolde swallowed the last drop and he was debating whether he was paralyzed or could still move, she slid up his body and kissed him on the mouth, her lips still wet with semen. Lifting her head, she smiled at him. "How was that? Do I please you, my lord?"

He smiled. "It was perfect, darling, and yes, you please me. I must send Fremont a thank-you gift."

"Not just yet," she sweetly said. "If you don't mind."

"Not while I still have a heartbeat," he replied with a grin, sliding a finger inside her as if her willingness was ever at issue. She was open and ready, her cunt slick and warm, pulsing around his finger. "The gates of paradise are ever open, I see."

"Always for you," she whispered, wiggling against his finger. Reaching up, she brushed the light bruises on his neck. "And these are for me."

He laughed when in the past he would have risen and left. "Is that a fact?"

Her smile was bright and she spoke not rationally, but with her heart. "They mark you as mine."

"In that case I'll have to make you *mine*," he drawled, fully rational and proficient at this game, his cock apparently engaged in some endurance contest. Rolling over her, he slid her under him with practiced ease and plunged into her slick sweetness with the unclouded concentration of a libertine in full command of his much-practiced talents. "This is mine," he whispered, withdrawing completely and driving in again. "And this . . . and this . . . and this," his lower body slamming into her on each blunt utterance.

She gasped at each forceful downstroke, a soft, breathy pleasure sound, and on each upstroke, she clung to him— loathe to lose him.

It was never enough—no matter how many times they climaxed that afternoon.

They were filled with lust, vibrating with lust.

Seething, feverish, out of control.

Until wild-eyed and hysterical, she shoved him away, fell on her stomach, and shuddered uncontrollably.

Oz gently stroked her back until her tremors ceased.

She rolled over then, her eyes wet with tears. "Hold me."

He gathered her into his arms, settled her on his lap, and leaning back against the sofa arm, held her with unaffected tenderness. He whispered all the love words, the play words, the amorous phrases meant to soothe and placate and disarm. He knew them well, glibly some would say, but his make-believe wife pleased him and he willingly uttered the words of affection.

She fell asleep quickly, like an exhausted child after too much excitement.

He waited for her breathing to settle before carefully shifting his position and easing her onto the sofa. Placing a pillow under her head, he covered her with a paisley shawl, and in an unprecedented gesture of sentiment, bent and kissed her cheek.

Conscious of the time, his dressing was swiftly accomplished, and when he left the room, he closed the door with the utmost quietness.

Going directly to the conservatory, he ignored the pointed interest of the young seamstresses and apologized to Mrs. Aubigny. "I understand the delay is a serious inconvenience with time so limited. Allow me to offer you a substantial monetary incentive to both forgive the interruption and bring in additional help to complete my wife's gown. I do apologize," he said again.

"There's no need to apologize," the Frenchwoman said, fully conscious of Lennox's wealth as well as the power of amour. His lordship was still sweating, his hair damp. "My lady has a mind of her own. It alleviates the boredom, I wager."

"Indeed," Oz replied with a faint smile. During the past two years, he'd spent considerable time in Mrs. Aubigny's shop with one woman or another; he and the modiste were on friendly terms.

"I'll need the fabric, of course," she said with a lift of her brows.

"A servant will fetch it. Ask Josef for whatever else you need and he'll see to it. Davey will bring you the additional bank draft for your trouble, and when my lady wakes, I'll see if she's available for another fitting. Although, I'm not sure," he carefully said, "if she will be or not."

"I have her measurements."

His expression cleared. "I thought you might. Excellent. By seven then."

"Yes, my lord."

He bowed with grace. "I'm in your debt."

She watched him walk away, the brilliant light in the conservatory betraying the bruises on his neck as well as the bite marks on his ear left by his wife's passion. Despite his bride's look of innocence, they appeared well matched. As for Lennox, his wildness was common knowledge. He was also as experienced as any man when it came to amour. He wouldn't have been marked unless he'd allowed it.

Oz went next to meet with the jeweler.

"Sorry to keep you waiting, Martin," he said, walking into his office and smiling at the heavyset man who looked more like a prizefighter than a jeweler. "Did you get coffee? Good. I hope you have pearls."

"Some very fine ones, sir. The kind that rarely come on the market."

"Sounds intriguing." Oz pulled up a chair beside the jeweler. "I'm sure my wife will appreciate them," he said with such obvious good cheer Martin was taken aback.

Martin, as the premier jeweler to those of prodigious wealth, had served Lord Lennox on occasions too numerous to count, but none in which the baron had appeared in such jovial spirits. He wasn't a man one would characterize as jovial. Or even animated; his natural reserve was as notable as his willfulness.

Martin briefly wondered at his lordship's sobriety. He was known to drink away his days with some frequency. But after a surreptitious glance as he was laying out the splendid necklace of large matched pearls, Martin saw that the baron was surprisingly sober.

He gently arranged the pearls in a circle on the pad of black velvet he'd set on the small table before him. "This exquisite piece was a Napoleonic trophy brought back from Italy—from a Venetian collection. The maker's mark on the diamond clasp, however, indicates Constantinople as the original provenance, with the original recipient Empress Theodosia. See—here—the imperial cipher."

Oz leaned forward to witness the imperial stamp. "I'll take it," he said, sitting back and offering Martin a smile. "I don't suppose you have earrings to match?"

"Unfortunately not. Sets rarely survive the centuries. But I have some superb pearl pendant earrings you might appreciate."

"I'm sure I will. Your taste is always impeccable."

Martin spread out a collection of expensive baubles; Lennox only wanted the best. A design question from the baron, another about a diamond clasp, a query as to gemstone quality, one about a goldsmith, and their business was quickly done. Lennox generally knew what he wanted, but then Martin understood the baron owned ruby mines in India. He wasn't a novice with gems. In short order Martin left Lennox House with a light step and a broad smile. The baron never quibbled over price, but more surprising—as gossip suggested—he seemed enamored of his new wife. His lordship had purchased all the jewelry shown him, including the diamond and onyx tiger brooch that was so dear even the Prince of Wales had balked at the price.

Needless to say, the faint scent of sex clinging to the young lord's person, in addition to the disheveled state of the baron's clothing and hair, bore witness to the fact that he'd only recently left his wife's bed. As any jeweler knew, such gratifying creature comforts lent themselves to a certain generosity on the part of husbands.

CHAPTER 9

ISOLDE'S GOOD HUMOR was as fulsome as Oz's when she woke, or rather when he woke her with a kiss.

Drowsy with sleep, she wrapped her arms around his neck and whispered, "I need you for a few minutes if you don't mind."

"I don't mind, but my valet will," Oz lightly said, untwining her arms from around his neck. "Karim's been fussing over me for the past half hour."

Isolde eyes snapped open. "You're dressed!"

"As you see." Oz was splendid in full evening rig, diamond studs sparkling down his shirt front, his black unruly hair schooled into place.

"Good God, how long did I sleep?"

"It's seven."

"Seven!"

"You needn't panic, darling." His voice was particularly indulgent—a contrast to long held custom, the afternoon of wild, frantic sex no doubt cause for his conversion. "Your bath is being drawn, Mrs. Aubigny and servants are awaiting your commands in your dressing room, and Achille has sent up a small collation to tide you over until he serves his lavish reception repast. You have well over two hours."

She groaned. "I find you thoroughly disagreeable."

He smiled. "No you don't." Her orgasmic screams were still vivid in his memory. "One evening, sweetheart, and you're free of any further appearances. Your obligation to society and to my inflexibility on the subject will be over."

"Then I may be rude to you again without fear of your ruthless temper?" she sweetly said.

"As rude as you wish."

"Arrogant man. As if I can resist you."

"Hold that thought," he said with a grin, "and we'll both better survive this tedious affair. Thank you, by the way, for this afternoon. You're damned entertaining, and my bites and bruises hardly show."

She blushed furiously. "Oh Lord, what will people think?"

"That I'm a very lucky man. Now come, darling, a good number of people are awaiting you."

"Must I?"

"Duty has it own rewards," he drolly noted.

"How would *you* know?"

"I believe one of my tutors had me write that phrase a thousand times. But in your case, I'd be happy to serve as *your* reward."

"How can I refuse?" she purred.

"How indeed when you haven't had an orgasm in three hours." At the look in her eyes, he quickly put up his hand. "Afterward, darling. If I disarrange so much as a hair on my head, Karim will sulk for a week."

"In the interests of household amity," she said with a pout not altogether feigned, "I suppose I must renounce my desires."

"I'll make it up to you."

Her smile was instant. "How nice."

* * *

OZ TOOK CURIOUS pleasure in watching Isolde bathe and dress, even sharing in the light collation Achille had sent up, when he'd previously steeled himself with a good deal of liquor for occasions such as this. How many times had he impatiently watched some lover taking overlong to outfit herself or primp before a mirror for his benefit, how many times had he counted the minutes and drunk to excess? Tonight he was practically sober, his drink at hand but barely touched, his enjoyment of the intimate scene affording him a degree of contentment long absent from his life.

He'd recognized how restful his wife was their first morning together, and so she was now—allowing the maids to bathe and dress her without complaint or direction, doing what was necessary with amazing good humor.

It was simply a matter of keeping her well fucked, he decided.

A task he was more than willing to assume.

She smiled at him over the heads of her maids from time to time, and he smiled back from his chair across the room, his libido reacting to her smile. At which point, he invariably felt like ordering everyone out, tossing up her skirts, and saying to hell with their guests. But ultimately, sanity prevailed; he softly swore and silently consigned the bloody reception to perdition.

She heard him, and at the last, watching him in the mirror as the hairdresser finished pinning her glossy curls into an artful arrangement, she dulcetly inquired, "Can I help you?" knowing full well what he was thinking.

"I wish you could," he murmured, glancing at the clock with a significant look. "Thirty minutes, darling." In thirty minutes, they'd be standing at the top of the stairs offering imitation smiles to everyone who arrived to ascertain the reasons for and authenticity of their hasty marriage.

"My compliments, Mrs. Aubigny. You outdid yourself,"

Oz said as Isolde rose from the dressing table and turned to him. The dressmaker had performed her office superbly, the gown fit to perfection: bared shoulders, half-bared breasts, the slenderness of Isolde's waist enhanced by the subtle drapery, the curve of her hips prominent with the current snug-fitting styles, the glittering diamant ornament on the dark velvet calling attention to the low décolletage.

"My lady's beauty enhances any creation," the modiste replied, although it was obvious she was pleased with the result. "And the pearls are superb."

Even Isolde hadn't begrudged the pearls. The necklace was stunning, its history a thing of romance, Theodosia's rise to empress a spellbinding tale.

Equally spellbinding was the sight of the gleaming pearls resting on the sumptuous curve of her breasts, Oz reflected, drawing in a breath of restraint. She was an amazingly beautiful woman. With another glance at the clock, he decided they'd escape the throng at midnight no matter what.

Mrs. Aubigny opened her arms with a flourish. "She's all yours, my lord. An ornament to you and the ton."

Isolde might have taken issue with being spoken of as an object if Mrs. Aubigny hadn't been of such enormous service. She'd called in a hairdresser, procured exquisite new lingerie, had a shoemaker at the ready with a selection of evening slippers suitable for Cinderella herself. "I'm in awe of your talent, Mrs. Aubigny." Isolde offered the modiste a glowing smile. "Thank you so very much."

Oz felt like a proud parent at the success of Isolde's toilette—or as close to the feeling as he could imagine. She was breathtaking. And so he told her, to which she blushed so prettily he had to further control his libidinous urges. It was all the excitement, he told himself, for he couldn't blame liquor tonight. Although, perhaps it was nothing more than the pretense of having a wife that prompted such lust—a prurient notion for a confirmed bachelor.

He rose to his feet, walked to Isolde, and with a graceful

bow, offered her his arm. "May I have the pleasure of your company tonight, darling? We are, it seems, about to play husband and wife before the world." He grinned. "Are you up to it?"

"Do I have a choice?"

"Regretfully, no," he gently said, moving toward the door, leaving the retinue responsible for his wife's elegant appearance beaming behind them.

"In that case," Isolde said with a sigh, "tell me when to smile and don't expect me to remember names."

"Your smile, of course, must be unwavering. As to the names, it doesn't matter. Our guests are here to see us, not the other way around," he said, walking through the door held open by a servant. "In any case, they'll all soon turn into a blur."

"You speak from experience?"

"I do, but then that's what a majordomo's for. Josef is nonpareil when it comes to names and titles. I rely on him completely," he said, strolling down the corridor. "And if someone should be rude don't be shocked at my response."

"Will they be?"

"Of course. In the ton manners are uncertain, snideness is an art form, and we are perceived as a divertissement of the first water. You already saw as much during our at-home."

Reminded, Isolde softly groaned. "Promise to save me."

"I believe I already have," he said easily, "but I shall again tonight. Consider this my Lancelot phase."

"If only you weren't so wicked, you might aspire to a Lancelot."

He shot her an amused look. "Who says I'm wicked?"

"Who doesn't? Although I'm sure all your admirers mean it in the sweetest way." The tittle-tattle was impossible to ignore, whether below-stairs whispers or those she'd overheard at their at-home. Or her own personal assessment of the spoiled young lord who'd done her the huge favor of marrying her—temporarily. "As do I, darling. Have I told you that you intrigue me mightily?"

"No, but I rather have that feeling with your, shall we say, captivating enthusiasm for my person."

"For your cock, darling. Be more specific."

He laughed out loud, causing the many servants still crowding the corridor to look their way. "You don't know how pleased I am to have stumbled into your little drama that night at Blackwood's. I haven't been so pleasantly entertained in ages."

"We're pleased we amuse you," she dulcetly replied. "So long as the next amusement isn't too long delayed."

"Midnight at the latest. You're not the only one waiting."

"How sweet. May I say you're the most charitable and obliging of husbands."

"You make it easy, puss. Everything in life should be so simple."

He was in too fine spirits to question the motives behind that ease. Or the reasons why his wife had become of such material interest to him. It had been an extremely busy few days he would have said, had the question been posed to him.

But it wasn't.

Which was perhaps just as well.

Because then he would have been required to think about a woman in something more than sexual terms for the first time since India.

CHAPTER 10

SEEING JOSEF APPROACH, Oz turned to Isolde. "I invited a friend of mine and his wife to meet you before the reception." He looked as his majordomo drew near. "Are they here?"

"In the Dresden sitting room as you requested, sir."

"The time?"

"Eight forty, sir. This way." Josef walked alongside Oz.

"Fetch us at nine."

"Of course, sir," Josef said with mild affront.

"Sorry, Josef. Nerves."

"I very much doubt that, sir."

"You're right. I dislike the fashionable world."

"With good reason, sir."

Oz shot an amused glance at his majordomo. "You think you know everything, don't you, Josef?"

"I was the one who carried you to your father on the day you were born. Begging your pardon, sir, there's very little I don't know."

Oz grinned. "Then I must pray you never resort to black-mail."

"If you prayed, sir."

"Darling, see what happens when one allows too much license in one's household?" Oz pointed out, suppressing a smile. "It's anarchy."

Between Oz and Josef, she rather thought they could set an army into the field, but this was no time to disagree. "I'm sure you're right, dear."

Oz gazed at her, one brow raised. "Now *that* must be nerves."

"I relinquish sedition for the greater good, my lord," she sweetly said.

He chuckled. "*Until later*, I assume."

"We're both waiting for midnight, my lord."

He leaned over and whispered in her ear, "I might be willing to strike a bargain for eleven o'clock."

"Done."

"Witch," he murmured, but the word was velvet soft. With a glance at Josef, who'd come to a stop, Oz took Isolde's hand and smiled, "Curtain up, darling."

Josef nodded at a footman to open the sitting room door.

"You needn't announce us." Oz waved Josef away. "Groveland and I are past such drills." Both habitués of London's finest brothels until Groveland's surprise marriage last fall, the men had been companions in vice, sharing common pleasures and women on more than one occasion. Not, however, since Groveland had dropped from sight and left that prodigal world. Oz was meeting his wife for the first time.

"Evening, Fitz," Oz cheerfully exclaimed on entering the room. "Thank you for coming early."

The Duke of Groveland had risen to his feet. "Our pleasure. Allow me to make my lovely wife known to you." He turned to a stunning redhead seated on the sofa behind him, the yellow silk upholstery perfect foil for her hair and Nile green gown. "Rosalind, Oz."

"I'm pleased to meet you at last," Oz said with a graceful

bow. He drew Isolde forward. "I'd like to introduce my beautiful bride. Isolde, Countess Wraxell in her own right, Rosalind and Fitz, the Duke and Duchess of Groveland."

Smiles and the usual banalities were exchanged, Isolde and Fitz took seats, and Oz moved toward the liquor table. "I refuse to face the mob sober. Let me bring us something to ease the strain."

"I may have a head start on you," Fitz waggishly noted. "I never face these entertainments sober. With your marriage the talk of the town, you have even more reason to indulge in an extra drink or three. To deal with the guile."

Rosalind smiled. "As you can see, Fitz isn't keen on mingling with society."

"Who is?" Isolde frankly replied. "Oz is the one insisting on this affair."

"Because your husband knows the best defense against the inquisitive is a preemptive offense," Oz offered over his shoulder as he poured the drinks. "In case you can't tell, we've been arguing about this soiree."

"And as you can probably tell," Isolde said with smile for their guests, "I've lost the argument."

"You can win the next one," Oz cheerfully offered, returning with the drinks expertly balanced on his large palms. "I understand congratulations are in order." He offered Fitz a drink, set his aside, and handed champagne to the ladies. "When is the blessed event?"

The duchess blushed and the duke took her hand. "May we're told," Fitz said. "Apparently, the timing of these matters isn't always certain."

The duchess added, "We're both complete tyros as well."

Isolde was surprised to experience a small lurch of jealousy, outrageous of course and instantly dismissed. "How pleased you must be. Is this your first?"

"Yes. And I'm more delighted than most expectant mothers because I never thought I could *have* children," Rosalind said, squeezing her husband's hand. "It's a miracle of sorts."

"My wife was a widow when I met her," Groveland explained.

"And my husband was a confirmed bachelor, so you and I have something in common," Rosalind teasingly remarked, smiling at Isolde. "We both astonished the ton by successfully luring these men into marriage when so many before us had failed."

"We must be two very clever women," Isolde playfully observed, responding to the duchess's levity.

"Or perhaps we're two remarkably clever men," Oz countered gallantly.

"I'll drink to that." Fitz raised his glass.

"I'll drink to anything tonight," Oz said, lifting his glass to Fitz.

The men drained their brandies, the ladies exchanged conspiratorial glances, and Oz rose to refill their glasses. "The champagne's not to your liking?" He nodded at the women's untouched drinks. "Josef can bring something else if you wish."

"My stomach is uncertain at this stage," Rosalind said in demur.

"I don't dare drink too much or I might be excessively rude to someone," Isolde declared.

Oz glanced at Fitz as he walked away. "Then it's up to us to maintain the family honor."

Groveland laughed. "Never a hardship, especially at times like this. How many curious guests are you expecting?"

"Two hundred."

Isolde gasped. "You never told me."

Oz turned from the liquor table. "I didn't dare. You scream."

"I *certainly* do not."

"I'm sure you have good reason," the duchess sweetly observed. "And disregard Fitz's rudeness. We're pleased to be here. As for these men, I'm sure they need someone to scream at them from time to time. They're much too familiar with male privilege." While Rosalind had never met Oz, Fitz had mentioned they were good friends and she knew what that meant for men of their repute. Or in her husband's case, his previous repute.

Isolde couldn't help but smile at Rosalind's pithy viewpoint. "I'm afraid my husband has an excessive need for authority," she mockingly lamented.

"Mine as well," Rosalind agreed with playful forbearance.

"You forget I've promised to be on my best behavior tonight," Oz pointed out, returning with two very full glasses. With the blood sport about to begin, he needed a bracing tonic.

Isolde grinned. "Rest assured, I shan't forget."

Oz rolled his eyes. "As soon as you marry them, they start giving orders."

"And yet the trade-offs are exceedingly pleasant," Fitz said with a lift of his brows.

"Agreed." Oz smiled, Isolde blushed, and a sudden silence fell. "Speaking of trade-offs, two or three hours in society is my limit. After that everyone can go to hell."

"If we can help in any way to ward off the obnoxious," Groveland offered, responding to Oz's note that had asked him to do just that. "Consider it done."

"Thank you." Oz held Fitz's gaze for a telling moment. "If I'm called away for a moment or two, I'd appreciate you stepping in."

"We'll be Isolde's phalanx against the unruly rabble," Rosalind submitted. "I'm becoming wider every day, and Fitz can be masterfully rude. His mother tells me he had much too much practice," she added with a bright smile for her husband.

The duke accepted his wife's assessments with a beneficence any of his friends would have found incomprehensible short months ago. Groveland had been distinguished for his shameless indifference to his lovers; as for his rudeness, his mother was right. "We'll protect Isolde, never fear." He expected Oz was concerned about his former lovers who'd try to lure him away from his wife. "Do you have any cognac?" Fitz asked, rising to his feet.

Oz quickly stood. "Of course."

As the men strode away, Fitz quietly said, "I wished to mention Compton. You must have heard what he's saying."

Oz nodded. "He concerns me. It's the main reason I'd like you to stay by Isolde's side if I'm absent. Compton's creditors are about to become vindictive I understand."

"Does he harbor expectations even now?"

"So I gather. He claims the marriage is a hoax, which implies that even if Isolde has a child, he remains the legitimate heir."

"Is he serious?"

"I'm not sure. But with someone like him—" Oz shrugged.

"I know . . . a cheat and a bounder. It might take more than threats to send him on his way."

Oz looked up from his pouring. "An excellent idea. I have ships regularly leaving London."

"Think about it then. If you're concerned with the niceties"—Fitz raised one brow to discharge the consideration; they were both men of unlimited power—"you might think of it as saving Compton from his creditors. A benevolence as it were. If you recall, he tried to extort money from Topham last year, threatening to inform his wife of the little wench Topham had set up in St. John's Wood."

"And?"

"You know Topham's temper. He paid Compton a visit. In any event, no one would miss the scoundrel."

"But his mother," Oz drawled.

The duke smiled. "Maybe she'd enjoy an ocean voyage as well. Beresford spent a year abroad in involuntary exile after the Tranby Croft affair, as have any number of other nobles who've unwisely strayed from the path of righteousness," he sardonically murmured. "And surely Compton is not in the least righteous, nor is his dreadful mother."

They were both men of enormous wealth who understood the advantages allowed those of great fortune. The world was neither democratic nor fair, nor—sacred opinion aside—did the meek inherit the earth.

Oz dipped his head in acknowledgment. "I'll let you know how things transpire."

"Just send me their sailing date. I'll understand. By the way," Fitz added with a grin, "those bruises and bites will draw comment. I expect your wife requires protection from leers and snickers on that score as well."

"If you don't mind."

Fitz grinned. "I expect it was worth it."

Oz grinned back and handed Fitz his drink.

While the men quickly tossed off their cognacs and had another, Rosalind and Isolde conversed with comfortable ease. They were both women who'd lived lives of relative freedom.

"I don't know if Oz told you," Rosalind said, "but Fitz and I married as precipitously as you. Against all reasoned practicalities, he managed to sweep me off my feet. I couldn't say no."

"I can understand why. He's not only gorgeous, he obviously dotes on you. Even on short acquaintance that's evident."

"Fitz *is* a sweetheart. Although it seems that Oz was as insistent on marrying you." She smiled. "Neither man has any regard for convention. They rather do as they like. You hadn't known Oz long, had you? Fitz didn't think so," she added, seeing her question had unsettled Isolde. "Forgive me. I'm sure it's none of my business."

"No, really, it shouldn't matter. I was simply debating whether to present the fiction Oz had promoted at our first appearance in public.

"If it helps, Fitz told me you're not related."

Isolde exhaled in relief. "Then I needn't dissemble. The truth is that we met at Blackwood's Hotel quite by accident and married the same night."

"How wonderfully romantic," Rosalind exclaimed. "Love at first sight—a thing of beauty! I once wrote romances, so I firmly subscribe to the notion. Although Fitz and I rather disliked each other on first meeting."

"Obviously that changed."

Her smile was affectionate. "Fitz can be very persuasive."

"Oz as well," Isolde softly replied, not altogether sure she wasn't beginning to care too much for a man whose genius for persuasion was apparently much in demand.

"Your delightful story is safe with me and rest assured with Fitz as well. Fitz and Oz were quite close in their prodigality; two of a kind," she added with a grin. "Or rather I should say, *were* two of a kind."

How to respond when her husband was still the prodigal rake?

"He'll change with marriage," Rosalind assured Isolde, as if reading her thoughts. "I had my reservations as well. Who wouldn't with men like them?"

"You're happy, I can tell," Isolde said rather than deal with the brevity of her and Oz's future.

"Over-the-moon happy. My life had been one of struggle, so I'm grateful beyond words for Fitz's love."

Such unalloyed happiness triggered a wretched and utterly useless ache of misery. No happy ending would befall her, Isolde reflected, although salvation from Compton certainly would be the sweetest of triumphs. And at the moment, Oz was everything she could possibly desire. "I'm equally grateful for Oz's kindness. He's incredibly benevolent."

What an odd choice of words, Rosalind reflected. But rather than voice her thoughts, she said, "I'm so pleased for you both. Ah, here come our darling husbands. I miss Fitz dreadfully the minute he walks away. I expect you feel the same way about Oz."

"Yes, very much." Simple words, complicated emotions, and no fairy-tale ending in sight.

"So have you men settled the affairs of the world?" Rosalind inquired, having noticed their quiet conversation.

"More or less," Fitz blandly replied.

"Provided we get through this evening unbloodied," Oz said with a grin.

"Pshaw. As if anyone will dare speak out of turn to either of you. To be perfectly honest," Rosalind declared, "*I'm* rather looking forward to all the spite and malice. The evening should be as amusing as a Sheridan play."

A single rap on the door interrupted the conversation.

Josef entered and bowed. "Nine o'clock, sir."

The men exchanged glances as if before battle, drained their glasses, set them down, and offered their arms to their wives.

This evening was warfare of another kind but equally strategic. Tonight was meant to be a deterrent to a perceived enemy—Compton—as well as a chivalrous mobilization against the fashionable world that could be tiresomely vicious. Oz wished to protect Isolde from both. And as with any duel, he felt it easily within his power to prevail.

A few minutes later, Isolde and Oz stood at the top of the stairs waiting to greet the first guests ascending the flower-garlanded and footman-lined staircase. The Duke and Duchess of Groveland were seated within sight of their hosts but beyond the need for conversation with the visitors. Josef had placed a small table with a bottle at Fitz's side, the duchess had an iced lemonade at hand, and both were intent on the coming performance.

"You needn't get up, dear, if you don't wish," Fitz said. "If Oz leaves, I'll take his place."

"I'll see how I feel," the duchess answered with a small smile. "There might be one or two of your old paramours I might wish to send away with a flea in her ear."

"Be my guest."

"Lady Buckley for instance."

Fitz laughed. "I warn you, she's a bitch. Don't expect me to save you."

"I already know she's a bitch, darling. We've met. And I won't need saving."

The most avidly curious were the first to arrive, and as Josef announced them by name, Isolde and Oz smiled the required smiles, uttered the prescribed courtesies and polite trivialities, countered the expected malice with suave malice of their own, and in general averted any overt belligerency with dulcet impudence or in Oz's case, with the occasional warning glance.

Nell's transit of the reception line passed without controversy since her husband was at her side and in consequence she was muzzled. Lord Howe had come specifically to meet the woman who'd lured Lennox away from his wife. While Nell was resentful of Oz's new bride, her husband was intrigued. Well aware of his wife's sexual expertise and agility, Lord Howe suspected that Lennox's wife was highly imaginative in the bedchamber.

"A prodigious pleasure to meet you, Countess," Lord Howe said, his voice silken as he gracefully bowed over Isolde's hand.

"The pleasure is all mine." Withdrawing her hand, Isolde spoke with counterfeit warmth. "Do enjoy yourself tonight." She was surprised that Lord Howe was so good-looking. For some reason she'd naively thought Nell's search for pleasure was predicated by an ugly husband.

"Thank you, I will." Lord Howe turned to Oz with an urbane smile. "Congratulations, Lennox. You've found a beautiful diamond of the first water. Dashing and spirited I don't doubt. Why else would you marry?"

The insinuation was plain, the word *spirited* pronounced with a certain small emphasis.

"Thank you. I consider myself fortunate." Oz cooly met Lord Howe's amused gaze. "Did you enjoy Paris?"

"Not as much, apparently, as you did London in my absence."

"Ah—no one new in the corps de ballet? I heard a young dancer from Hungary was all the rage."

Lord Howe didn't so much a blink an eyelash at the allusion to his latest adultery. "You must have better sources than I."

"I do, of course. Mine are excellent. Enjoy our little soiree. My chef has outdone himself it seems, but then one must allow him his romantic fervor. I don't get married every day."

"Indeed. Brooks's betting book was inclined to wager—never."

"Then someone won a tidy sum." Oz deliberately turned to the next person in line, dismissing Lord Howe and his wife. Not that the following couple was an improvement. Another of his lovers had come with her husband, and unlike Lord Howe, the Earl of Dugal took issue with his wife's infidelity.

"Will married life rein in your debauchery, Lennox?" the Scottish earl demanded in his heavy brogue.

"Marriage has brought it to complete standstill, Dugal. What about you?"

The elderly man turned a mottled red and cleared his throat. "I don't see how that concerns you," he growled.

"Nor does it, no more than my life concerns you," Oz said, an edge to his voice. "Now make your bows to my lady wife and go off and drink my liquor. Unless you have something more to say."

Dugal's pretty young wife smirked behind her husband's back, dipped her head to Oz, and turning to smile at Isolde, said with sweet innocence, "I wish you well, my lady. Lord Lennox is exceedingly kind."

"I know. Thank you." She almost felt sorry for the young wife who gazed at Oz with such longing. If she were married to a frightfully old as well as unfaithful man, she'd be looking for love elsewhere, too.

And so it went, the men offering their good wishes with leers at Isolde, the many women who'd slept with Oz predictably offering him seductive smiles and winks and whispered asides. Then there was the general herd who'd come to gawk or scrutinize or hope to ferret out the freakish and unaccountable explanation for Lord Lennox's marriage. And last but not least, Achille's reputation was well-known due to Oz's wild bachelor parties. A small percentage of guests with epicurean tastes had come for the haute cuisine alone.

Those who dared mention Oz's bites and bruises were ignored if Oz was in a lenient mood or were warned off with a look even the most obtuse recognized if he wasn't. Also as promised, he was ever gracious and adoring to his wife, so much so that those who didn't actually believe in love were given pause. If cupid's arrow could strike a reprobate heart like Lennox's, surely the concept was more than a matter of poetic license.

Isolde had long ago given up any notion of publically exerting control over her husband. Oz was at his charming best in any event, and at base she found herself indifferent to all but the pressing need for escape.

An hour had passed, Josef had brought Oz several brandies, the number of arriving guests had dwindled, the drawing rooms were crowded—and still no Compton.

Oz was impatient. He needed Compton; he wanted this over.

Isolde was relieved. If she never saw her cousin again, she'd be content.

A footman jogged up the stairs, spoke to Josef, who in turn spoke to Oz. "I think we've done our duty long enough, dear," Oz said. "Why don't I have Fitz and Rosalind escort you into the supper room. Try some of Achille's special dishes. He did it all for you. It seems that Sam has something he can't deal with. I'll be right back."

A look of fear came into her eyes. "Is it Compton?"

"No, a matter to do with our departure tomorrow. It's nothing serious." Turning, he signaled to Fitz. "Would you escort Isolde into the supper room? I won't be gone long."

He waited until Isolde and the Grovelands had disappeared into the crowd before quickly making his way downstairs.

"Sorry to bother you," Sam said as Oz entered his study. "Davey thought you wanted him to go with you," he added, indicating the secretary. "I said I thought not. He's wondering whether he has to pack your business ledgers and papers tonight. Tell him what you want him to do."

Oz glanced at the clock. "I have to get back. Compton

hasn't come yet. You're staying in London, Davey. Follow me and I'll explain what I need."

As the two men walked down the corridor, Oz gave directions in crisp, rapid-fire accents: he needed a daily courier between London and Cambridgeshire; more than once a day if matters were urgent; Davey could sign anything that wasn't of singular importance; he particularly needed the shipping schedules of his fleet. "The exact times of departure, dates, hours, the captains, destination. Everything."

Davey was half running to keep up with Oz's long stride. "Are you shipping an important cargo?"

"I might. It depends. Make sure that the departure schedules are current—to the minute." They were entering the entrance hall. "If you have any more questions, we can talk in the morning." Oz scanned the empty stairway.

"Will you be staying in the country long?"

"Only as long as I must. Not very long as far as I can tell. I'll let you know." Catching sight of the man he'd been waiting for out of the corner of his eye, Oz came to a stop. "We'll talk later," he murmured, waving off Davey before turning to his right. "What are you doing skulking in my entrance hall, Compton?"

Isolde's cousin stepped from behind a malachite pillar into the light, a petulant thrust to his jaw.

"No answer? Have you seen all you wish to see?" Oz's brows lifted faintly. "Mute tonight? Very well," he calmly said. "Since you're here, go upstairs and wish Isolde happiness on her marriage."

"*If* she's married," Compton blurted out. "You of all people married?" he sullenly added. "I'm not the only one suspicious."

"Would you like to see the marriage license? Your hired minister brought it to the hotel as I recall."

"He seems to have disappeared."

Oz looked amazed. "Are you sure?"

"You know damned well he's gone," Compton spat. His solicitor had immediately attempted to see the minister.

"You may find this hard to believe, but men of the cloth

are of no interest to me." Oz's gaze was direct and pointed. "Nor will they ever be."

Compton's expression took on a cunning look, and his voice turned silken and sly. "Ministers and licenses aside, perhaps the question should be instead—how long will your marriage last?"

Had Compton heard him answer Davey's question? Perhaps. Did it matter? "Rest assured, my marriage will last longer than you can wait," Oz bluntly said, for realistically that was *all* that mattered. "Your creditors are becoming anxious, and Bedlington has been known to break legs and fingers. Time isn't your friend."

Compton sucked in his fat belly and puffed up his chest. "I'm still the Wraxell heir. That means something."

"Good luck in that regard. Isolde's only twenty-three. She might soon have an heir of her own." *Not that I'll be involved, but she can marry again and start a family.* "Ask Bedlington if he'll wait fifty years for his money or how he'd feel about never getting paid if Isolde has sons."

"Will they be yours?"

"Surely you're not so unwise," Oz said very, very softly, "as to question my wife's fidelity to my face."

Compton immediately took a step back, the lethal threat in Oz's eyes turning his blood cold. "No, no, of course not. I meant— nothing . . . of the kind," he stammered. But beneath his trembling fear, he knew what he'd heard. Then again, perhaps not.

"Go and wish your cousin happy," Oz growled. "And don't be rude or you won't have to wait for Bedlington to break your fingers."

As Compton scuttled away and made for the stairs, Oz watched him with a frown. Had he overheard his discussion with Davey? *Merde.* As if he needed another complication from the little worm. Oh, hell, he'd best be standing at Isolde's side when she spoke to Compton.

He ran for the stairs.

Just as Isolde's back stiffened at the sight of her cousin making his way through the crowd, Oz came up behind her.

"I'm here. Relax." He nodded at Fitz and Rosalind, who flanked his wife. "Let me deal with this."

"In that case, I think I'll speak with Lady Buckley," Rosalind said, smiling up at her husband. "She keeps looking your way. You don't mind, do you?"

"Of course I do. There's no reason to bother with her."

"But I wish to gloat, of course. Come now, indulge me."

"Just for the record," Fitz grumbled, "it was a long time ago. Clarissa's no more than a blur in my memory."

"Only because there were so many, dear. You must allow me this satisfaction. Did I tell you she came to the bookstore once and was exceedingly rude? Go and get yourself a drink. I can handle this perfectly well."

When it came right down to it Fitz wasn't so cavalier as to allow his wife to face Clarissa without protection. "I'll get a drink afterward. I'll need it. Let's get this over with if you insist."

"You're so incredibly sweet."

"Only because you give me enormous pleasure."

"I do, don't I?" the duchess said with a sultry glance.

It was left to Fitz to deal with Clarissa, however, for the moment they met, Clarissa took one look at Rosalind and curled her lip. "I see you didn't waste any time breeding."

"Nor was it the immaculate conception," Fitz cooly said. "How are *your* children?"

"Good God, you can't mean Buckley's loathsome brood."

"Buckley's heirs, aren't they?"

"How tiresome you can be, Fitz. You know perfectly well, I'm getting my share."

"In bath soap?" Rosalind dulcetly asked. "Someone said your husband is giving Pears soap stiff competition."

"I'm sure I wouldn't know. I don't deal with such bourgeois matters."

"Other than bourgeois husbands, you mean," Rosalind said in honeyed accents.

"What a vicious little cat you have for a wife, Fitz. Does she amuse you?"

"Every minute of every day." Fitz turned to Rosalind. "Darling, please, I need a drink. Now," he growled.

"Of course, sweetheart. Why didn't you say so before? If you'll excuse us, Lady Buckley."

"I hope you're satisfied," Fitz muttered as they walked away. "Christ, I don't—"

"—know what you saw in her?" Rosalind supplied. "I suppose you didn't talk much," she angelically noted.

Fitz shot her a disgruntled look. "You're enjoying yourself, aren't you?"

"Very much. Thank you."

He smiled. "You can thank me when we get home."

"Whatever do you mean?" the duchess purred.

"I mean I'm going to keep you up all night."

Rosalind lowered her lashes and offered him an enticing smile. "Maybe we should leave now."

Fitz glanced at Oz and Isolde over the heads of the crowd. "We'll check with Oz as soon as Compton's gone." He looked down and grinned at his wife. "And you're not allowed to talk to anyone else."

"None of your former lovers, you mean."

"That's exactly what I mean," he whispered, leaning over to kiss her without regard for the public. "Start thinking about what you want first . . ."

COMPTON DISPLAYED NONE of his sullenness or pomposity when he stopped before Isolde. He merely said, subdued and ingratiating, his gaze nervously flicking to Oz, "My compliments . . . on your marriage, cousin. I wish you the best." He saw Oz frown and quickly added, "And much happiness . . . in the future. Naturally . . . from Maman as well."

"Thank you, Compton," Oz remarked, bringing the stumbling recitation to an end. "We appreciate your kind regards.

I'm sure Isolde and I desire all the very best for you as well," he offered in a meticulously gentle tone. "Might I tempt you with some of my chef's offerings or a drink perhaps," he added, taking Compton's arm in a hard grasp. "If you'll excuse us, darling." Isolde was ashen. Catching Fitz's eye over the crowd, he nodded at his wife and drew Compton away.

"You're shaking," Rosalind murmured moments later, taking Isolde's hand. "I'm so sorry."

"I shouldn't be so fainthearted," Isolde said with a small sigh. "Frederick's been intimidating me too long, I think. I'll be fine in a minute."

Rosalind looked up at her husband.

"We could put an end to that intimidation," Fitz said, reading his wife's gaze. "Oz and I."

"No, no, please—that's not necessary." The duke sounded just as Oz had when he'd threatened to shoot Frederick. "I'm sure my cousin will leave soon. Perhaps if I sit for a minute . . ."

"Of course," Rosalind said. "Would you like Fitz to fetch you a lemonade? Good. Fitz, darling. We'll go and sit down over there."

Moments later, Fitz returned with Oz and the lemonade.

"He's gone," Oz said, unruffled as he'd been throughout. "Here, dear, take a sip, although you probably could use something stronger."

Isolde drank down a good portion of the lemonade before handing it back to Oz. "I'm feeling more myself now. Thank you, everyone. I didn't mean to make a scene."

"Nonsense. You may do as you wish."

Isolde experienced a great wave of relief at the transcendent power in her husband's simple words. He lived his life without restraint, uncowed and undaunted. And with Frederick's menacing image still vivid in her brain, she deeply appreciated the confidence and strength that lay beneath Oz's glittering charm. "If you mean it," she said, astonished at the timidity of her tone, "perhaps we might—"

He smiled. "End this charade?"

She nodded, suddenly exhausted in body and spirit.

Oz turned to the Grovelands. "Many thanks for your support and assistance tonight. I'm sure you're as ready to leave as we."

"You don't have to ask me twice," Fitz said, taking Rosalind's hand. "I hope you're more yourself in the morning," he gallantly added with a smile for Isolde.

"I will be, I know. I so appreciate your company."

Oz met Fitz's gaze, the men of a height, temperament, and understanding.

"If you need anything, let me know." Although in terms of human management, Oz's skills were impeccable. Turning to Isolde, Fitz offered their good-bys.

"We must have dinner when you're back in town," Rosalind said, their earlier conversation touching on their departure for Cambridgeshire.

"Yes, thank you," Isolde said, because it was expected of her.

Oz nodded. "We'll call on you."

A moment later, Oz quietly said, "Would you like me to carry you?"

"Heavens no!"

He smiled at her alarm. "You have to learn not to give a damn, darling. I'll teach you."

"Just not at this moment if you don't mind," she quickly said, coming to her feet. "I'm fine . . . really—perfectly fine." She held out her arm. "Look—a steady hand."

He liked that toughness she prided herself on—occasional moments in reference to Compton notwithstanding. Her stubborn intrepidity was what had first endeared her to him. Not that her independent streak didn't turn mutinous at times, but then that only added to her allure. He wasn't bored yet when he always was long before this.

"Am I allowed to take your hand?" he sportively inquired, doing just that.

"No."

"Thank you," he murmured, tightening his clasp. "You're always so accommodating. That must be why we get along."

"We get along because I can keep up with you in bed."

"And even exceed me at times." He shot her a grin as they moved toward the corridor. "I find that exceptional flair most attractive in you."

His hand was large and firm and reassuringly warm. "While I find you exceptionally difficult." She was smiling though.

"But loveable."

"If only so many other women didn't think so as well."

"How can it matter?"

"So practical, Lennox."

"We both are." His voice was relaxed. "Practical with regard to this marriage."

"And with regard to the sex."

"Especially the sex. Which provides me uncommon delight."

She wanted to ask, *For how long?* but consoled herself with knowing that he was feeling perhaps as beguiled as she.

And in that she took solace.

But it turned out to be a night quite separate from anything so tame as beguilement. It was a night of hot, steamy sex, of frenzied, furious sex, of sex with a hint of violence at times, but not without a fanatical degree of pleasure as well. Until Isolde finally cried, "No more!"

"Are you sure?" Oz panted, trying to drag air into his lungs. "Sorry," he whispered, meeting her gaze. "You're sure." Exhaling softly, he rolled onto his back, gathered her into his arms, and watched her fall asleep in seconds.

His heart was still pounding like a drum.

He felt as if he could last a week, a month.

She was amazing.

He was looking forward to his conjugal duties with real pleasure.

CHAPTER 11

Isolde's traveling carriage, brought to Oz's from Blackwood's after the wedding, was at the curb outside Lennox House the next morning. Oz had been up early as usual and came up to speak to Isolde when she woke. He had a few arrangements to make before he could leave, he explained. One of his ships was due in port that morning. He'd ride up later. He wanted to have his favorite thoroughbred with him in Cambridgeshire.

Achille fussed over them at breakfast, so they smiled at each other more than they spoke, both of them pleasantly relaxed after their night of wild passion. Although they frequently took note of the time: Isolde was anxious to return home; Oz had a call to make.

After breakfast, Oz escorted Isolde to her carriage. In anticipation of the scandal accruing to the published reports of her denouement, she'd chosen to avoid the train. "I shouldn't be long in London," he said, offering her his hand to step up into the carriage. He was already dressed for travel in a dark coat, chamois breeches, and riding boots. "I may even overtake you before you reach home. Lift your feet." He took a foot warmer from a waiting footman and slid it under her booted feet. "You're sure you don't want a lady's maid with you?"

"I'm sure. I'll be home in a few hours." Pulling her fur-lined cape over the skirt of her traveling gown, cleaned and pressed by Oz's staff, she wiggled her toes against the heat of the ironstone container filled with hot coals.

She was incredibly self-reliant. Unlike the ladies he knew who never traveled without dozens of pieces of luggage and a full array of servants. "Then I'll see you at dinner if not before." Shutting the carriage door, he raised his hand in farewell and signaled the driver to move off.

He watched the coach pick up speed. Once the carriage disappeared from view, he turned suddenly. Crossing the pavement in two strides, he took the stairs in a bound, nodded at Josef who was holding open the door, and said with a grin, "Don't say I'm becoming responsible just because I'm obliging to my wife."

Josef's mouth quirked. "I wouldn't dream of it, sir."

"Has Sam come down?"

"He's waiting in your study."

"I may be away from the city for some time," Oz said over his shoulder as he strolled away.

"So I understand, sir."

Knowing Josef could command the Queen's household if necessary, there was no question his would be left in good hands. Although Oz *was* wondering how long he'd manage to remain civil, cooped up in the country with a wife. The sex aside, of course, which was a considerable attraction. But his business was in London, as was Brooks's, not to mention his habitual vices weren't likely to be found in the country.

"She's off?" Sam asked as Oz entered his study.

"Yes, on her way to Cambridgeshire—and pleased to be. Is our pigeon home?"

"Compton staggered in at four I'm told."

"In that case, he'll still be half-drunk." Oz picked up the overcoat that had been left on a chair for him and slipped it on. "I'll have to speak slowly so he understands. He was being difficult last night."

"These should help." Sam held out two pistols.

Oz's brows lifted. "Always useful in gaining someone's attention." Taking one of the pistols, Oz shoved it in his pocket. "Has Achille left?"

"They're loading up now. You're not taking your chaise?"

Oz shook his head. "We'll ride. I want Sukha with me. Isolde rides every morning. Ready?" At Sam's nod, the men left the study and moved down the hall toward the front door. "If Compton listens to reason, we should overtake Isolde before she reaches home."

"If he doesn't listen to reason—what then?"

"Plan B, I suppose."

"You don't have a plan B."

Oz shrugged. "Maybe he'll inspire me. Although, I don't have a lot of patience for a man who'd force a woman into marriage."

"For gambling debts no less."

Oz grunted. "It's hard to have much sympathy for a prick like that."

"You're taking on enormous responsibility for this woman." It was a question rather than a statement. Not since Khair had Oz shown concern for a woman.

Oz grinned. "When I haven't of late, you mean?"

"Damn right." Sam gave a lift of his brows. "And I've known you a long time." Sam had come to work for Oz years ago in Hyderabad after being cashiered from the king's tenth fusiliers.

"I expect my wife will soon tire of me. I'll accommodate her with a divorce, and life will return to normal." Oz shot Sam a cautionary look. "For your ears only."

"Acknowledged, sir." *Now this curious arrangement makes sense.*

A few moments later they were striding down the street, making for Compton's apartments. Two men in a hurry.

"I hope Compton finally realizes that his choices are limited. He argued with me last night. About his rights as heir."

"Which he has so long as the countess is childless. Will you accommodate her there as well?"

"Hell no. So," Oz added with a significant look, "Compton must be dealt with once and for all—firmly and finally. Not that a loaded pistol shouldn't prod his understanding."

"I'm not so sure, sir. Stupid's stupid. Stevens took a bullet in the head rather than listen." Sam had been flogged for refusing to lead his men into an ambush. The brash, inexperienced Lieutenant Stevens had been killed soon after leading the charge instead—Sandhurst military tactics the kiss of death in the Hindu Kush.

"I doubt Compton has martial spirit."

"What if he does?"

Oz grinned. "Then I'll try not to get blood on my boots."

Shortly after, as they approached Compton's lodgings, Oz murmured, "Stand guard outside his door."

"Yes, sir. Although if you'd like my advice, I say get rid of the scum."

"I can't just shoot him in cold blood."

"I sure as hell would."

Oz smiled. "I sure as hell would like to."

Pulling out a flask from his jacket pocket, Sam held it out. "A wee dram? Pure and fine, sir." Sam was a big, strong, sandy-haired Highlander.

Taking the flask, Oz swallowed a long draught. Smiling, he handed back the flask. "Excellent as usual. Now, tell me about Compton's debts. What do I have to deal with?"

"Five to the moneylenders, four for chits at Brooks's—"

"Due by Friday next."

Sam nodded, the men's clubs rules, like jockey club rules, were etched in stone. "And a thousand more give or take to the gambling hells."

"That's not so much."

"It is for anyone but a nabob like you."

"But since I am," Oz drawled, stopping before the entrance to the building, "let's see what it takes to buy my wife's peace of mind."

The foyer of the building that catered to bachelor apartments was silent, the lack of activity no surprise considering the early hour and the late-night habits of London's young bucks. The third floor where Compton resided was equally deserted. When they reached his door, Oz glanced at Sam.

Pulling out a slender metal pick from his pocket, Sam inserted the makeshift key and after a few deft twists, stepped back and softly turned the latch.

Drawing his pistol from his coat pocket, Oz eased the door open, quietly entered a narrow hall, and shut the door behind him. With the efficiency of a man impatient to finish an unpleasant task, Oz hustled Compton's manservant out of his bed in a small antechamber, made him understand his silence was required, and locked him in his room.

Entering Compton's bedchamber a few minutes later, Oz glanced at the snoring lump in the bed, then moved to the window and threw open the curtains. When no movement from the bed ensued, Oz picked up a liquor decanter and let it drop from his fingers to the marble floor.

As it shattered with a crash, spewing glass splinters and liquor across the floor, Compton came up on his elbows. "What the hell?" He squinted against the bright light. "Shut the bloody curtains, Standish!"

"Your man's indisposed at the moment."

The familiar voice, no matter its mildness, brought Compton awake with a jerk. "How did you get in?" Struggling into a seated position, he peered at Oz standing at the foot of his bed.

"The usual way. We need to talk."

"I have nothing to say to you." Petulant and rude, Compton was emboldened by the residual alcohol coursing through his blood. Not to mention the overheard conversation that had significantly altered his plans.

"I have a few words of advice for *you*, however," Oz mildly returned, raising the pistol he held at his side.

"You won't shoot. I'm unarmed." There were rules, gentlemen's rules.

"Once you're dead, whether you were armed or not is irrelevant."

The indifference in Lennox's voice drained the color from Compton's face, and too late he recalled his adversary's barbaric background. "My man would notify the authorities," he warned, sweat beginning to bead his brow.

"Your man might be killed in the melee," Oz silkily replied. "You went berserk. Everyone knows you've been drinking a lot."

"You wouldn't get away with it," Compton blustered.

"Of course I would. The only real question is whether you survive this meeting. I suggest you listen to my proposal and more to the point, agree to it."

"Do I have a choice?" Encouraged by the word *proposal*, however, Compton's native venality came to the fore.

"No."

Nevertheless, it looked as though Lennox was here to deal. Further emboldened by recall of what he'd heard last night, Compton rallied his confidence. "Say what you have to say then," he sneered. "Although, I might have plans as well. Have you thought of that?"

"Unless it involves you having a weapon in your hand right now—and you don't appear to have one—you're fucked," Oz pleasantly said. "So I'd listen if I were you. You've a count of three to make up your mind before I blow your head off. One, two—"

Oz's finger tightened on the trigger, and Frederick's false courage evaporated. "Don't, don't!" he screamed. "I'll listen!"

"Excellent choice." A soft, expressionless statement. "How much do you owe in gambling debts?"

"I'm not sure." Hedging, his mind racing to find deliverance from this madman, Compton mumbled, "I'd have to add it up."

"Don't bother. Five to the moneylenders, four to Brooks's, one to the gambling hells. Is that about it?"

"It could be; I'm not sure." Where the hell was Standish? Would anyone hear if he screamed for help? Would it matter whether they heard or not if he was dead?

"Don't be tiresome," Oz growled, irritated by the man's petty evasion. "I'm trying to be reasonable. God knows you don't deserve it. Look," he said, exhaling softly, "I'm willing to pay your debts and give you an additional five thousand if you agree to keep your distance from Isolde."

"My debts and ten thousand," Compton quickly countered, greed overcoming his fear.

"Very well—ten." It was more than he deserved, a fortune in fact.

"My debts and fifteen."

"Don't get reckless, Compton. Decide."

"It seems I don't have a choice." Although, the sum he was willing to spend meant Lennox wanted to please his wife. For a fraction of a second Frederick considered holding his ground.

Oz steadied himself against iniquitous impulse and said with forced calm, "Of course you do. You can choose to die, and I'd save a helluva lot of money."

"Very well," Frederick said, grudging and surly. "I'm at a disadvantage, unarmed."

Oz's nostrils flared at the man's insolence. Stifling an urge to shoot and be done with it, Oz said taut and cold, "You may draw on my banker, Simms." Turning on his heel, he strode away before he completely lost his temper.

"Smug bastard," Oz muttered as he exited the apartment.

Sam nodded in the direction of the open door. "Let me take care of him."

"If not for Isolde, I'd say yes." Oz shut his eyes, slowly

counted to ten, opened his eyes, and said through his teeth, "She'd be appalled. Let's get the hell out of here."

The men walked in silence for several blocks before Oz tamped down his fury. "I have to see Simms to arrange the payments to the half-wit. It won't take long."

"If you don't need me, I'll go back to the house and settle a few matters."

"With Betsy."

"Aye. She's a bonny lass, and I won't be seeing her for a while."

"Bring her along. Take my chaise."

"And Jess?"

"Of course, Jess. Bring them both." Achille's sous-chef, Robbie, had gone to the aid of his sister when Betsy's husband had run off and left her. She was learning to cook.

Sam smiled. "Much obliged."

Oz shrugged off the thanks, distracted by his thoughts. Could he trust Compton to comply? Yes, no, maybe? Realizing Sam was waiting, Oz looked up. "I'm not sure I can trust someone as venal as Compton."

"Do you want him watched?"

Oz shook his head. "Let's not—at least for now. I don't want to think about him." Should he though? The man had no ethics.

"Whatever you say, boss."

Oz's gaze snapped up.

Sam grinned. "Just making sure you were listening." Oz disliked that designation; they'd been friends too long.

THE MEN PARTED near St. James Street.

Oz found his banker having his breakfast ale and rasher of bacon at his desk. "Don't get up, Simms. I'll be brief."

The elderly man who carried his years well leaned back in his chair and smiled. "Congratulations, my lord. I heard the good news."

"Thank you. There comes a time in every man's life," Oz replied with a roll of his eyes.

"The betting books lost money on you," Simms noted. "You surprised everyone. Marriage offers a certain contentment, though, and after nearly fifty years of connubial bliss," he said with a smile, "I know of what I speak."

"Good God. Fifty years and you haven't killed each other."

"No, sir. Never even thought of it."

"I'm encouraged." Oz grinned and dropping into a chair across the desk from the man who'd been his father's banker in London, added, "You'll have to give me some advice on marital goodwill."

Pushing his plate aside, Simms spoke with the imperturbability that came to a man of his years and experience. "The golden rule is useful, my lord. I recommend it."

Oz smiled faintly. "That might take a personality change."

"On the contrary, sir, you do much good with your wealth. Benevolence in marriage is no different." Oz contributed vast sums to charitable enterprises.

"Ah, but unlike charities that can be satisfied with an anonymous bank draft, one's wife is at the breakfast table every morning."

"I'm sure you'll become used to it, sir."

"I doubt that," Oz said lightly. "Speaking of uncomfortable situations, I've come to tell you that a despicable little man will be calling on you soon."

"What would you like me to do with him?"

Oz chuckled. "A question I'd best not answer. What I can say is that Frederick Compton is my wife's cousin and I've agreed to pay off his gambling debts as well as give him an additional ten thousand to save my wife irritation. He apparently feels he deserves a share of her wealth."

"He's not the first relative to think so, my lord. But his debts plus ten thousand is a right good sum." Simms spoke in measured tones.

"Noted, but it must be done. If you'd personally see to his gambling debts, I'd appreciate it. He's a double-dealing knave who'd otherwise likely keep the money. The ten thousand, however, is his to do with what he likes. I suspect he'll gamble it away, after which he can go to hell with my blessing."

"Would you mind if I make some inquiries about this fellow?"

"Not at all."

"Should he have other debts you're unaware of, I could deduct them from the ten thousand."

Oz shook his head. "I promised him ten, so ten he'll have. If you discover other debts, pay them and give me an accounting. I don't wish my wife to be bothered by him."

"Very good, sir. I'll see that the business is appropriately managed."

"I expect he'll be in today. I apologize for asking you to deal with him, but"—Oz put his hands on the chair arms, preparing to rise—"I'll be out of town for an indefinite time. If you wish to contact me, Josef has my direction in Cambridgeshire." He rose to his feet. "My wife prefers her country home to the city."

"I don't blame her, sir. Winter in the city is insalubrious with all the coal smoke and fog."

"My apologies again for saddling you with this noisome individual."

"No need, sir." Simms smiled. "In my business one learns to deal with all kinds. I'll send you a message when the transaction is complete."

CHAPTER 12

WHEN OZ LEFT London, he had every expectation of overtaking Isolde.

But her carriage was built for speed, her bloodstock prime, and she liked to travel fast. Reaching Oak Knoll in under six hours, she jumped out as the carriage rolled to a stop and smiled at her gypsy driver. "Excellent time, Dimitri. That's a new record, isn't it?"

"By ten minutes, Miss Izzy."

"You're the best driver in England." No one knew horses like Dimitri. "Tell Grover you won the bet, and tell him not to grumble about the sum. I really thought I'd win," she cheerfully observed.

Since news of her wedding had been carried to Oak Knoll by one of her grooms directly after the ceremony, her staff rushed out to greet her as she stepped down from the carriage. Everyone from her butler and housekeeper to her lowliest footman and scullery maid swarmed around her, offering their congratulations and best wishes.

Their pleasure at her marriage was doubly relished after the insult she'd suffered at Lord Fowler's hands; his treat-

ment of Isolde had been taken personally by a staff who
doted on their mistress. And to have wed a handsome nabob!
What better revenge, they all agreed!

"Yes, yes," Isolde replied to the polite, hopeful inquiries
concerning her husband's appearance. "He should be here
directly. He had some business to deal with, and I just
wanted to get home." She grinned. "To see you all."

"You're looking right chipper, Miss Izzy. Like a blushing
bride!" Mrs. Belmont, the housekeeper who'd overseen the
household since before Isolde's birth, beamed. "I expect your
nice Lord Lennox will be wantin' a hearty meal right soon
after he arrives." She didn't say that the chef had been scour-
ing his repertoire for dishes from India. Nor did she say
they'd heard all the gossip about the handsome young lord
who had money to burn—one of the groomsmen had ridden
hell-bent for leather to bring them the news.

"I'm sure Lord Lennox will enjoy a fine meal," Isolde
said with a smile for Mrs. Belmont. "And see that our best
brandy comes up from the cellar."

"Indeed, Miss Izzy. With a nice cognac for you?"

"Thank you, yes. Now, if you'll excuse me, I have a bit of
business to discuss with Grover," she said, turning to smile at
her steward.

He gave her a very correct bow because Grover prided
himself on the civilities. "I'm at your disposal, ma'am."

With a smile for her staff crowded around her on the
drive, Isolde exclaimed, "It's *wonderful* to be home again."
After three hectic days in London, she was indeed grateful to
return to the familiarity of her own residence.

The moment she and her steward had made themselves
comfortable in his office, she explained her concern. "I'm
afraid Cousin Compton is not at all happy with my marriage."

Her steward smiled wryly. "Deprived as he is of his expectations of marrying you."

"Indeed. For which I'm vastly pleased as you may per-
ceive." Relaxing in the old worn chair her father had favored,

she gazed across the ancient desk at the man who'd taken care of Oak Knoll well before she was born. "However, he might decide to call, and you can be sure he won't be up to any good. I wished to alert you to the possibility because I doubt he'll come alone. In London he bearded me with hired roughs at his back. The staff should be warned."

"Frederick was always a knave." Grover's voice was chill, his beetled brows drawn together in a scowl. "Even as a child he was constantly up to some wickedness and his ambitions are common knowledge. We'll be on the lookout, miss."

"Thank you. Compton is imprudent at times, that's all. I can't be sure what he might be planning. Lord Lennox tells me his debts are at a point that Frederick himself might be in danger from the moneylenders."

"Then, as usual, he'll be coming to you for money. If you don't mind my saying, Miss Izzy, you've been too generous with him in the past. He quite forgets the Wraxell fortune is yours."

She shrugged. "I have so much; it didn't seem right to begrudge him."

"He wants it all, though," her steward gravely said. "Without a thought for the illegality of his claim or a care for your rights or happiness. There's a point, Miss Izzy, where one can't continue to overlook his callous greed."

Her brows lifted. "You're telling me that point has been reached?"

"Long since, miss," Grover quietly said. "As to the present, might I suggest you stay inside for a time?"

"Surely, that's not necessary." Isolde smiled at her steward's solemn expression. "You know my morning ride is sacrosanct."

"Take a groom with you then, Miss Izzy. A modicum of caution is always sensible." The entire household understood their mistress's untrammeled nature. She'd been allowed free rein by her indulgent parents and staff and in consequence was not a model of conformity. "Now," Grover continued, his thin hands steepled on the desktop, his voice quietly diplomatic, "how would you like your cousin dealt with should he step foot on the estate?"

"I'm not sure. What do you think?"

"I'd call the constable, Miss Izzy."

Isolde's eyes widened.

"As a precaution, Miss Izzy. We're all agreed."

"The staff has spoken of this?"

"For some time." He dipped his shiny pate, and his blue eyes twinkled for a moment. "Cousin Compton is universally abhorred."

She smiled. "I don't know whether to take issue or be grateful for my staff's good judgment. But really, Grover, I'm afraid the constable might be a bit much."

"Compton's a nobleman, Miss Izzy. And right familiar with doing as he pleases."

"Oh dear." She hadn't considered having him arrested.

"It would be for your own safety, miss. Constable Hawkins abides by the letter of the law, whether noble or working man."

Isolde sighed. "Let me think about it."

"Of course. The decision is yours. You do look right happy, miss, if I do say so myself," the steward added with a smile. "Everyone is pleased about your marriage." The scandal sheets hadn't reached the remote country neighborhood, nor might they ever.

"You'll like Lord Lennox, Grover. He's a most charming man," she remarked. Time enough to define the pragmatic nature of her marriage at some later date. For example, when she announced her divorce plans.

"We all wish you the very best, Miss Izzy. You deserve it. Now if you'll excuse me," he politely said, coming to his feet. "The sooner I inform the staff about Compton, the sooner you'll be protected."

"Protected from what?"

At the familiar voice, Isolde turned to see Oz walking in,

booted and spurred, and shrugging out of his coat.

"Grover, allow me to present my husband, Lord Lennox. Oz, my steward, Grover. We were speaking of Compton and the possibility he might call."

"A pleasure, sir," Oz said, nodding at the steward as he strode forward, spurs clinking. Dropping his riding coat on a chair, he raked a hand through his hair as he moved toward Isolde. "As for Compton, I believe he's checkmated. I spoke to him this morning. Threatened him, as a matter of fact. You travel fast, darling," he murmured, ignoring Grover and protocol, pulling her up out of the chair and into his arms. "I thought to overtake you."

She blushed, but the feel of him was much to her liking. "My carriage is built for speed. You made good time as well."

"I missed you," he whispered, dropping a kiss on her nose. "So tell me," he said in a normal tone of voice, releasing her and turning to Grover, "what sort of protection are you planning?"

"It's just a matter of having the tenants and staff look out for him. They're sure to recognize Frederick," Isolde explained. "He might attempt some mischief, particularly if he's in his cups."

"In other words, force Miss Izzy to give him more money," Grover explained. "That's the only reason he ever travels this far."

"I see. Are you expecting him?"

"It's a very real possibility, my lord," Grover asserted.

"Then I wasted my money."

"You gave him money!" Isolde exclaimed. "You shouldn't have."

"I thought it worth a try. He seemed to understand my position when we spoke," Oz said.

"Only because you threatened him," Isolde said with a smile. "Naturally, I'll repay you."

"You'll do no such thing. It was the merest bagatelle."

"Still, Oz, I'm in your debt."

"Nonsense. You're my wife. Tell her not to give it another thought," he said, swiveling toward Grover.

"His lordship is most kind, Miss Izzy." Oz immediately found favor with Isolde's steward, for his generosity in bribing Compton to stop harassing Miss Izzy, for his obvious concern and affection for his wife. After Lord Fowler's grievous behavior in breaking off their long-standing engagement, Lennox's solicitude was especially gratifying. "If you'll excuse me, Miss Izzy, I'll see that the staff and tenants are alerted."

As the office door closed on Isolde's steward, Oz said with a grin, "Alone at last. Show me your bedroom."

Isolde smiled. "I'd love to if only the entire staff wasn't all atwitter to meet you, if the kitchen wasn't busy making dinner for you, *and* if I wouldn't be hideously embarrassed disappearing into my bedroom with you in the middle of the day."

"It's our honeymoon, darling. Everyone expects us to lock ourselves away in the bedroom." He moved toward her.

"Don't you dare," Isolde whispered, backing up at his approach.

His smile was cheerfully wicked. "I didn't ride my horse into a lather in order to worry what your servants think. As for daring, sweetheart, you're talking to the wrong man."

"Oz, please," she begged, holding out her hand in deterrence. "At least wait until after dinner."

"And if I do," he softly replied, forcing her back against the door and dipping his head so their eyes were level, "tell me what I get?"

"My eternal gratitude," she said to the teasing light in his eyes.

"You'll have to do better than that." His gaze was amused. "What do you want?"

He chuckled. "As if you don't know by now."

"After dinner, I promise."

"An early dinner I hope."

She nodded. "We keep country hours."

He smiled and stepped away. "Then I shall restrain myself, but I warn you, I eat very quickly."

"Thank you for your forbearance."

Her relief was so apparent he said, "Your staff means a lot to you, don't they?"

"They're my only family now that my parents are gone."

"So I mustn't play the tyrant before the staff," he remarked.

"Or at all if you know what's good for you."

"As I recall," he said, soft as silk, "you like orders now and again."

"God, Oz, don't start. I'm trying to be sensible."

He liked the heat rising on her cheeks, the slight tremor in her voice. He liked that she wanted him because he'd thought of little else on the ride north. "I'll be virtuous, darling. But it won't be easy. I'm in constant rut with you." Drawing in a breath, he stepped away. "I need a drink."

"Are you sure that's wise?"

"I'm very sure," he said, his voice rough with restraint. "But don't sit too near me."

CHAPTER 13

Oz WAS AT his most charming when introduced to Isolde's staff, so much so that even her butler, Lewis, who prided himself on his dignity, was seen to smile. Mrs. Belmont, less starchy by far, was instantly captivated by Oz, his admiration for her mother's cameo she always wore at her throat bringing forth blushing giggles that only subsided at a warning cough from Lewis. As for the young footmen and maids, their adulation was plain—a paragon of manliness had come into the family. The staff of the neighboring gentry would be green with envy.

The pleasantries concluded, the newlyweds retired to a small drawing room to await dinner. While still midafternoon, the winter light was beginning to fade, and the blazing logs in the fireplace lent a snug coziness to the chamber. As did the comfortable, well-used furniture from an era long past; it was Isolde's favorite room.

Oz lounged on a needlepoint settee stitched by some early Wraxell lady of the manor. His jacket was unbuttoned, his booted feet, devoid of spurs now, were draped over one of the curved armrests. An open bottle of brandy, loosely grasped, rested on his chest.

Isolde sat well away from him, framed by an exquisite tracery window purloined from one of the monasteries sacked by Henry VIII. She was doing her best to carry on an essentially one-sided conversation.

"Are you even listening?" she asked after a particularly lengthy period of silence from her husband.

He turned to her and smiled. "You were telling me about your stables. Go on, Miss Izzy," he added with a grin.

"Don't laugh."

"I'm not. I like the name. It suits you."

As he lifted the bottle to his mouth once again, she marveled at his capacity for drink. He appeared perfectly sober, neither slurring his words, nor becoming disorderly. Her father had held his liquor like that. "You're drinking my father's favorite brandy. It apparently meets with your approval."

"Indeed. He had good taste." As though to underscore the point, he drank another long draught, after which he said in a ruminating tone, "My father drank claret even though it didn't travel well. Habit, I suspect."

"Perhaps it reminded him of home."

"He was born in India."

Her surprise must have showed because he added, "As was his father. Our family has deep roots in India."

"And yet you're here in England."

"After everyone died there was no reason to stay."

His words were almost inaudible. "I'm sorry. Your memories must be painful."

"Not with this." He lifted the bottle slightly. "My anesthesia." He suddenly smiled. "As are you in a much more pleasurable way."

She dipped her head, responding to his more lighthearted comment in kind. "Pleased to be of service, sir."

He grinned. "Hold that thought until after dinner."

"If you must know, I think of little else."

"Not another word," he gruffly said, stabbing her with his glance. "I'm barely holding on."

"Should I leave?"

"No." Quick and curt. "Talk to me. Distract me with some more benign conversation. What do you read, for instance, or how did your crops fare this year? Does Mrs. Belmont always giggle like that? Who made that hideous traveling gown you're wearing?"

Her gaze narrowed. "I beg your pardon."

"Throw it away after dinner. I'll buy you ten better ones."

"Tut! Do I complain about your tailor?"

"I should hope not. Poole even manages to make fat Wales presentable."

He was exquisitely dressed, dusty boots notwithstanding, his tailoring expensive, elegant, and deliberately austere. "I shall tell you what I'm reading of late," she primly said. "Prepare to be edified."

He groaned.

Exacting vengeance for his rebuke of her dressmaker, she went on at some length about her recent reading. The books she favored were generally agricultural publications having to do with new crop hybrids and livestock breeds, and when he'd not taken a drink for some time she rather thought he'd nodded off. "So I decided to plant pineapples and bananas on my acres and had a most successful harvest," she finished with a flourish.

"Unlike you, we actually grow them in Hyderabad," he drawled, turning his amused gaze her way. "As for edification, I've been translating a rare Urdu manuscript, an ancient romance with warring kings and armies on the march. You may read it once I'm finished. Now, when are we going to eat?" He shook the brandy bottle. "This is damned near empty."

The drawing room door opened as she was about to answer and an agitated footman stood on the threshold. "Lord Fowler, my lady," he nervously announced, only to be shoved aside by the man she'd once thought to marry.

"What the *hell's* this about you *marrying*!" Striding into the room, tracking mud with each step, his gaze hot with temper, Will Fowler bore down on Isolde like a man possessed. "The news is all over the neighborhood!"

"This must be Will."

A man's voice, languid and softly mocking, brought Lord Fowler to a standstill, and Isolde thought, *Oh dear.*

Spinning around, Will saw a man undraping himself from the settee and lazily coming to his feet. "Who the *hell* are you?" A rhetorical question, fractious and cross as a bear.

"Will, allow me to introduce my husband," Isolde quickly interposed before someone tossed down the gauntlet. "Osmond Lennox, Baron Lennox; Will Fowler, Baron Fowler."

Will's gaze swiveled to Isolde. "You never told me about him," he snapped.

She bit back a similar comment about his wife, unwilling to enter a verbal skirmish of no practical use to anyone.

"Ours was a whirlwind love affaire," Oz said sweetly, setting down the bottle he was holding. "The moment we met, we fell head over heels, didn't we, darling?" A ghost of a smile on his face, Oz inclined his head slightly toward Isolde.

"Indeed, we did," Isolde agreed, performing her role.

"Ah, the magic of love—easy as falling off a log and yet more baffling than the riddle of the universe. Would you care to stay for dinner?" Oz continued with exquisite grace, ignoring Isolde's forbidding look. "I'm told we sit down to table soon."

"I'm sure Will is expected home for dinner. Aren't you?" The pleasure she derived from her innocent query was tawdry perhaps but wholly satisfying.

Oz watched his wife with a discerning gaze, and playing the indulgent husband, pressed Lord Fowler to stay. "Why not send Lady Fowler a note so she needn't worry? Isolde was telling me I must get to know the neighbors."

How wicked and sweet of Oz, Isolde decided, exchanging

a whimsical glance with her husband. "One of the grooms can ride over with the note, Will. Do stay."

"I can't," he retorted, his voice still brusque with temper, his gloved hands clenched in chafing rage. "We have guests coming for dinner."

"A shame. Some other time perhaps," Oz murmured, walking over to Isolde and curling his arm around her shoulder. "Although, we may be keeping to ourselves rather more than not," Oz roguishly added, pulling Isolde close and holding her gaze. "You promised me a full month for our honeymoon, didn't you, dear?"

"Hush, darling, you're embarrassing me." A demur glance for effect.

"Nonsense, my sweet. Lord Fowler understands a man's needs are a man's needs." Oz surveyed Will with good humor. "Isn't that so?"

"I'll talk to you later, Isolde." Taut and curt, Will choked out the words, then whirling around, stalked from the room.

"Dear Will reminds me of Nell's tantrums," Oz murmured, releasing her and moving back to the settee and his bottle. "Some lovers take issue with a fait accompli. Don't they know possession is nine points of the law?"

"If your many lovers who came to call in London are any indication, I'd say no," she drolly replied.

"Nor did Will appear ready to give up his ownership stake," Oz gently observed.

"Too bad." Dropping back into her chair, she contemplated her lounging husband with fondness. "Thank you, by the way. You were superb."

"You're more than welcome. Since Will seemed unwilling to relinquish his claims, I thought it only right that he be made aware of our deep and *passionate* regard for each other."

"And so you did most excellently. Although I very much doubt Lady Howe or any of the other ladies who came to call are ready to give you up, passionate regard or not."

"Ah, but he's close and they're not."

"I doubt he'll be back."

"I guarantee you he will."

Strangely, she didn't care. For the first time since Will's marriage, she no longer experienced a feeling of loss or having been forsaken. "It doesn't matter. Don't look at me like that. I mean it. Something was different today." She smiled. "You were here as buffer, I suppose."

His grin flashed. "You also took pleasure in his discomfort."

"Yes. Is that so bad?"

"Not at all. In fact I wish him pleasure in his richer-than-you heiress. Gold is little satisfaction in the end. That I know." At which point, he upended the bottle, drank the remaining dregs, and setting the bottle on the carpet, said with a touch of weariness in his voice, "Ring for someone. I want dinner now."

CHAPTER 14

An hour later, Oz was leaning back in his chair, his half-lidded gaze on Isolde seated at the distant end of a long table, the huge room quiet save for the sound of her spoon occasionally striking the side of her dish. "Do you always dine so formally?"

"In traveling clothes, you mean?" she answered with a smile.

"Should I have changed?" Quizzical and light as down.

"It didn't sound as though you were inclined to wait."

His brows lifted. "So you normally adhere to ceremony."

She shook her head. "The staff is showing off for you. Or were." Oz had dismissed the footmen once coffee and dessert had been served. "I usually dine in the breakfast room. It's smaller, cozier, and my dozens of ancestors are not looking down their noses at me."

"I'm relieved."

"You don't stand on ceremony?"

"A waste of time. Speaking of which—are you finished eating?"

"Are you?"

"Long ago. I've been observing the courtesies. That's your third dessert."

"I, on the other hand, haven't been counting your brandies."

"I applaud your restraint. So?"

She smiled. "Such impatience."

"On the contrary, I've been exceedingly patient. You could take that blancmange with you if you like."

"I might."

"Excellent." He pushed his chair back and stood.

Setting down her spoon, she watched him walk toward her, serenely smiling, relaxed, his tall form gilded by lamplight. "Would you think me absurd if I said I'm feeling different about"—she half lifted her hand—"this."

"Sex?"

"Now that I'm home," she rapidly finished as he stopped beside her.

He picked up her spoon and bowl of blancmange. "Let me change your mind," he gently said.

The house was strangely empty of staff as they made their way to Isolde's bedroom. "Did you say something to the footmen when you dismissed them?" she asked. "There's not a soul in sight."

"I said we'd be retiring soon. Did I put them to the blush?"

"How exactly did you say it?" A maid or footman could generally be seen in the midst of some task or errand.

"Politely. Unlike, I might add, your Will's belligerence."

"He's not mine, but point taken." She abandoned the subject. Oz was her husband, at least in her staff's eyes; he could issue orders as well as she.

Oz had no intention of pursuing the discussion either, and as they made their way to Isolde's bedchamber, he politely inquired about the various portraits they passed, about the date of a splendid solarium they walked through, why she'd chosen so small a bedroom for herself. The last query uttered as he stood on the threshold of her childhood room.

"We'll need a larger bed," he said once she'd explained.

"I'll have one sent up from London if you don't mind. One with bunny rabbits painted on it," he added with a grin. "Although that might take an extra day or so."

"Very humorous. I like my old bed."

"I might too if I could stretch out my legs. What of your parents' rooms, or is that—"

She wrinkled her nose.

"I understand. Surely in a house this size you have other choices. Perhaps some state rooms are available? Queen Elizabeth must have slept here once or twice; she did in every other Tudor mansion, I'm told."

"Is that so?"

The small, quick petulance in her voice prompted a tactful reply. "I was merely alluding to common lore." *And to Amanda Hawthorne's annotated tour of her Tudor palace one weekend when her husband was in London.* "But if you prefer your bunny bed, I'll manage."

She softly sighed. "I have no earthly reason to be jealous."

"Nor I." He lifted his brows. "Or at least not until Will returns."

"Enough said on that score," she muttered. "I apologize again for his presumption."

Oz put up his hand and grinned. "Please—talk of Will affects my amorous mood."

"I'm surprised anything can affect your libido," Isolde said drily. "For which I'm naturally grateful. Come." She crooked her finger. "We'll find a bed better suited to your size."

He followed her down several more hallways of the sprawling house, which had obviously been enlarged over the centuries by Percevals with a penchant for building. She stopped at a small door framed by two beautifully carved female figures attired in gilded medieval courtly dress. "Bend your head going in," Isolde warned, opening the door and reaching for the light switch. "The room itself is commodious, but Grandmama had a fancy for follies."

"Along with modern conveniences," Oz remarked, taking

note of an elaborate chandelier suddenly aglow with faux candles as he dipped his head and walked through the doorway. He entered a spectacular room constructed in the English Gothic style, the white-painted ceiling a spiderweb of delicate, soaring arches, its decorative gilt agleam. Tracery windows embellished with scenes from troubadour chronicles lined two walls, the theme mirrored as well in the splendid carpet modeled after the famous unicorn tapestry from Amiens. "Very impressive," he said. "Including the bed. Thank you." The vast, canopied bed was large enough to sleep six.

The Gothic revival had been popular midcentury. *His* grandmother had built a summer house in Hyderabad in a similar style. He said as much, then added, "My cousins and I used to sling ropes over finials like those"—he pointed to the decorative moldings on the ribbed vaults—"and climb the walls. Speaking of ropes," he murmured, his gaze studiously bland.

Isolde laughed. "I have none. Although, come to think of it," she said, "tying you up *might* be interesting."

"We'll toss a coin."

"*I* don't like being tied up."

"You speak from experience?"

"Do you?"

"Does it matter?" he replied with composure.

"What if I were to say it does?"

"I repeat, we'll toss a coin."

"Or we could just do it the usual way."

"Which usual way?" Oz pleasantly inquired. "Although we've plenty of time for whatever you like. I'm not going anywhere."

Isolde's sudden smile warmed her eyes. "I'm very happy you're staying."

He debated making his position clear in terms of *staying* but decided against disturbing her good humor. "While you make me happy in countless ways."

"Even without rope?"

"Keep it up and I'll rip those cords from the bed curtains and we'll see who likes what. Speaking of likes—where do you want this?" He held out the dish of blancmange.

"Whatever do you mean?" she purred.

He laughed. "Focused on sex, are we?"

"You aren't?"

"I believe I'm quickly becoming focused on blancmange." He smiled. "Then bondage. And don't say a word about your staff. This room is built like a medieval fortress. No one will hear a sound."

She offered him an unblinking look of amusement. "Should I be alarmed?"

"You should," he said with amiable delicacy, setting the dish down on an oddly shaped table carved from an oak burl. "But having waited through a long afternoon and an extremely lengthy dinner, I'm first inclined to end my abstinence—if you don't mind."

"And if I do?"

He smiled faintly. "You never do."

"I could."

"Why don't we see?" He shut and locked the door.

"Are you going to take off your boots?"

"No." Catching her by the arms, he turned her and backed her toward the door.

"You *are* in a hurry."

He couldn't say he'd not gone without sex for an entire day in years. "Watching you at dinner took its toll on my restraint. I promise to be more polite next time." As she came to a halt against the oak panels, he leaned into her, his arousal blatant between them. "Feel that?" he whispered, swiftly opening his trouser fly. "He's about to explode."

She normally would have taken affront at such bluntness, but then nothing had been normal from the moment she'd met Oz; she had but to *feel* his hard, rigid cock and every erogenous portion of her anatomy turned feverishly rapacious. "Me first," she insisted, as selfish as he, as impatient and greedy.

Hell no. But she was busy hitching up her skirts and untying her drawers, so calling on all his charitable impulses, he drew in a breath of constraint and muttered, "Spoiled brat."

But he was saying yes, she understood, and he finished unbuttoning his underwear just as her drawers slid to the floor. "I won't keep you waiting long," she whispered, grateful for his benevolence.

"Damn right you won't."

And the newlyweds who in the past had always eschewed adolescent frenzy, surrendered once again to their raging passions. Lifting her off her feet with ease, he wrapped her legs around his waist while his heart pounded in his chest, his erection stretched higher, and consummation took on a life of its own. Covetous and lustful, she clung to him and dizzy with uncontrollable need, began to seriously believe in sorcery. All else disappeared but her craving to feel him inside her.

Way, way inside her.

Hard and deep and forceful.

Coincidentally, Oz was warning himself not to run amuck and use her too roughly. With more than usual caution, he guided his erection to her sex, and nudging her sleek vulva with the head of his cock, paused, inhaled, and prayed for restraint. Having regained a modicum of sanity, he was able to smile when she wiggled her hips and impatiently hissed, "What are you waiting for?"

"The return of logic, or in this case, your orders," he said with a grin, and bending slightly, he pressed her against the door for better traction, straightened his legs in a powerful upward thrust, drove deeply into her hot, slick cunt, and felt her gratified sigh warm his cheek. He didn't move for a breath-held second after her silken flesh closed around him, occupied with the lunatic concept of having come home. But too disciplined to give in to delusion for long, he slid his hands under her bottom to raise her for the next sumptuous plunging descent.

"No, no, don't!" Isolde cried, a creature of impulse rather

than discipline, not inclined to relinquish the pleasure washing over her in heated waves.

Ignoring her exclamation as well as her fingers digging into his shoulders, Oz lifted her bottom until she shuddered on the crest of his erection, panting and pleading for more. When he released her, she immediately slid down his cock with such force, he caught his breath at the strumming rapture.

"If you could just stay right *there* for a week or so . . . ," she whispered.

He brushed her lips with a smiling kiss. "Greedy puss."

"Yes, yes . . . yes, yes, yes."

But he moved despite her protests because he couldn't last a week or even five minutes at this point, which was a startling admission for a man who had always been able to control his ejaculation.

It turned out to be a very close race to the finish, the feat accomplished only by sheer will and incredible control on Oz's part. With intense concentration he curtailed his orgasm, exerting himself to pleasure his wife, his powerful legs propelling him upward again and again until Isolde's orgasm crested and her screams brought him to a standstill deep inside her. Only waiting until her cries began to fade, he jerked her off his cock, dropped her on her feet, ripped his shirt tails from his trouser waistband, and just barely managed to save the carpet from semen stains.

Moments later, still breathing hard, his head braced against the door above her shoulder, he inhaled the perfume from her hair, her warmth, felt the softness of her body against his, and offered up a prayer of thanks to whatever gods had initially guided him to room thirteen at Blackwood's.

"That—was . . . fantastic—wasn't it?" Isolde breathed, so filled with bliss she felt lit from within.

"Yes," he whispered without moving.

"Perfection."

"Yes." Lifting his head, he inhaled deeply, took a step

back, shrugged out of his jacket, and began unbuttoning his shirt. "Yes to everything, darling."

Her nostrils flared at his facile reply. "Don't patronize me."

He paused in his unbuttoning. "Sorry. You'd prefer I disagree?"

"No, no." She waved her hand in a little absolving gesture. "I didn't mean to be fretful. I'm just feeling more in thrall to pleasure than I'd like—to you . . . him—sex with you." She made a wry face. "It's not your fault, though, it's mine."

"As you know," he replied with a lift of his brows, "you're not alone in your craving." Not that he didn't have every expectation those cravings would abate. They always did. "Let me wash up," he said, pulling his shirt over his head with a jerk, bundling it up and dropping it, "and we'll deal with our mutual randiness."

"I'm feeling odd in other ways, too." *Dependent. Necessitous.*

Women always wanted to talk about their feelings. He'd learned to politely agree. "It's probably due to the oddity of our marriage," he said over his shoulder. "You have to admit we didn't do a lot of planning." Because he was drunker than usual.

"In contrast to my previous detailed wedding planning," she wryly noted.

"There, you see? That's why you're unsettled. You're not accustomed to rash behavior."

On the other hand, rash behavior had it's advantages, she decided, contemplating her husband's powerful physique, his naked torso tautly muscled, the width of his shoulders impressive like his lovely, resilient cock. That he was still booted was perversely arousing as well. Or maybe everything about him provoked her lust, magnificent male animal that he was. If this was obsession, there was pleasure in embracing it.

Quickly washing up at a small sink in the corner, Oz stripped off his boots and remaining clothes. Quickly crossing the room, he stopped before Isolde still motionless against the door, the torpid warmth of fulfillment pulsing through her body. "If you can hear me," he teased, dipping his head to meet her lethargic gaze, "might I interest you in some less frantic conjugal sex?"

A slow smile lifted the corners of her mouth. "So you don't mind being my husband?"

"Hell no. I'm delighted to be here. If you'll allow me, I'll show you how delighted I am."

How many times and to how many women had he so casually offered his services? And how could it possibly matter in this business arrangement of theirs? But it must have because she heard herself say, "Would you still be delighted if I said I wanted to tie you up?"

One dark brow rose. "Is this a test?"

"Perhaps—I don't know. May I?" If not a test, it may have been a means of stabilizing the inordinate power he commanded over her senses and passions, over what had always been an unfettered will. Compensation, too, at some inchoate level, for the serried ranks of his lovers. "Think of it as a minor conjugal obligation."

He hesitated for a fraction of a second, not sure he liked the word *obligation* or the act of submission itself. "Why not?" he finally said.

Conscious of his small hesitation, Isolde felt nominally redeemed, more herself. Perhaps she wasn't slavishly obsessed, nor just another of the bevy of ladies in his life, but the woman of independence she'd always been. "Where should I tie you up?" she murmured, half musing.

"It depends what you want."

"Meaning?"

"Do you want sex standing, sitting, or lying down?"

"This is all familiar to you?"

"Come, darling, you know what I am. Everything's familiar to me." He knew better than to goad her, but he was being goaded, too—and not entirely sure he liked it. Raised in princely wealth, he was a golden child, the world at his beck and call. Submission wasn't and never would be his strong suit. But in the interests of civility along with the prospect of his future plans for the night, he chose to comply.

Moments later, he lay on the bed, watching his wife unwind the tasseled tiebacks from the bed drapery, and fleetingly debated his choice. The green silk cord would look much better against Isolde's pink skin, while the thought of her in bondage to him was profoundly erotic. He briefly took issue with his baffling need to dominate her; sex had always been about amorous sport, not supremacy. On the other hand, his darling wife was unusually independent. Perhaps therein lay the reason for his novel impulse.

"You have to listen to me."

He glanced up to find his wife kneeling beside him, her mouth sweetly pursed.

He smiled. "I was thinking about changing roles."

"You can't."

It took him a second to politely respond. He didn't mind her giving orders—within limits. "Maybe later," he pleasantly said, this man who'd been indulged from birth.

"We'll talk about it," Isolde returned, relishing her position, no longer mindlessly surrendering to passion.

"As you like." Amused at her air of command, he asked, "Are you enjoying yourself?"

"Very much, as a matter of fact. Hold out your hand." When he did, she deftly tied a slipknot around his wrist, tossed the braided cord around one bedpost, and smoothly secured it with another slipknot.

He nodded at his wrist. "You're handy with a rope."

"Anyone who deals with horses can tie a slipknot. Unlike you, though, I'm new at this game."

"Is that so."

"You don't believe me?" She looped a cord around his other wrist.

"I'm not sure it matters to him"—he glanced downward—"whether I do or not."

"Excellent. We're all of a mind then."

"So it seems. When it comes to sex, we're extremely well matched."

"Are you not with other women?" she asked, securing his wrist to another bedpost.

"No."

"Liar."

Why do women always want to know about their rivals? "Not like this," he said, competent at love play.

"How charming you are. Spread your legs a little so these ties reach the bedposts. I'm beginning to wonder about Grandmama's need for such a large bed," she added, circling his ankle with a tie.

"I'm sure the bed is simply a reproduction like everything else in this room."

She looked up from tethering his ankle to the bed. "You should be a diplomat."

I am very much at the moment. "If only I had the time," he smoothly replied.

"From all your debauch."

But she was smiling as she spoke, so he felt it permissible to say, "Yes."

"I'm not inclined to take issue when your expertise affords me such pleasure," she cheerfully noted.

"Very sensible."

"I think so. There." Sitting back on her heels, she surveyed him spread-eagle and secured to the bed. "Now what should I do?"

A number of answers leaped to mind. "Be selfish of course. I'm at your command." Although his suggestion was not without motive, having her impaled on his cock high on his list of priorities.

"Maybe I'll make you wait."

"Suit yourself." *This from a woman who couldn't wait.*

She wrinkled her nose. "Such composure. Do you ever get agitated?"

He smiled. "I seem to quite often with you."

Mollified by his boyish smile as well as his answer, she softly sighed. "I don't know why I'm so petulant with you. I dislike petulance. It's so . . . so . . ."

"Willful," he finished. "I like that about you."

"In contrast to all the fawning women in your life."

He stopped smiling. "I'm tied to your bed—a first for me, darling. Don't quibble about other women."

She grinned. "Is this really a first?"

"In countless ways, my darling wife," he drily said.

Her smile was one of untempered delight. "So you're being particularly agreeable."

"I'm trying."

An irrepressible constraint underlay his soft reply, prompting a little shiver to race up her spine. After quickly surveying his bonds, reassured, she whispered, "I promise to be gentle."

"I'm not sure that's a requirement."

"And you would know, of course."

Definitely petulant. His lashes shaded his eyes. "I only meant to give you license."

"I believe I have all the license I need with you trussed up hand and foot," she snidely countered.

Already going above and beyond in terms of congeniality, he tamped down his temper with effort. "This isn't armed combat, darling. Or at least it shouldn't be."

"You're right," she replied, telling herself to be sensible; jealousy was a useless emotion with Oz. "Sex is sex is sex better suits the occasion."

"The golden rule of dalliance," Oz said with brevity. "And my cock would prefer less talk and more action if you don't mind."

One glance at his enormous erection caused a predictable flare of desire; really, she was shamelessly captivated by his beautiful penis. As was every quivering sexual receptor in her body.

"Please," he said, whether candidly or designedly he wasn't sure.

Her gaze came up and met his. "In a minute," she answered, in her case designedly, and slipped off the bed.

He recognized his phrase, understood her possible motive, considered breaking free, taking his pleasure of her and putting an end to this bit of foolishness. But since he intended to prolong his visit for an undetermined length of time, a certain civility was required. "Take your time," he said with just enough impertinence to salve his pride.

She swung around, the dish of blancmange in her hand. "You're not in the least tractable, are you?"

He shook his head slightly. "*Resigned*, I believe, is the word."

"I must see that you're better reconciled to your condition."

"You talk too much," he grumbled. Conversation was not a salient feature of his sexual encounters.

"Let me remedy that," she blandly offered, climbing back onto the bed. "As you said to me that first night, *Observe*." Setting down the dessert dish, she pulled his rigid erection away from his stomach until it was perpendicular to his body, and holding it with one hand, dipped the fingers of her other hand into the blancmange.

Controlling his breathing, his senses, the impulse to break his bonds, Oz watched from under his lashes as his wife slowly smeared the length and breadth of his upthrust cock with pudding.

The coolness should have shrunk his penis, but under his wife's ministrations, with her lush breasts close enough to touch under normal circumstances, and anticipation of the finale to her bedaubing inflaming his lust, the possibility of contraction wasn't an issue.

"If you keep getting bigger, I'm going to run out of pudding."

Oz gazed reflectively at his wife. "You could do something about that."

"Whatever do you mean?" she cooed.

"You know what I mean. Even under the best of circumstances *I* couldn't taste that pudding."

She resented his ability to keep his voice so normal. "I might just be amusing myself."

"And I might be the king of Siam."

"Rather than the prime stud of London."

"Who is tethered to your bed for your pleasure," Oz softly reminded her.

Licking her fingers, she set aside the dish, reason restored with his comment. But beneath the reason a small unjustifiable jealousy remained. "And yours as well," she said with a touch of acerbity.

At her tone he unconsciously braced himself only to meet her dazzling smile.

"Worried?"

"A little."

"Good." Her grip tightened at the base of his erection, and she bent her head.

He flexed arms heavy with muscle, testing the strength of the silk cords.

Glancing up, her mouth inches from the slick head of his cock, she murmured, "You're not going anywhere."

"That depends on what you're planning to do."

"On the contrary, it depends on the solid wood of this bed and that heavy braided silk cord. You're at my mercy. Ah . . . you find that arousing—look at him swell. I think he wants me to kiss him."

He shut his eyes as her mouth closed over the swollen crest of his penis, the enigma of wanting and not wanting mystifyingly unclear when the warmth of her mouth, her tongue, the light friction of her teeth on the thin-skinned, highly impressionable nerves of his cock was obliterating rational thought.

"There now," she murmured, the hum of her words on the

head of his erection a provocative buzzing jolt to his senses.
"He likes that."

At the moment, he was willing to acknowledge a fondness
several degrees more enthusiastic than *liking*, but in the grip
of gut-wrenching sensation he was incapable of speech. Particularly with his wife beginning to suck on him with increasing pressure.

Less experienced, Isolde had no way of knowing that the
fierce vibrations throbbing through her vagina had more to
do with the object of her attentions than the actual act of
bondage. What she did know, however, was that she had no
intention of wasting the gloriously large penis in her mouth
when she could apply it to better purpose.

Swiftly sweeping her tongue up the rigid length, then
down, once, twice, three times, she licked off all the sweet
blancmange before moving to position herself astride Oz's
thighs. "This is mine by right of marriage," she said, brushing her fingertips up the distended length of his erection. "To
do with what I will," she playfully added.

The residue of pudding glistening on her lips was starkly
erotic, the lingering sensation of her mouth on his cock fuel-
ing his impatience. "I'd help you if I could," he murmured,
his penis twitching in expectation.

"I like that you can't." Rising to her knees, she reached
for his massive cock.

Maybe he did, too, if his fierce lust was any indication.
But thought gave way to feeling as she slowly slid down his
turgid length with exquisite deliberateness. And when she
finally came to rest fully impaled on his cock and softly
sighed, rapture took on an incorruptible purity for them both.

It shouldn't matter who was riding his cock, he thought.
Yet it did. He gave her high marks for allure.

How was it that Oz's erection felt more wildly arousing
than anyone else's, she mused?

Why was every susceptible nerve ravished yet insatiable,
gloating yet gluttonous, they both wondered in that brief

moment before Isolde rose to her knees, slid back down once again, and made the world disappear.

When that prolonged moment of excess passed, she moved, but without haste—unlike her usual impatience; perhaps she was taking a lesson from Oz. Or maybe the tactile sensation of slick skin-to-skin friction was so acute and prodigal, she tempered her normal impetuousness to better experience the ostentatious pleasure. Whatever the reason, each leisurely ascent left her breathless for more, each slow, velvety descent was a melting, yielding avaricious search for the sublime.

So facilely supplied by her well-endowed husband.

Lost in his own carnal fervor, Oz struggled for control at the very depth of her downward glide when his cock was buried in her hot cunt and paradise took on an earthly form. He resisted the urge to break free and caress her lush breasts gently bobbing and quivering as she rode him, broke into a sweat at the thought of slipping his fingers between her legs and fondling her clit, wondered how much longer he could play the docile husband. Until he reached that ungovernable moment, however, he deferred to Isolde, adjusting his rhythm to hers, allowing her to direct the activity, restively performing his *conjugal obligations*.

He even graciously satisfied her first two orgasms, his legendary endurance put to good purpose. But finally, having tolerated considerable orgasmic pressure for sometime, he reached a critical point of no return. "Get off!" he gasped, breathless, every muscle taut with constraint.

"Soon," she said as if his exclamation was inconsequential.

"Now," he said through gritted teeth, curtailing his ejaculation with every cognitive technique he'd acquired in his youth and had perfected over time.

"Hush." Coming to rest on his thighs, she shut her eyes and with a soft moan, swiveled her hips in feverish quest for orgasmic bliss. Twisting, rocking, grinding against his rigid cock, heedless to all but the mounting rapture, she impatiently sought surcease.

Curbing his orgasm with stubborn resolve, tense with the effort, Oz managed to repress his ejaculation if not his temper until Isolde climaxed. At which time, well beyond the cultivated graces, he rapped out in quiet fury, "Untie me or I'll break this bloody bed."

Isolde's eyes flew open and she stared at him as if coming awake from a dream. "You're angry."

"Damn right. I almost climaxed in you."

It took a moment for his brusque words to register. "You didn't, though," she said, mildly—imperturbable, postorgasmic.

"No thanks to you," he snapped, incensed by her casual reply. "Untie me."

Suddenly aware of his implacable rage, her contentment dissipated beneath the savage fury of his anger. But equally quick-tempered, as disinclined as he to take orders, she snapped in return. "What if I don't?"

"This game's over." His voice was grim, a heavy pulse beating in his neck. "Do as you're told."

"I don't think I like your tone."

Any of his late enemies would have recognized the danger in his gaze. "I don't care. Untie me or this bed goes."

"You're not that strong."

He drew in a breath through his nostrils, his gaze hard and intent. "What the *hell* do you think you're doing?"

"What the hell are *you* doing?"

Reining in his temper, understanding when it came to a fight she was grossly outmatched, he softly sighed. "Could we please stop? Just untie me."

"No."

"I'm asking nicely," he said not entirely nicely after her crisp refusal.

"And I'm telling you no nicely," she replied, looking smug.

Flexing biceps that would have been the envy of a galley slave, Oz came up off the bed in a brute, explosive lunge that snapped the bedposts like matchsticks. Grabbing the silk cords, he checked the rocketing trajectory of the shattered posts, shoved Isolde onto her back, slipped his wrists free, and extricated his ankles a second later. A second after that, his wife was pinioned beneath him and his fingers were lightly circling her neck.

"Just for the record," he said, glowering, "I have no intention in hell of fathering a child on you."

"Nor would I wish you to," she hissed.

His fingers tightened. "Then you should have gotten off me when I bloody asked you to."

"It wasn't a good time," she insolently retorted.

His eyes went shut, and when his lashes lifted he said in a dangerous voice, "That was *deliberate*?"

"It was not! I couldn't move if you must know. Is that better?"

"Fuck no."

"Well, I'm sorry. Apparently, we can't all be as responsible as you."

"This isn't going to work out," he muttered, unclasping his hands from her throat and beginning to rise. "I'm not going to ruin my life because you're irresponsible."

"Wait," she cried, shocked and confused, her feelings in tumult.

But he didn't; he swung his legs over the side of the bed.

"I'll never do that again. I promise," she impulsively blurted out, overwrought, her body still tingling. "Don't go! Oh hell," she muttered, disconcerted to feel tears welling in her eyes, embarrassed and wretched and not altogether sure she wasn't coming apart at the seams for indefensible reasons.

Turning back he saw her pale and distraught, her eyes wet with tears, and hesitated. He was uncomfortable with women's tears; he normally gave them wide berth. But then Isolde sniffled in an attempt to stifle her little hiccupping sobs and she looked so innocent, her pale hair tousled and disheveled, her cheeks flushed, that he recklessly disregarded the dangers in her overwrought passions. Turning, he lifted her into his arms, settled her on his lap, and as his cock instantly came to attention, he found himself overwhelmed by lust.

Even then, he may have suppressed his impetuous libido if Isolde hadn't slipped her arms around his neck and lifting her tremulous, wet gaze to him, artlessly whispered, "I'll be better. I'll be good. Please don't go."

It was no contest.

He softly exhaled, silently denounced himself for a fool, and then heedless of precedence and practicality, quietly said, "Don't cry. We'll work something out. Although," he added, gently wiping away her tears with his knuckles, "I can't do this alone." He smiled faintly. "You have to help."

"I know," she said, sniffling. "I will. Word of honor."

He accepted her promise when he wouldn't have given it credence even as a callow youth. And years past such folly, he knew better than to trust her discretion. But then he was operating outside the pale, in some never-never land of sexual delight, and in that fantasy world he understood that the responsibility for not impregnating his wife was primarily his. Obviously she wasn't trustworthy—solemn promises notwithstanding. "I'll be more cautious, too," he kindly remarked.

"Thank you," she simply said, her smile radiant. "Thank you for understanding, for giving me such unbounded pleasure. I don't even care that I'm like every other woman you know who's enamored of you. I don't, and I am—so there," she said with a pretty moue.

"Believe me, darling, you're unlike every woman I know," he honestly said, their sexual compatibility rare, the delight she carried within her rarer still. "And I'm sorry about the bed. I'll have it fixed or replaced tomorrow."

"No, no, it was my fault entirely. You may beat me if you like."

But her voice was sultry and low, her blue gaze provocative. "Don't tempt me, you little vixen," he said with a grin. "Or I might."

"Would it hurt terribly?" she whispered, shifting her bottom slightly against his rock-hard cock.

"If you didn't obey me, it would." His voice was velvet soft as he eased her back onto the bed and settled between her warm thighs.

"I'll obey you, darling, in every possible way. You have but to ask and . . ."

Her words trailed away as Oz slid gently inside her, and when he came to rest against the mouth of her womb and said, "You have to wait for me this time," she shivered, powerless against the vaulting desire flaring through her senses.

"Yes, sir," she replied, feverish and breathy.

A practiced libertine, Oz understood the orgasmic sequence might require altering. Fortunately, her tears had minimally dampened his lust and he was always capable of a certain restraint in any event. Not that it was ever necessary to wait long for his bride to reach climax—one of her endearing qualities.

As it transpired, they did indeed take turns that night. Both conscious of their recent row, they were careful to mind their manners in terms of who climaxed when. But Oz was infinitely more indulgent. Having long enjoyed an intemperate life with sexual revel commonplace, he was less frantic than his bride, who'd only recently been introduced to prodigal sensation.

That wasn't to say he didn't find his lovely wife exceptionally desirable. He did.

As for Isolde, she was wholly smitten.

But then every woman Oz dallied with was equally enamored, she understood. There was no point in being foolish.

CHAPTER 15

FAMILIAR WITH OZ'S early rising habits, Isolde wasn't surprised to find her husband bathed and dressed when she opened her eyes. "How do you do it?" she murmured.

"I get hungry," he said with a grin.

"Then go by all means. I think I'll loll in the tub this morning."

"Would you like to ride after breakfast?"

"I'd love to. I'll show you Oak Knoll."

"Sam will have messages for me from Davey. I'll speak with him over breakfast and meet you later. I might be out in the stables. Sukha likes reassurance when she's in a new home. Send someone for me when you're ready to ride."

Oz's use of the word *home* was gratifying, even though she knew it was casually uttered, and she was careful to keep her voice as neutral as his. "The weather looks as though it's cooperating," she said, glancing out the window. "The rain has stopped."

"A rarity this time of year. Perhaps the gods are looking on us with favor."

"I ordered it for you."

"In that case, order me a few hours in bed with you this afternoon as well," Oz said with a grin.

"It would be my distinct pleasure. Now go, before I have you undress again."

Sam was waiting, so Oz said, "I'm gone." With a wave, he walked from the room.

But one look at Sam's face when he met him in the doorway of the breakfast room and Oz knew he had more for him than Davey's messages. "What's on your mind?"

Sam frowned. "Grover came to me early this morning. Compton's in the village. One of the tenants saw him at the inn."

Oz lifted his brows. "I'm surprised at his speed. I assume he didn't come alone."

"No. Grover says a few bully boys and—"

"His solicitor."

Sam nodded.

Oz sighed. "How many men did you bring?"

"A few. Enough."

"Come then," Oz said, Sam's competence never in question. "We'll talk to Grover. He knows the neighborhood better than we."

Grover rose from behind his desk the moment Oz walked into his office. "Thank you, sir. I've been waiting for you to come downstairs."

"Sit." Oz waved him into his chair, and he and Sam took chairs on the other side of the desk. "Tell us what you know. Start at the beginning."

"The grooms were riding through the village to the downs for the horses' morning gallop and saw Frederick big as life walking from the inn."

"With others, Sam said," Oz prompted.

"Three thugs and a man in a suit."

"Where were they going?"

"To the livery stable it appears. Naturally, the grooms turned back to warn me."

"Has he entered the property?"

"Not as far as we can tell."

"You have men who can handle a weapon, I presume," Oz said.

"Every man jack hunts, sir. Miss Izzy allows shooting and snaring on her land—for the cook pot. It keeps the rabbits in check."

"I'm going to have Sam organize your men and send them out with mine to patrol the property. I would prefer Compton be on his way back to London before the end of the day." He glanced at Sam. "Is that possible?"

Sam nodded. "We'll find him."

"Compton's been listening to his mother's praise too long. He actually thinks he deserves more than he does." Oz softly exhaled. "My little chat with him in London apparently wasn't sufficient, so we'll move on to other options. Here's what I'm thinking." Briskly sketching out his plan, Oz added at the last, "There's no point in waiting to see what Compton's planning. Whatever it is will prove unpleasant for Isolde. At base, he seems unwilling to accept our marriage." Oz didn't mention Compton's possible eavesdropping at the reception. It was irrelevant. He wanted Compton well away from Isolde, and to that purpose he was willfully disposed. "If the knave behaves, he can come back to England later." Once Isolde was remarried. "Now, for the solicitor. Is he going to be a problem?"

Sam shook his head. "I expect he can be bought off for very little. Or so our sources tell me. The man lives on the fringes of the legal world."

"Then do it," Oz crisply said. "See that the man understands he's not to so much as whisper a word about Compton. Take the two men back to London separately so they won't plan something nefarious. Pay off the hired ruffians as well. I expect they don't care who pays their fee. Then see that Compton ships out tonight. Hatch is ready to sail. There's no reason for you to go into London, Sam. Send Jimmy and his crew. As for Isolde, I'll find a way to tell her"—his brows lifted—"some reasonable story when Compton's disappearance becomes known."

"His flight won't surprise anyone," Grover pointed out, flat and direct. "Not with the state of his finances."

"It might surprise his mother. Although a note from her son should mitigate any alarm. Have Davey arrange it, Sam." Oz suddenly smiled. "The way I see it, we've done a service to the community . . . and more specifically to Isolde—which is the point. Thank you, Grover," Oz said, "for your attentive staff. Give your men a bonus; Sam has funds." Oz came to his feet. "Are we all agreed?"

"I know I speak for the entire household when I offer you our thanks, sir," Grover said with a soldierly straightness to his shoulders and a lift of his chin. "The blackguard should have been struck down long ago."

"Nevertheless, he'll have money enough to live abroad, Grover. I don't want him on my conscience for Isolde's sake. Having said that, you're more than welcome for my help in seeing him off on a lengthy journey beyond England's shores. If everyone could remain silent, though, until I find the appropriate time to tell Miss Izzy, I'd appreciate it."

Grover was smiling broadly at Miss Izzy's new husband, who'd calmly contrived to see to his wife's comfort. "Rest assured, sir, no one will say a word."

"Excellent. Now, if you want to gather your men and meet Sam at the stables, our plans will be translated into action."

A few moments later, Oz and Sam watched Grover hurrying down the hall.

"I want Compton alive," Oz quietly said. "Because Isolde would wish it. Is that clear?"

"Yes, sir. Although it goes against my better judgment."

"Alive, Sam," Oz gruffly said. "No excuses. Swear on whatever god you honor."

Sam met his gaze and nodded. "I swear."

Oz's smile was instant. "As for yourself," he said with a

friendly slap on Sam's shoulder, "what would you like for seeing this mess through for me? A house? One of my race-horses? A new commission in the Queen's army? I am as you can see, extremely grateful that Compton will be going on holiday. Any possible stress on my wife will disappear and—"

"She won't be distracted—"

"From my hot-blooded pursuits," Oz softly finished.

Sam met Oz's sardonic gaze; this was not a man in love. "A house for Betsy, then. Nothing grand."

"Buy whatever you wish. Let Simms know." Oz reached out and gripped Sam's hand. "I'm indebted to you as usual. Might we be hearing wedding bells for you soon as well?"

Sam shrugged. "Who knows."

"At the moment I highly recommend it."

"Talk to me in a month," Sam said, humorless and knowing. "As I recall you quickly grow weary of sameness."

"True. Perhaps it's the fresh country air," Oz replied, his voice mild.

"Until the weather turns," Sam remarked, his gaze mildly ironic. "You've spent days with various lady loves, testing the limits of your cock more times than I can remember, and never had any problem leaving."

Oz grinned. "Go. You're ruining my mood."

CHAPTER 16

EXPLAINING COMPTON'S DISAPPEARANCE turned out to be a simple matter.

Simultaneously with news of Frederick's absence from London, a rumor surfaced that he'd been seen boarding a ship bound for Australia with Beresford and Huxley. Since both men had talked of little else in the clubs the last many weeks, Compton's addition to the party was entirely plausible. Shortly after, Lady Compton received a note from her son in which he explained that the increasing pressure from his creditors had prompted his spur-of-the-moment flight. Lady Compton, of course, put forward that her son was off on an Australian adventure—the dear boy so loved to travel.

Davey had arranged the rumor and note.

Both had adequately served their purpose even while there were some who chose not to believe Lady Compton's story. But for those of a more cynical bent, gamblers escaping abroad to elude their creditors was so common as to raise little comment.

Three days later, Isolde leaned back in her chair at the

breakfast table, wide-eyed and smiling. "Is he really gone from England? Are you sure?"

Oz handed her the message from Davey. "Read for yourself. Davey checked out the rumor and found it authentic. Apparently your troublesome cousin accompanied two friends to Australia." Oz lifted his shoulder in a faint shrug. "I expect his creditors may have had something to do with his sudden decision."

"He's truly gone?" A note of cheer rang in her voice.

"Without a doubt," Oz said, reaching for his coffee cup. Indeed, Sam's men had carried him aboard the *Sea Mist*. "His gambling losses were considerable if you recall."

"But you paid them," she murmured, quickly scanning the brief note.

"Knowing him, he ran up more losses." A polite lie.

She looked up. "So we may thank Frederick's incompetence at the gaming tables for this peaceful interlude."

He swallowed and set down his cup. "It appears so."

Her eyes lit with delight, Isolde grinned. "Tell me, how long does it takes to sail to Australia and back?"

"A *long* time, darling," he said, his answering smile tender. "There's always numerous ports of call along the way." More than ever this time, nor was the voyage routed through the Suez Canal. "I could have Davey find out the particulars from the shipping line if you like."

"No, no, don't bother. However long he's gone will be divine."

"Speaking of divine . . ."

"Oz! We just came downstairs!"

Laughter stirred in his eyes and something splendidly provocative as well. "Can I help it if your dressing gown is revealing an enticing amount of cleavage? Although, I'm more than willing to wait until you've finished eating."

"How very kind," she sardonically murmured.

His smile was lazy and assured. "I'll be even kinder upstairs. Or would you like to test the softness of the window seat over there?"

"You're impossible." But she was smiling, too.

"And you're a darling to put up with me." Leaning back in his chair, he pushed his coffee cup aside and reached for his perennial brandy bottle. "Take your time."

THE MONTH THAT followed was as close to paradise as an earthly existence allowed. Oz and Isolde spent their days in a free and easy companionship unique to two people who'd lived alone for so long. When Isolde asked Oz once whether he was bored with their lack of entertainments in the country, he'd said, "You're my entertainment." His long lashes had lifted then and their dark seductive gaze surveyed her serenely. "You may exhaust me at times, sweet Izzy, but no one could accuse me of being bored."

They rode every morning regardless of the weather because it was Isolde's custom and Oz willingly indulged her. The rare Urdu book had been sent for, and Oz continued his translation while Isolde often curled up on the sofa and read as he worked. He sat in on her daily meetings with Grover, occasionally offering a suggestion on farming that no longer surprised her; his interests were cosmopolitan, his expertise varied. In addition to his banking and shipping interests, she discovered that he administered several plantations in India via telegraph and surrogates.

Davey sent messengers from the city, coming himself at times with the most pressing of Oz's business affairs. One time when Davey had delicately inquired whether Oz knew when he'd be returning to the city, Oz had glanced at Isolde, smiled, and said, "Not just yet."

Achille took great pleasure in offering the newlyweds superb delicacies that Isolde's chef was beginning to master— no grievous competition there. And of course, inspired and beguiled by gluttony of another kind, the young couple made love with unfettered license. Here and there and everywhere.

The servants learned to knock loudly before entering a room when formerly, Isolde's casually run household had required no such prudence.

The first time the pair had been surprised in the library, Isolde had turned ten shades of red and Oz's impatient gaze had driven the servant out without a word. Later that day, Oz had spoken to Lewis; no further unannounced entrances ensued.

In time, Oz even consented to call on the neighbors with Isolde. His agreement to so public a display of their connection pleased her and didn't displease him so far as he'd admit. As to the rest——why he did it at all——he chose to ignore. Like so much during this idyll in the country, he was operating on instinct alone.

The first time he accompanied Isolde to a hunt breakfast, he'd been admiring a Stubbs painting of a stallion from racing history when he was distracted by a thin, plain woman who came up beside him. She was staring at him with such narrow-eyed attention he was tempted to say, *I'm not for sale.*

"We haven't met. I'm Lady Fowler," she crisply declared as he turned to her.

Ah, the heiress; poor Will, he thought, with a connoisseur's eye for beauty. "A pleasure, ma'am," he answered with an exquisite bow. "I'm Oz Lennox."

"I know who you are."

He found himself being scrutinized again—with a cool arrogance this time as though he were being measured against some lofty standard and found lacking.

"You're in shipping, I hear. How interesting." It was meant to belittle, her words, the sneer in her voice marking him as inferior. To be involved in trade was considered a failing by some in the peerage.

"I understand your father made his fortune in coal. An equally interesting business," Oz blandly replied.

"The coal is on our lands."

"I have ruby mines on my estates," he pleasantly remarked, ignoring her direct stare. "A hazardous occupation, mining. How do you manage your workers' safety? We've instituted various safeguards and haven't had an accident in years."

"I have no idea," she said with a sniff. "Miners' safety doesn't concern me."

"A shame," he answered, polite and unperturbed. "Production and profits are directly related to working conditions."

"I'm sure my father has menials to see to such things," she said in haughty rejoinder.

It always amazed him when certain peers found it necessary to impress him with their superiority because of his Indian background. As if the Lennox bloodlines weren't centuries old. Or it amazed him as much as his careless indifference allowed. "Did you have some question you wished to ask me?" he softly inquired. "Instead of this very ambiguous conversation."

"Of course not," she cooly countered.

He surveyed her with a misleadingly innocent gaze. "Allow me to clarify a few points, ma'am—in the event you have some future questions. People often wish to know if I'm as wealthy as rumor has it." He smiled. "I'm even wealthier. People are curious as well about the shade of my skin; my grandmother was a native of Hyderabad, India. If you were wondering about your husband, he's come to call. Apparently he was upset with Isolde's marriage. Is there more?"

"They said you were shameless!" she said with a peevish snort.

"More than you'll ever know. But then I like my women with a bit of meat on their bones." As her color rose and she worked herself into a withering reply, he gently added, "If you'd like a little advice, I'd put a curb on that husband of yours. From what I've seen, he's likely to wander."

"How dare you!" she hissed, her sharp nose twitching with indignation. "What right has someone like *you*—"

"Ah, there you are, darling," Oz said fondly as Isolde came up to save her husband from Anne Verney's obvious wrath. "Lady Fowler and I were comparing our mines."

"We were doing no such thing!" Anne furiously exclaimed.

"Mines?" Isolde cast a questioning glance at her husband.

"I have ruby mines. Didn't I mention that?" he said, lazy and cool.

"No, you didn't. How very nice. If you'd excuse us, Anne, Pamela hasn't met Oz yet. Come, dear, you'll like *her*." She needn't have been rude, but she couldn't resist. Anne always glared at her as though she were the Antichrist; there was no question either that she was being uncivil to Oz. Her scowl had been visible from across the room.

"Will's wife's an arrogant cow," Oz lazily said as they walked away. "I can see why he's hell-bent on renewing your friendship. She's not only pompous, she's ugly, poor thing. Christ, you'd have to shut your eyes to fuck her."

"Hush, Oz," Isolde reprimanded, suppressing a smile. "She can't help it. The entire family is pompous as the pope."

"With no good reason from all appearances," he said, smiling a little.

"They're very wealthy."

"Many people are, darling. But I see I'm going to have to keep an eye on you. Will must be desperate to bed you again."

"You needn't keep an eye on me. I'm quite content with your—"

"Cock?" he murmured with a sparkle in his eyes.

"Yes, now hush, don't embarrass me; here's my very best friend." Taking Oz's hand, she smiled at a pretty, slender young woman dressed in russet velvet to match her hair. "Pamela, I'd like you to meet Oz."

Pamela was immediately charmed, but then Oz put himself out to be charming, a talent honed to a fine pitch long ago. And once all the pleasantries were exchanged, conversation turned to mutually satisfying subjects having to do with horses and racing—a topic much on the mind of everyone in the environs of Newmarket.

"Isolde tells me you have some splendid bloodstock from the Hindu Kush."

"You're welcome to ride them anytime," Oz offered with unimpeachable courtesy. "They're sweet and well mannered."

"And they run like the wind," Isolde interjected with a smile for her husband. "My morning rides have quite improved since Oz brought them up."

"With the spring meets about to begin, we'll have to see how they perform." Pamela followed the race meets with the avid interest of someone who owned a prime stable. "I warn you, my husband, Elliot, prides himself on his racing wins."

Oz smiled. "We'll have to exchange a friendly wager."

"What wager?" The Earl of Petworth joined his wife.

"Elliot, have you met Isolde's husband? Oz, Elliot. We were talking about the new race season. Oz has some bloodstock from India."

Several others joined the conversation at talk of racing, and before the hounds were brought up and breakfast over, Oz had met a great many of Isolde's neighbors.

But after his encounter with Lady Fowler, Oz monitored Isolde that day with more than ordinary vigilance. Will Fowler's interest in Isolde had nothing to do with friendship— his angry response to news of her marriage a case in point. And after having seen Fowler's wife, it was clear that the man had coldly and calculatingly married for money. Nor had he the decency to treat his wife civilly; Will hadn't come near her at breakfast.

Nor had she mounted up with the others. She'd stayed behind.

Hours later, after an exhilarating hunt over miles of green, rolling countryside, Oz and Isolde were riding home slowly, the sun low on the horizon.

"You needn't have played duenna all day," Isolde lightly teased. "As you very well know, you've spoiled me for other men. I have no interest in Will."

There was a small silence. "That may be, for which I thank you," he said with a faint smile. "But I don't trust Will. I may have to call out the dog if he doesn't stop sniffing around you."

"Don't you dare," she quickly said.

"Warn *him* off, not me. I'm just protecting my own." There was a faint hint of anger beneath the flat tone.

"You're mistaken," she said in a deprecating voice. "Really, Oz, I don't need your protection."

"Believe me," he cooly said, "with Will, you do."

While she might disagree, Oz's jealousy pleased her—regardless its motivation or degree. "I'm sure you're wrong, but rather than risk having you call out Will, I'll take care to avoid him."

He turned an impersonal gaze on her. "And I'll see that you do."

"I don't respond well to orders," she softly said.

"Sometimes you do."

"I'm serious, Oz."

The flexible charm was automatic as was the smile that warmed his eyes. "I humbly beg your pardon, darling," he gently said. "I had no intention of offending you."

He rode with animal grace, she thought; the same grace he brought to the bedroom; the same grace she could no more relinquish than she could contemplate life without him, she thought with an unpleasant lurch of her heart. "I don't want to fight," she murmured, shaken by her feelings.

"Nor I," he said with forced calm, her feelings clear to see.

* * *

In the course of the blissful days that followed, Oz told himself he could take his country holiday in stride; care, but not too much; love his new wife with passion but not with his heart; above all keep the ravishing pleasures they shared in perspective.

Isolde warned herself she was getting in too deep, allowing herself to be swept away by rapture, becoming too attached to a man who played merely a stopgap role in her life. But then Oz was celebrated for his many charms; meeting his legion of lovers in London served to confirm the fact. Why wouldn't she be equally captivated? More to the point, why shouldn't she enjoy her ephemeral pleasures while she may? *No reason at all*, she recklessly decided.

Nothing could have stopped them in any case, their need for each other beyond reason. They spent their nights playing at love while their days were given up to the country social calendar, their intimacy and closeness a sumptuous, personal la dolce vita, the very breath of life.

Oz escorted Isolde to the neighbors without complaint when in the past he would have found such company tame. He briefly questioned his pleasure in such peaceful pursuits but as quickly decided it was irrelevant. Since when did he question degrees of gratification?

CHAPTER 17

A FEW DAYS LATER, Isolde and Oz were at Pamela's dinner party. Since Will and Anne were also guests, Isolde had taken care to stay by Oz's side—not a hardship by any means. She preferred keeping her distance from the Fowlers.

But after dinner Pamela had taken her away to see her new Worth gown, which turned out to be as spectacular as claimed—embroidered and jeweled green velvet; the masterful Worth had surpassed himself. A maid had come in as they'd been viewing the gown, calling Pamela away to the nursery over some minor crisis, and Isolde made her way back to the drawing room alone.

Catching sight of Anne Verney waiting in the corridor outside the drawing room, she almost turned around. The last person she wished to see was Will's fretful, sullen wife who constantly glowered at her. On the other hand, she wasn't so craven that she'd let herself be intimidated over something so silly.

"Has the dancing begun?" she asked as she approached the woman who managed to look frumpish even in an expensive creation of sparkling silver tulle. The violins could be heard through the closed doors.

"I have no idea," Anne icily replied. "I have something to say to you."

God help me. "If it's about the flowers for the church, my gardeners tell me the hothouse roses are in bloom. You're more than welcome to them."

"You insolent hussy. Why would I care about the flowers for the church? I want you to stay away from my husband," she spat, caustic and malevolent. "I saw you staring at him all through dinner."

"I did no such thing!" Isolde retorted, her shock plain. "You're grossly mistaken."

"Don't play games with me, you slut." A mottled flush colored her thin face. "I saw you trying to catch his eye."

"I have absolutely no interest in your husband," Isolde calmly said, not wishing to engage with this angry woman. "I'm married and more than content. You needn't be concerned."

"You duplicitous little bitch. Don't try and placate me with your lies. You always wanted Will. But he's mine. I bought him!" Blunt as a hammer.

"Everyone knows you bought him," Isolde snapped back and instantly contrite, quickly added, "Forgive me, I shouldn't have said that. He's yours, Anne, truly he is—in every way." She felt foolish for ever lamenting Will's loss, embarrassed as well that she'd been so blind to his lies.

"I don't need *you* to tell me he's mine. He was never yours," she said with deliberate malice. "*Never.* He told me so—that you were always in hot pursuit, trying to entice him into your bed, using your body to lure him, you witch!"

Isolde could have disputed who had pursued whom, but more than ever, she wanted this confrontation to end. The malicious glitter in Anne's eyes was alarming enough to motivate a quick retreat. "There's no need to argue over Will, Anne. He's indisputably yours. I wish you both much happiness."

"Spare me your spurious good wishes," she snapped, her color high, the pulse in her neck beating violently. *"Just stay away from my husband!"*

"I most certainly will," Isolde soothingly replied, edging away from the enraged woman. No longer concerned she might appear fainthearted, she fled, jerking open the drawing room door and slipping inside like a thief in the night.

"I needn't ask how she was," Oz murmured, pushing away from the wall beside the door as Isolde entered, white-faced. "I saw Anne go out, but I thought Pamela was with you."

"I wish she had been." Isolde shivered faintly. "The woman's crazed."

"Poor darling," he gently said, taking her hand and drawing her away from the door. "But consider, dear, you're outrageous competition for a plain sparrow like Anne."

"I've never given her any indication that I covet her husband. In fact, I told her in no uncertain terms I had no interest in Will."

"And she didn't believe you."

Isolde grimaced. "She said I was looking at her husband during dinner—I wasn't."

"He was looking at you."

"He was? Oh God."

"He was looking at you with prurience, lust, and adultery on his mind," Oz delicately said.

Isolde groaned. "Don't start, Oz. I'm sorry I ever met the man."

A smile transformed the trifling unease in his eyes. "In that case, would you care to dance?"

And so the drama continued in the small exclusive world of dinner parties and country entertainments.

Will was restive under his wife's constant guard.

Oz was mildly watchful and surprised that he was.

Isolde, with nothing to hide, openly enjoyed her husband's company and wasn't amazed to discover that Oz also danced better than anyone she'd ever met. But then he did everything better than anyone she'd ever met.

Which meant she must remember her life was her own and not lose her grip on it. Oz exerting the full power of his charm made one forget.

CHAPTER 18

A LOVELY, IDYLLIC week later, one in which the newly-weds had refused to leave Oak Knoll, they finally foreswore their hermitage because a singer Isolde particularly liked was performing at Constance Banning's afternoon musicale.

"Do you mind?" she'd asked the previous day as she and Oz lay hot and sweaty in the shambles of the bed.

He'd turned his head as he lay panting beside her, a faint smile lifting the corners of his mouth. "After—that last orgasm—how can . . . I refuse you . . . anything."

"How lovely, how sweet—"

"How likely . . . I am to fuck you again . . . as soon as I catch . . . my breath," he'd rasped. "Yes to the musicale—now come here . . . I have something to show you."

WHY IS HE here? Isolde thought as she and Oz entered the Bannings' sunny music room. Will disliked sopranos, music in general, and Constance Banning.

Well, well, if it isn't the ex-lover in hot pursuit. Oz knew very well why Will Fowler was here.

But after greeting their hostess, Isolde took a seat well
away from Will and joined the gathering of well-dressed
gentry who were fond of music. The audience was primarily
female—no surprise. Oz had come out of consideration for
his wife, as had a handful of other husbands. Will was alone
and here out of consideration for himself.

A boy prodigy Constance had brought up from London
performed first, his virtuoso skills on the violin breathtaking
for someone so young. Isolde was entranced, leaning forward
slightly as though drawn to the beautiful sound.

His head resting against the back of his chair, Oz watched
her, aware of the violent passion she evoked in him, equally
aware that his normal impersonal dealings with women had
altered. As the boy's dazzling technique brought Tchaikovsky's
fantasia to life with nimble-fingered energy and brio, the
audience listened in breath-held silence, and Oz wondered,
mildly disturbed, if he was less indifferent than he wished.

But the music came to a precipitous end, the crowd
erupted in applause, and Oz's musing gave way as everyone
came to their feet in homage to the boy.

In the interval between performances, Constance Banning's footmen carried around trays of champagne and
sweets, the audience fell to gossiping, and Oz was drawn off
by the few husbands in attendance where talk turned naturally to horses. Newmarket was the Nirvana of bloodstock
fanatics, and Oz's racers had won all the early meets in the
neighborhood. The men were anxious to hear how best to
obtain entree to the mountain tribes that bred Oz's racers.

Oz noticed Isolde leave the room with Constance, and
shortly after their hostess returned alone. Scanning the room,
he saw that Will was absent as well, and experiencing an
unbridled rush of anger, he excused himself from the group
of men with a smile and a bland excuse and went in search of
his wife.

Unfortunately he found her.

At the soft footfall on the threshold of a nearby drawing

room, Isolde snatched her hands from Will's and turned to meet the hard, ruthless gaze of her husband.

He was standing in the open doorway, challenge in his stance, in the merciless set of his mouth, menace in his gaze. "Am I intruding?" His voice was meticulously soft.

"No, not at all." She was doing nothing wrong; there was no need to blush. "Will just called me in to tell me he's going to be a father. Isn't that wonderful news?"

Oz turned his unpleasant regard on Will, then his lids lowered slightly, there was a fractional pause, and he said in a controlled voice, "Congratulations." He sketched Will a self-contained bow. "If you'll excuse us. Come, Isolde. The Florentine soprano's about to begin."

Will was as tall as Oz, and heavier, a solid, handsome man with grey eyes that contemplated Isolde with more than a casual claim. "I'm not sure Izzy wishes to leave. You needn't, Izzy."

As Oz took a threatening step into the room, Isolde hurriedly said, "I'm perfectly fine, Will. I'm looking forward to Miss Rossetti's performance. Do give Anne my best." Quickly moving toward the door, she brushed past Oz and hastened away down the wainscoted hall adorned with portraits of Banning thoroughbreds.

Walking very fast, Oz's swift tread behind her, she'd almost reached the music room when she was jerked to a halt and spun around. Grabbing her shoulders, his effort at self-control obvious in the slight tremor in his arms, Oz growled, "What the *hell* was going on?"

"Nothing. I told you," she said, bracing herself against his implacable gaze. "I was on my way back from the powder room when I met Will. He told me that Anne's having a baby. That's all." She tried to pull away. "You're hurting me."

His grip only tightened, his long slender fingers like vises. "He couldn't tell you that in the music room?"

"We met by accident."

"The hell you did," said Oz shortly.

"Oh, very well. He may have been waiting for me."

A muscle clenched high over his cheekbone, and when he spoke his voice was like steel. "In the future, I suggest you keep your hands to yourself if you don't want to make Fowler's wife a widow. Do you understand?"

"Don't be ridiculous." She met his cold gaze with a determined lift of her chin. "I don't respond to male tyranny; you have no jurisdiction over me."

"On the contrary, my *dear* wife," he said with sudden impatience, "I have considerable jurisdiction over you. The law is not yet in your favor, and while the double standard is deplorable, in my current frame of mind it is not entirely objectionable."

He sounded like any rich man, assured and confident of his place and power in the world, female autonomy no part of his life. She had a choice of further provoking him with bravura challenge or calming the waters and thereby avoiding a possible embarrassment should someone come out of the music room. "For heaven's sake, Oz," she said, her voice deliberately unruffled, "if you recall, our marriage is temporary. There's no need for this autocratic display of temper. You're making too much of an innocent encounter. Will and I've been friends forever and—"

"Slightly *more* than friends as well," said her husband, his lip curled in a sneer.

"If only you weren't an infamous libertine," she shot back, "you might have cause to take issue with *me*." A lifetime of indulgence was unlikely to long sustain a spirit of submission.

"Men can do what women can't."

"Allow me to disagree!"

"Just stay away from him or I'll put a shot through him," Oz said, his voice ruthless and uncompromising. "I won't wear cuckold horns."

"Unlike all the husbands *you've* crowned with horns?" Flaring irritability in every word.

"They chose to accept it. I don't," he answered with enormous self-control. "Nor do I fancy being made to compete for my wife's favors."

"No more than I fancy being ordered about by you," she said tartly. For a moment she thought he was going to strike her, and whether prompted by panic or the oppressive atmosphere, she suddenly felt a wave of nausea roll up her throat. Hastily slapping a hand to her mouth, she said faint and unsteady through her fingers, "Oh dear."

Oz dropped his hands as if burned. *Say it isn't so*, he thought, even as he understood that it was not only possible but also highly probable considering their single-minded obsession with sex. Softly swearing under his breath, he pulled his handkerchief from his pocket, shoved it into Isolde's hand, leaned over, picked her up, and praying she wouldn't vomit all over them, carried her down the hall, down the stairs, and out the door.

The fresh air helped Isolde's roiling stomach, and by the time they reached her carriage she was feeling marginally better. Oz lifted her in, jerked his head toward Dimitri, ordered, "Drive slowly," and climbing in, dropped into the opposite seat. Leaning back, he stretched out his legs. "Feeling better?" he asked as the carriage rolled down the drive, his voice notable for its restraint.

"Slightly, yes," she whispered, ashen to the roots of her pale hair. "Tell me it's not what I'm thinking."

"Perhaps something you ate is the cause," he said, not above negotiating with the gods of anarchy and disorder.

"Do you think so?" A glimmer of hope in her eyes.

"It's possible." But even as he spoke, he knew he was lying, his imagination racing unchecked toward disaster. He'd practiced coitus interruptus—normally effective—but the risk increased with constant repetition and he'd been on permanent stud duty for weeks.

"You're right. We *have* been careful, haven't we?"

"Fuck no."

She bristled at his blunt repudiation, at the sullenness of his tone. "Are you blaming me?"

"I don't suppose," he said, gently, "it would do much good at this point."

"You do have some responsibility," she said, pithy and acerbic, annoyed at his insolence. "Whether you like it or not."

"Yes, I know. Could we talk about this later?"

"When later?" she said, affronted by his soft and savorless voice.

"When I don't feel like strangling someone."

"Me, you mean."

"No, I don't mean you. I mean the whole bloody world," he said sharply.

"It might turn out to be nothing."

"I don't want to talk about it." Blunt and brusque.

"We're going to have to talk about it sometime."

"But. Not. Now."

Her temper was rising. "You're acting like a child."

He shot her a gelid look. "And you're acting like a shrew."

"How dare you call me a shrew," she hissed.

A muscle twitched over his stark cheekbone, and silent, he fixed a cool eye on her.

"Just like a man," she said, flushed and petulant. "Mute and muzzled when there's the devil to pay."

He rolled his eyes but gave no answer, and from that point on, no matter what she said or how she prodded him, he refused to respond. Even when she lost her temper, lunged forward, and slapped his face, he just grimaced, grabbed her, and tossed her back on her seat. Then, bracing his foot against her seat cushion as if to ward her off, he slid down on his spine, shut his eyes, and promptly went to sleep.

Openmouthed, she sat transfixed, reminded of their first night together when he'd said to her, "Observe," and proceeded to shock her with his instant erection. In the same astounding fashion, he'd fallen asleep, his mastery over his senses extraordinary.

She swore under her breath, debating an outright attack. Not that she was likely to prevail. Nor would such behavior solve her dilemma.

This particular problem required a cool head and thoughtful reflection.

Not that it wouldn't be satisfying to punch him a few times as well.

If it would only help, she brooded.

Although, if nothing else, the turmoil and fury had served as remedy to whatever had been ailing her. She felt quite herself again.

Except for being mad as a hornet.

CHAPTER 19

WHEN THEY REACHED Oak Knoll, Oz helped Isolde alight. In the presence of grooms and footmen, with Dimitri looking on, he said with cultivated grace, "Would you like me to call your maid?"

"I'm perfectly capable of calling my maid," she said, bristling at his cool detachment.

He smiled tightly. "If you'll excuse me then, I'm going for a ride. Don't hold dinner for me." He found himself addressing the air. Isolde had turned and was walking away.

He wasn't obtuse; he understood her anger. But he needed time to sort out the turmoil in his brain, come to terms with the burden of his past. Reconcile what was to have been a temporary marriage with this *current dilemma*.

As the door closed on Isolde, he swiftly made for the stables. Too restless to wait while a groom saddled his horse, Oz rigged and harnessed Sukha himself. A chestnut stallion from the mountains beyond the Hindu Kush, Sukha had been bred for speed and endurance, and once horse and rider cleared the stable block, Oz let the leathers slip through his fingers. With extended rein and curbless mouth, Sukha was soon racing flat out over the downs.

Literally escaping entanglement, Oz rode fast and hard over the green hills and dales, eyes narrowed against the wind, his hair disheveled by the breeze, his ears deaf to the thunder of calamity riding his coattails. He didn't want to reason or debate, referee or adjudicate; he just wanted to bolt.

Evade and avoid.

Until he no longer could.

The banner of defeat hoisted itself at the signpost for the village of Upper Framton, where his exhausted mount stumbled and nearly went down. Leaping from the saddle, Oz apologized to Sukha, who'd carried him across most of India as well as along London's fashionable gallops, and turning back, he walked his lathered horse until the huge chestnut was rested enough to take his weight again.

His return to Oak Knoll proceeded at a gentle pace, the March light slowly fading, a light mist rising in the low ground as evening approached. No matter how often he tried to flee—whether from formidable memory or disquieting emotion—Khair's memory remained fixed in his mind: beautiful and full of grace, her skin like alabaster against her dark hair, her eyes smiling, her soft voice teasing and playful. They'd grown up together at the court in Hyderabad, had always assumed they'd marry. But his suit had been rejected, her family committed to a union that would ally them to a powerful northern prince. Not that her family had had a hand in her death, but they'd been the reason she'd taken her own life rather than marry a man she didn't love.

A part of him had died with her that day, and in the years since, he'd not found the means to salvage his life. Immediately after Khair's funeral, he'd fled to England, where he'd dealt with his anguish in his own dissolute way. He was there when his father and mother had died, both prey to a summer fever that decimated the Anglo community. And ironically, while his English ancestry had cost him the woman he loved, the fact that his grandmother had been a native of Hyderabad permitted him to inherit the largest bank in India. Not adequate compensation for so heavy a loss of those he loved, but at least his road to destruction was paved with limitless gold.

Long accustomed to his particular method of escape, he was case-hardened to withdrawal, untaxed by the sensibilities that touched other men, thick-skinned with practice, and wholly selfish. Devoted to no living soul, when he finally came to a decision apropos Isolde, it was unequivocal. His certainty would have come as no surprise to those who knew him.

The moon was pale on the horizon when he rode into the stable yard, all turmoil and doubt resolved.

Isolde, unable to evade the behemoth in the room, had spent the ensuing hours fretting and stewing and in general working herself into a pet. It wasn't that she was blaming Oz completely; naturally, she shared responsibility. Nor was she irrational when it came to the necessary decision making *if*— there was still the remote possibility she was jumping to conclusions—*if* she should be pregnant. However, she didn't think herself unduly difficult in expecting Oz to discuss the situation. Although that might be too demanding for a man who'd apparently avoided permanence in his relationships. More to the point, a man who'd offered her his name with the clear understanding that there existed an express time limit to the offer.

It was her mistake, she ruefully thought, to have become so enamored and infatuated that she'd surrendered completely to passion and neglected the most fundamental prudence. Resting her head against the chair back, she softly groaned.

She should have known better.

The door to the small drawing room opened so softly, she wasn't sure for a moment whether the sound was real or imagined. But the familiar voice, drawling and languid with impudence, brought her head around.

"I see you've eaten with your usual appetite." His dark gaze surveyed the remnants of several dishes on the small table near the fire as he walked into the room. "You must be feeling restored."

Isolde had eaten supper in the cozy chamber as was her habit prior to Oz's arrival. "I do feel better, thank you. And you?" She was capable of sarcasm as well. "You look wet."

His hair and clothes were damp from the evening mist. "It's always wet in England." He stripped off his gloves as he approached and tossed them on a chair.

"Should I apologize?"

"Not unless you control the weather as well as my passions."

Her brows rose at the caustic edge to his voice. "Allow me to set your mind at rest concerning the weather at least."

"As to the other, I'll contrive to master that myself." He stood before her now, his large form silhouetted against the firelight, his face half in shadow, a restiveness to his stance. "I'm not staying."

"Fine."

"What do you mean, fine?" His surprise showed for a fleeting moment before, more clear-eyed, he saw his advantage.

"Did you think I'd beg and plead for you to stay?" She held his gaze for a moment. "On the contrary, should I be pregnant, it's my problem, not yours." She'd had plenty of time in his absence to deal with the practicalities. You could no more hold Oz in bondage than you could shackle the wind.

"You might not be pregnant at all." He stood there splendid, half-tamed, unencumbered.

"I agree."

"Naturally, if you are, I'll assume any financial responsibility," he said, cool and businesslike.

"There's no need. My fortune is considerable." She smiled faintly. "And thanks to you, secure. Sincerely, Oz, I'm most grateful." Her smile widened, and her eyes sparkled in the firelight. "For all your many services rendered."

He forced himself not to move, even as powerful lust urged him to pick her up, carry her over to the sofa, and fuck her until hell froze over. "I think I'll leave tonight." Sheer self-preservation. What had appeared sensible and reasonable on his ride back no longer seemed so astute, logic and lust seriously at odds.

"I'll have Lewis help with your departure." She picked up a small bell. "Although Betsy and Jess should wait until morning before they set out for London."

For a flashing second he debated plucking the bell from her fingers and changing his plans.

They'd been together long enough that she read that small hesitation.

And out of hope, she waited a second more.

"I'll have Sam tell Betsy," Oz said in a neutral voice. "And if you need anything at anytime, don't hesitate to let me know. My resources are at your disposal."

A shame you aren't, she thought, although he'd been clear about his role from the start. "If I should prove to be with child, would you mind if the divorce waited until after the birth? As a matter of clarity."

How often he and Khair had spoken of having a family. And now he might become a father by a woman he'd known a few weeks. A sudden disquieting thought raced through his brain. "As a matter of clarity since Will's already married and your child needs a father, you mean?" His voice was suddenly soft with malice. "I don't recall you having your menses since we wed."

A blush of disbelief washed up her face, replaced an instant later by a look of burning outrage. "How dare you suggest such a thing!"

"Then tell me," he said, unsympathetic and hard as nails, "how do I know this child is mine?"

"There might not be a child," she cooly replied.

"One can but hope," he drawled.

She went utterly still, her eyes held his for a stark moment, and with an equal measure of sarcasm, she softly said, "I'll thank you to shut the door behind you when you leave."

He was as motionless as she, his gaze knife sharp. "Coloring like mine runs true." He flicked a finger toward his face. "We'll find out the identity of the father soon enough."

"All I need from you is a divorce." Clipped and curt.

Anger flickered through his eyes. "Except not just *now*."

"*Anytime*," she said grimly. "I'll send Malmsey directions." She took a small breath, and her eyes were dark with rage once again. "Do you think I care what people say? If I did, I'd never have spread my name in all the scandal sheets. So you're free to go back to London and your women—"

His dark eyes, full on her face, narrowed. "And you to Will."

"No. Unlike you, I don't break up marriages."

"Nor do I," he said suavely. "I just make life bearable for the wives."

"How commendable," she said, ten generations of ice in her voice. "I wish you well in your benevolence. Now, if you won't go, I will." She came to her feet.

"Relax, darling," he said without inflection, a faint smile on his lips. "I'm leaving."

CHAPTER 20

Oz was back in London by ten, and by half past he was slipping into a chair at one of Brooks's gaming tables, in command of his feelings once again.

"You win, Harry," young Telford said with a grin. "You bet seven weeks. Evenin', Oz," he cheerfully said. "Marriage worn thin?"

"Don't they all."

"Could have told you." The young marquis had been married four months.

Oz flashed the table a grin. "It seemed like a good idea at the time."

"You were probably three parts drunk."

"No probably about it. What are the stakes? I'm in the mood to gamble."

And as was normally the case with the wealthy and privileged young noblemen who amused themselves at Brooks's, talk of wives and marriage was quickly exhausted. Play was high that night, thanks to Oz's reckless mood, and liquor flowed like water—that, too, due to Oz's largesse. He was drinking heavily in an effort to dislodge the images saturating his brain and raising havoc with his peace of mind: Isolde in bed, in the bath, in his arms, her voluptuous body warm against his, her honeyed sweetness his paradise on earth—his irresistible temptation.

The irresistible part unnerved him; it pissed him off.

Reaching for his remedy for aggravation, he found his glass empty. He shot a gimlet-eyed glare at a footman, the servant quickly filled his glass, and so it remained—never less than brim full—the rest of the night.

He consistently won, of course.

Didn't he always?

But he was drunker than usual, or more accurately, drunk when he stood on the pavement outside the club and squinted against the morning sun.

"Ready for some cunt?" Harry inquired in slurred accents.

Oz turned and surveyed him for a speculative moment. "I'm not sure," he said regretfully, "I've the stomach for it just yet."

"Marriage can sour you, that's a fact," Harry commiserated, five years' married and a father three times. "Just don't think about it. That's my advice."

It was advice Harry's wife pursued as well. Rumor had it her last child was Paxton's. Oz's brow knit in a black scowl; like the child of questionable paternity his wife might be carrying. "I'm off to bed," he muttered. "I've a helluva headache."

"Hair of the dog, Oz. It's the only way. Let's go to Marguerite's; her brandy's fine, and if you change your mind, the ladies are finer."

"Some other time. You go. Give Marguerite my regards."

"She's been asking for you, you know."

Oz shrugged. "Maybe tomorrow." The gilded brothel, and its equally resplendent owner, had been a habitual home away from home for Oz in recent years. "I'm bone tired, brain weary, and out of sorts with the world; you'll have to fuck 'em without me," he said over his shoulder as he moved away.

When Oz entered his house a short time later, Josef greeted him with studied civility.

"Don't look at me like that," Oz said, shrugging out of his coat, his voice entirely prosaic, not a hint of drink in his tempered syllables. "She *told* me to go, and if someone told you something different, they shouldn't have had their ear to the door."

"Yes, sir," Josef said with scrupulous restraint, having heard it all from Achille. Taking Oz's coat from him, he nodded to his right. "You have a visitor in your study, sir. Mr. Malmsey."

"That was quick," Oz said drily.

Josef didn't have to ask what he meant; everyone at Oak Knoll knew what had transpired. Nor would he have asked in any event with Oz's mood unchancy. "Would you like coffee brought in?"

"Why not, although I doubt this is a cordial call. You'd better bring me some brandy, too."

Entering his study a moment later, Oz greeted Malmsey with a natural grace uninhibited by drink. "This needn't be awkward, Malmsey." He waved him into a chair. "You'll find me completely amenable."

"Thank you, sir. You've been most agreeable; my client is grateful."

"Pray be candid," Oz said, dropping into a chair opposite the solicitor, "or we'll be talking circles around each other. I know why you're here." Leaning back, he crossed his legs and lazily smiled. "Let's deal with the ledger pages of our mutual responsibilities impartially. You'll find me willing to sign most anything."

"Very well, sir." Given leave to dispense with the preliminaries, Malmsey went directly to the primary consideration. "If there's a child, the countess would like full custody."

Oz's brows rose. "That'll take more than a conventional divorce, won't it? I'm no solicitor, but women's rights are limited in practice if not theory."

"Naturally, it would have to be a private agreement."

Whether impelled by some primal patriarchal impulse or whether he felt Isolde was asking too much, Oz hesitated when faced with the finality of giving up his child. Should a child even exist, he reminded himself. Not a certainty at this point. "Is that common? A private agreement?"

Malmsey didn't quite meet his gaze.

"Ah," Oz murmured and a malicious glitter entered his eyes. "The countess is taking matters into her own hands—as usual."

"Your marriage was outside the norm, sir—if I might be so bold to say. Its dissolution need not necessarily conform to precedence."

Oz's gaze was half hidden by his lashes. "Does she always get her way?"

Malmsey studied the floor for a moment before he replied with diplomatic obliquity. "As an only child, she was indulged, my lord. Furthermore, an independent title and great fortune confers added scope to one's freedom. But the countess is kindhearted and obliging, sir, and well respected by all."

She was indeed obliging in bed. You couldn't fault her there. But then Will knows that, too. "There's a small issue of paternity," Oz said with careful detachment. He glanced up as the door opened and a servant carried in a tray.

The men sat in silence while coffee was served, Oz's brandy was poured, and the servant departed. Quickly drinking down his brandy, Oz leaned forward, set the glass on the table beside him, and picked up the bottle. "As I was saying," he pleasantly went on, uncorking the bottle, "the issue of paternity may be in doubt. But should the child be mine, I hadn't contemplated relinquishing my paternal claims. Isolde's request for sole custody"—he shrugged—"could be a sticking point." Lifting the bottle to his mouth, he drank deeply.

"She didn't think it would be."

"Then we have a dilemma," he cooly said. At Malmsey's look of chagrin, Oz's expression altered, and in a completely different tone, benevolent and affable, he added, "Other than the custody issue, I'm quite willing to oblige her."

"I'm sure she'd be willing to pay you whatever you like to, ah, reach some agreement."

Oz smiled angelically. "I have too much money, Malmsey, not too little. I can buy this country and barely touch my wealth. Now if it was Will you were dealing with," he sardonically noted, "you might be able to negotiate. For my part, I'll have to wait and see." There was a small pause, and then a trace of mockery lightened his voice. "Tell her if it turns out to be my child, it's not for sale."

Malmsey had known before he'd come that Lennox's wealth would hinder negotiations. A few questions in the right quarters had brought to light the vast extent of his fortune. "Other than custody, however," Malmsey said, methodical and deliberate, "you have no objection to the divorce?" A solicitor's question, clarifying the boundaries.

"None."

"Very well. I'll relay the information to the countess." Malmsey stood and picked up his leather portfolio.

"How is she?" Oz asked, his voice guarded.

"I couldn't say, my lord. Her note was brief."

Oz grinned. "And full of spleen, I warrant."

"I couldn't say, sir."

"I commend your loyalty, Malmsey. She's lucky to have you on her side."

"If she wishes to compromise, I'll come back."

Oz lifted his brows. "Not likely that, eh, Malmsey?"

This time, the pink-faced solicitor betrayed a modicum of feeling in the calibrated neutrality of his face. "I was told she was unhappy," he slowly said. Then, turning, he walked from the room, leaving Oz mute.

WHILE MALMSEY WAS presenting her case in London, Isolde was lying abed at Oak Knoll, weary and fatigued after a sleepless night, her stomach in questionable straits, her mood sulky. In an effort to overcome her joyless spirits, she reminded herself she'd only known Oz seven weeks. There was no point in falling into some vaporish or resentful gloom over the departure of a wild, charming, irresponsible man who never intended to stay. Before long, she'd look back on his sojourn at Oak Knoll as no more than a tiny blip in the full and vital continuum of her life. *Except for the child in your belly*, a little voice pointed out.

Which observation triggered a wave of nausea she fought down because she was too tired to get out of bed and she wasn't about to vomit where she lay. Drawing air into her lungs, she breathed shallowly and slowly until the queasiness receded, and as if gaining control over her stomach somehow translated into fresh authority over her life, she felt refreshed. Sliding into a seated position against her pillows, she decided, rationalizing furiously, that the delicacy of her condition was no doubt the cause of her sleeplessness and melancholy. There was a very good possibility that neither circumstance had anything to do with Oz. It was purely physical.

Good; that was settled.

She'd always had a disgust for females prone to megrims.

Now that her recuperation was in hand—as if on cue—a soft knock on the door indicated her breakfast had arrived. She bid her maid enter.

Ah, the comforting familiarity of a daily routine.

She smiled. Nothing had changed.

She was alone at Oak Knoll as she'd been for many years. She was healthy and young; Grover was no doubt waiting to discuss his plans for the day. He'd be pleased she was ready to assume the estate duties she'd abandoned while Oz had been in residence.

With regard to the routines of local society, she was also pleased that she wouldn't have to deal with Anne Verney's triumphant looks. She wouldn't have to concede victory to her on pregnancy at least. Bitchy and trite though it might be, irrational as well, Isolde's feelings of satisfaction and redress were gratifying. As for her being pregnant, she was relatively certain of her condition with her morning nausea so pronounced.

While her feelings for Oz might be muddled and moot, or more to the point, useless, she had no such doubts about this child. She was excited, elated, filled with delight. She had been from the first.

Taking the tray from the maid, she arranged it on her lap, wished Libby a cheerful good morning, and tucked into her breakfast.

After all, she was eating for two.

LATER THAT MORNING, she went to see Betsy and Jess before they left. Betsy, who had the same bright hair as her son, was finishing her packing and she turned when Isolde entered her room. "The baron has a temper, my lady. But he always gets over it, Sam says."

"Izzy, Izzy!" Jess dropped the wagon he was playing with, jumped up, and ran to Isolde, his arms wide open.

Isolde scooped him up and hugged him hard. They'd become good friends in the weeks he'd been at Oak Knoll.

"We going London!" Jess squealed, his smile wide. "You go, too!"

"Maybe I'll come later. Grover needs me to help with the farming right now."

"Me stay help." He glanced at his mother. "Me stay, Mummy?" Jess had attached himself to Grover and spent hours every day accompanying Isolde's steward on his rounds of the estate.

"We can't stay now, darling, but we'll come back," Betsy said, knowing how to pacify an insistent toddler. "Miss Izzy'll tell you so."

"Of course, sweetie. If I don't see you in London, you make sure you have your mummy bring you back for a visit."

"When, Mummy?" A wide blue gaze swerved to his mother.

"Next week."

"Fer sure?"

"For sure, Jessie," Isolde lied, kissing his plump cheek and swallowing hard to stanch her tears.

Seeing the wetness in Isolde's eyes, Betsy distracted her son. "Come, darling, show Miss Izzy your new wagon," she said with a smile, taking Jess from Isolde.

"Grover found that toy wagon in the village," Isolde said, as Betsy set Jess down by his new toy. "It's rather sweet, isn't it?"

"It go faaasssst!" Jess exclaimed, launching the wagon across the floor like a projectile, quickly scrambling after it. Like any two-year-old, he was easily diverted.

"How are you feeling, miss?" Betsy quietly asked as Jess was once again engrossed in his toy. "Better than yesterday?"

Everyone knew; not that she'd thought otherwise. "I felt a little unwell when I first woke, but once I ate"—Isolde smiled—"I'm quite myself again."

Betsy smiled back. "I know what you mean. Those first months can be a trial. Me and Sam wish you all the best, miss. Men can be a right handful, and I should know," she said with a grimace. "My Richie left me God knows why. But things are bound to work out—for you and Lord Lennox. Sam says he's never seen his lordship so over the moon for a woman; I thought you should know."

"Thank you. His lordship is very loveable in turn, but life takes strange directions at times." *And I don't believe for a minute that Oz would ever be over the moon for a woman.* "I'm very pleased with the child, though; I'm grateful to my husband for that." She took a small breath to steady her nerves, talk of Oz and the baby adversely affecting her composure. "Now please, come and visit anytime. You and Sam and Jess."

"Sam's buying me a wee house, so you must visit us as well."

"I'd love to. Send me your direction when you know it."

A short time later, as she stood on the drive and waved good-by, Isolde felt less forlorn knowing she could visit Betsy and Jess again—without having to see Oz. In the past few weeks she'd become attached to the adorable, affectionate little toddler and she'd miss him.

She'd become attached to an adorable big boy, too.

A shame he was no longer on her visitor list.

CHAPTER 21

Both Isolde and Oz set about restoring their lives to a cultivated and intentional normalcy, working very hard to rebuff or rout any memories of the weeks they'd spent together.

There was no point in dwelling on the past, Isolde decided, especially after having heard from Malmsey. Oz was going to be difficult about the divorce—no surprise from a man who conducted his affairs very much as he pleased. Not that she wasn't grateful for all he'd done to save her from Frederick. But the original agreement had established a clear-cut time frame to the marriage. And so it would remain. Furthermore, it suited her purposes that he wished to wait until after the birth of the child to divorce. She'd avoid unwanted gossip, and since few noblemen played nursemaid to their pregnant wives, an absent husband wasn't unusual.

Naturally, news of Oz's departure spread quickly through the neighborhood, as all gossip did in a small, insulated community. Isolde's staff protected her by bruiting abroad that Lord Lennox had business in London.

Isolde said as much when Pamela called on her the day

after Oz left, knowing full well the time would come when such bland pronouncements would no longer serve. In the meantime, however, she smiled at her dearest friend and said with a sigh, "Men and their business. He wouldn't be deterred."

"Isn't that always the way with them," Pamela commiserated over tea. "Although, if you ask me, it's hard to keep any husband in the country for long."

"I'll admit I don't exactly mind," Isolde replied, half-truthfully. "I'm much more familiar with my own company."

"You always were a bit odd." But Pamela was smiling kindly. "We never could induce you to spend much time over cards and gossip."

Isolde returned her smile. "I have my acres to care for and my stables. And as you well know, I detest cards."

"Still, you must miss your darling husband now and again. He's a proper handsome devil with a smile that can charm the birds out of the trees."

"If I miss him too much, I'll hie myself to London," Isolde dissembled. "Tell me about Annabelle's new baby," she said, deliberately changing the subject, Pamela's sister having recently given birth. "She must be pleased to finally have a daughter."

"She's in raptures and writes of nothing else. The child is a paragon of every earthly virtue according to Annabelle, although I fail to see how even a mother can tell at three weeks of age."

"How are her boys dealing with their new sister?"

"I doubt they noticed, roughnecks that they are. They spend every minute out-of-doors. Not that their father is much of a homebody." She raised her brows in reproach.

"At least he's in the hunting field and not in some hussy's bed." *Oh dear, a stabbing reminder of Oz's favorite activity.* "Speaking of husbands," she quickly went on in an effort to distract her thoughts, "is Elliot at home or in the city?"

"Don't ask," Pamela said in chafing accents.

Isolde was sorry she had for Pamela went on at length describing Elliot's loathsome family and how he'd had to run to London and set to rights some Simpson dispute. The disparaging comments continued apace, a largely one-sided conversation as was often the case with Pamela. But Isolde didn't mind. While her friend detailed the lunacy of her husband's family, Isolde had the leisure to reminisce about recent, pleasurable events in which a devilishly handsome man with a charming smile played a major role.

It was all well and good to logically dismiss the weeks of her marriage as nothing more than a pragmatic alternative to Frederick's harassment. It was quite another matter to quash the enchanting memories of that blissful interlude.

Clearly, Oz had lived up to his prodigal reputation.

In due time Pamela ran out of invective. "Dear me, do stop me when I rant on like that," she ruefully muttered. "I apologize."

"Nonsense. You've listened to enough of my grumbling and laments over the years. At least you aren't in London dealing with the unruly Simpson mob; consider yourself fortunate."

"You're right. Elliot's mother orders everyone about like a despotic harpy; I have to constantly refrain from saying something rude to her." She waved her hand in a little dismissive gesture. "That's enough—on to more pleasant subjects. Can I coax you to come to Cassandra's luncheon tomorrow? She promises us a lecture on dahlias, which in itself isn't enticing, but apparently, the young landscape specialist giving the lecture is very, very handsome. Irish." She winked. "You know those dark Irishmen are absolutely delicious."

"No, I don't know," Isolde said with amusement. "Nor do you."

Pamela smiled. "We can at least look."

"You look. I've promised Grover we'd purchase some new Scottish cattle he's excited about."

"Good God, darling, you should have been a man with your outrageous interest in farming. Wherever does it come from?"

"From my father as you well know. Papa was a very accomplished farmer."

"My father's expertise was in vingt-et-un. Fortunately, he was good at it."

"And you're the richer for it," Isolde lightly said. "Never a bad position to be in as a woman. Particularly since the law now allows us control of our property."

"Speaking of which, what were the terms of your marriage settlement? We all discovered what Will was looking for in marriage. More than your considerable fortune, the greedy man."

"So it seems. I was naively unaware he had a market price on marriage."

"You were coddled from the cradle, darling. How could you possibly know the world wasn't all sunshine and moonbeams. Try growing up in a family of five brothers like I did. Now, Oz didn't want your money, did he—a nabob like him?"

"No. He insisted I keep my own property, so my world is unchanged." And she had a fortune in new jewelry as well, Oz generous in all but his constancy.

"Lucky you. A rich, handsome, deadly charming husband who doesn't make demands on your wealth. Surely, he's an anomaly in the beau monde."

"I suppose he is." But rather than continue a discussion that would only require her to contradict portions of it when her divorce was announced, Isolde said instead, "Do convey my apologies to Cassandra, but you know I'm not interested."

"Of course; she won't be surprised you've declined." With a glance at the clock on the mantel, Pamela began gathering up her gloves and bonnet. "My dressmaker is coming over to fit that Worth gown, so I must be off." Placing the velvet confection on her curls, she tied the ribbons under her chin. "I could say don't be such a stay-at-home," she said, slipping on one glove, "but since you are, I'll come over again soon and regale you with the latest gossip."

"Thank you." Isolde grinned. "I shall wait with bated breath."

The second glove in place, Pamela smiled. "Enjoy your Scottish cattle purchasing."

Isolde dipped her head. "I shall."

But after Pamela left, Isolde hadn't even had time to finish her cup of tea before Will was announced.

"Your wife will hear of your visit," Isolde remarked as he strolled into the drawing room, the image of a well-tailored country squire in chamois breeches, riding boots, and a tweed hacking jacket. "You must have met Pamela on your way in."

"Can't I visit a neighbor?" he murmured with a smile. "You're looking as beautiful as ever. I've always liked you in that gown."

"Thank you." Short months ago, she would have glowed with happiness at not only his compliment but also his visit. And now his words were no more than pleasantries anyone might have uttered—a brother, for instance, or a familiar cousin from childhood. The glorious Lord Lennox had rendered her good service in more ways than one when Will no longer caused her distress. "Honestly, though, Will, Anne won't appreciate you calling on me." Anne Verney had made her feelings crystal clear, although she couldn't bring herself to openly disparage his wife. "You know how servants gossip," she blandly said instead.

"Don't worry about Anne. I don't. I never did."

She was not only surprised at his candor, but she was also unprepared for her lack of pleasure at his admission. How she would have longed to hear such words short months ago. "Harboring such feelings," she said with a practical logic no longer hindered by pangs of unrequited love, "why did you marry her?"

"You know why." He stripped off his gloves and tossed them on a nearby table. "My family insisted."

"Your family insisted on securing Anne's dowry, you mean. And you willingly complied. I wouldn't have thought you so dutiful." *And so willing to relinquish the affection we shared.*

"We can't all be financially secure," he bluntly replied, dropping into a chair he'd sat in so many times before and stretching out his legs. "Could we talk about something else?"

She'd been unaware of his callousness. Although surely her husband's callousness was of a kind. She'd not considered herself so naive and yet . . . the implication was clear. "What would you like to talk about?" she asked, telling herself she was capable of civility. "My marriage? *Your* marriage? The price of cattle?" she lightly queried.

"I've missed you," he said, ignoring her levity, his smile warm and intimate, familiar. "I heard your husband went back to the city. I thought you might like company. Or do you find marriage less boring than I?"

Boring was not a word she'd use to describe her marriage. "I'm sorry you're bored; I'm quite content." A lie but he was the last person she was likely to confide in.

"Even abandoned by your bridegroom as you are?"

"He has business in the city."

"Will he be back soon?"

"Really, Will, do I inquire of Anne's schedule?" She sat up a little straighter, unwilling to continue in this vein. "Speaking of your wife, you must be aware she takes exception to me," she ambiguously noted. "I'm not sure you should linger. And I do have a meeting scheduled with my steward and farm manager soon."

Will gazed at her from under his lashes and slowly smiled. "Are you giving me my congé? After our long and affectionate relationship?"

So he wasn't denying it. "Former relationship. You married first."

His gaze narrowed. "You're still holding that against me?"

She slowly exhaled, his unwillingness to accept responsibility so unabashedly selfish, she was mortified at her obtuseness. *Love is blind* was a sobering fact, as was a degree of personal naivete she'd rather not acknowledge. "I'm not holding anything against you," she said, neither angry nor wounded, but awakened now to a sumptuous pleasure Will could never offer her. "I'm simply pointing out that you and I are both married," she kindly said, "and not in a position to enjoy each other's company in the same way we once did."

"You have to admit, darling, we were very good together," he softly said, holding her gaze. "We could be again."

"We can't call back yesterday. Too much has changed." How easy it was to be gracious and affable when one's emotions weren't involved. She began to understand Oz's casual urbanity.

Unchastened by her words, Will's smile was smug. "You like sex, darling. We both know it. All I'm saying is if your husband doesn't find time to return to Oak Knoll anytime soon, I'd be more than happy to accommodate you. Anywhere, anytime, day or night."

Her brows rose. "And your wife? What do you say to her?"

"Don't concern yourself with my wife. Remember, darling, anytime . . ."

Suddenly intent on ending this disillusioning conversation, Will's casual infidelity reminding her too odiously of her husband's, Isolde came to her feet. That she'd been so blind to Will's faithlessness was disturbing to a woman who prided herself on being levelheaded. That she wanted no man other than Oz who was cut from the same cloth was even more disturbing. "I *do* have a meeting, Will. If you'll excuse me. You know your way out." And in a swirl of plum silk, she turned toward the door and quickly left.

CHAPTER 22

BACK IN THE city, Oz threw himself into work and dissipation with signal zeal. By the third day, his staff was rolling their eyes and trying to stay out of his way. He was short-tempered, short of sleep, and savagely critical of anyone who dared to question him. Only Jess escaped his temper. Even Marguerite bore the brunt of his resentments one night when she suggested he delay opening a third bottle. He turned to her and in a freezingly hostile voice said, "Pray don't advise me. I have all the managing women I need in my life."

When he came awake in her bed the next morning, he offered her a blanket apology—not exactly sure what he'd said or done, but at the sight of her wary gaze, he understood that he'd been rude or worse. When he returned home, he had his secretary send her a large bank draft with a written apology, then he soaked in the tub until his head stopped pounding. After which, he dressed, went down to breakfast, drank two brandies with his beefsteak and eggs, and began another day much the same as the previous one.

It was Sam who had the nerve to confront him in his office at the end of the second week. Standing just inside the door, he surveyed Oz's languid pose, the taut fatigue of high living evident on his face, the slackly lidded gaze.

"You may go, Davey," Oz said without lifting pen from paper, smiling faintly as his secretary quickly came to his feet. "I believe Sam has something unpleasant to say to me."

Both men waited in silence until the door closed.

"I don't suppose," Oz said, putting his pen down, his dark brows level, "it would do any good to say, 'Go away.' "

"You haven't been sober since you returned to London," Sam said, clearly not relishing his task. "Do you think it might be wise to slow down?"

Sliding lower in his chair, Oz put his fingers together on his chest and very gently said, "Did you draw the short straw in the household vote?"

"They thought me better able to deal with your drunken charm," Sam said, sardonic and disapproving. "I was delegated to tell you you're going out of your way to piss off everyone."

Oz smiled. "I'm not going out of my way."

"If your wife bothers you so much you're drinking day and night," Sam said sharply, "why don't you go and see her?"

"Why would I do that?"

"So you might be less overdrawn on sleep and less pickled in alcohol."

Oz softly sighed. "Go back to my needlessly worried staff and tell them they're all remembered in my will. And tell them, too," he said, his voice grating very slightly, "it's my affair how I go to the devil."

But that evening, Marguerite confronted him as well, although in a more tactful way.

"Oz, darling, you're losing weight drinking, not eating, rarely sleeping. I worry about you." The proprietress of one of London's elegant brothels was seated across from Oz, a small fire in the grate between them, the lights dimmed in her sitting room because Oz found bright lights objectionable of late.

"I'm fine." Since that night he'd been vicious to her, he took care to be civil. "I've never needed much sleep."

"You do need *some*, though."

"I sleep at home," he lied.

She didn't argue nor say he spent a good portion of his time in her apartments—not sleeping. Nor talking. Nor touching her—which betrayed the state of his spirits more than anything.

Monkish, Oz was not.

"Sam was over," she quietly said.

He didn't look up, his gaze on the glass balanced on his chest as he lounged in his chair, his eyes heavy lidded. "Ignore him."

"They're worried about you."

"Ignore them all," Oz crisply said, and lifting the glass to his mouth, he drained it and reached for the bottle on the table beside him.

"You know Fitz, don't you?"

He looked up from pouring. "Groveland?"

She nodded. "He didn't quite know how to deal with love either," she said, not sure she wouldn't be tossed out of her sitting room for mentioning the word *love*.

His gaze sharpened, a spark of anger visible even in the shadowed light. But when he spoke he'd sufficiently curbed his temper. Setting the bottle aside, his voice was mild when he spoke. "Spare me your romantic sentiments, darling. My drinking has nothing to do with love. I don't give a tinker's damn about love. I'm bored with life in general and my life in particular and overset with ennui. I wish to be insensate."

"You should talk to Fitz."

"You overstep," he said very, very softly, his gaze over the rim of his glass touched with violence.

"I know. Someone has to when you're acting like an undisciplined child."

"I may give you a thrashing again," he said, lightly mocking. "Have you thought of that?"

"I'll call for Jeremy. He's bigger than you and sober."

Unblinking, Oz placed one hand on his coat pocket. "But does he have a weapon?" His smile was faint, his voice passionless. "Just so you know before you call him."

Her fine nostrils flared. "How tedious you can be, Oz." Coming to her feet in a rustle of rose silk, she said in a voice brittle with temper, "Go and talk to your wife for God's sake!"

He stared at her back as she walked away, then at the door that closed behind her, nothing moving in his lounging pose for so long he might have been comatose. Even his breathing was indistinguishable. Until finally, he set his untouched glass aside, ran his fingers through his hair, uncut since leaving Oak Knoll, exhaled softly, and heaved himself to his feet.

Emptying his pockets of money, the sum capable of launching a midsize business, he dropped the bills on Marguerite's desktop and slowly walked from the room.

He couldn't go home yet. It was too early. In the morning he could be distracted by the daily transactions necessary to the efficient functioning of his shipping line and merchant bank. Each day at eight o'clock sharp, he bestirred himself to listen to Davey's recital of cargoes loaded and unloaded, of ships arriving and embarking, of telegrams received from his Indian banks; he dutifully signed all the new documents prepared for him and issued what orders were required. Those few hours were the only respite he had from the persistent, damning thoughts of Isolde that confounded and perplexed and in general screwed with his mind. Her physical loss had unsettled him more than he'd expected, complicated his life more than he'd expected. Left formless doubts abrading his spirit.

He glanced at his wristwatch as he stood on the pavement outside Marguerite's. Eleven. So—where now?

He was in St. James, close to all the clubs and brothels.

He smoothly turned as Marguerite's front door opened, his physical facilities unimpaired by drink. "Harry!" He smiled. "Just the man to join me somewhere—anywhere, so long as the liquor flows and the company amuses."

"I don't know about the company, but there's liquor aplenty at Harvey's," Harry said, swiftly descending the stairs. "I promised my wife I'd be there an hour ago. Come and shield me from her sharp tongue and sharper temper."

"You might want to change first," Oz pleasantly said. "You reek of cunt."

"You can stand in front of me. She'll think it's you."

"By all means, allow me to be your shield and protection from domestic outrage," Oz cheerfully intoned.

"Better you than me," Harry grunted, taking Oz's arm at the elbow and propelling him down the street.

The entertainment was in full swing at the Harvey's in Grosvenor Square, the curb lined with carriages, every window alight, the sound of music faintly heard as the men approached the entrance.

"Why the hell are you obliged to make your bows?" Oz asked as they moved up the stairs. "It's not as though you and Vanessa share many social occasions.

"Something about her mother," Harry mumbled. "I didn't listen. But she made it clear I was expected to play husband tonight and smile when required. Christ, she's going to be pissed; I should have been here long ago." He grimaced as the front door opened. "I'm expecting you to take the brunt of her displeasure. I'm blaming my tardiness on you."

"And how exactly have I postponed your arrival?" Oz asked with sardonic deference as footmen took their coats. "Give me a hint."

"Jesus, I don't know," Harry muttered as they made for the rose-garlanded staircase. "Think of something. Who better than you knows how to make excuses to women?"

It was true of course; he'd made it a practice the past few years. So moments later when they found Harry's scowling wife tapping her foot outside the ballroom, Oz smiled winningly. "It's my fault entirely, Vanessa. I forcibly conscripted

Harry in the interests of the nation. We were entertaining Wales. Daisy's in Paris with her husband and Wales is moping." The Prince of Wales's newest affaire was in that frenzied early phase of overwrought passion.

"Mother's been asking for you." She shot a vexatious glance at her husband, who was partially concealed by Oz's large, well-developed frame, although everyone knew an invitation from Wales was a royal command. "Come, darling," she said, her tone modified by understanding, her gaze quickly swiveling to Oz so the diamonds in her ears twinkled. "I'm sure Oz can find someone to amuse him."

As Harry followed his wife, he shot Oz a raised-brow look over his shoulder. Clearly he had no idea why he was being summoned by his mother-in-law.

Oz entered the ballroom a moment later and stood preoccupied and attractively powerful on the verge of the floor for no more than five seconds before a bevy of females descended on him like vultures spying a fresh carcass. Very pretty vultures as it turned out and as determined as their bird-of-prey counterparts to plunder the spoils.

If only his senses responded to the lovely, perfumed throng dressed in courtier gowns, glittering with jewels. If only he gave a damn about all the fawning females. But their bare shoulders and low décolletages displaying comely breasts like so much ripe fruit, the smiling mouths and seductive glances paying homage to him, the salacious double entendre that passed for conversation reminded him instead of the sameness he'd come to detest. Restive and moody, he replied to their artifice and banter with disinterested courtesy even as he was tempted to say, *Pick a number between one and ten and I'll take you in turn.* Or, he thought, surreptitiously scanning the room over their perfectly coiffed heads, a quick retreat would satisfy more.

He shouldn't have come to this pointless affair. What had in the past served as amusement no longer amused; what had passed for diversion now left him indifferent. Whatever hu-

man impulses had served him in the two years since India
hadn't survived his departure from Oak Knoll, his ability to
conjure up tender emotion gone.

Having listened to the fifth or tenth or twentieth sweetly
insinuating remark about his new singleness, he'd just decided to make his excuses and leave when he was tapped on
the shoulder and a familiar, honeyed voice said, "Finally, the
prodigal has returned."

Turning around, he saw salvation of a sort outfitted in
cloth of gold and smiling up at him. "Nell," he said with a
freshening sense of appreciation. His dark gaze drifted down
her splendid body, flauntingly festooned in shimmering gold.
"I thought you were abroad."

"I was. Excuse me, ladies," she crisply said, taking Oz's
arm. "Lennox promised me this dance."

He hadn't danced since he'd danced with Isolde at Pamela's, but Nell's sophisticated chatter, the comfortable feel of
her in his arms, her indifference to emotion, made her safe,
helped his demons recede—if only temporarily.

But it was enough after a fortnight of alcohol and too
vivid dreams.

It was enough not to shrink from a woman.

Everyone watched, of course, as they always did with a
new scandal brewing. Beautiful Nell, known for her passionate appetites, her glorious red hair foil for her glittering
gown, melted against Oz's tall dark form as they gracefully
glided across the ballroom. Her pale cheek rested on his la-
pel, her curvaceous back, bared to the waist, lured every
man's eye, envy in their gazes. Women, too, watched with
envy, wishing they were held in Oz's powerful arms.

He was very drunk, very charming, and recklessly irresponsible.

As usual.

Indifferent to the shocked appraisals and whispers, the
handsome couple swirled past the avidly curious in their

circuit of the ballroom. *Look where his hands are, so low on her back, curved around her neck! Look how tightly he's holding her! You can't even see her right hand—the little slut! My God, she kissed him! He kissed her back! He's drunk! He's always drunk! She left her husband in Egypt! He abandoned his wife in the country!*

Everyone knew how close they'd once been, how torrid their love affaire, how Nell had hysterically bearded Oz on his wedding morning, how he'd thrown her out and given orders she wasn't to be admitted again.

They knew everything; everyone always did in the ton.

What they didn't yet know was that the moment Nell had heard Oz had left his bride, she'd come back—her journey from Cairo more tedious than it should have been, her husband more difficult about her leaving than he should have been.

But the pyramids would always be there, and Oz, restless and changeable, might not.

They didn't dance long.

They left midway through the waltz, leaving a buzz of gossip in their wake.

And retired to Blackwood's.

"EVENING, FREMONT," OZ said a short time later, entering the hotel with Nell on his arm. "What do you have for us?"

"Good evening, my lord. The Wellington Suite happens to be available." It was Lady Howe's favorite.

"Perfect. Have some brandy sent up." He turned to Nell. "Any requests?"

"Nothing Fremont can help me with," she murmured, tugging on his arm.

Oz shot a look at Fremont. "We know our way."

"A pleasure to see you again, my lord," Fremont said, knowing better than to publically address the lady.

"It's good to be back."

Fremont smiled as the young couple walked away. He liked young Lennox. He'd heard all the gossip, of course—about the surprising marriage, the not-so-surprising separation, Oz's return to London. It was the lifeblood of his business to know who was with whom and when in order to avoid awkward encounters; husbands, wives, and ex-lovers were never lodged in close proximity. "You heard," he said to a footman standing by. "Lennox's brandy in the Wellington Suite, some champagne and petit fours for Lady Howe as well. She prefers the almond fondant icing."

The Wellington Suite was on the garden side of the hotel, well away from the bustle of the street. Not that Nell cared for gardens or quiet. Rather, she enjoyed the overlarge bed and sumptuous marble tub in the mirrored bath. But what she enjoyed *most* was the man at her side.

"I'm so *vastly pleased* I found you tonight," she said, slipping her arms around Oz's waist the moment he closed the door behind them. "The trip from Cairo was *endless* . . . but with *you* as my prize it was worth every minute."

"And you saved *me* from another night of boredom."

"So very pleased to be of service," she purred, gazing up at him with a seductive glance.

"In what way?" His smile was wicked.

"Since I thought of little else but *you* on my awful trip home I have several ideas. First, I'm going to undress you and admire your strapping young body," she said with a sultry smile, sliding her hand upward over the diamond studs on his shirtfront. "Then you can lie in bed, watch *me* undress, and tell me how *much* you missed me."

"Desperately, of course," he said with a faint smile.

"Of course," she whispered, profoundly grateful to have her favorite lover back.

Neither mentioned the occasion when last they'd met the morning after Oz's marriage. This was playtime, after all, not harsh reality. Which precluded mention of the subsequent collapse of his marriage as well.

Oz had no objection to Nell's agenda, knowing he'd be suitably rewarded for his acquiescence as would she. In the meantime, he was here to forget. As she slowly removed his evening clothes, he found her idle chatter soothing, familiar. Nothing was required of him but an occasional smile or nod, while her obvious relief on escaping her husband mirrored his own on fleeing his marriage. At base though, they were of a kind: she was as self-indulgent as he, eminently versed in the game of love and unlikely to demand anything of him other than sex—casual sex. Which was exactly what he wanted. Wasn't it?

Fortunately, she dropped to her knees at that point to remove his trousers and he wasn't compelled to face the vexing truth.

"Mmm . . . my lovely stud," she murmured a moment later, his trousers and underwear cast aside, her fingers measuring the length of his erection in pleasant anticipation. "You have the most beautiful penis, darling," she added, glancing up at Oz. "I suppose you hear it all the time."

"Never," he politely lied.

"I want him to wait for me, though, so go now," she ordered, rising to her feet in a flurry of gold cloth and gardenia scent and pointing to the bed. "And think about what you want me to do for you while I undress."

Fuck me into oblivion. "You decide. I'm amenable to anything."

"Aren't you always," she dulcetly returned, reaching up to pull the pins from her hair.

"Rule one on the road to excess."

"We agree on everything," she lightly said, looking forward to remapping that route with England's most talented cocksman.

A knock on the door broke into the amorous banter and

undeterred by his nudity, Oz called out, "Enter." Pointing to a table, he waited while the footman deposited his burden, thanked him, then immediately set about pouring himself a drink. As the door closed, Oz drained his glass, refilled it, and smiled at Nell. "Your audience of one is ready to be beguiled." Moving to the bed, he disposed himself in a comfortable sprawl, the glass balanced on his chest, and gave her a nod. "The stage lights are up, sweetheart."

After executing a dramatic bow, Nell struck an elegant pose that showed her stunning form to advantage. "For your pleasure and divertissement, my Lord Lennox, I took dancing lessons in Cairo."

He grinned. "Why did I know that?"

A frown marred the porcelain perfection of her forehead. "Don't say this is the twentieth time you've seen such a performance," she pettishly retorted.

"No." A courtesy lie. "I just knew what would interest you in Cairo."

"Sex—if you'd been there," she playfully replied, her good humor restored.

"And since I wasn't there?"

"I found something else to amuse me."

"Something or someone?"

"Really, dear, need you ask?"

"I only wish to point out that we are both faithless"—his brows lifted—"and not likely to change."

"Yes, yes, I know," she said with a little sigh. "I shouldn't be pettish."

"Nor will I," he said with pallid amusement. "Show me what you learned."

After she unclasped the few hooks at her back, her gown slid to her waist and her large, flamboyant breasts were on full display.

"Did your teacher take a fancy to your lovely breasts?" he murmured, wondering if her minimum clothing tonight was planned for him or anyone.

"*She* did as a matter of fact," Nell said, perjuring herself without a qualm. "And I took the lessons for you."

If so, news of his abandoned marriage had traveled fast. "I'll have to do something for you in return."

"All night long and often," she said in a sultry contralto.

He smiled. "Whatever you say."

Sliding her glittering gown down her hips, clad only in white silk stockings and gold slippers, she posed for him, arms raised, her smile dazzling, knowing she was unabashedly desirable.

"Breathtaking as usual." She was a sumptuous, showy female with pale skin and auburn hair, flaunting breasts and ripe, rounded hips—a perfect companion in his current frame of mind. A vixen to titillate his senses without stirring his emotions.

"I expect you'll also be impressed with my new skills," she murmured with a little swish of her hips.

"I'm impressed already," he said. "As you can see."

"And *I'm* getting wet just looking at your huge erection," she said softly, her gaze trained on the object of her lust—the holy grail for her long journey home.

"How wet?" he quietly asked.

Slipping her hand between her legs, she drew in a skittish breath as she slid her finger palm-deep into her vagina.

"I can do better than that for you," Oz silkily remarked.

Lost to feverish sensation, it took a moment before Oz's voice registered and a moment more before she held up her index finger for his perusal. It was pearled with moisture.

"I suggest you start dancing or your recital will have to wait," Oz drawled. "We're both primed."

"No, no . . . don't you dare. I want to show off my new skills."

"By all means then, do so."

"Because you can always wait," she grumbled.

He shrugged. "If I have to."

A femme fatale by nature, she objected to Oz's self-control in the face of what was to most men her irresistible allure. "I suppose we can't all be raised in India," she sulkily muttered.

He smiled. "I can't help but think you'd have been a willing pupil of Vatsyayana. But please, entertain me—and then I'll entertain you."

"It's up to me to say when, though." A sop to her inner femme fatale.

"Naturally." Or not. He wasn't a eunuch.

Having mastered the intricate manipulation of stomach muscles so necessary to the dance—thanks to a very charming young male instructor—Nell swiveled and rolled her curvaceous hips in a splendidly appropriate rhythm perfectly in sync with the sinuous undulations of her upper body. Her large, full breasts quivered and bobbed in provocative counterpoint to her gyrating hips, and when she twirled, her heavy breasts swung out in a spherical eddy that raised Oz's cock an appreciable distance more.

She'd learned her lessons well; the dance was meant to arouse, titillate, and excite. And it did.

The moment she came close enough, he intended to assuage his lust. After weeks of celibacy, self-control was a relative term, and Nell was the perfect antidote to his collective frustration. She offered him what he realized he needed: worldly sexual pleasure and nothing more. He was grateful.

Suddenly, putting his glass aside, he set about curtailing her performance. "If you don't come here, I'll come there. Literally."

She giggled. "You who can always wait?"

"It must be your new dancing skills," he smoothly replied. It wasn't; an image of Isolde lying in his arms had abruptly pervaded his brain and he needed to extinguish it. Quickly.

Having thought of little else for days, pleased at Oz's rare impatience, Nell was more than willing to oblige. And Oz was so thankful for the instant obliteration of his unwanted memories that he obliged *her* with three quick orgasms before he found release.

"You're absolutely . . . worth my . . . dreadfully . . . long journey," she breathed, lying beside him, softly panting. "God, Oz . . . you're so much better than I remembered."

"I find it equally pleasing that you came back to London." He meant it; she was the distraction he needed from haunting memory. Arching his back, he lazily stretched, his demons put to flight. "When you've caught your breath," he gently said, "you can do something for me."

Turning her head on the pillow, she held his gaze. "I'd love to."

He knew she would; that's why he proposed what he did. After two more drinks and champagne for the lady, Nell was reclining against the pillows, her feet comfortably clasped behind her head, her acrobatic flexibility beautifully showcasing her pouty vulva.

Kneeling before her, Oz contemplated the sleek, pink, pulsing flesh, the piquant offering enchanting. There was something about a creamy cunt in all its full-blown glory, ripely expectant and primed, that racheted up the pleasure scale of lust. Inhaling softly, he leaned forward, guided the swollen head of his penis to Nell's delectable slit and penetrated her marginally. Then, once joined, he eased his hands under her bottom, lifted her slightly to allow him better ingress, and slid in another small distance.

Embedded midway in her pulsing flesh, the fullness of his cock pressed against the highly sensitive erectile tissue on the top wall of her vagina, that vividly impressionable area having been described in detail since medieval times in various Urdu texts. Since his youth, Oz had understood the subtleties of female arousal apropos that tiny spot. And he also knew what Nell liked. Remaining fixed in place and utterly still, he served as willing instrument to her pleasure as she panted and twitched in escalating delirium, absorbed the increasingly fierce, seething rapture, and eventually climaxed. Over and over and over again.

She was infinitely easy to please. But then they were well matched when it came to selfish carnality.

Their reunion turned out to be an exercise in politesse and hedonism. Careful to stay within the prescribed perimeters of urbane friendship, the night passed in a mellow exploration of ravishment and ecstasy. And when morning came, Nell decisively said, "I'm going to preempt your leisure time. Don't argue. It's not as though you have anything more pressing to do."

He didn't argue. "I'd be delighted," he said.

They went to Blackwood's often in the following days.

Oz didn't have to think with Nell.

He didn't *want* to think. Or talk—other than suave pillow talk without substance or humanity.

And Nell didn't care as long as Oz exerted himself to please her.

It was no exertion; it was automatic for him, and that in itself offered relief. He wasn't obliged to face his discontent during the hours he spent at Blackwood's. Nor was he apt to be grilled on his marital situation. It was the last subject Nell was likely to bring up.

CHAPTER 23

WHILE OZ WAS exorcizing his demons at Blackwood's, Isolde was coping with Will's unwanted visits. No matter what she said or did to discourage him, he refused to listen. He'd ride over with a message from his steward for Grover; their estates shared a border. Or he'd carry over an invitation from his wife for some social event when they both knew the invitation had been coerced. Will had even taken to meeting her on her morning rides, which thoroughly spoiled one of her favorite pastimes. His persistence was vexing to a very large degree.

She'd even pleaded a headache once, the ache in her temples instant and real the moment he'd been announced. She'd sent a message down by her maid only to have him come back an hour later with a cordial recommended by the village doctor. And she'd not been able to eject him for hours.

She was beginning to consider threatening to inform his wife of his frequent visits if he didn't stop. She'd finally said as much one morning when he'd met her on the downs, swung his mount alongside hers, and matched her pace. "You're being much too attentive, Will," Isolde fretfully muttered. "I'm tempted to talk to Anne. I doubt she'd approve of your constant calls."

"Your husband's taken up with his former lover. Did you know that?" he said as if she hadn't spoken.

With considerable effort, her reply was cooly composed although the color had left her face. "Like you, you mean."

His smile was bright with good cheer. "On the contrary, darling, I'm still only hopeful."

"Allow me to dash those hopes. I'm not interested in renewing our friendship, not now, not ever. I hope I make myself clear."

"Allow me to disagree, Izzy, darling," he pleasantly countered, immune to her rebuff. "You're a passionate woman who'll eventually require sexual satisfaction. And from all appearances, you won't be getting that from your wandering husband."

"Perhaps one of the stable boys is servicing me." The blood had returned to her face, her smile was flawless.

"Lucky fellow."

"For God's sake, Will. Stop. I have no interest in discussing this."

"When you do become interested, darling," he softly said, "I'd like to be first in line."

She shot him a sharp look. "You certainly have tenacity. But, pray, take me off your list of hopeful conquests and *don't* speak to me of this again!" Whipping her mount, she raced away from Will's unwanted company and more from his unwanted news. She'd expected it, of course, but all the same, on hearing of Oz's infidelity her stomach had risen to her throat. How unfortunate to have fallen in love with a wild young man who bewitched without even trying, who masterfully practiced the art of pleasing in bed untrammeled by feeling or regret. Who'd walked away without a backward glance even knowing she might be carrying his child.

Even more unfortunate, that same wild young man had spoiled her for all others. No matter she'd been trying mightily during the past fortnight to disabuse herself of the notion—there it was plain as day.

The sight of Will left her cold. Annoyed her, in fact.

While Oz's beguiling image was a permanent fixture in her brain.

Damn. Life wasn't fair.

As if to emphasize that point, Pamela came to call that afternoon, looking so uncomfortable that after five minutes of prosy, pointless conversation, Isolde said, "I already heard about Oz." With pride she controlled her anger and distress. "You needn't feel awkward."

Pamela didn't quite meet her gaze for a moment, then said with a sigh, "I thought you should know if you didn't."

"Will was pleased to inform me of the news when he disturbed me on my morning ride again," Isolde replied, even as she braced herself to hear another version of the gossip.

"You know then that Oz has taken up with Nell Blessington again."

She nodded. Even braced, even knowing, it hurt to hear the words. So much for logic. She was consumed with jealousy and sorrow, the thought of her husband lying with the splendid Nell, disheartening. "She's very beautiful," Isolde said as calmly as she was able. "And I hardly expected faithfulness from a man like Oz."

"Or most men," Pamela said with a sniff. "I'm so sorry for you, dear. Especially now."

Isolde glanced up from her tea.

"I don't know if others know, but I've suspected for some time." Pamela smiled. "It's always the breasts that give it away." She half lifted her hand. "Your gown's getting tight. Are you happy?"

"I am. Very happy."

"Then the rest doesn't matter."

"I agree. This is *my* baby."

"Is he gone then?"

"I don't know," Isolde said, setting down her cup. "We

quarreled and he left." She couldn't yet bring herself to disclose their divorce plans. It was foolish, of course. Pamela's silence could be depended on. But matters of the heart didn't yield to reason, nor was passion so easily repudiated.

"Have you tried writing to him?"

Isolde shook her head. "I don't relish being rebuffed. He was quite determined to leave."

"Are you heartbroken?"

"It wouldn't do me any good if I were. I keep busy; the child I carry brings me enormous joy. I have too much goodness in my life to be despondent."

"Do you want me to explain to our friends?"

Isolde softly exhaled. "Strangely, I don't care. If you and Will heard the gossip, others did as well. As for my pregnancy, that too will be obvious before long. What I do wish you'd do is find some way to keep Will from coming to visit. He's driving me mad."

"Do you want me to tell Anne? That could put an end to it."

Isolde frowned. "I don't know if I want to stir up trouble."

Pamela smiled. "At least you're not pining over him anymore."

Isolde laughed. "Indeed. I can thank Oz for that at least."

"And for the baby."

"Yes, very much for the baby."

"Do you want a boy or girl?" Pamela had one of each.

"I don't care in the least. Come," Isolde said, quickly rising. "Let me show you the layette we're assembling. The staff is over the moon at the prospect of a baby in the house."

"Good God, they know and haven't gossiped?"

"They know everything and haven't breathed a word. They're family." Isolde smiled. "Apparently, I'm to be protected."

"You must be the only one who ever was protected by their staff," Pamela replied with a lift of her brows. "My household thrives on gossip."

CHAPTER 24

TWO DAYS LATER, Grover handed Isolde a flyer. "Tattersalls is finally having the Deveral dispersal sale."

She scanned the single sheet. The old earl had died some time ago, but the family had been squabbling over the will. "The younger son lost out." He was a celebrated aficionado of the track.

"So it appears. The new earl is selling the entire stud."

"We must go, of course. I want that filly out of Persimmon."

"Everyone does."

"But I intend to acquire it."

"Yes, Miss Izzy," her steward said with an affectionate smile. "I thought you might."

She briefly debated the possibility of meeting Oz at so distinguished a sale, but her keen desire for that fleet-footed filly outweighed any awkwardness she might encounter. Certainly the London set knew Oz had left her. Nor was discord in aristocratic marriages uncommon. She was perfectly capable of facing down the tittle-tattle. "We'll go into London the night before. Have the house opened."

"Will we be staying?"

"Just the night." She smiled. "We'll bring the filly home directly."

A week later, Isolde and Grover entered the yard at Tattersalls where the sales were held, prepared to pay whatever was required to purchase the extraordinary filly.

The yard was crowded with every horse lover and breeder in England, Deveral's stable celebrated. Very few women were in attendance, which may have accounted for the throng parting like the Red Sea as Isolde and Grover made their way to an advantageous position bordering the courtyard. Or the silent attention as she passed may have had to do with the scandal of her marriage.

But Isolde ignored the stares and the buzz of conversation that rose behind her, having expected nothing less. Oz was well-known in the fashionable set; naturally his estranged wife would draw eyes. In fact, she'd specially dressed for the occasion, her new gown designed to accommodate her expanding bosom, the violet silk walking costume attractive with her fair hair. She particularly liked her new hat embellished with flowers; it was fresh as spring.

In the first round of bidding, Deveral's less illustrious thoroughbreds were sold off. The second round was just beginning when the main door into the yard opened, people turned to look, and a sudden hush fell over the crowd.

Oz had walked in with Nell on his arm.

Alerted by the tomblike silence, even the auctioneer having gone mute, Oz quickly scanned the crowd and saw Isolde. Without a word, he and his companion turned, reversed course, and shortly after he reappeared—alone.

Everyone in the breathless throng would have given anything to have heard the conversation between Oz and Nell. Lady Howe was a force unto herself; she did very much as she pleased and to have so readily deferred to Oz's wishes suggested a threat of huge proportions or a very expensive pound of flesh on Lennox's part.

The latter had been the case.

Making his way through the crowd, Oz emerged on the verge of the courtyard opposite his wife, braced his back against one of the marble columns supporting the loggia, and proceeded to bid on several of Deveral's prime racers. He'd bought six thoroughbreds when the filly, Pretty Polly, was finally led into the courtyard.

Pushing away from the column, he moved closer to the yard and was first to bid on the filly.

"Three thousand."

The sound of breaths sucked in wafted in the air.

He was starting high.

Grover glanced at Isolde, she nodded, and he said, "Four thousand."

Two other men came in at four thousand two, and four thousand four.

"Six," Oz said quietly, the sound clearly heard in the hushed courtyard.

"Seven." Isolde spoke up herself that time, her cheeks flushed, her sumptuous bosom gently rising and falling in her seething agitation.

"Nine."

"Ten." Crisp and taut, challenge in her lifted chin.

"Twelve."

No one else was bidding, the price outrageous; an entire, tolerable stud could be purchased for twelve thousand.

"Fifteen," she carefully said, her nostrils flaring, the fingers of her gloved hands tightly twined before her.

"Thirty."

A communal gasp swept through the crowd.

Abruptly spinning around, Isolde made her way through the throng, everyone leaping aside to let her pass—Grover in her wake. The moment the main door closed on her, conversation erupted in the Tattersalls yard.

Ignoring the busybodies and voyeurs, the curious and overcurious, the tittle-tattle and speculation, Oz walked up to the accounting clerk, spoke a few words to him, and swiftly followed his wife.

He didn't know why he was chasing after her, no more than he knew why he'd not let her have the filly. Sour discontent, exasperation, defiance, the fact that she looked like some voluptuous fertility goddess with her flamboyant breasts on display for all to see. That most of all.

Damn her!

Isolde was so bitter, rankled, and out of humor that on reaching the carriage she was literally quivering with rage. "I'm going to walk off my tantrum, Grover," she said through her teeth. "You take the carriage back."

"Are you sure, Miss Izzy?" He'd never seen her in such a pet.

Drawing in a deep breath meant to calm—ineffective as it turned out—she said tightly, "I'm sure. Please, Grover," she added more softly, "I wish to be alone."

"Yes, Miss Izzy," he replied, dutiful and loyal. But he stood by the carriage as she stalked off toward Hyde Park and watched her, concerned she was without an escort in the city. He glanced up at Dimitri. "We'll follow behind to see that's she's safe. Lennox bought the filly for thirty thousand."

Dimitri softly whistled. "Deliberately?"

"So it appeared."

"Maybe he cares after all."

"If he does, he has a queer way of showing it," Grover muttered. "Oh Christ!"

Dimitri turned his attention back from Isolde and saw Oz approaching.

"She's not here," Grover said, surveying Oz grimly as he stopped at the carriage.

Oz glanced into the carriage just to make sure, Grover's expression unfriendly as hell.

"She doesn't want to see you."

There, a speck of purple in the distance. Turning back to Grover, Oz gently said, "Why don't I ask her?"

"Don't make trouble," Grover growled.

"I thought I'd give her the filly." A sudden impulse, unrelated to logic or reason or Grover's growl.

"Then you should have let her buy it."

"I should have."

He started running.

CHAPTER 25

SHE HEARD THE racing footsteps as they neared, turned, came to a shocked standstill, and thought, *Why didn't I take the carriage?*

"I'm sorry," he said as he came up. "You can have the filly."

"I don't want her."

"You can have her anyway." *God, she looks good.*

"Why the sudden change of heart?"

He smiled; she rarely screamed when she was angry. She usually spoke in that cool voice of disdain. "Seeing you at close range makes me feel in charity with the world, darling."

"I'm not your darling. I believe Lady Howe is at the moment."

"I sent her home."

"Am I supposed to be appeased?"

He felt like saying, *You should be because it practically cost me an arm and a leg to get her to leave,* but he didn't because he was the transgressor. "Could we go somewhere and talk? Seeing you—"

"Reminds you of your impending fatherhood?"

"I was going to say, makes me think of you fondly until you effectively tempered those feelings," he said drily.

"I suspect you're just looking for a change of partners for the afternoon to avert the boredom. Perhaps fondness isn't a requirement after all."

He smiled, capable of overlooking arch derision for a greater purpose. "You might be right. You probably are. But you look delectable in that gown. Come talk to me at least; I'll attempt to restrain my baser instincts."

"Do you dare be seen with me?" she said, snide and abrasive. "How will you explain it to Nell?"

He never explained anything to Nell, but rather than aggravate his wife's fractious mood, he decided to eliminate some of the obstacles from the landscape. "Would it help for me to say I was sorry?"

"For which licentious offense? Surely you don't confine your amusements to Nell."

"How's Will if we're into full disclosure?" he acidly inquired, his gaze suddenly cool like hers.

"Annoying. Can you say the same for Lady Howe et al?"

"I could." A mirthless smile lifted one corner of his mouth. "But that wouldn't be very gentlemanly of me. How often does Will annoy you?" Fine-drawn malice at the last.

She softly sighed. "Why are we doing this? It can't matter in the least."

"No, I suppose not." Struggling to keep his temper in check, he reminded himself that Will was there before him and so it would remain. "Tell me," he diplomatically said, "how are you feeling?"

Her smile was heart-stopping when it shouldn't have been, when it shouldn't have mattered to him one way or another, when he'd been trying for weeks to forget that sunny smile.

"I'm feeling fruitful and happily pregnant. The staff has assembled a lovely layette and"—*short of missing you*, she thought—"I'm quite content. How about you?"

"Disgruntled and sullen. Although you could make me feel better." He smiled sweetly, better seduction than actual feeling. "Come, darling. I promise to behave if you wish. Talk to me, that's all. Davey can sit in the room with us if you like."

She shouldn't. She was just exposing herself to more heartache; he was more beautiful than ever even with the dark circles under his eyes. "I shouldn't," she said.

"I shouldn't have asked. Come anyway. We'll worry about the practicalities later."

"Don't you always."

He grinned. "I could think about changing for you."

It was smooth and suave and untrue. "No need for such a sacrifice," she said, smiling herself, suddenly jettisoning better judgment because she was being offered a few moments in Elysium. "Perhaps I can stop by for a short time."

"Thank you," he quietly said, surprised at the shocking degree of pleasure he felt. Offering her his arm, he half turned, raised his hand, and signaled for his carriage, which had been following behind.

"I should tell Grover," Isolde mentioned as he handed her into his closed landau a few moments later.

"Send him a message when we reach my house. Or would you like to drive back and tell him?"

"No, a message will do." It was too embarrassing to face her steward after succumbing so readily to Oz's invitation. But then love made one foolish.

Dimitri and Grover watched Oz's carriage drive up, watched Isolde step inside, looked at each other, and lifted their brows.

"It's good," Dimitri said. "She wants him. Why shouldn't she have him?"

"Because he doesn't want to be had," Grover muttered. "Damn him."

CHAPTER 26

As THEY ENTERED his house, Oz said to Josef, "Have Achille prepare some refreshments for my lady."

"That's not necessary," Isolde quickly interposed. "Really, I'm not staying long."

"He doesn't mind. Brandy for me, Josef. And send a message to—" He glanced at Isolde.

"Perceval House, Mayfair. Give Mr. Grover my direction."

"There now, all is in order," Oz pleasantly said. Leading her across the hall, he opened the door into a small drawing room. "Please make yourself comfortable."

She hadn't seen the little jewel of a room before, but then she'd not been in residence long and the house was very large. "How lovely." Standing on the threshold, she surveyed the octagonal room, brilliant with sunlight, the window walls framed with gilded moldings, the painted ceiling a pale blue sky filled with colorful birds.

"My mother's room," he said. "She painted."

"This?"

"Some of it." He eased past her. "Come, sit down. I'll

send the filly up to Oak Knoll tomorrow. Consider it an apology for my various sins."

"An expensive apology." She followed him in.

"Only because of my vicious temper," he said and turning, offered her his practiced smile. "I have no excuse. You'll enjoy her, though, so maybe the gods were in charge after all."

"Any special god?" Arch riposte to his facile smile.

Unmoved, Oz said, "Take your pick," then added in a more agreeable tone that took in account the reason he'd invited her here and the pleasure he felt for the first time in weeks, "Please, sit here." He indicated a sofa. "You can put up your feet."

"I don't *need* to put up my feet."

"Ah," he murmured, cool tempered to her pet. "That's how little I know about pregnancy. Sit where you wish then." Dropping onto the sofa, he swung his booted feet up onto the flowered chintz, crossed his ankles, and resting against the upholstered arm, slid into a comfortable sprawl. "I didn't know you had a house in town."

"I didn't know you had an estate in Kent." At Tattersalls she'd heard him order the first horses he purchased be sent there.

He smiled. "We should talk more."

Feeling her face flush hotly, she said with equal nonchalance, "If only there had been time." Taking a chair across the room from him, she smoothed her skirts over her knees in unconscious resistance to the beautiful, faithless man lounging on the pale flowered sofa in his mother's jewel of a room.

"There never is, it seems. Perhaps we could take a few minutes today to exchange confidences," he offered, impervious to her sarcasm. "Take off your lovely spring hat and stay awhile. I won't attack you, I promise."

"I wasn't concerned," she comfortably returned, untying the ribbons and placing her hat, purse, and gloves on a nearby table. Assuredly, Oz had never been obliged to attack a woman. "But I can't tarry long. Grover and I are driving home this afternoon. You look tired," she abruptly said when she shouldn't have, when she should have restrained her impulse. When Oz's needs were already sufficiently catered to by numerous women.

He didn't seem to notice or at least didn't resort to some quelling retort. He only said, "I haven't been sleeping well." Or much at all, those close to him would affirm. "Davey is working me hard; some of my business partners have turned difficult lately." An understatement of vast proportions. "Actually, I may have to go to India if the situation doesn't improve."

Her stomach lurched, and like some innocent young maid, she blurted out, "Will you be gone long?"

Ignoring his bride's outburst, he shrugged. "Who knows. It depends"—he exhaled a noiseless sigh—"on the degree of malfeasance in India. But Davey would stay behind, and if you need anything, he'd be available in my stead."

Not likely for the role she wished. "I appreciate your thoughtfulness." She said what was expected this time even as melancholy washed over her. Deep in her psyche the hope had burned that romantic dreams might become reality someday. And now—her cool and assured husband was leaving to go halfway across the world.

The small, lengthening silence spoke of absence along with the elaborate courtesy of not giving utterance to the thought.

Achille suddenly walked in, a footman in his wake.

"Ah, Achille, thank God, my brandy." Oz thrust out his hand. "That was quick," he said, grasping the proffered bottle and glass. "Isolde has come for a visit. Isn't that nice."

"Indeed. Hello, my lady. I brought you cake and sandwiches, and if you'd like I could make you something more substantial as well." He didn't say for the baby, but clearly that was what he meant.

Isolde blushed. "Cake and sandwiches will be fine. Oh,

that lovely chocolate ganache, I see," she murmured as the footman placed the silver tray on a table before her.

"The cherry cake as well, my lady. Enjoy." He swung to Oz. "Is there anything more?" he delicately inquired.

Oz shook his head, raised his glass to his mouth, and drained it.

Another small silence ensued once the door closed on Achille.

"He's been hoping you'd come back," Oz said into the hush. "He complains I don't eat."

"You should. You've lost weight."

"Tomorrow." He smiled and poured himself another drink. "Now tell me how things go at Oak Knoll."

As she ate, she spoke of her daily activities, the new cattle she'd bought, the visits she made, the small entertainments she'd attended, leaving out any mention of Will, concentrating instead on the farm and livestock.

He listened without reply, quietly drinking and watching her from under his lashes, restraining his impulse to get up, lift her from her chair, and carry her upstairs.

"Am I boring you?" she finally said.

"Not at all. I like the sound of your voice. I like to look at you. I'd like other things as well, but I promised to behave."

He might have reached out and touched her, her body's response so hot spur. "Don't," she said on a caught breath, setting down her teacup with such force the tea splashed on the cloth.

"Forgive me. I've missed you." He hadn't known until then just how much.

"You can't walk away like you did and then expect me to—"

"Make love to me?" he said with impeccable charm.

"I won't," she whispered, furious at his cool insolence, her astonishing willingness, at all the women in his life.

"How can it matter if you do?"

"Because I *dislike* what you are."

"That doesn't have to affect the pleasure or play."

"No, Oz. No!"

She was holding her hands tightly in her lap, as if white-knuckled restraint would serve as a deterrent to desire. *As if saying no actually meant no.* Setting his glass aside, he slowly came to his feet to play gallant to her desperate passions. Workmanlike and competent, he knew the signs of arousal, could recognize them blind in the dark.

A moment later he was lifting the small table away, and a moment after that, he leaned over, took her clenched hands in his, and drew her to her feet. "Feel my heart race," he said, placing her closed fists on his chest. "This is like the first time for me."

"No. I'm the thousandth, not the first."

He shook his head, the movement small and faint. "You're wrong. I've been waiting for you."

He shouldn't have said that, she thought, because she'd been waiting for him, for this, for the feel of his body next to hers, with utter, unequivocal longing since he'd left. The realization was so undeniable, tears welled in her eyes, and she sniffed and hiccupped, struggling to discipline her emotions.

"Don't cry," Oz whispered, gently wiping away the wetness trickling down her cheeks. "I'm sorry for whatever I did, for all I did, for what I didn't do—for everything."

"It's not . . . your fault . . . you walked into my room . . . that night."

"But I stayed." He smiled. "And then stayed some more." Abruptly picking her up, he said, "You may chastise me upstairs in more comfort." Carrying her effortlessly, he strode to the door, shoved it open with his foot, and walked toward the stairway.

How smooth he was, how pliant his conscience, how gracefully he offered pleasure. And if her heart wasn't involved she might argue, reject, and refuse. But she loved him, she understood now if she'd not known before, if by some spurious logic she'd discounted the truth in the past days and weeks. "I love you," she whispered, like some foolish, naive, overly sentimental female being carried off by her Prince Charming.

She felt him tense for a moment in his swift passage up the stairs.

"I love you, too," he said a fraction of a second later, telling himself words were only words, there was no point in being rude. He had what he wanted, and if in some small corner of his soul he acknowledged more than his sham nuptial tie, he was quick to dismiss that incomprehensible thought.

The door to his bedroom had been opened by some invisible hand, she noted when they arrived, although no servants had been evident as they traversed the quiet corridors. And a fresh bottle of brandy shared space on a small table near the bed with a tray of sweets and a carafe of scented tisane.

"They anticipate your every move," she said with a wave of her hand at the display. "Or are arrangements like this commonplace?" Did Nell like tisane?

He came to rest just inside the room, glanced at the delicate pastries, the mild aperitif. "On the contrary, this little offering is unprecedented. Achille wishes to please you. As do I," he added softly. "You have but to tell me what you want."

She knew better than to tell him the truth—that she wanted him beyond the perimeters of their agreement. "Would you think me terribly selfish if I asked for ten orgasms?"

Any other woman offered carte blanche would have been less modest in her demands; in his experience expensive jewelry generally led the roster. "No, of course not," he agreeably said. "Is that all?"

Her expression brightened. "Perhaps more then if you don't mind."

He smiled. "How much time do I have?"

"I'll let you know."

He liked that her timetable was vague; he liked more that she was in one of her insatiable moods.

Carrying her across the broad bedchamber, he reached the high four-poster bed and seated her facing him on the stark white coverlet embroidered with colorful tropical birds.

"This is different," she murmured, running her fingertip over a bit of scarlet silk embroidery replicating exotic plumage. The last time she'd been here, the coverlet had been pale blue.

"My mother's large collection of embroidered linens. The house is relatively unchanged." He shrugged. "I'm not home much."

He was too polite to say he didn't often sleep at home, she thought. "Your mother's decorative sense is lovely."

"Lovely like you," he said, abstractly exercising his charm, his focus on consummation. "You look very stylish today." He reached for the gold filigree button at the collar of her bodice.

"I found a new dressmaker."

Aware of his comment about her previous modiste, he ignored her pointed remark. "She's very good," he mildly said, his gaze flicking downward to her breasts before returning to her face. "It takes superb tailoring to contain such voluptuousness. You turned heads at Tattersalls. In fact," he added with a fleeting smile, "I expect every man there would like to be doing what I'm doing right now."

"Speaking of Tattersalls and sex, how did you dispatch Nell?" A blunt question perhaps, but she knew he wasn't about to throw her out in his current state of arousal—his erection impressive as usual.

His smile faded and he paused, his fingers motionless on the third ornate button. "She responds to money," he mildly replied, resuming his unbuttoning. "Unlike you."

"I have enough money."

He glanced up. "Apparently." He didn't say, *I know because you tried to buy my child.*

"I'm jealous of her when I shouldn't be, when your life is your own." Isolde envied his cool restraint, her own feelings in tumult.

"She means nothing to me, nor I to her."

How was it that he could cooly dismiss a woman linked with him by gossip and she didn't see him as heartless. She only saw the man she loved. Although, she'd be sensible to remember that this occasion was about sex, not love, and to that purpose, she said, "I shouldn't have mentioned Nell. It was tactless of me."

"Say anything you like." His smile was indulgent, his voice untouched by umbrage. "I'm just happy you're here." The buttons freed, he slipped the violet silk jacket over her shoulders, down her arms, and over her hands. Tossing the garment aside, he stood for a moment surveying her, a forceful sense of droit du seigneur suborning his better judgment. "Your breasts are—"

"Larger."

My property by law. "Stunning," he said instead, her splendid breasts straining the delicate silk of her chemise, his libido in a decidedly proprietary frame of mind. Locked rooms suddenly inviting his interest.

"Pamela tells me it's the first visible sign of pregnancy."

He took a small breath to steady his brutish impulses. "You're sure then, about the pregnancy."

She smiled. "Very sure."

An unmistakable concern entered his gaze. "Is it all right—that is . . . would there be any reason to—"

"Sex is permitted if that's what you're wondering."

He exhaled. "Good. Thank you," he simply said. "I'm very much a novice when it comes to this."

"We both are."

"Indeed," he softly agreed, the full impact of Isolde's pregnancy suddenly undeniable. His gaze examined her with naked interest. "If I should touch you in any way you find uncomfortable," he said, precise and delicate, "please let—"

"Oz, stop," she said with exasperation. "I'm just the same. Other than perhaps being slightly more demanding sexually," she added with a lift of her brows.

The term *sexually demanding* gave him pause when in the past he would have greeted it with delight. "Perhaps we should think about this. How can you be sure it's safe?"

"Good God! Don't tell me you've brought me this far to begin to equivocate! I won't allow it! Do you hear?"

He looked at her for a considering moment. "So I must perform no matter what," he said with a sliver of a smile.

"Surely it's no hardship."

"And if I don't?" he lightly inquired.

"Then perhaps I'll go somewhere else and—"

"Don't say it," Oz said in sudden anger, Will, too convenient, too available, as unmarried as he.

"I was joking. Unlike you," she said, her blue gaze direct and open, "I've not been entertaining at night."

He felt a fleeting surprise, followed by an elation he chose not to decipher. "I apologize. I spoke out of turn. Allow me," he blandly replied, "to render whatever services you require."

"I should reject such a cooly dispassionate offer. And if I wasn't so famished for sex," she said, leaning back on her hands and shrugging faintly, "I might. But you're here and I'm here and—"

"You're famished," he finished with a practiced smile. "I remember your charming impatience." Her uncorseted breasts were raised high in her languid pose, the taut nipples and plump contours conspicuous through the sheer white silk of her chemise. "And I'm not in the least indifferent to you. In fact, I'm deeply moved by your presence in my home and bed."

"While I look forward to being deeply moved by your presence in *me*," Isolde sweetly replied, amusement in her clear-eyed gaze.

"We always did agree on that," he drily said. "Even when all else was at odds."

He was standing quite still, his gaze unreadable. "I feel as though I'm negotiating something of grave consequence instead of an afternoon of sex," she said just a trifle shortly. "Is my pregnancy prompting your reluctance?"

"No—yes . . . no," he gruffly concluded. "I beg your pardon again." He smiled faintly. "I'd be very much obliged it you'd make love to me."

"Finally," she said. "I thought I might have to attack you."

He grinned. "An irresistible concept. If only I didn't prefer my own rules of war."

"War? Should I have come armed?"

"You already are, darling, in every way known to man." And reaching out, he grasped her bare shoulders, dipped his head, and kissed her with a fierce, pent-up desire he'd held in reserve the weeks past—apparently for her alone. His erection stood waist high, horniness and lust a hard, pulsing ache so intense he could feel the rush of blood coursing through his veins, his nerves oversexed and skittish. He attributed his unique response to Isolde's long absence, although the uncharacteristic involvement of his entire nervous system was staggering. Not that he gave a damn, though, when he was moments away from burying his cock in the hot little cunt that had haunted his dreams for weeks.

While she kissed him back with frenzied yearning, he smoothly untied the ribbon at the neckline of her chemise, unfastened the small buttons running down its front, and unwrapped her arms from around his neck long enough to slide off her chemise. "Your skirt," he said against her mouth as she clung to him once again. "Let go a minute."

She was feverishly panting as he freed himself from her fierce grip, the small irresistible sound ringing every randy bell in his libidinous memory as he quickly disposed of her skirt and petticoats.

Smiling up at him, her gaze heavy lidded and heated, she whispered, "No one else makes me feel this way—desperate and ravenous, weak with longing."

"Lucky me." He took pleasure in her admission when even the hint of exclusivity had been anathema to him in recent years. Untying her drawers, he slid them off along with her silk stockings; his weeks of deprivation were nearly at an end. Inhaling deeply, he cautioned himself to restraint—her condition and the battering ram of his libido a ruinous mix. "Are you sure ten orgasms might not be excessive?" Had he ever in his life opted for sexual moderation?

Her rampant desires running high, Isolde took a moment to fully comprehend his question and a moment more to breathlessly say, *"Excessive?"*

"Considering your, er, condition."

"Is ten too much for you?" Explicit demand in every acid syllable.

He smiled. "My darling little bitch." He flicked a finger downward. "You tell me."

The stretched fabric of his trousers sent an anticipatory shiver up her spine. "I thought London amusements may have sapped your vigor."

Whether she was goading him out of spite or toying with him mattered little now that the rules were clear. Ten and carte blanche. Kicking off his shoes, he pulled off his socks and shrugged out of his jacket.

"Hurry."

Ah, his imperious, randy wife of fond memory. "I am, darling." Swiftly unbuttoning his waistcoat and shirt, he pulled them off and dropped them to the floor.

"Oz, have pity," Isolde pleaded, her eyes half-shut, her hips undulating faintly, flame-hot need in her ragged whisper.

Wrenching open the last button of his trouser placket, he saw her clench her thighs together in an effort to repress the peaking turbulence. Experienced, he moved quickly, shoving her upward into the center of the bed, spreading her legs with an agile brush of his hands, and in seconds he was fully engulfed in her warm, honeyed sweetness.

Her blissful sigh echoed his soft grunt of pleasure.

"Please," she begged, leaving nail marks on his back, urging him on with little importuning whimpers. "Please, oh God, please . . ."

Where would you like me to go? But never one to contradict an impassioned female, he cautiously eased forward.

She gasped and he recoiled, his heart drumming in his chest.

"Don't you dare stop!" she hissed, bloodying his back in her impatience.

Ultrasensitive to the yielding resiliency of her vaginal tissue, scrupulously unselfish even in extremis, he moved forward warily—fucking pregnant women outside his area of expertise.

Not that there weren't decided advantages to the situation.

Coitus interruptus was no longer required.

Sex au naturel in all its glory. A first.

Less intellectually engaged, Isolde was in the grip of a hot, roiling passion inundating her senses in overwrought waves of pleasure, warming her heart and soul, offering her unprecedented rapture. Filled to overflowing, utterly gorged, Oz's virility and power gratifying every trembling nerve and cell, beguiling every impressionable sexual receptor, she was being transported toward orgasmic bliss with an expertise that anticipated her every wish.

Like now.

Sliding his hands under her bottom, he lifted her slightly, drove forward minutely, and reading her shuddering response, whispered, "Now darling, *now*."

His voice alone was enough to incite her palpitating genital nerves into an orgasmic spasm that hurtled through her vagina, up her spine, and spiked through her fevered senses in a wild, violent, long overdue climax.

She wondered after that first fast and furious orgasm

whether the raw, breathtaking ecstasy was due to Oz's long absence, her pregnancy, some flawless synthesis of hot lust and sweet love, or a combination thereof.

Then his grip tightened on her bottom, he dragged her closer, and shocked by the sudden prodigal sensation, her thoughts yielding to tempestuous feeling, she gave herself up once again to flame-hot avarice. Breathlessly clinging to him, her vagina silken with liquid desire, she melted around his hard, rigid length as he plunged deeper and deeper still, his rhythm practiced, facile, delicately expert.

In the ensuing velvety flux and flow, with her warm, soft body offering him all—bliss and ravishment, passion and raging fervor—the game of dalliance took on a capricious and volatile new scope. An unquenchable longing pricked his previous sangfroid; wistful sentiment overrode the sophisticated worldliness of carnal lust, and moments later, when he joined her second orgasm and poured his hot seed into her, the fury of his climax matched the ferocity of her screams.

Perhaps it was her wild cries that provoked his novel emotions, he decided afterward with postcoital pragmatism.

Or perhaps her voracious appetites gratified his vanity.

Or maybe she was nothing more than a rollicking change from Nell, he thought as his breathing slowed, reason returned, and he lifted his forehead from the mattress.

Isolde's lashes fluttered upward, her gaze heavy with languor and only inches away. "I may not survive many more of those," she whispered.

"I guarantee you will," he murmured, a smile twitching at the corners of his mouth, amorous play replacing quixotic emotion. "As I recall, your record is more than ten."

"Never like these. I feel as though I've been drugged."

"A good drug apparently," he drawled.

She shifted her hips the merest distance and smiled up at him. "You're still gloriously hard."

Oz smiled. "He likes you."

"I can tell." Oz's erection was undiminished. "Take off the

rest of your clothes . I want to feel your skin on mine—not just him"—she wiggled her hips—"but everywhere."

"At your service, ma'am." With a quick kiss, he withdrew, slid from the bed, and swiftly stripped off his trousers.

"Only at *my* service," she playfully charged. "Humor me, darling," she said to his suddenly cool gaze. "A half truth will do."

He bowed. "Consider me exclusively at your service, darling. I shall be a monk outside your company," he promised.

Her darling Oz—ever the graceful hunter. "How terribly sweet of you," she said with equal urbanity. Surveying his hard, muscled body nude save for his white linen underwear, she lazily arched her back and considered her next orgasm with explicit delight. "Wasn't it opportune that we both went to Deveral's dispersal sale. Otherwise we wouldn't be here enjoying—oh dear," she murmured, "I'm dripping on your bed. I need a towel and then you, my splendid stud. Or just you if you don't mind stickiness."

In his current mood, he'd willingly fuck her anywhere, anyway, but he also knew where to find towels, and moments later, naked now, his arousal freshly washed, the blood wiped from his back, he returned from the adjacent bathroom with an armful of white towels. He tossed them on the bed. "Stickiness makes no difference to me. You decide."

"How charmingly amenable."

Slipping off his rings, he grinned. "I intend to charm the hell out of you, darling, until you cry *stop* or I die trying."

Placing his rings on the bedside table, he joined her in bed, picked up a towel, glanced at her with raised eyebrows, and at her nod, wiped his semen from between her legs. "Ready?" he said, throwing the towel on the floor.

"I'm not only ready, I'm shamelessly besotted, ravenously lustful, and indifferent to everything but having your cock inside me."

He laughed. "Tell me how you really feel."

"Why shouldn't I when I see you so seldom. The point, it

seems to me, is to take full advantage of your splendid capacity for fornication." Reaching up, she patted his cheek. "Now be a dear and do what you do so well."

For a brief moment he took issue with her flippancy but quickly decided there was no point in splitting hairs. He was what he was, and realistically, sexual pleasure always took precedence over minor affront. "Speaking of seldom seeing you, allow me to scrutinize this newly maternal body of yours. I'm intrigued."

She smiled. "You're a neophyte, as am I. But be my guest, although I warn you, I'm much more easily aroused in my fecund state. I masturbate more." Her brows flickered sportively. "You should come home. I could use you."

A more tempting invitation had never been offered him. And he said so.

"But," she murmured.

"I have my business in town," he answered with well-mannered courtesy. "Otherwise I'd be more than willing to take over the duties of stud for you."

She sighed with a touch of drama. "Alas, then, I must take full advantage of these hours." She threw her arms wide, spread her thighs, and grinned. "Touch me at your risk and my pleasure."

He laughed, her candor delightful, along with her unquenchable craving for sex. Not to mention her comment about masturbation suggested Will wasn't a constant in her bed—pleasant thought. Lightly brushing his palms over her flat belly, he said, "Nothing shows here yet."

"It's too early, Pamela tells me."

"But these are sumptuous and flourishing." He covered her breasts with his hands, fingers splayed, and experienced a warm content as her eyes went shut and she softly moaned.

How compatible they were when it came to sex.

His cock was always at full mast when his darling wife was near.

It almost made one contemplate marriage with fondness.

"Your nipples are bigger," he said, gently stroking the taut pink crests. "Do they feel different?"

She smiled up at him. "Everything feels different. More sensitive and tender, oversensitive at times," she answered, arching her back against the tingling tremors sliding downward from Oz's gentle stroking to her pulsing sex. "You're a man of finesse, are you?"

"I try to be. Would you prefer roughness?" he asked, his gaze speculative.

"Heavens no. Whatever you're doing is sublime. Do. Not. Stop."

"Yes, ma'am," he happily said.

"And you needn't look so smug."

"No, ma'am."

"Arrogant bastard," she grumbled.

"Uh-uh. Grateful as hell, darling, to have you in my bed."

She smiled. "You can be *such* an absolute sweetheart."

He didn't feel it useful to contradict her; he was very much not a sweetheart, as any of his acquaintances would testify. "Thank you. We try," he said instead. "See if this is sweet enough for you." Bending his head, he drew her left nipple into his mouth, slid his hand between her legs, found the nub of her clitoris with his forefinger, and began to softly suck on her jewel-hard nipple.

She was right about the changes pregnancy had wrought on her sensitivity levels. It was almost too easy to make her climax; very little of his virtuoso skills were required to send her over the edge. She literally climaxed in seconds.

He glanced at the clock on the bedside table from under his lashes as he switched his ministrations from her left nipple to the right, as he redirected his attentions to her swollen clitoris once again. The image of a fertility goddess in all her voluptuary ostentation entered his consciousness, reminded him of erotic temple sculpture back home, reminded him even more vividly of his youthful pilgrimages to shrines and sanctuaries that extolled the glories of sexual enlightenment.

It took considerable restraint to suppress his selfish impulses as his erection swelled higher. But Isolde's appreciation for his largesse was so lavishly profuse after each of her several precipitous orgasms that he honestly replied, "It's my pleasure, darling."

"You're outrageously benevolent," she breathed, brushing his cheek with her fingers. "I must be making up for lost time; I don't how to thank you enough."

As he lay propped on one elbow beside her, he almost said, *You're having my child. That's thanks enough.* But relatively sober, he wasn't lost to all reason. "You can thank me later."

"Just tell me what you want me to do. Really—anything."

"You probably shouldn't say that to me right now," he said, his voice a low rasp.

"You don't frighten me. You're not at all like your reputation."

"You encourage my better impulses."

"In contrast to those—"

"Who don't." At which thought, all the untidy perversions in his life came to mind. "I need a drink. Would you like a tisane?"

He was already off the bed and halfway to the brandy bottle. "Was it something I said?" she teased.

She seriously complicated his life, his future, and his peace of mind. Fortunately, there was a time limit to her visit, he decided, pouring himself a drink. Drinking it down, he grimaced at the odd taste in his mouth, and poured another to wash away the sour, acidic tang. Then, carrying the plate of sweets, he set it on the bed, went back to bring the carafe, a cup, and his brandy. Sprawling on the bed beside her a few moments later, he said, "Try the strawberry ones. They're the best."

"I will. I'm hungry all the time now. Would you like one?" She held up a small tart.

He leaned forward and she put it in his mouth.

As they ate, a small, increasingly uncomfortable silence fell.

"If you have something else to do," she said in the awkward hush.

"No." Curt and abrupt. "No, nothing at all," he added in a more conciliatory tone. "I seem to be having trouble with my temper today. It's not your fault. Please stay. You bring me pleasure."

"The pleasure you give me is oceans wide, darling. I'd love to stay."

"Do you sail?" He chose a subject less fraught with sentiment.

Recognizing she'd overstepped the bounds of amorous play, she gracefully said, "I'm a farmer, darling. Sailing's outside my normal venues."

He grinned. "And a very lovely farmer at that. I'll take you sailing sometime if you like. I have a yacht at Dover."

She couldn't say *I'd sail to the ends of the earth with you* without causing him alarm. "When the weather becomes warmer perhaps." She congratulated herself on her measured reply. Her acting skills were improving.

"Anytime. Just let me know. I'll send a carriage for you."

If he could affect the role of bland acquaintance, she could as well. In terms of their future child, it would be useful to cultivate a cordial relationship. "Do you ever think of our child?" she impulsively asked. "Sorry," she quickly said at his startled look. "You needn't answer. I have no wish to provoke you with my pleasure at stake."

"Don't worry. I'm not exactly uninvolved in terms of pleasure. As for the child"—he lifted his shoulder in the faintest shrug—"the answer is no. I've not yet come to terms with the notion, although I'm sure I will with time," he diplomatically remarked. *Depending on the identity of the father.* "Have you tried the almond tarts?" Picking up the plate, he held it out to her. "They're excellent."

"Thank you." With talk of babies having been politely but summarily curtailed, she took a tart. "Where do you usually sail?" she inquired, as capable as he of casual conversation.

"Anywhere. North to Scotland occasionally, across to Calais at times on my way to Paris, to the Isle of Wight during race week."

"To India?"

"No."

His instant withdrawal was palpable. "Maybe you should pick the topic of conversation," she said quickly.

"Or we could dispense with talk."

"As you wish, of course." Her faint smile was sardonic.

"You don't mean it."

"I want sexual satisfaction from you, and to that end," she said frankly, "I mean it. You set the agenda."

"Even at the risk of offending you?"

She lifted one brow. "Better my temper than yours."

"That's true. Are you finished?" He nodded at the plate of sweets.

"I certainly can be."

His grin this time held a degree of warmth. "Do I detect a renewed interest in sex?"

"I wouldn't say renewed so much as persistent. I didn't wish to pressure you while you were relaxing."

He beat down the resurgent image of a locked room with his wife inside, waiting for him, for sex—her unquenchable passions a libertine's dream. "Why don't you put that away," he suggested with a nod at the food, "and we can get back to business."

He watched her gather the items on the bed, taking note of the subtle changes in her body. Her sumptuous form was even more curvaceous now, her hips rounder, her waist slightly less slender, her plump breasts ripening and enlarging in anticipation of the future babe. That may or may not be his.

"Do you want me to take your glass?"

Startled from his musing, he saw her point to his glass.

"Penny for your thoughts."

"I was admiring your beauty," he urbanely said, handing over his glass.

"Thank you. I, in turn, appreciate your magnanimity." Setting the glass on the silver tray, she returned and climbed back onto the bed. "You're much, much better than my dildo."

"I should hope so," he negligently said, "or all my practice has gone for naught."

"Let me assure you it hasn't. You're the very best, darling, not that my experience is as wide and varied as yours, but—"

"Pray desist from mentioning your experience," he brusquely returned.

She mimicked locking her mouth. "I apologize most profusely."

"Because you need me."

"Very, very badly as a matter of fact."

Such unequivocal eagerness required a moment of restraint to curb his first intemperate impulses. Would *anyone* assuage her sexual yearning? He didn't allow himself to answer that question, although his temper showed in his voice as he tautly commanded, "Up on your hands and knees then."

She immediately complied, curtness marked in his soft order. When he neither moved nor touched her for some moments, driven by her own intemperate needs, she glanced over her shoulder. "Is there something more?"

"No," he gruffly replied, struggling to curb his treacherous thoughts. Her need for sex was insatiable, damn her, and talk of dildos aside he suspected that Will might be a frequent visitor at Oak Knoll after all. *Breathe in, breathe out, relax. Keep in mind she might be the mother of your child; taking out your temper on her isn't right, proper, or even legal anymore.*

Coming up on his knees, he moved behind her. Running his hands over the soft, silken curves of her bottom, he slid one finger over the slippery wetness of her pouty vulva—what he viewed as her eternal readiness evident in the sleek, hot flesh. As if further testing her receptiveness—unnecessarily, he sullenly thought—he gently stroked her prominent clitoris, and at her shuddering gasp, a covetous jolt pulsed up his cock.

The worst kind of heavy-handed tyranny suddenly over-whelmed his senses, the feelings unnatural for a man who generally played at love. For some ungodly reason, Isolde brought out the brute in him. He should send her home before he hurt her.

Then like a sorceress inducing him to succumb, he heard her soft plea.

"Please, Oz, I need you," she implored, impelled by her own demons, lust a constant whenever she was within sight of her husband, reason yielding to incomparable need.

He took a deep breath, still marginally in control. "I might hurt you."

"You won't. You can't. Please, Oz," she whispered. "I'm not in the least fragile."

"In the event you turn out to be wrong, scream or hit me if I get out of hand," he cautioned. "I mean it."

"I'll hit you if you don't give me what I want," she hotly retorted, swiveling around to glare at him, wanton desire an irrepressible pulsing ache inside her. "I don't need politesse. I need you *now!*"

Could any man refuse? Although the fact that she suddenly reached behind her, grabbed his erection in a fierce hard grip, and swung her hips back to meet the swollen crest of his cock served as added incentive.

And quickly resolved his qualms.

At which point, he obliged her or she obliged him; it wasn't absolutely clear who ultimately did what to whom. But he rammed into her luscious cunt as he'd promised himself he wouldn't, and she welcomed the hard, lusty pounding with an equally gluttonous fervor.

Neither had ever felt such desperation, nor equated sex with violence, or felt the smallest impulse to engage in wild, brute fornication with others. But then neither had ever felt the faintest jealousy with anyone else or cared so much as to be desperate—not that such outré emotions were acknowledged in the course of the fiery, tempestuous mania that re-sembled a combat zone more than what passed for dalliance in the fashionable world.

When Oz eventually climaxed, his ejaculation left him momentarily lightheaded and gasping for air.

Isolde hadn't thought her orgasms could get any better, but this one did, shocking her senses with a hot, intense blaze of glory and a flying-too-close-to-the-sun ferocity that left her prostrate.

"I should move," Oz murmured, semicollapsed on her back, his weight lightly supported above her.

"Don't," she breathed, shifting slightly to better feel his hard cock. "You feel wonderful."

"Speaking of wonderful." Flexing his thighs, he forced his erection deeper, gently testing the limits of her vagina. "You keep me in constant rut."

"And that's a good thing."

"How good." He drove deeper.

"Better than anything."

"Damn right," he whispered, his voice husky. "I've been thinking of locking you in a room and keeping you here for sex."

"I might let you."

"You might not have a choice."

"Better yet." She felt his laugh on her back and inside her, and if it were possible to measure pleasure and happiness, hers would run off the charts.

"My bewitching little wife. How the hell do you do it?"

"I could ask the same of you. Perhaps it's karma."

She wondered afterward what in those few words had ir-revocably altered the mood. She never did know, but he sud-denly withdrew, shoved a towel between her legs, and left the bed to pour himself another drink.

He didn't throw her out; he wasn't so discourteous. He just reverted to the charming, practiced rogue who enjoyed sex, who gave pleasure in full measure, who amused with cool versatility and politesse.

Whether he actually counted her orgasms or not, there came a time when she saw him glance at the clock twice in a short span of time.

"Grover's going to be wondering what happened to me," she tactfully noted, kissing him lightly on the cheek as he lay beside her, resting from their most recent climax. "I can't thank you enough for your hospitality this afternoon."

His dark lashes lifted, and turning his head, he smiled at her. "Come again. You're always welcome."

A dismissal, however gracious.

In the course of their dressing, he spoke of trivialities with an urbanity that bespoke of other times like this when leave-takings had turned awkward.

He helped her with her toilette, laying out a brush and comb, shaking the wrinkles out of her skirt with a practiced hand, offering to have his servants iron her gown if she wished.

"No, that's not necessary," she said, thinking he always knew the right tone to take. "The long drive home will only add more wrinkles anyway." And she accepted the comb he held out to her with a smile.

CHAPTER 27

A SHORT TIME later, standing utterly still in the vast entrance hall devoid of servants, Oz said, "I'd be happy to accompany you back to Perceval House." He was barefoot, dressed only in a shirt and trousers, his hands loose at his sides, his gaze completely shuttered.

Like his heart, Isolde thought. "Please don't," she said, conscious of the dearth of servants, wondering if he'd been expecting a scene. "It would only make things worse."

There was no reply that wouldn't offend. But he murmured "Thank you for coming" very softly and meant it—that small corner of his soul momentarily exposed.

"You're entirely welcome." Her reply was neutral, as if they'd completed some business transaction of no consequence. Then she glanced at the door, Oz quickly moved to open it, and looking out, she saw Sam waiting at the curb.

A moment later, as the carriage pulled away, Oz closed the door and turning on his heel, swiftly made for the bathroom off the entrance hall where he was violently sick.

When it was over, he was white and shaking, gasping for

breath. Pushing himself off his knees, he slowly rose to his feet and walked to the green travertine sink. The man in the mirror was wan and gaunt with dilated eyes, his skin moist with sweat. He looked away, turned the faucets on full, rinsed out his mouth, then shoved his head under the stream of hot water until he stopped shaking. Straightening, he smoothed his wet hair back with his palms, wiped his face with a towel, and walking out into the hall, said to Josef, "Don't let anyone in you don't know."

"A problem, sir? Do you need help?" Oz was sweating profusely.

"Not just yet." And he made for the kitchen, sheer will keeping him upright.

Once there, he waved for Achille to follow him into his apartment and told him to shut the door. As Achille gazed at him with alarm, Oz sat down heavily, spread his arms on the kitchen table as if for support, and lifting his black gaze, said, "I just retched up a deal of blood along with my breakfast. My guts are raw and mutilated. I'm wondering who poisoned me."

"Christ! You need a doctor!"

"No. There's nothing he can do anyway. I need to know if we have any new help in the kitchen, in the house, for that matter. Have any tradesmen you don't recognize been around lately—anyone out of the ordinary?"

"I haven't noticed, but I'll ask the staff. Let me get you something—water, coffee, lemon juice and sugar?"

"Water—bottled." Oz followed Achille with his eyes as he hastened to a cabinet. "I'm dying of thirst. Thank you," he said a second later as Achille handed him a bottle of Apollinaris, uncapped as he watched.

As Oz drank a small amount, his swallowing impaired by the poison, Achille said, "Someone in India ordered this. Do you know who?"

Oz blinked to clear his blurred vision. "The lovely cartel trying to take over my banks, of course."

"Have they tried before? You were sick a few mornings ago."

"I don't know." His voice was weak, the room wavering around him. "I thought I'd just drunk too much. But this time there's no question—I've all the symptoms. My heart's racing, my eyes are dilated so much the light hurts, blurred vision, can't swallow."

"Belladonna," Achille said shortly—a favorite in India. "You threw up, though. That should help."

Neither man said what they were thinking; there was no known antidote.

"Here's hoping." Oz clenched his fists against an involuntary tremor convulsing his body. "I feel like shit."

"We *should* call a doctor."

Nothing moved in Oz's braced body but his gaze. "No."

"I'll make you some broth. Something to soothe your stomach."

Oz grinned faintly. "Not unless you kill the cow yourself. Do you have some cans of anything?"

Achille looked affronted, then quickly said, "I'll go out and buy some soup myself. I'll open the can in your room, warm it on the grate."

"Later. I feel like sleeping."

Achille knew better than to express his disquietude. Oz had slept erratically or not at all for weeks. The poison must be taking its toll. "We'll watch over you. Don't say a word; none of us wants you to die in your sleep." Convulsions, coma, and death—in that order—were typical of belladonna poisoning.

"Least of all, me." Oz's brows flickered. "Especially after my wife's very agreeable visit. Perhaps I can induce her to call on me again."

Achille scowled. "She would have stayed if you hadn't sent her away."

"Romantic soul," Oz said gently. "No, she wouldn't have."

"Surely you could have convinced her. She's having your child for Christ's sake."

"Ah—the mystery child."

"You're an ass," Achille said with disgust. "But time enough to lecture you when you're not on your deathbed. You're going to faint where you sit."

Oz raised weary eyebrows. "How kind of you to notice. Now, could we get back to more relevant issues? Throw out all the food and liquor—particularly the brandy. It tasted like hell. My enemies chose to poison the liquor, I expect. Fortunately, Isolde drank nothing but tea. Dispose of everything where some scrap man doesn't scavenge it and die because of me. In the morning—the gods willing—I'll deal with my detractors."

"I'll send a telegram to my friends in India."

Achille had met a motley crew during his sojourn in the Maldives.

"Thank you, but no," Oz said. "My relatives will take care of my enemies in Hyderabad for me." Oz supported an extended family of second and third cousins in India in regal splendor. They, in turn, were grateful, not to mention capable of retaliation—subtle or cold-blooded; Oz's sense of vengeance was equally vindictive. "And I'll talk to Davey and Sam about my London rivals." If he lived, those who'd done this to him would regret it.

But grey with pain he did nearly faint when he rose from his chair, and instead of going to his office, Achille helped him to his bedroom. Davey and Sam arrived shortly after, both careful to disguise their apprehension at Oz's appearance. His skin was turning blue as he sat in bed, his hair damply matted on his head, and even with a quilt thrown over his shoulders he was shivering uncontrollably.

"You know the names of those in the cartel, Davey. Find their cohorts here in town." He inhaled deeply, and the men saw the effort it took to speak. "I'll see them tomorrow. Send a telegram to my relatives in Hyderabad. They know what to do."

"You have to drink liquids to rinse the poison from your system," Sam said, clutching at straws, knowing the poison as well as anyone, knowing it was too late.

"I will, thank you," Oz politely said, the toxins already in every cell and tissue, in his coursing blood and ravaged guts.

"Don't worry, sir, Sam and I'll take care of everything," Davey interposed. "No one must have thought to mention your size. It may have saved you."

"We'll see." Oz's voice was very weak. "Are . . . we . . . done?" He lay back, his rapid pulse making his head spin; whoever had done this to him was of less concern right now than trying to keep his lungs working.

"We're done," Sam firmly said, signaling to Davey that he was staying.

Oz's secretary looked back as he followed Achille from the room, a last question on his lips.

But Oz was already sleeping or unconscious or dying.

Sam, Achille, Davey, and Josef took turns watching Oz that night, fearful he might stop breathing—the drug capable of paralyzing the nervous system. Or he could deteriorate further into a coma. More than once during the long night, they considered sending for his wife.

But ultimately, none dared breach the barricades Oz had erected against sentiment after Khair's death and those of his parents.

None of his attendants slept that night, each intent on making Oz as comfortable as they could: changing the bed-clothes when they became soaked, offering him water when he'd wake in a daze with dry lips and a parched mouth, talking to him in his delirium, offering succor when his nightmares raged.

Everyone watched the clock, waiting for sunrise, as if daylight signaled a degree of success. And whether it did or not, everyone exhaled a sigh of relief when dawn broke.

Oz had survived the night, his breathing was improved, as was his color; he was sweating less, and the convulsions had stilled. That he was young and strong was in his favor. They were all hopeful now when they hadn't been so many times during the long hours of the night.

Sam left to marshal his men, Davey to see if he had any responses to his telegrams, Achille to personally shop for Oz's breakfast. While Josef sat with Oz, thinking as always that his young master reminded him more of his mother than his father; no blunt, sober, reliable Lennox lay before him, although the former baron had unequivocally loved his rebellious, intemperate son. Oz had all his mother's charm; they could both delight with word and smile. And now the young boy he'd watched grow to manhood would live to see *his* child born, Josef pleasantly thought. He was in touch with the staff at Oak Knoll, as would be any conscientious retainer.

Oz woke to find Achille cooking his breakfast over the bedroom grate. "Scrambled eggs the way you like them," his chef said, smiling over his shoulder. "I bought and cracked every egg myself."

"I can't be dead," Oz croaked, "because I feel so bloody rotten."

"You'll feel better after you eat."

Oz turned his head, was gratified to find that his eyeballs didn't explode, and slowly pushed himself up into a sitting position. He was lightheaded and unsteady, and everything from head to toe that could ache, ached. "I think," he said, conscious of his stench, "first I need a bath." Carefully swinging his legs over the side of the bed, he waited until the ringing in his ears stopped before he tried to stand.

Achille was at his side, his arm out to steady him. "You're hard to kill."

"My enemies will discover that to their regret," Oz said, waving away his help, closing his mind to the pain. "Catch me if I fall, and thank you, by the way. You haven't slept, I presume."

"I will tonight. One question," Achille said with a grin, walking beside Oz as he made for the bathroom. "If you don't mind."

"I fear something vulgar with that grin. Would it help if I said I minded?"

"Not after all the years we've known each other. I was just wondering how you managed to function during your wife's, er, visit when you were being laid waste by poison?"

Oz smiled. "At first belladonna stimulates the central nervous system, and later," he said, exquisitely sardonic, "although the effort was increasingly harrowing, the prize was worth the discomfort."

CHAPTER 28

JUSTICE WAS SWIFT and efficient, Oz directing it with no fuss and a carafe of ice water on the desk by his right hand.

The five men who had the most to gain from his death had been brought together by various means, from their homes or clubs, offices or mistresses' beds, one from his morning ride in Rotten Row. They were now seated, sweating and fearful, in a row of hard-backed chairs opposite Oz's desk in the building that housed his shipping line. Sam, Davey, and Sam's troops lined the walls.

It was early morning—not yet nine—Oz was fed and fresh from his bath, his tailoring impeccable, his smile bland, his hands loose on the smooth mahogany before him; only his cold-eyed gaze reflected his vicious state of mind. •

"I have no intention of hurting you," he began when the silence had become unendurable to the coerced men who had never before been treated with such violence, who had only given orders to brutalize others from the safety of their fine homes or offices. "Unless you choose to be uncooperative. As you see, I survived your attempt on my life. Allow me to point out that I'll not be so derelict should it be necessary to end yours." He offered them a look of serene and arrogant calm. "I hope I make myself clear. Now then, as to your associates in India——they are no more; my relatives are less lenient than I. Pray take a moment to acknowledge the good health you still enjoy because of me."

No one moved, not his captives, nor his retainers, the air crisp with catastrophe.

After the small pause allowed for personal reflection, Oz pleasantly said, "I should kill you all. Normally I would with any man so stupid as to try and rob me of my banks. If you continue to press me, I *will* kill you *and* perhaps your families as well. I suggest you watch what you eat, what your wife and children eat, watch the servants who attend you, the retainers at your clubs, anyone who gives you a cup of tea, a plate of food, a glass of wine. If you don't already know fear, make another attempt on my life and you'll know it with certainty. Then you'll die." He exhaled softly. "Now get out."

There was a ragged moment of silence.

The prominent, influential men who set great store on their consequence, who had always felt the execution of the law was in their own hands, looked white-faced one to the other, unsure whether to move, terrified they might suffer for such a misstep. The young man before them was half their age or younger even, indifferent to their prestige and power, unforgiving, violent.

"You'll be watched," Oz said, visibly impatient now. "Every movement, every minute. *Now go.*"

Then he leaned back in his chair and shut his eyes.

A few minutes later the room was silent.

"Christ, we're going to have to hire a bloody army to watch them all," Oz said into the quiet.

"Fortunately, it won't be a problem."

Eyes still closed, Oz smiled. "How many times is that now," he wearily said, "that wealthy swindlers have set out to rob me of my fortune?" Then he opened his eyes, clasped his hands lightly on the desktop, and said with the extraordinary degree of self-control that only rarely deserted him, "One too many. I should have killed them."

"You should have." Sam stood alone by the door, the throng dispersed. "You're young; they think you're vulnerable."

"Next time I will," Oz said flatly, pushing himself out of his chair, his strength depleted, the effort it took to come down to his office and deal with his adversaries costing him dearly. "We'll prepare the surveillance lists at home." Moving around the edge of his desk, he slowly walked to the door. "I wonder what my wife's doing while we're chastising the extortionists of the world?" he said with a sudden smile.

"Farming."

Oz laughed. "Christ, I forgot. You're right."

SAM WAS HALF-RIGHT.

Isolde was following her head gardener, Forbes, through the drifts of daffodils that ran down her south lawn to the river.

"Just a wee bit farther, Miss Izzy. You ain't never seen such a sight. Now hush, mind, or they'll hear us."

As they reached the border of the lawn, where the daffodils gave way to a small copse of beeches planted long ago by an earlier Wraxell, the gardener put his finger to his mouth and then pointed.

Following the line of his arm, Isolde peered through the dappled shadows under the trees and saw the rare sight promised by old Forbes, who'd seen all there was to see on the Wraxell lands. On a bed of green moss, in the curve of its mother's body, lay a snow-white fawn, tiny and delicate. Isolde unconsciously sucked in her breath, and the small sound brought the doe's head up.

She and Forbes stood motionless, scarcely breathing, until the doe's attention returned to her fawn. Then, slowly backing away until they were out of range, they returned to the house.

Standing on the drive, Forbes said, "I were wondering if'n we should snare the pair and carry them into the paddock so the young'n ain't harmed by the hounds or mayhap a wild pig."

"It might disturb them too much; the fawn looks new-born."

"Still, miss, yon might be kilt if we don't take a hand."

Isolde softly sighed, the helplessness of the little fawn triggering a rush of maternal emotion. "Moving them could be traumatic. Might food be set out for the doe without frightening her? Then she wouldn't have to leave the security of the copse."

"Mayhap we could."

She couldn't tell if he agreed or was being polite. "Talk to Grover. I'll defer to his judgment."

"Yes'm."

But she couldn't rid her mind of the tender image—the vulnerable fawn and protective mother, the aching beauty of the scene. Or maybe seeing Oz yesterday made her more susceptible to emotion. She should have been sensible and refused him, but then what woman could? He made the world disappear with a smile or a single word; she had no proof against such disarming appeal. But allowing him to entice her into his bed, to have yielded to his sweet and versatile talents only made her sense of loss worse.

She had in the weeks since he'd left her reconstructed her life; she'd even thought she'd reached a stage of rational equilibrium where she could meet him with stoic self-command.

And now those barricades must be erected all over again.

As defenseless as the young fawn, as vulnerable, she went to the nursery that was being prepared for her child—for Oz's child—and shutting the door behind her, sat in the rocker that had been brought out of storage, and quietly broke down and cried.

She'd had the misfortune to fall in love with a man who

was adored by every woman who came within range of his magnetic, effortless charm. And with the exception of their passionate sexual encounters, he otherwise treated her as he did all women once the heat of desire had cooled—with patient kindness . . . until they left.

She wondered if he ever thought of her—of his child.

Or if she and the child were forgotten as were all the other women.

She wondered if it was only vanity that had tears leaving wet paths on her face but knew better before the thought was even finished.

It was unfortunate, that was all.

She'd fallen in love with a man who, once the sexual play was over, could ignore with equanimity the displeasure of a great number of women. And would continue to do so in the future.

That her eyes were open to his faults did not in any fashion absolve her from the ensuing heartache.

A timid tap on the door interrupted her gloomy thoughts, and quickly wiping the wetness from her cheeks, she said, "Enter."

It was Grover, who out of politeness averted his gaze. "You'll be pleased to know that the fawn and mother are safe, Miss Izzy. Forbes said you'd wish to know."

"Yes, thank you," she answered, her self-possession restored. "Did you bring them into the paddock?"

"No. We gently nudged them along until they entered the sanctuary of the old oak grove. It's fenced high, and once the fawn is older, the gate can be opened again. They're quite safe."

Isolde smiled, more relieved than she would have thought over a wild creature, more relieved than she would have been a few weeks ago when babies were far from her thoughts. "How wonderful. Thank everyone for me."

The staff knew what had happened yesterday, of her visit to Lennox House. Her melancholy since acquainted them with the outcome of the visit. Grover briefly debated revealing his second bit of news.

She saw the hesitation. "Is there more?"

"Pretty Polly just arrived," he quietly said. "She's in the stable if you'd like to see her."

It took considerable effort to hold back her tears, to speak with composure, but if she were to surrender to grief at every thought or mention of Oz, she'd be crying from morning to night. "Thank you, Grover. I'll be out to see her directly."

"She's a right fine beauty," he said, his manner more comfortable with his mistress's calm reply. "She'll win you a monstrous number of races."

"Yes, I expect she will. It was very generous of Oz."

Grover bowed and quickly left; Miss Izzy's bottom lip had begun to tremble.

A quarrel erupted in the kitchen a short time later, some of the staff advocating that Miss Izzy's errant husband be kidnapped and brought back to her bound hand and foot. Others cautioned calm, saying Miss Izzy would never agree to coercion to keep her husband. They all glumly agreed, though, that she loved him.

A sentiment in accord with those of their mistress, who was surveying the nursery one last time before making her way downstairs. As she closed the door on the newly painted murals, the fresh carpets and curtains, the Tudor cradle brought downstairs, the shelves filled with new books and old, she sensibly reminded herself that very few marriages— whether ones of convenience like hers or those marked by normal bonds—were founded on love or long sustained by love. Hers was no different.

Once the child was born, her marriage would cease to be in any event.

And with it, the useless debate.

CHAPTER 29

IN THE FOLLOWING days, Oz recuperated, worked long hours with Davey and Sam, shocked everyone by no longer drinking, and irritated one and all at Brooks's by continuing to win every game he played. By the end of the week he was considerably richer, not that it mattered.

Not that anything seemed to matter.

He even took no joy in his enemies' discomfort. Sometimes he thought he should have killed them and been done with it for all the satisfaction the role of warder afforded him.

Jess alone gave him pleasure. Oz had taken to coming down to the kitchen during the day with some new toy to entertain the young boy. He'd sprawl on the floor and talk softly to Jess as he entertained him with the new trinket. Or sometimes he'd just silently watch the toddler absorbed in play.

The little fair-haired boy was Oz's restorative in a hindered world, indulging the toddler affording him uncomplicated pleasure, buoying his spirits. In more brooding moments, though, he recognized that Isolde's child might be neither brown haired like Will, nor dark like him, but bright haired like its mother. What then of the father's identity?

And how much did he care?

The first time the treacherous question entered his consciousness, he dismissed it out of hand. But the troublesome thought returned, restive and refractory, perfidious.

Demanding an answer.

Which he didn't have.

ONE NIGHT OVER cards at Marguerite's, with all the players drunk but Oz, the Earl of Barton, too inebriated to know better, unwisely said, "Sober again, Lennox? Can't call yourself a man if you don't drink."

The silence was thick enough to touch.

Oz set down his cards, leaned back in his chair, and gave all his attention to the earl, who'd belatedly noticed the sudden quiet. Then Oz unexpectedly smiled, glanced back at Marguerite who stood behind him, and gently said, "Bring me a bottle, darling. I do believe Barton's right. Sober, the world's exceedingly grim."

Marguerite closed her doors to the earl after that gross stupidity.

Whether a moment of truth had transpired or the strain of sobriety had reached crisis point, Barton's drunken remark served as impetus for Oz to revert to his former regimen; brandy at breakfast, lunch, and dinner, and the hours between.

Several nights later, understanding personal issues were taboo but increasingly uneasy about Oz's liquor consumption, Marguerite said, "You've not yet fully regained your strength after your brush with death, darling. Perhaps it would be wise to moderate your drinking."

"I'm grateful for your concern," he replied gracefully and without temperament, "but I'm quite recovered." And he poured himself another drink.

He *hadn't* completely recovered, of course, nor might he ever after the mistreatment his body had undergone.

"Come now, sweetheart, don't pout," he softly cajoled a moment later, reaching out his free hand and drawing her close as he rested against the bolsters of her bed. "Consider, I've tempered my violent streak. I haven't called out anyone in weeks. And I'm more than happy to give you my undivided attention at night." Dipping his head, he kissed her lightly on her temple. "Surely, I'm allowed one vice."

She looked up and held his gaze. "Everyone worries about you, that's all."

"Tell *everyone* not to worry." The thinnest edge shaded his voice.

She was tempted to say, *Should I tell your wife, too?* But she didn't because it wasn't her place to inform him that he uttered Isolde's name in his sleep. Nor would anyone who ran a business requiring discretion. On the other hand, should she do nothing while he continued to drink himself into his grave? Surely that was misspent discretion. "Do you ever think of your child?" she asked, thinking to prod his charitable impulses. He'd not mentioned Isolde's pregnancy, but her intelligence network was the envy of the government.

He didn't answer for a very long time. "No," he finally said. "And if you insist on taking the pleasure out of my evening, have another bottle sent up first."

Understanding she'd been imprudent, she offered a conciliatory olive branch in apology. "Would you like me to play Liszt for you instead?"

His smile was instant and equally cordial; they were, after all, two people who knew how to play the game. "Please do."

She was an accomplished pianist, trained at the Sorbonne in her youth, and she favored him with all his favorite pieces while he lay, eyes closed, drinking. Later, he took over from her and played with technical flair and fury, the wild, explosive music a means—however temporary—of escaping his hellish obsession with his wife.

Since the Tattersalls auction, Oz had given up Nell, his

parting gift of the race box at Ascot she'd been coveting so lavish she'd not taken issue with her dismissal. Perhaps she thought he'd come back in time as he'd done before. Or perhaps she'd recognized a restless volatility in him distinct from his previous capriciousness. He hadn't been the same since his marriage, so much so that she'd actually considered the shocking notion that he might be in love with his wife. That, more than anything, prompted her to accept her congé with good grace and then take up with young Sullivan, who wasn't quite so beautiful as Oz, nor as talented in bed, but his eagerness was charming. Furthermore, his father owned several railroads, a fact that more than made up for young Sullivan's occasional clumsiness.

In the absence of Nell, Oz spent a good deal of time at Marguerite's, although he was no longer interested in prodigal pleasures. Rather, he wished other entertainments from her: companionship, conversation, a level of peace, and only occasionally sex. But even his lovemaking had changed. He was detached, polite, careful to please her—intuitively proficient, *and* preoccupied.

On more than one occasion, he'd unconsciously said aloud, "Isolde."

After his second bottle one night, when he inadvertently called her Isolde again, Marguerite decided perhaps it was time to lose a customer and instead help a friend. Rising well before him the next morning, she wrote a note calling in a favor, had it delivered by a flunkey, and saw that the breakfast table was set for three.

When Oz woke, he glanced at the clock and quickly rose; his carriage would be waiting to bring him home for breakfast with Jess. As he stepped into his trousers, he heard a man's voice in the adjoining room and curious, went to investigate. Opening the bedroom door, he came to a sudden stop. "What the *hell* do you think you're doing?" he growled.

"You two know each other," Marguerite pleasantly said, as if Oz wasn't standing half-nude in her doorway, hot tempered and scowling. She indicated Fitz, sitting across from her, with a graceful wave of her hand. "I invited Fitz for coffee."

The duke shrugged faintly. "Rosalind made me come. Women are romantic."

"I don't appreciate this, Margo," Oz curtly said, quickly closing his trouser placket with deft fingers.

"Fitz was kind enough to come. Talk to him at least." Marguerite came to her feet, more familiar than most at dealing with difficult men in difficult situations. "Why don't I leave you alone."

As the door closed on her, Oz shot an irritated glance at Fitz. "I'm not doing this," he muttered and turned to leave.

"Marguerite tells me Isolde's expecting. I imagine she's looking forward to the new baby."

Whether it was the unexpected disclosure, or the temperate tone, Oz slowly turned back and said, cool and precise, "How did she know?"

"You know Margo's intelligence service." Fitz shoved his coffee cup away and leaned back in his chair. "I give you my word Isolde didn't send me."

"So Margo called you here to reform me," Oz muttered, sullen and gruff.

"I only came as a favor to Rosalind. Sit down; I have no interest in reforming anyone." Fitz smiled. "That's Rosalind's favorite undertaking from which I try to steer clear, present case excepted, of course. I understand your feelings. I was a confirmed bachelor, too; I was thirty-five when I married."

"Now there's a reasonable age to succumb to the ball and chain." With a sigh, Oz finally submitted to Marguerite's well-meaning interference; at least she hadn't called in a priest. "Thirty-five is a *perfect* age if you ask me," Oz said flatly, walking to the table.

"And yet?" An explicit query, gently put.

"I was drunk."

Fitz laughed. "You're not the first."

Oz dropped into Marguerite's vacated chair. "Nor the first to sober up and repent his actions."

"Isolde's a disappointment?"

"Only so much as she's my *wife*." Oz kept it simple; the truth was byzantine.

"At the risk of interfering"—Fitz smiled at Oz's quick sardonic glance—"I have a certain affection for Marguerite, so bear with me; I promise not to lecture. She tells me you've called her Isolde on several occasions. Were you aware of that?"

Oz's surprise and recovery were nearly invisible. "Our conjugal relations were . . . I suppose the word is—*stimulating*."

"Certainly an asset in a marriage," Fitz replied with exemplary tact.

"But not sufficient reason to give up one's freedom," Oz countered. "As you know, sex is readily available."

For men of wealth, a statement not open to debate. "What of the child?" Fitz asked instead. "Is that a factor at all?"

Oz hesitated, anger briefly flaring in his eyes. "The child is not open to discussion."

The hard set of his mouth gave added warning the subject was off-limits. "Forgive me; I'm sure it's a private matter. As I said, Rosalind encouraged me to respond to Marguerite's note. I find myself unable to refuse her anything—a matter of considerable embarrassment for a man like myself." He smiled faintly. "But then love is unrelated to reason, I've discovered."

Slumped low in his chair, Oz gazed at Fitz from under his long, dark lashes. "Wanting what you want is unrelated to reason as well," he irritably said.

"Marguerite says you're drinking too much. I did the same, attempting to avoid entanglement."

"Apparently, it didn't work."

Fitz's brows rose. "Does it ever?"

There was a short silence before Oz lifted his gaze fully and with obvious reluctance asked, "What changed your mind?"

"I thought I'd lost her."

There was a long interval that Fitz took care not to break.

"Lost her to another man?" Oz finally asked with restraint, a note of weariness in his voice.

"No, to my own stupidity." If Oz was dealing with a third party, there was reason for his aggrievement.

"In my case," Oz said in measured tones, "the other man is also married, and I'm not feeling stupid so much as resentful of the ménage à trois. Not to mention even under the best of conditions, I'm still too young to be married." Oz didn't mention their union was to have been temporary; he wasn't so discourteous.

"How old are you?"

"Twenty-two."

Fitz's eyes widened. He knew Oz was young but not *that* young. He had no argument for so youthful a marriage; at that age he wouldn't have listened to God himself advocating matrimony. And a third party in the picture changed everything. Had Marguerite not known? He shoved his chair back. "If you ever want a sympathetic ear, I'm always available either at home or at the bookshop. As I mentioned, Rosalind's obsessed with helping people. I merely serve as banker to her many charitable impulses." His smile was benign. "A considerable shift in my priorities."

"While I'm not interested in altering my priorities," Oz said shortly.

Fitz came to his feet. "I understand. Give Marguerite my regards."

Oz poured himself coffee with a tot of brandy as Fitz left, drank it down, and poured himself another. He glanced up as Marguerite entered the room. "I should beat you."

Marguerite's smile was as sweet as the frothy pale yellow dressing gown she wore, her temper as well maintained as her beauty. "You're too enervated by resentment and discontent to exert the effort, darling," she said. "I wonder when you're going to admit you want your wife."

Oz flinched. Then keeping his temper in check, he said, "I

appreciate your misplaced concern and all your trouble in bringing Fitz out so early in the morning. I don't recommend, however," he continued, lightly acerbic, "that you marshal any more forces in your mistaken attempt to save my marriage. It's my business, not yours," he finished, a flicker of anger in his dark gaze.

BUT LATER THAT morning, after breakfast with Jess, Oz found himself standing outside Bruton Street Books. He had no idea how he'd happened to come this way, but he was enough of a mystic to yield to the randomness of fate. Although, he expected his time with Jess had brought to the fore a certain preoccupation with babies and pregnancies and by association, Rosalind and Fitz's invitation to visit.

He wasn't sober, of course, which proved an irresistible force as well.

Walking up to the canary yellow door, he pushed it open.

The store was busy. Standing to one side of the entrance, he surveyed the large interior. Two clerks were behind a counter to his right, displays of books were arranged down the center of the main aisle, customers were perusing books on shelves lining the walls, and colorful paintings were on display through an open archway at the back of the store.

As he searched the crowd for either Fitz or his wife, the door opened behind him and a familiar voice said, "You came. Let me show you around."

Oz turned. "I have no idea why I'm here."

"It doesn't matter," Fitz said with deliberate courtesy. "Come say hello to Rosalind. She's in back."

Fitz led the way through the store into the gallery, and coming up behind his wife, dressed in soft apple green silk tussah, he kissed her lightly on the nape of her neck.

She swung around slowly, her pregnancy advanced. "That didn't take long," she said with a warm smile for her husband. "Ian must have had the new drawings ready."

"He did; I approved them. Demolition begins next week." Stepping to one side, Fitz said, "Look, darling, Oz stopped by."

"What a pleasure to see you again," Rosalind pleasantly said, keeping her counsel about the earlier visit. "Would you like tea, coffee"—she lifted her brows—"something stronger perhaps?"

"We'll both have a brandy," Fitz said, having drunk his breakfast often enough in the past to keep Oz company. "Come, sit down, Oz. I'll shut the door so customers don't wander in."

A few moments later, they were seated in a corner of the gallery in comfortable chairs and had been served tea and sweets for Rosalind and brandies for the men.

"How are you feeling?" Oz impetuously asked, his gaze concentrated on Rosalind. "You look lovely. Healthy"—he smiled—"I believe the word is *glowing*."

Rosalind and Fitz exchanged an affectionate glance. "At this stage," she said, turning to Oz and indicating her belly, conspicuous beneath the soft silk, "I mostly feel fat. But thank you for the compliment."

"Isolde's pregnant." While softly uttered, Oz's declaration was a precipitous rush of words.

"That's what Fitz said," Rosalind smoothly replied. "Congratulations."

It remains to be seen whether congratulations are in order. But as capable of politesse as his companions, Oz graciously replied, "Thank you. Isolde's extremely pleased."

"Do you have any questions about"—Rosalind again gestured at her swollen stomach—"pregnancy in general or in particular?" He'd not taken his eyes off her since he'd walked in.

"A thousand." He smiled. "I won't bore you. Have you picked out a name?"

Rosalind glanced at her husband, then at Oz. "We're arguing about names," she lightly said.

"We're *discussing* names." Fitz grinned. "I expect I'll lose in the end. Not that I mind, darling, considering you're doing all the work."

"Indeed. Although I've been feeling wonderful from the first. Since I never thought I could have a child," she said on a small exhalation, "I'm not inclined to complain in the least. Oh my," she murmured, placing her hand on her stomach, "the baby's kicking again; the little dear's getting stronger every day."

The movement was obvious beneath the fine silk.

"May I feel it?" Oz's voice was low, constrained, his dark gaze fixed on her belly. "Forgive me," he added in a normal tone. "You must think me exceedingly rude."

"Not at all. Fitz was just as fascinated, weren't you, darling? Remember the first time the baby kicked?" She turned back to Oz. "We were all agog. Here, put your hand right here."

Leaning forward in his chair, Oz reached out and delicately placed his fingertips on her belly.

"Put your palm down so you call really feel the movement. Don't be shy."

He did as instructed, the baby suddenly kicked, and Oz jerked his hand back. His heart was racing.

"When is Isolde due?" Rosalind asked, Oz's expression one of wonder.

"I don't know. She's not far along yet."

Fitz caught his wife's eye and warned her off. "I don't suppose you have any suggestions for names." Fitz tactfully changed the subject.

Grateful for the civility, Oz collected himself, and when he spoke, no evidence of his emotions remained. "With my background, my repertoire of names is more Indian than English. I wouldn't be much help."

At that point, the conversation turned to India, a country

Fitz had visited several times. Rosalind was fascinated, asking a multitude of questions. With India the crown jewel in Britain's empire, the store's stock of books on India was considerable. Later, the men compared hunting experiences, India fertile ground for exotic game.

But as they conversed, Oz's glance would drift back to Rosalind, his fascination with her pregnancy profound. He was young, Rosalind thought, a novice in dealing with the event; she understood his interest. Fitz understood other factors were in play as well, questions of paternity perhaps, although no one had explicitly said so.

After a convivial hour of conversation, Oz took his leave with an open invitation from Fitz and Rosalind for dinner or tea or a visit of any kind.

Fitz escorted Oz out.

"I don't pretend to know your situation," he said as they stood on the pavement outside the store, "but if I were to give a single piece of advice, I'd say, don't burn your bridges." He smiled. "You never know until you know."

Oz laughed. "Since I'm currently in limbo, I won't find it difficult to follow your advice. Now, if only I experience some epiphany before I drink myself to death."

"At least you're not involved in a duel every other day."

"True. Marriage has emasculated me in that respect."

Ftiz grinned. "I'm sure the members of Brooks's are relieved."

"No doubt." Oz put out his hand. "Thank you. You and Rosalind are an island of calm in a highly volatile world."

Fitz gripped his hand. "Come visit anytime. I'm always ready for a brandy."

Later that day, Fitz sent Marguerite a brief note:

Oz is beginning to question his resentments. He came to see Rosalind and was enthralled with her belly. If he doesn't drink himself to death in the meantime, I feel that a suspension of hostilities is possible.

CHAPTER 30

AT THE SAME time Oz was riveted by the spectacle of a heavily pregnant belly for the first time in his life, Isolde was riding hard after the hounds. Will and Anne had invited her for the neighborhood hunt they were hosting that week, and since Pamela and Charles had promised to serve as shield to Will's unwanted attentions, Isolde had accepted the invitation. In a few weeks, she'd no longer be able to ride hell-bent for leather but would have to content herself with a more gentle pace.

True to their word, either Pamela or Charles were at her side throughout the day as well as at dinner that evening. Isolde enjoyed the exhilarating afternoon, the soaring jumps and wild gallops, the warm spring temperatures and lush green countryside, the agreeable company of her neighbors, other than the Fowlers. All in all, she had a most gratifying time.

Even dinner was pleasant, with Charles and Pamela on either side of her at the table, the conversation animated, farming and horses favored topics, the food excellent. And when it came time to retire—the company staying over as was usual—Pamela saw her to her bedroom.

"I'll wait to hear you lock your door," she said as they reached Isolde's door.

"Thank you, and thank Charles. I had a wonderful, peaceful day with no harassment from Will."

"He was exceedingly grumpy by the end of the day, but you made Anne happy, if you care."

Isolde shrugged. "Why not. As long as I escaped his attentions, I can afford to be magnanimous. Although," she said with a smile as she opened her door, "the reviling looks sent my way by our hostess were not in the least charitable."

"The poor girl doesn't have a charitable bone in her body," Pamela returned. "Although knowing her parents, it's no wonder."

"None of which is my problem," Isolde airily noted, and with a wave, she entered her bedroom and locked her door.

But she didn't immediately sleep that night, as was the case since Oz had left. It was most difficult to distract her thoughts once she was alone, when the activities with which she kept herself occupied during the day were at an end. She'd learned to run through the litany of all that was good in her life to remind herself there was recompense for her loss. But she missed him nevertheless.

She expected she always would.

CHAPTER 31

TWO DAYS LATER, Oz was deep in a high-stakes game at Brooks's, debating which of several good cards to discard, when a player newly come to town said, "I saw your wife at Fowler's the other day." Ignoring the frantic shaking of heads from those standing behind Oz's chair, the young Earl of Quarles continued walking into the lion's den. "She's not only dazzling, but she rides like an Amazon. She outrode everyone in the hunting field."

Oz had stopped breathing.

The silence was so profound, the hiss and crackle of the fire could be heard from across the room.

Smoothly recovering himself, Oz's gaze, judiciously blank, rested on the earl's face. "At Fowler's you say?"

Quarles, suddenly aware of the hush, more aware of the sleek chill in Oz's voice, began to sweat. "I may . . . have . . . been mistaken," he stammered.

Feeling not only cold but also bloodless, Oz set down his cards and pushed himself upright in his chair. "I doubt it. She rides well. Not that I'm sure she should be riding in her condition," he murmured, his dark gaze so punitive no one dared respond to the startling admission. "Was she there long?"

"I—that is . . . you see—"

The buffeting, obsessive sensations so long held in check broke free, and abandoning reason and the role of complaisant husband, Oz said in a voice held steady only with effort, "Tell me or I'll cut out your liver."

"She was still there when I left after dinner," the young man choked out in a rush of words, ashen and cringing under the lethal gaze.

"And what time would that have been?" Whisper soft, knife sharp, murderous.

No one dared interfere, the men at the table silent, the entire room hushed and expectant. Oz in his cups was a child of danger; drunk for weeks, he was the prince of darkness.

"Eleven," Quarles answered, white-eyed and barely breathing.

"You've been most helpful," Oz said. Picking up his cards again, he swept the table with a glance. "Are we playing or not?"

Disaster averted, the buzz of conversation resumed, although Quarles took the first opportunity given him to escape. Oz didn't even look up as he left the game, his thoughts divided between his cards and his morning's schedule.

The conversation between Oz and Quarles was repeated like a drumbeat throughout the club rooms, the tantalizing news soon carried farther afield by noble young sprigs leaving the club for other social pursuits. By morning, the story in all its explosive detail had raced through the beau monde, spurred and energized by the stunning news of Oz's impending fatherhood.

Not only had the perennial bachelor been snared.

But a child was also on the horizon . . . and so quickly.

People immediately began counting on their fingers.

What lovely tittle-tattle! Would he discard his lovers? Or more to the point, how often would he visit his breeding wife in the country? No one seriously expected him to relinquish his lovers. Although, with poor Quarles having only narrowly escaped serious harm, it was deliciously apparent that Lennox was jealous of his wife.

Astonishing!

It quite staggered the imagination!

CHAPTER 32

THE MORNING FOLLOWING Quarles's disclosure at Brooks's, Isolde had finally reached the limits of her patience. Will had arrived as she was having her breakfast for heaven's sake! Jumping up, she advanced on him in a rage, "This is too much, damn you! I'm telling Anne! I swear I will!"

"Calm down. She'll only blame you for it."

"For heaven's sake, Will. How can—"

Suddenly the door to the breakfast room swung open, crashed into the wall like a mallet, toppling a small curio cabinet and catapulting a collection of Meissen figurines to the floor.

His mud-spattered riding coat swinging against his filthy boots, Oz stormed in, his heels crushing the shattered porcelain, his hard, haggard gaze leveled on Will. "Get the hell out of my house!"

"My house," Isolde snapped, instantly provoked by her husband's misplaced authority.

Oz shot her a look as though noticing her for the first time. With a shrug, he said, "Her house. Now get the hell out!"

As Will hesitated, Oz pulled out a pistol with dizzying speed, cocked the hammer, and in a voice cold with outrage, snarled, "Stay away from my wife."

"Maybe we should ask Isolde what she wants," Will hurled back. "She and I were friends long before you came along!"

Isolde had never seen the blood drain from a man's face. Frightened, she went still, the pale, stark planes of Oz's face conspicuous in the morning light, the blank look in his eyes terrifying, the pistol aimed at Will's chest held, white-knuckled.

"Don't be a fucking hero," Oz murmured, slurred, softly goading.

And completely drunk, Isolde suddenly realized.

"Go, Will, for God's sake!" she gasped, unable to breathe, understanding now why Oz had looked right through her.

"There, you see," Oz softly said, his nerves flinching at Isolde's concern for her lover. "Tell him again, *my darling*," he said with overdrawn sweetness, "how you fear for his life."

Even without looking, she could feel the contempt in his gaze. But she wouldn't be the cause of Will's death, and ignoring her husband's indolent sarcasm, her face closed, she whispered, "Please go, Will. Think of Anne and your child."

Whether it was the terror in Isolde's voice or the annihilating indifference of the man holding the gun, Will bowed to Isolde, turned, and tramping over the scattered bits of Meissen, passed through the open doorway.

His footfall echoed down the hall, the sound slowly fading.

A hush descended, the brilliant sunlight glinting off the silver on the breakfast table, the air taut with aggression and insult.

Oz stood swaying gently on his boot heels, his eyes half-shut, a gauntness to his face even more pronounced since she'd seen him last. Then his lids slowly lifted, he eased the pistol hammer back in place, tossed the weapon on a chair, and turned a jaundiced gaze on Isolde. "You seem to have been amusing yourself rather nicely in my absence despite your protests to the contrary."

The word *absence* kindled a sudden thought, and she glanced at the open doorway. In all her busy, well-staffed household, not one of the scores of servants she employed was visible. Honest surprise raised her brows. "How did you threaten them?"

"I told them I'd kill you."

"And will you?"

A vein beat rapidly along his temple. "I haven't decided."

"Am I supposed to plead?"

"Please don't. And don't make excuses," he said evenly.

She wouldn't plead, no more than she'd beg him to love her. "You're being a little presumptuous, aren't you? Jumping to conclusions?" She had nothing to hide.

Turning the full weight of his anger on her, he said with a cruel and deliberate malice, "I arrive to find *him* here at breakfast? And *I'm* jumping to conclusions? Spare me your fucking lies."

"You're drunk."

"I wonder what his wife says when he drags home stinking of you?" he growled as if she hadn't spoken.

"You're wrong. When you're sober, I'd be happy to explain."

"My ears work drunk or sober."

"But does your brain?" With Will gone, so was her fear. She could feel it in her bones, intuitive and independent of reason. Just as she suspected Oz was jealous, if extravagant dreams were allowed. "You look tired," she said, wanting to take him in her arms and soothe the scowl from his face. Wanting more that he might have come because she mattered to him.

"Tired and abysmally drunk." The faintest of smiles twitched across his fine mouth. "You don't look tired at all."

"Unlike you, I have no one making demands on my energy at night." She lifted one brow. "I'd appreciate no lies from you on that score if you please."

He felt a twinge of guilt for the first time in his life, and as if to mollify that culpability, he said, "Then we won't exchange lies."

"I have none to exchange. Ask any of the staff. In fact, I was in the process of threatening to tell Anne of her husband's visits if he didn't stop calling on me. Will's been annoying me worse than ever, if you must know."

Oz's grin was instant and disarming. "I should have shot him."

"I'm almost in a mood to agree. But I'll leave it to his wife to bore him to death instead."

"Tut, tut," Oz murmured, his gaze limpid.

"You met her," Isolde said, charmed by the uncalculated warmth in his voice. "Admit, she's boring."

"Hell yes. I'd shoot *myself* after a week in her company."

"What a sweet thing to say."

"At the risk of ruining this charming rapprochement," he said, his gaze suddenly alert, "I have a question."

"I didn't, if that's what you want to know."

He watched her for a moment, then slowly said, "Why did you go on his hunt?"

"Because I like to ride. Who told you?"

"Quarles. I almost hurt the poor boy."

"I was sent an invitation. The entire neighborhood was there. Pamela and Elliot were my duennas."

"You stayed late."

"No later than most."

"Did you stay the night?"

"Yes," she said, steady and composed. "Everyone did."

"Not Quarles," he replied, clipped and cool.

"He and his wild party left for more intemperate pleasures in Cambridge."

"And what," he said, holding her gaze, "was the extent of intemperate pleasures at the Fowlers'?"

"What were the extent of your pleasures in London?"

His dark brows floated upward. "Are you picking a quarrel?"

"Am I not allowed a wifely question?" she delicately asked.

"Not that one," he placidly replied.

"Which ones am I allowed?"

There was a small silence, and then he smiled. "Let me get out of these muddy clothes and I'll tell you."

"Just like that? No apology for your false accusations?"

"That, too, I can better do upstairs."

"What if I were to say no?"

"You'd be lying."

"So sure?"

"Very sure," he pleasantly said and offered her his arm.

"Apologize," she said, because she would not be so easily seduced or worse, trifled with.

He dropped his arm and stood still, not speaking for a moment as if gathering his thoughts. Then he quietly said, "I apologize for insulting you, for leaving you here and in London, for questioning the paternity of your child."

"Our child."

"For that," he graciously said, willing to take the child, whether his or not. "My life is no longer my own," he said, open-eyed and softly, his earnestness so heartfelt it stole her breath away. "I say it humbly and without pride. I need you to make the sun shine and bring the stars out at night. I need you to make my life sweet again and stop the weeping inside me. I need you."

She smiled, happiness warm and fathomless, the music of the world in her ears. "I love you. I have from the first."

"I love you, too." His eyes scanned her face. "Is there more?"

She shook her head. In time, she knew, he'd speak those words of love with feeling. Taking his hand, she drew him to the door. "I must warn you, darling," she calmly said, glancing up at him. "My passions seem to have increased with pregnancy; I may be demanding. Do you think you can stay awake?"

His smile unfurled and filled his eyes. "No sleeping. I promise."

When they reached her bedchamber, he quickly stripped away his muddy boots and clothes, leaving them in a pile at the door. Then pulling off his rings, he dropped them into a small Imari bowl on the dresser. As the emerald twinkled against the orange and blue design, he knew he wouldn't be wearing Khair's ring again.

The past was the past.

He'd be a father soon. The concept was strange but pleasing, he thought, smiling faintly.

"Why are you smiling?"

He turned to find his wife half-undressed, her pale hair tumbled on her shoulders, her blue gaze speculative and watchful. "I was thinking about fatherhood. You must tell me what to do."

"Love us both."

"That's simple enough. And until such a time, I'll love *you*."

Her smile was pure sunshine. "How?"

"Any way, every way. And I apologize. I smell of horse."

"Would you like to bathe?"

"I did before I rode up, but if you want me to."

"No. I don't know why I said that."

"Nervous?"

"Yes."

"Don't be. I've decided to become a farmer. Even if you want me to leave, I won't."

"So you can be troublesome coming or going," she playfully noted.

"In some ways I'm not troublesome at all." He moved closer and taking her face in his hands, kissed her gently. "Let me show you."

A sharp rap on the door was followed by Grover's voice. "Do you need anything, Miss Izzy?"

Isolde's eyes widened. "I don't believe Grover has ever stepped foot in this wing."

"He's here to save you," Oz kindly said.

"I already have someone saving me. Let me tell him."

Finding a robe, she went to the door and opening it a small distance, assured her steward of her safety. Shutting the door a few moments later, she turned to find Oz facedown on her bed in a dead sleep.

Drawing up a chair near the bed, she sat and studied the wild, young man she loved to distraction. His breathing was deep and slow, the dark shadows under his eyes indication of his exhaustion, of his wastrel ways, of the overindulgence that marked his life. Would he cease his debauch for her? Could he? Was she a fool to think he might? Was she a bigger fool to think she could tame his headstrong ways and turn him into an obliging husband?

She softly sighed.

He came awake with a start, instinctively scanning the room as if waking in strange places was habitual. His gaze stopped on Isolde, and he smiled the beautiful smile that had charmed across three continents. "Have I been sleeping long?"

"A few minutes. Sleep, though; I can wait."

"I can't." Rolling on his back, he held out his arms. "Come here and tell me about your farming."

"In an hour I'll tell you about my farming," she quietly said, rising and slipping off her robe.

He grinned. "That's what I meant."

As it turned out, they didn't speak at all unless whimsical, sporadically uttered love words could be characterized as speech. Or screams, sighs, and pleasurable growls.

And when, finally, both were sated and it was possible to consider that a world lay beyond the confines of the bed, Oz lifted his head from Isolde's shoulder, smiled down at his wife, and content now beyond his wildest imagination, softly said, "I have come to rest now from my travels."

With his black hair brushing her cheek and the pulse of her heart beating wildly with love, she met his affectionate gaze and smiled. "Welcome home."

Keep reading for a preview of the next
historical romance by Susan Johnson

SWEET AS THE DEVIL

Coming soon from Berkley Sensation!

CHAPTER 1

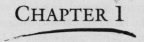

London, July, 1893

"JAMIE, DON'T YOU *dare* leave! I *need* you. *Jamie!*"

Already sliding from the bed, James Blackwood turned back, leaned over in a fluid ripple of honed muscle, and kissed the countess's pouty mouth. "I would stay if I could, darling," he said, sitting up and smiling at her. "But I'm already late. Drinks at eight. John's new wife was quite emphatic."

"Pshaw on little Vicky," Countess Minton peevishly noted. "What about me? I haven't seen you in almost a year. And it's only drinks. You won't miss dinner, I promise. You can't say you're not *interested*," she murmured, her sultry gaze drifting to Jamie's blatant erection, her smile sly and knowing.

"You keep a man interested, Bella—no doubt about that."
The voluptuously nude woman sprawled in the shambles of
the bed was well aware of her sensual allure. And her charming capacity for innovation was also an accomplishment of
no small merit. "Unfortunately," he said with a truly regretful
sigh, "duty calls." There were degrees of lateness and politesse apropos his cousin's wife and he was pressing the
boundaries of both. He began to turn away.

Rolling up on one elbow with breathtaking speed, Bella
seized Jamie's upthrust penis in her pink nailed grip, swiftly
bent her head, and seized the moment.

Christ! Jamie's breath hissed through his teeth, his cock
oversensitive after the hours they'd spent together, Bella's
assault a shock to his nerve endings. But a heartbeat later,
his twitching nerves adjusted with indecent speed to licentious pleasure and he softly exhaled. *Now what?* With Bella
performing fellatio in her usual masterful fashion, assessing
the relative merits of duty and lust required a degree of
rational observation that was fast eluding him. Yet, a modicum of reason still remained in the nether reaches of his
brain; he glanced at the clock.

Bella suddenly nibbled a trifle overzealously, perhaps deliberately.

He gasped, the fine line between pleasure and pain not
only taking his breath away, but effectively ending his debate. *What the hell.* Shutting his eyes, he gave himself up to
prodigal sensation.

One good turn deserved another . . . and an hour later, lying face down on the bed, panting, Bella gasped, "No . . .
more."

Sprawled on his back beside her, laboring to drag air into
his lungs, Jamie finally became aware of the censorious voice
inside his head that had been trying to warn him for a considerable time that—*Vicky's going to be really pissed!* Silently swearing, he lifted his head from the pillow, took a
disgruntled breath, and sat up. Why had he made plans? He

never made plans. Raking his fingers through his dark, ruffled hair, he wondered how much time had passed since he'd
been so felicitously persuaded to tarry.

Oh Christ. The face of the small bedside clock jerked him
back to reality. Swinging his legs over the side of the bed, he
scanned the floor for his trousers.

"Don't go."

He glanced at the flushed woman who could keep his
cock hard indefinitely. "You said no more."

Her smile was Circe's. "I take it back."

His dark lashes lowered slightly. "Be reasonable. I'm already later than hell."

"I don't care. Stay—*please, please.*"

For a moment he actually debated staying; it was incredibly late. He still had to return to his apartment and change—
which would make him even later. Dare he ignore Vicky's
invitation? And his cousin's displeasure? Knowing the politic
answer, he twisted back with the fluid grace of an athlete,
whispered in Bella's ear, and quickly quit the bed before his
libido regained the upper hand.

He found his trousers where they'd been hastily discarded
that morning after he'd stopped by to talk to Charlie about a
prime cavalry mount he wished to buy and had found Bella
in dishabille instead.

Charlie was out of town, she'd explained with a seductive
smile. "But there's no reason to hurry off, Jamie dear," she'd
purred. "We haven't seen each other in ages. Do tell me all
the gossip from Vienna."

She hadn't meant it of course.

She'd meant something else entirely.

And now he was damnably late for Vicky's dinner.

HE MADE HIS excuses to Vicky and his cousin, John,
Baron Reid, and to all the guests who'd looked up from their
desserts as he'd entered the dining room, and they greeted

him with sly smiles and curious gazes. No one believed for a minute that he'd been detained because of an accident on the Windsor road because Vicky had chanced to mention over drinks that Jamie had gone to see Charlie Bonner on the matter of a horse, to which Freddy Stockton had pointed out that Charlie was in the country. Everyone also knew that Bella had a penchant for handsome men and Jamie Blackwood in particular.

But since the fashionable world viewed fidelity in marriage much as they viewed children—as something to be ignored—amorous peccadilloes were not only commonplace but generally viewed with amusement.

So after the initial raised brows and roguish scrutiny, conversation reverted to the usual tittle-tattle and gossip that passed for social intercourse in the frivolous world of the beau monde. Several earlier courses were brought up from the kitchen for Jamie while the other guests indulged in a sumptuous variety of sweets. John's chef was superb, the wine free-flowing, and Jamie, famished after having exerted himself as stud all day, tucked into his meal with gusto.

"Worked up an appetite I see," Viscount Graham sportively noted.

Jamie turned a bland gaze on the man to his left. "There's no opportunity to eat when your carriage's stalled in traffic."

"The road to Windsor you said?" the viscount pronounced with unsullied cheer.

"Yes, Windsor." Jamie set down his knife and fork, his dark brows lifted faintly. "Would you care to tell me why you are asking?"

Graham smiled widely. "Hell no." While Jamie served officially as attache to Prince Ernst of Dalmia, he was, in effect, bodyguard to the prince, and in that capacity had gained a reputation for efficiency or more pertinently, violence.

"I didn't think so." Jamie signaled to have his wineglass filled and returned to his meal.

* * *

MUCH LATER, WHEN all the guests had departed and Vicky had gone off to bed, Jamie and his cousin retired to John's study to share a decanter of whiskey.

"Allow me to apologize again for arriving so late," Jamie immediately said. "It was—"

"Bella's engaging charm?" his cousin interposed with a grin. "Along with her inexhaustible desires?"

"Indeed." Jamie dipped his head. "Not that I'm complaining. You no doubt speak from experience."

"Previous experience. I'm a happily married man now."

Jamie raised his glass in salute. "To your brilliant marriage. You love Vicky and she obviously loves you. A nice change from the beau monde's penchant for marriages based on balance sheets and quarterings." With a smile for his cousin, he drank down his whiskey.

"Thank you. I consider myself very fortunate. *You* should consider marriage. I heartily recommend it. Women are always in hot pursuit of you," John said with a lift of his brows. "Why not let yourself be caught?"

"No thanks." Swift and certain. "The Isabelles of the world suit me just fine."

"So it seems. My personal bet was you wouldn't make dinner."

"I almost didn't. It was a matter of not wanting to disappoint your lovely new bride."

"And you'd had enough of Bella's charms," his cousin perceptively remarked.

Jamie smiled. "That too."

"Someday the right woman is going to change your mind about marriage."

Jamie gently shook his head. "Don't waste your breath. Unlike you, I've never been enthralled with the concept of love. Several of your youthful infatuations come to mind," Jamie added with a grin, "if you'd like me to refresh your memory."

"God, no. In any case, Vicky's different."

"Which is why you married her. I'm not questioning your sincerity. I just lack the necessary sense of devotion." Leaning over, Jamie picked up the decanter and refilled his glass.

"I used to think as much."

Jamie shot his cousin a jaundiced glance, but rather than argue his cousin's past history with women, Jamie set down the crystal container and politely said, "Even if I were inclined to endorse the notion of love and marriage, *at the moment*, I'm up to my ears in risky ventures. As you well know, the Hapsburg Empire's in decline; every petty despot with an army at his back is jockeying for position."

"Including Prince Ernst."

"Including him." Leaning back in his chair, Jamie met his cousin's gaze with his usual immutable calm. "He's as ambitious as the rest. And why shouldn't he be? Twenty generations of Battenburgs have ruled that piece of prime real estate, offered up their resources and sons to the emperor when needed, and played a significant role in the Hapsburg prosperity."

"As your family has for the Battenburgs." Jamie's forebears had fled Scotland after the '45 defeat and sold the services of their fighting clan to the Duchy of Dalmia.

"With due compensation," Jamie serenely said, John's red hair gleaming in the lamplight reminding him of his mother's. Their mothers had been cousins. Shaking off the melancholy that always overcame him on recall of his mother's unnecessary death, he pushed up from his lounging pose and said, "You heard, of course, that Uncle Douglas came back from India with a fortune."

"And a native wife."

"A very beautiful wife. He's looking to invest his money. I told him to talk to you. You've guarded my investments well," Jamie said with a grin.

"Anyone could. Other than upkeep on your Dalmian estate, you don't spend any money."

"I don't have time. Guarding Ernst is a round-the-clock commission."

"Speaking of guarding, who's protecting Ernst in your absence?"

"He's on holiday with his newest paramour, who rules a duchy of her own with a small army and a top-notch palace guard." Lifting his glass to his mouth, Jamie arched his brows. "Adequate deterrent to any assassin," he murmured and drank down half the whiskey.

"Which explains *your* holiday in Scotland."

"A much needed holiday," Jamie softly replied, lowering his glass to the chair arm.

John looked surprised. "Do I detect a modicum of frustration? Is Ernst spending too much time in libertine pursuits—silly question."

"Let's just say he doesn't have his father's sense of responsibility."

"Or any responsibility at all."

"He was perhaps too indulged." Jamie shrugged. "A problem at a time when Dalmia could use a ruler of insight and diligence."

"Haven't the Balkans always been a tinderbox?"

"It's worse now. The wolves are beginning to circle with the emperor's grip on power weakening. They smell blood. And rightly so. It's just a matter of time until Franz Joseph dies and all hell breaks loose." Jamie grimaced. "But screw it. I'm not there, I'm here. Tell me about your thoroughbreds instead. Rumor has it your chestnut brute's going to take all the major races next year." The last thing Jamie wished to dwell on was the crumbling Hapsburg Empire and the approaching deluge.

"You should plan on being here for the Derby next year," John pleasantly said, urbanely shifting topics. "Shalizar's going to win by ten lengths. You can bet on it."

"In that case," Jamie drawled, "I shall—heavily."

"As will I. A pity you don't have time to see my stud at Bellingham."

"Next time. I promised Davy I'd meet him day after tomorrow. He's coming down from the hills to meet me."

The two men, long friends—their family resemblance clear despite their disparate coloring—went on to discuss the merits of various horses and trainers, bloodlines and jockeys. The quiet study was peaceful, a temporary hermitage in a quarrelsome, perilous world and the fine highland whiskey served its purpose as well—lessening Jamie's disquiet. Neither touched on the serious or personal, both careful to keep the conversation companionable and toward dawn, cheerfully drunk, the two men parted ways.

John went upstairs to his wife.

Jamie strolled to Grosvenor Square, entered a large house through a back door, conveniently unlocked, took the servants' stairs to the second floor and entered a shadowed bedchamber.

"I didn't know if you'd come," Bella drowsily murmured, gazing at Jamie from under her lashes.

"I said I would." Quietly closing the door, he slipped off his swallowtail coat, dropped it on the floor, and, pulling his shirt studs free, moved toward the bed.

"How nice." Pushing up on her elbows, Bella smiled. "I don't believe I've ever met an honest man."

Jamie grinned. "I have an excuse. I live outside the fashionable world."

"Too far outside at the moment," she purred, tossing the covers aside. "Do come in . . ."

CHAPTER 2

THE NEXT MORNING, the sultry air heavy with the promise of rain, Sofia Eastleigh was cooling her heels in a small waiting room off the entrance hall of Minton House and becoming increasingly agitated. She didn't as a rule agree to paint society portraits, finding those in the fashionable world too spoiled or difficult to sit the necessary hours required to complete a painting. But Bella, Countess of Minton, was one of the reigning beauties of the day—not to be discounted when it came to publicity—and she was generous as well in terms of a fee.

She'd give her five minutes more, Sofia resentfully decided, and then the countess and her money could go to hell. With her artwork much sought after, Sofia didn't *need* the money. Nor did she appreciate being kept waiting like a servant for—she glanced at the splendid Boulle clock on the mantel—dammit . . . *thirty-five* minutes!

Rising to her feet, she was slipping on her gloves when the waiting room door was thrown open by a liveried flunky, Bella was announced, and a moment later, a radiant, blushing countess, obviously just risen from bed, swept into the room, trailing lavender mousseline and a cloud of scent.

"Good, you're still here. A matter of some importance delayed me."

The countess's partner in that important matter strolled into the room behind her and offered Sofia an engaging smile. "I'm sorry you had to wait. Please, accept my apology. Bella tells me you're an artist of great renown."

"The baron will keep me company while you paint," the countess briskly interposed, ignoring Jamie's apology. "We're quite ready if you are."

Understanding that Bella viewed an artist as a trades person, consequently not due the courtesies, Jamie introduced himself. "You're Miss Eastleigh I presume. James Blackwood at your service."

Even with her temper in high dudgeon, Sofia couldn't help but think, *Wouldn't that be grand to be serviced by a big, handsome brute like you.* The man was splendid—tall, dark, powerfully muscled, and all male, with the languid gait of a panther and the green eyes to match. Now there was a portrait worth painting. She'd portray him as he was, casually dressed in the remnants of last night's evening rig, his dark hair in mild disarray. He wore a cambric shirt and trousers, the shirt open at the neck, his long, muscular legs shown to advantage in well-tailored black wool, his feet bare in his evening shoes.

A faint carnal tremor raced through her senses.

Commonplace and not in the least disconcerting.

She found handsome men attractive and, in many cases, useful.

A modern woman, a bohemian in terms of cultural mores, Sofia enjoyed lovemaking. But on her terms. She decided if a man suited her, she decided when and if to make love, and whether to continue a relationship—mostly she didn't, preferring men as transient diversions in her life. Although, for a gorgeous animal like Blackwood, she might be inclined to alter her rules and keep him for a time. He had the look of a man who was more than capable of satisfying a woman. And the fact that the countess—who had a reputation for dalliance—was obviously captivated by him was testament to his competence.

TAKING JEALOUS NOTE of Sofia's admiring gaze, for a brief moment Bella debated canceling the sitting. On second thought, the pale, slender artist was hardly the type of woman to appeal to Jamie, who preferred women of substance who could keep up with him in bed. The little painter looked as though a good wind would blow her away. "Come, Miss Eastleigh," Bella crisply commanded. "I have another appointment after your sitting."

Following the women from the waiting room, Jamie contemplated the stark differences between the two beauties, the lively contrasts of blonde femininity intriguing. Miss Eastleigh was slender with hair the color of sunshine on snow, her pale loveliness poetic and ethereal—like an Arthurian Isolde who might bruise with the slightest touch. Bella, on the other hand, didn't bruise at all, as he well knew after two days of wild, untrammeled sex. Bella's golden splendor was that of a robust flesh and blood Valkyrie: passionate, impatient, demanding. He understood why Charlie preferred his sweet, young mistress in Chelsea from time to time if for no other reason than to rest.

A few minutes later, they entered the small sun-filled conservatory where Sofia had set up her easel. Bella disposed herself on the chaise in David's *Madame Recamier* pose, waved Jamie into a chair opposite her, and sweetly cajoling, murmured, "Darling, tell me how I might tempt you to stay. Surely, your Highlands can wait for a day or so." She spoke as if Sofia didn't exist. "And don't say you must go immediately because you don't when you're here for an entire fortnight."

"If Tom wasn't coming down from the hills to meet me I

could change my plans, but it's a long, rough trek for him. It wouldn't be fair to waste his time."

"He's your gilly for heaven's sake. Send him a telegram. He can wait for you in Inverness for a day or so."

"We can talk about this later," he quietly said.

"Why? Oh, you think Miss Eastleigh is mindful. Of course she isn't." A duke's daughter would, of course, hold such an opinion; servants were invisible.

"That's enough, Bella."

The countess offered her lover a sultry smile. "Will you beat me if I don't obey?"

"Of course not."

He spoke with soft restraint but something in his tone apparently struck home, for the countess said with a complacent sigh, "Very well. You must always have your way." She smiled. "For which I've been extremely grateful on any number of occasions my masterful darling."

"Are you quite done?"

"I suppose I must be with you frowning so. Was Vicky pleased last night that you finally arrived?" She knew when to be accommodating, particularly with Jamie. While they shared a mutual pleasure, he wasn't in the least enamored or adoring like so many of her lovers.

"Vicky was very pleasant," he said, relieved Bella was finally minding her manners. "John's a lucky man."

"His wife is as well. You and your cousin share a certain charming expertise. I was surprised when he married."

"He's in love."

"You don't say. How quaint."

"It happens."

"But fortunately not to you"—she smiled—"or me."

"Could we talk about something else?" *Or not talk at all?*

"Of course, darling. Did you hear that Georgie Tolliver left his wife for his children's governess? Isn't that droll?" At which point, Bella lapsed into a gossipy discussion of their various acquaintances who were involved in affairs of one kind or another—the favorite amusement of the aristocracy.

Sliding down on his spine, his eyes half shut, Jamie replied in a desultory fashion to her comments. He was tired, two days of fucking and little sleep had taken its toll.

Bella seemed not to notice, absorbed as she was in her frivolous recital, or perhaps she was simply content to have Jamie near.

It was like watching a bored animal, Sofia thought as she captured the countess's pretty features on the canvas, Countess Minton's lover politely biding his time, listening with half an ear to the countess's chatter, appearing to doze off on occasion. Although, apparently, he didn't, for he always managed to respond when required. Politely. With a cultivated civility at variance with his lassitude. He'd open his eyes and answer even the most banal queries with good humor.

The conservatory arm chairs were gilded faux bamboo, the attenuated metal dangerously light for a man his size.

Would it or wouldn't it collapse beneath his weight? Would he or wouldn't he actually fall asleep, Sofia wondered as if she were somehow his keeper. Or the countess's. As if either of them cared what she thought when they apparently dealt very well together.

Wresting her gaze from the stunning couple, Sofia curtailed her contemplation of the two lovers and applied herself to her work.

And so the sitting progressed, Bella chattering, Mr. Blackwood largely inanimate, Sofia finishing the depiction of the countess's large blue eyes and beginning to sketch in her nose with quick, sure strokes. Having defined the shape to her satisfaction, she was gathering a dab of pale pink paint from her palette for the highlights when the door to the conservatory abruptly opened.

A stylish young lady dressed in ruffled, beribboned white muslin burst in, using her parasol to shove aside a flustered servant who'd arrived in her wake.

"Your man, Walters, wasn't going to let me in, Bella," she irritably proclaimed, casting a censorious glance on the innocent footman who'd followed her on the butler's orders. "I knew perfectly well that you were at home with Jamie in town." She swung around in a rustle of silk. "Hello, Jamie, *darling*." Her smile was both dazzling and gloating; she'd successfully run her fox to ground. "You're looking utterly gorgeous as usual. Do give me a kiss."

While the countess scowled, Lady Winterthur, flushed with triumph, swiftly advanced on her prey, her parasol swinging from her wrist. "I should be in a pet with you, darling," she sweetly said with feigned chagrin. "You didn't stop by to see me."

James Blackwood had come to his feet before the lovely brunette reached him and, taking her hands in his, suavely saved himself from her embrace. Bending, he bestowed the requested kiss, held her at arm's length, and smoothly lied. "I'm just passing through London or I would have called."

"Since you've chosen to disturb our sitting, do sit down at least, Lily," Bella ordered, anxious to separate her rival from her lover. "And don't distract the painter," she said with annoyance. "We are under a time constraint. I have another appointment after this."

Taking a seat next to Jamie, Lily Chester slanted a sly glance at the countess. "How perfect! I'll take Jamie off your hands then. We'll find something to do to amuse ourselves, won't we, darling," she brightly said, smiling at her quarry.

"You'll do no such thing," Bella snapped. "He's staying here!"

"Ladies, I prefer not being handed around like a Sacher torte," Jamie drily said. "I'm off to Scotland at five in any event."

"What a shame. We won't have time to *play*," Lily murmured. "You've been terribly selfish, Bella," she chided, turning on her hostess, "keeping him all to yourself." She glanced at Jamie, her gaze openly avaricious. "Perhaps on your return to London, darling, we could share a *moment or two*."

"We're done here," the countess rapped out, her color high.

It was unclear to whom she was speaking, until she rose from the chaise, and dismissed Sofia with a flick of her fingers. "Really, Lily, have you no shame?" she hissed, turning a vengeful eye on her guest. "Do I intrude when you have company? We are *done* Miss Eastleigh," she repeated, sharply.

"She's putting her brushes away, Bella. Be civil." Rising from his chair, Jamie walked toward Sofia, stopping just short of her easel. "Ignore her," he softly said. "May I help?"

"Thank you, no," Sofia replied, wiping her brushes. "This will take just a minute." Dropping her brushes one by one into a jar of turpentine, she closed the lid on her paint box.

"I apologize for them both."

"You needn't. I'm familiar with—"

"Outspoken females?"

He'd formed the word bitch, Sofia noticed, but changed his mind. "Yes, with them," Sofia said, giving her hands a last wipe. "Have a pleasant journey."

"Thank you." He nodded toward the painting. "The likeness is superb."

"The countess is very beautiful."

He smiled faintly. "Let me see you to the door. I'll be right back, Bella," he called out, ignoring his lover's scowl, offering Sofia his arm.

As they exited the room, he said, "My apologies again. Lily is always troublesome and Bella is—well, Bella. She's a spoiled child."

"And yet?" Sofia shot him an amused glance.

He grinned. "I have no excuse. Have you been painting long? You're very good."

"All my life. Both my parents are artists."

"Ah. That explains it then. My forebears were all soldiers."

"That explains it then," she said, mimicking him. "You have a powerful physical presence. As an artist, I notice such things."

He could have said most women noticed his size, but on his best behavior, he said, "I hope Bella's paying you well for her discourtesy."

"Yes, very well. I'm quite content and, no offense, but I don't really listen to women like her. Aristocratic women are entirely wanting in occupation." She grinned. "Which is where you come in I expect."

"It does pass the time," he said with a broad smile.

"But you're on your way to Scotland."

"Yes, and none too soon."

"I noticed your boredom."

"Too much of a good thing," he drolly replied. "I'm looking forward to little conversation and fewer people at my home in the Highlands."

"Then I wish you safe journey."

They'd reached the front door where two flunkeys were waiting.

Jamie nodded to them.

The door was opened and with a graceful bow he sent Sofia on her way.

Praise for Lindsay McKenna

"Captivating sensuality."

—*Publishers Weekly* on *Wind River Wrangler*, a
   Publishers Marketplace Buzz Books 2016 Selection

"Moving and real . . . impossible to put down."

—*Publishers Weekly*, starred review on *Wind River Rancher*

"Cowboy who is also a former Special Forces operator?
Check. Woman on the run from her past? Check. This
contemporary Western wraps together suspense and
romance in a rugged Wyoming package."

—Amazon.com's Omnivoracious, "9 Romances
   I Can't Wait to Read," on *Wind River Wrangler*

"Set against the stunning beauty of Wyoming's Grand
Tetons, *Wind River Wrangler* is Lindsay McKenna at her
finest! A *tour de force* of heart-stopping drama, gut-
wrenching emotion, and the searing joy of two wounded
souls learning to love again."

—International bestselling author Merline Lovelace

"McKenna's dazzling eighth Shadow Warriors novel is a
rip-roaring contemporary military romance novel with heart
and heat."

—*Booklist* on *Running Fire* (starred review)

"McKenna does a beautiful job of illustrating difficult
topics through the development of well-formed, sympathetic
characters."

—*Publishers Weekly* on *Wolf Haven* (starred review)

Also by *New York Times*
bestselling author
Lindsay McKenna

WIND RIVER WRANGLER

WIND RIVER RANCHER

WIND RIVER COWBOY

WRANGLER'S CHALLENGE

KASSIE'S COWBOY (novella included in
CHRISTMAS WITH MY COWBOY)

and coming in September 2018

WIND RIVER LAWMAN

Published by Kensington Publishing Corporation